MW01234610

OZ

A BATTLE IN ATLANTA

BOOK THREE

By

Michael Osborne

Copyright 2023 by Michael Osborne

All rights reserved. This book or any portion thereof may not be reproduced or used in any manner whatsoever without the express written permission of the publisher except for the use of brief quotation in a book review.

ISBN 978-1-961017-97-9 (Paperback)
ISBN 978-1-961017-98-6 (Ebook)

Inquiries and Book Orders should be addressed to:

Leavitt Peak Press
17901 Pioneer Blvd Ste L #298, Artesia, California 90701
Phone #: 2092191548

CONTENTS

THE LONG BIKE RIDE

Two hard hours on the back of Sifu Cho's chopper had passed. Mike's butt was burning, a rash wore his thighs raw. Each bump, on the road aggravated the searing pain. Needless to say, Mike remained quiet. The loss of Sifu Stephen was still on his mind. Neither Cho nor Mike said one word, between them. Not a word was said, when they made their first stop at a filling station, to fill the gas tank. It was hot on the road from the overhead sun. Every part of the bike absorbed the heat, giving the effect of sitting on a stove. Only the cool breeze traveling help keep the heat at bay. Any one out in the sun was sweating, but neither Sifu Cho or Mike showed the effects from the heat others were experiencing, if they cared to have taken notice.

Back on the bike for another long joust, Sifu Cho, and Mike rode. Soon, they came to a vista overlooking a large city looming ahead. Sifu Cho turned onto another road avoiding traveling through, the large city.

Mike peered at the immense size of the city driving a parallel course pass the city. He recognized several buildings from his time on his long road home. It was Atlanta.

After several miles, on the road parallel to Atlanta, Sifu Cho again made a turn, then another, and another, until it was impossible for Mike to track his position.

Another hour and Sifu Cho came to a dirt road. Without moments pause, they turned down the road heading full speed, kicking up a huge cloud of dust behind the chopper. Up ahead, was a turn off through a fenced in drive. Cho slowed. The cloud caught up with the bike, quickly both Cho and Mike were entirely overwhelmed with a thick layer of dust.

Neither Cho nor Mike felt a single dust particle. Cho revved his chopper, both scooted through the mist, leaving a gaping hole where they once paused to turn into the drive. Mike looked back at the funnel hole closing. The cloud remained in place, collapsing to the ground, similar to a splash in a pool of water after a rock was tossed into it. Up ahead, was a house.

"Wasn't much to look at, Mike thought. This can't be the place, it looks deserted. The paint is nearly removed and replaced by gray, dry wood. What shutters remained around the windows ware barely still clinging to the walls. Some are hanging crooked and missing shutter blades. The roof is an entirely different matter. It looked almost new. On one side of this house, I can see a fire-place chimney. No smoke is coming from the top. This house looks bad with any standard I compare it too." Mike continued to make observation riding on the back of Sifu Cho chopper.

"Wow! Many bikes are parked all about. No order, just a random assembly of bikes. A few seemed to be sprouting from shrubs. Apparently, those bikes had no choice to where they were placed. Their riders must have been under the influence," Mike wondered with awe.

Sifu Cho parked near the front door. Steel bars were across each window. A light shown through the thickly smoked covered window-paned glass. Music was heard, after Cho stopped the engine, to his chopper.

Mike sat on the seat, until Cho hopped off. Slowly, Mike slid off the rear of the seat. Cho was watching. A slight smile creased his lips. Mike saw the grind grow across Cho's face, slowly peeling his butt from the seat.

Sifu Cho watched the pain, Mike was feeling. A memory long passed from his first long ride on a bike. It gave Cho both a giggle and a sense of shared experience to the pain, he remembered. Still, he could not help preventing the grind creeping across his face.

Mike stood by the chopper straighten his back, then slowly took his first steps toward, the front door.

Cho watched Mike bowed legs, waddle toward the door. Mike pulled on the door; it creaked opened. Smoke, immediately fled out.

"From the amount of smoke coming through the door, one would think a fire was blazing inside," thought Mike.

Mike quickly brushed the plume of bellowing cigarette smoke away, holding the door opened for Sifu Cho to enter, first. Once inside the door, Mike followed.

Inside, was a typical home converted into a bar. The bar area was many times larger, than the whole of the house. Many tables and chairs were placed along the walls away from the center. The center was reserved for two pool tables. Only one music box, parked in a corner, playing rock-in-roll music, was the sole source of music. Low hanging lights hung in the center of the ceiling, lighting the pool tables, but not the tables. Every table remained partly in a shadow. people sitting at the tables were slightly visible to observers entering the house. Only, until a person's eyes adjusted to the gloomy dim, were the tables visible, but omitted any sign of patrons sitting at them. This was a purposely done, arrangement. It prevented new-comers entering, from seeing the whole content of the bar.

Looking about, Mike spotted on the opposite side of the room a long bar with many stools gathered across the length and breathe it spanned. Beers bottles littered the bar top. Three times as many bottles were to bikers strewn at the bar. Some biker's heads laid upon the bar top drunk. Others were teetering on the brinks of falling off their stools. What was left, were bikers hoisting beer bottles. Each yelled forth, his toast to falling comrades.

"Here's to Sonny, my best friend. I'll miss him. One for Jesus, the dang baddest trick rider among the lot of us. Here's for Teddy Bear, a mountain of a man. Yeah, he made three of any of us," another shouted out.

Cheers reverberated throughout the house with each toast. Every fallen biker was called out and saluted with a toast. Over and over again, the names were shouted out and given a toast.

Mike figured, "the toasts would end with the last biker lying prone, on the floor."

Mike looked back toward an isolated corner noticing a woman, standing by several men, sitting around a table. Sifu Cho was making his way toward that table. Mike, immediately recognized all the sitting people at the table. His eyes had adjusted to the heavenly laden room, filled with smoke.

One person, caught his attention, "Bell." She was hard not to notice. Tall, well busted, and having those beautiful blue eyes staring in my direction. It felt as if those eyes were reaching out to me," thought Mike. They were.

Mike's eyes filled with tears slowly making his way behind Sifu Cho to the table. Tears coming from the noxious odors, emitting from the boozy breaths of bikers, scattered like confetti in a parade mixed with cigarette smoke. One tear came from Mike's memory, of Bell's tender caring.

Bell quickly worked herself from around the table. She wangled around the tight corner space, left from the large men squeezed into the corner. After some effort, she managed to step out from the table, making her way to Mike, cradling him in her arms.

Mike often felt Bell treated him like a child, maybe her child. She and Chopper never had children. Bell seemed to have adopted him. "It was good to have someone feel that way, about him, Mike thought with her embrace. Still, her big boobs never fell to smack him in his face. It wouldn't have been so bad, if not for her burying his face between the two boobs. He had to pull free, just to get a breath of air.

Razor stood with his hand reaching to Sifu Cho. With a quick nod to Mike. It was no use to try and git between Bell and Mike, when she had a hold on him. Chopper sat smiling at the sight. A beer was handed to Cho, once he found an empty chair to sit in.

Razor popped the cap, before handing the bottle to Cho, then signaled the bar keeper to bring a soda for Mike. Cho sat between Razor and Jack knife across from Chopper. Nothing was said, until Bell completed her hugging, allowing Mike to sit. A bottle of pop was waiting for him, before he had a chance to wash the dirt from his mouth, Bell had a tight grip around his neck.

Chopper seeing Mike plight, asked Bell to release him. "Babe allow the kid to drink his soda. Bell, let the poor kid be for a while. He just got here and from the looks of Cho and him, they could use a drink, to wash all that dirt down." Chopper gives Mike a short nod and a smile.

Mike lifted his soda; the same time Cho did his beer. Quickly, both bottles were drained. Two new bottles quickly appeared on the table.

"Thanks Chopper, you read our minds," Cho said.

"Been there, Cho," replied Chopper. Everyone laughed agreeing.

Bell resumed her bear hug around Mike's neck. A chair was slid over to her, to sit next to Mike, holding unto his arm.

No one asked, but Chopper spoke the words on both Cho and Mike's mind. "The funeral is two days from today. Mike, Bell will take you shopping tomorrow, for some proper clothes. Cho, I assume you have something," asked Chopper? Cho nodded.

Cho glanced around the room, first entering the clubhouse bar and again before reaching the table. Slowly, he took a head count of the faces. Many he could identify in their prone positions, either on the bar top, or on the floor, drunk and out. Still, he observed several men, were unaccounted for.

Razor and Jack knife both noticed him taking count. When Chopper finished with his main thought, Razor told Cho about the missing men not.

"Cho, we have four men in the hospital and two will be coming back later. Should be here soon, with the others riding them here. Only Teddy Bear and Stephen our only losses, you and Mike knew. Several others are clinging to life, at the hospital. Best we can hope for now, is they make it," Razor followed with.

"To many, Razor, replied Cho, to many."

Mike heard the count, hearing Stephen and Teddy Bears names spoken, tears formed in his eyes. Bell saw them and resumed her hugging.

THE OUTBURST

A loud slam, from a door, occurred. Everyone at the table turned to see, who slammed the door. It was a tall woman, accompanied by a young girl, about the same age as Mike.

The woman had long brown hair, uncombed. She had a weary expression worn across her face. Tired and disrabbled was her dress, she made her way over to the table. The young girl followed. She was also crying, like Mike.

Bell stood, greeting her with a hug. The tall woman apologized to the men, sitting at the table for her appearance. Bell assured her, it was perfectly alright.

"Susan, don't be silly, we are here for you and Cheryl. We will always be here, for you." Chopper speaks up.

"Susan, we have taken care of everything. Don't worry one bit. Your family, and family, you always will be. You sit and rest. Let Bell tend to you."

"Bell, I am sorry to come and ask this from you, but, but could you please tend to Cheryl, for the day?"

"You know I will, Susan. What else do you want?"

"Well, I could use a ride to the funeral home."

"Sure thing, Susan."

Chopper spoke, "Susan, we have several people there, tending to what's needing to be done. Bell turns giving Chopper a stare to stop, "she doesn't need to hear that now look". Chopper stopped. He knew the look and what it meant.

Bell, seeing Susan's reaction on her face, from Chopper's poorly said comments, attempting to ease her anxieties, knew exactly what Susan was feeling. Chopper did not understand what she was trying, not to say. Bell knew, she wanted to sit with Stephen, alone.

Bell took Susan by her hand, walking her to two men, not yet fallen to the floor from the effects of alcohol. She instructed them to take Susan, to the funeral home. For added measure, reassured each of them, any problems along the way, she would personally deal with. It had a sobering effect on both bikers.

Razor and Jack knife stood, to git a chair for Cheryl. Two sodas were brought to the table. One for Mike, another for Cheryl. She was giving a seat next to Mike.

Chopper made the introductions. "Cheryl, you know most of the men sitting around the table. Heck, you know all of them, here. A slight giggle erupted around the room. Cho wasn't present on our raid against the gang, we attacked."

Cho reached over hugging Cheryl and softly spoke into her ear. Words of his love. Cheryl hugged Cho, back. Cho often was at their home for supper. He and Stephen were like brothers, Cheryl thought Cho, as an uncle.

The next words to leave Choppers mouth bought about a totally unexpectant result. Cheryl, the young man sitting to your side, is Stephen and Cho's student.

Cheryl abruptly stood pushing, her chair away. "You mean, I am sitting next to Mike. Is that Mike, the one my dad got killed for." Angered was in her voice. Hate followed the anger. Everyone turned, looking at Cheryl.

Mike sat there with his hands, still hanging in the air, to greet her. His mouth, gaping open to those words," he was the reason for my dad, Stephen being killed." Cheryl screamed looking about, to fine anything, to hurl her dad's murderer.

Susan turned, hearing her daughter say those words. She knew, the reason for her husband's death. Never did she feel it was someone's fault, much less, a boy. Stephen did his duty and that was, to save a life. No greater duty is there but to give one's life, for another. This, she heard Stephen many times say and this, she knew was in his heart. Her heart, too. She also hoped, was in her daughter's heart.

Mike sat feeling more alone, than he ever had been. Among friends, no, comrades willing to fight and died filling his mind. Now, he sat ashamed, "they died for me. I wasn't part of the action. My life wasn't part of the life and death of those fighting for him. I didn't have a stake in the choice and a gamble with the odds. The odds to live through the ordeal or to die during it. Now, I see what came from my actions. It didn't matter, if the choice was taken from me by the bikers. It still fell on me, for Teddy Bear and Sifu Stephen's deaths."

Cheryl reached for a chair and before she could level it upon the bent head of Mike, Razor had hold of her. Jack Knife grabbed the chair. She stood there yelling at Mike.

"Look at him sitting there. That chair, my dad would be sitting in, now. Look at that scrawny kid, skinny as a rail, the mighty Mike. Everyone so in awe of him. Sifu Cho chose him, to succeed him. My dad was Cho's student. He was far more the better man, than that kid. Look at him crying, whimpering like a baby. For what, not for my dad, you don't see me crying like a baby, no, not me. My dad made me tough, he taught me. He didn't teach that kid anything."

Before another word exited Cheryl's mouth, Susan was standing in front of her. Cheryl stopped her ranting. Razor released her. Cheryl fell into her mom's arms. Together, they walked to the front door. Bell followed; once outside, Bell returns to the table. Mike wasn't there. He walked to the bathroom. Several of the men wanted to follow. Cho stopped them. Cho turned to Bell waving her back. Cho went into the bathroom, alone.

Mike was standing near a wall leaning, barely able to stand from his appearance. Cho knew the hurt, he knew it well. Mike needed Cho, no others. He was his student and adopted son, needing his father. A hand touched Mike on his back.

Mike knew the touch and turned. He stood there; head lowered in shame. Cho grabbed hold of him. They remained in the bathroom for nearly an hour. Not many words were said, nor needed saying. Mike understood the reasons, for Cheryl outburst. Knowing the reasons different make the words hurt, any less. Cho understood Mike's ability to see the truth inside the veils often hiding it away. The same was for Cho, he understood, but the words, still hurt. It hurt Cho, as well. He too, was not present, for the finally fight. Those words inflicted toward Mike; Cheryl also unexpectantly inflicted at Cho.

"Each were alone, but together, as will be the case, until they die," Cho thought.

Both Cho and Mike exited the bathroom walking to the table, whence they were seated. Mike sat for a minute, then stood. Turning to Sifu Cho, asked if he could be excused. Then, turned to Chopper and repeated the request.

Sifu Cho stood asking Mike, "I will walk with you, if you please, Mike."

It was difficult to look at the faces around the table. Mike had cried in private. That act, each man knew occurred in the restroom, was evident to everyone at the table. After the remarks Cheryl made, it stung more the worst for them, to see Mike weep.

"Yes, I would like that, Sifu."

Both walked to the front door exiting the clubhouse. Outside, Cho asked Mike what he wanted.

"Mike, I know your heart, I know, talking is not what you need now. It is some alone time. What can I do, to aid you in this?"

"Sifu Cho, it is getting dark, I will need to find a place to stay."

"Mike, I have considered this, I am sorry to say, I had not yet prepared us for lodging. You may stay with me tonight, in my room at the local motel, or I will get you a room for yourself. I noticed your bags had a sleeping bag. Did you prepared for camping out?"

"Yes, I did. I didn't want to impose on others, for my lodging or food. I imposed enough; I don't want to feel any more, the burden, I now feel is upon me. I know Sifu, I would be welcomed by all and treated as such. After that rebut, I can't bear to be seen by them. I feel, they see me as Cheryl does, a whimpering baby."

Cho was about to speak, Mike stopped him. He knew what was going to be said, like Stephen often said about him, Mike had a strong sense of understanding. "I know what you going to say Sifu, it is what I feel. I need to work it out of my system, before I can face any of them. They already gave so much, for me."

Cho walked to where his bike was parked, assisting Mike in removing his gear. Mike held what few belonging he had, then pointed to a place where they rode passed, on the driveway to the clubhouse. Along the road, was a clearing, about a hundred yards from the road. It looked like a quiet place to set his bedroll down and make a fire.

"By the picnic tables, I will sleep."

Cho knew the place and waved Mike off. He stood watching his protege take a very long and slow walk down the road. Once Mike turned down the path leading him to the tables, Cho turned, re-entering the house.

Bell was the first to approach Cho, asking where Mike went. "Cho is Mike coming back inside? We haven't discussed where he will be staying. Besides that, you two haven't had anything to eat. We are thinking of going out to a Chinese restaurant. You think, he'll like Chinese food, Cho? He is hungry, isn't he, Cho? I know by the way you put food away, you are. Mike on the other hand, eats little."

"Bell, Mike will be camping out tonight."

"Where Cho? Does he have any gear for camping?"

Chopper stands, walks over to where Cho and Bell were talking. "Bell, stop your mother-Henning to Cho. He knows Mike better than any of us."

"Chopper, I can worry all I want, if you don't mind?"

"Sure Bell, all I mean is, Cho is his teacher and."

"And what Chopper, he ain't his mom?"

Chopper was about to remark on that fact, to Bell. He decided not to tell her, she neither was his mom, nor teacher. He knew, Bell formed a strong attachment to Mike. This was dangerous ground he was threading. "Your right Bell, Cho is his teacher and doesn't always understand what a young kid requires. He is a bachelor and never raised a child."

Cho stood still and quiet. I definitely want to stay out of this argument and could feel the wrong word or words were around the corner for a knockdown, drag out fight among Bell and Chopper, if I am not careful."

Cho quietly signaled Chopper, from Bell's backside facing off to Chopper. He tried to warn Chopper, to ease back. Chopper saw the signal and had already began is back tracking.

"Bell," her face was beet red; Chopper wanted her outside, to cool off, before the full storm swelling inside her, spilled out. Bell

OZ

ask Cho where Mike went, wanting to go check on him. No answer was forthcoming from Cho. That made Bell mad and madder when Chopper tried to interfere.

"It will be good for him to see you, Bell, Chopper said. You know that lad really likes you a lot." Before Bell could ask Chopper how he came by that conclusion, Chopper quickly explained to her how he knew that.

"Bell, remember when you were shot? Mike and I had a short talk outside his house, before Razor went to town to get food with Mike. He was really worried about you. He told me, he thought you were one of the prettiest women, he ever met. He really cared about you. He was really worried for you and kept pressing me, if you were going to be alright. I think, he has a crush on you? Besides Bell, you need to go and give the lad, the good news about us. He could sure use some, right about now. You think?"

"What good news are you talking about, Chopper? Bell, we never told him about that thing, on your finger. It was going to be our surprise. Now, it can be your surprise, to tell him." Bells eyes lit up. All thoughts of the discussion, that nearly got out of hand, turned to excitement. Quickly, she turns back to Cho.

"Well Cho, you gonna tell me where he is, or do you want me to drag you to where he is?"

"No, no Bell, Mike, he went down the drive turning into that open space, we have cookouts. He plans on setting up camp."

"Camp, camp outside, by himself. He just got here? What is wrong with you, Cho? We treat our people, better than that. Did you bother to notice the sky? It might rain, tonight. Does he have a tent, or just a sleeping bag?"

Chopper stepped back, and Bell unloaded on Cho. Cho looked back at Chopper for help. No help was coming when Chopper's arm went out to his side, to signal, sorry buddy, she is your problem, now. Chopper quietly and quickly made his way back to his seat, in the corner.

Everyone was watching Cho and Bell. Some of the men at the table couldn't help themselves and began making cute faces, with body gestures at him. Cho stood quiet allowing Bell to finish. Then,

11

he escorted her to the door. Once Bell was at the front door, Cho turned to the table. Cho had a very nasty look on his face looking at his friends. Everyone quickly turned away lifting beers, to honor Cho's bravery under fire. Cho could only smile and accepted a beer handed to him returning to the table. Bell stomps out of the bar. Both doors slammed opened barely able to return to their closed position.

Outside, Bell made a bee line straight down the road. Swiftly arriving at the path to the picnic tables. Quickly walking down the path, tempering each step to calm herself, before reaching Mike's make shift camp. His bedroll was down under the picnic table. Mike was about to start a fire, in the open pit, bikers used for cook outs and sensed a presence coming his way.

Mike heard Bells soft footsteps, nearing his camp. He recognized them, a women steps, sensing Bell. She was the nearest thing to a second mom, he had. Since coming home, his mom was glad, he came back but she soon fell into her old habits.

Mike being the only son among three women, soon felt left out. Bell was the first woman, beside his aunt, he could felt had some caring, for him. Before Bell had a chance to introduce her presence, Mike called out to come into his camp.

Bell was amazed, he was aware of her presents. She wanted to quietly approach and watch him. She wanted to make sure, he could take care of himself, out here. She remembered what Cho and Stephen, as well as the others had been saying. "He was gifted, with unique abilities far beyond, a normal person. He learned quick. His self-awareness for things around him, were as good as Sifu Cho. Cho even said this himself to Chopper and the others. Stephen reported he was performing well ahead of his training and no one, but no one wanted to fight him. He was quick, powerful, and dam good," cited Stephens in his reports, to Cho.

Bell walked over to where Mike laid a towel on the bench, to sit. Bell walked over seeing the towel. "Well, I'll be Mike, that isn't necessary for me. I sat on far worst places, than, a dirty bench seat. Thank you for the gesture." Bell sat on the towel close to Mike.

Mike remained quiet, waiting for Bell to voice her concerns. He knew her intentions but none the less, waited until she asked him, her questions. One thing Mike learned about Bell, you don't tell her anything, you ask her, or wait until she tells you.

"Mike, I am concern for you. That young girl, Cheryl loved her dad. She is just looking to blame someone. Mike, Stephen thought a great deal of you. As much as Cho does. Stephen had no son, and in many ways, you had become Cho and Stephen's son. They saw in you, what they would want in a son."

Bell gave pause, before she spoke again. Mike remained quiet. Hearing those words, confirmed to Mike what he had guessed and hoped. He too looked at both of them, as if they were his fathers.

"Mike, this is not meant to hurt you, but, I think, it is important for you to be told. Stephen spoke a great deal about you. His wife remarked to us ladies, about what Stephen often said. Cheryl, I feel may have heard most of that talk and most likely, has some jealous feeling against you. She loved her dad a great deal. Stephen was often sent on trips, for the club. The times he was home were treasured, by his wife and daughter.'

"Mike, all the women in this club, like the men, have been through training courses learning to handle ourselves. We were taught how to use firearms and self-defense fighting. Stephen taught every woman and child survival skills. Cho on the other hand, never taught any people his art. Stephen was but a handful, he entrusted. Stephen never received the kind of training Cho, is teaching you. He was Cho's best, but was never intended to be his inheritor."

"Mike, this is not why I came out here to talk to you." Mike sat quiet. He knew she was about to tell him some important thing. It was obvious, how Bell kept putting off her true reason for coming."

"Mike, I want you to know, I care about you very much. I feel the same as both Cho and Stephen does. This is why Chopper and I want you to know this and why we have chosen you."

Bell offers Mike her hand. Mike accepts her hand in his. Bell points to the ring on her finger. Mike looks down at the ring. Suddenly, it dawns on him. Bell, you mean, you and Chopper, Chopper and you got married?"

"Yes. But not yet. We wanted to have you here, for the wedding. Then, this happened. In two days, we will lay to rest Stephen and Teddy Bear. I will take you to town to git you some clothes, to wear. You can't stay out here, with those new clothes. Tomorrow, we will git you into a place to stay. I don't want to hear any argument about this." Bell looks into Mike's eyes and squeezes his hand. Mike understood, there was no saying no. Complying to her wishes was best and right.

"Cho tells me, you want to be alone. I understand. I still will worry; if you need anything, we will be here. Now, one more thing. I know you and Cho had a long bike ride and hadn't eaten. We will be going out to eat and you will be going with us. Be ready in an hour." Over in the corner, is a garden hose. Bell pointed to the faucet. Mike had already located it, within minutes arriving at the picnic tables.

"Sure Bell, as you wish. I will be ready and waiting by the roadside."

"Good, now finish up and I will tell the others."

Bell and Mike stood up. Bell grabs Mike, giving him a hug. Then turns, walking up the path. Mike started to begin his fire. Once the fire had a good burn, he extinguishes it.

Hem, good now, I will have hot embers to readily reignite my fire, when I return from dinner, Mike thought out loud. Now wash and get ready.

Several bikes roared to a stopped at Mike's camp site. Mike hopped on Cho's bike. A hot meal was not on his thoughts.

THE CONSPIRATORS

On a lonely street, by a park, in a neighborhood of many of the biker homes, a small group of friends met. The suburb children knew each other since childhood. As the years progress, so did their bonds. Some, grew with a strong bond of friendship. Some, even had amorous nature. This was not shared with the biker newcomers. They were left out of any subdivision activities.

Among the small band of biker children friends, Cheryl was in the fore front, as their leader. Bobby, one boy every one followed, allowed his amorous feelings toward Cheryl, relinquishing his leadership role, giving her control. A decision that had been solidified among the group.

It was nearly high noon, all of biker children in Cheryl's group had been sitting around the swings, for an hour. The topic, was Mike. Each, heard the stories their parents spoke about. The battle and the plan to take down this gang threating, Mike. Some of the other facts, were missing. Those small facts were not required their decision, how to deal with the new kid. A kid, every member was impressed with. He came to the club with Master Cho. He was his new student. He acquitted himself superbly, defending people at a haunted home. He was nearly killed, saving their lives. Their parents spoke about the student with awesome abilities.

Several small facts were omitted, it was a fight with three gang members at his home. The second, was the haunted house and movie producers. Five men attacked Mike's friends, intent on killing them. Mike sacrificed himself, to save them. That night, he was serious hurt. The wounds was the cause Mike was not in the battle in Atlanta, Stephen and Teddy Bear were killed; also, Cho staying behind to keep the Rama kids and Mike safe.

The only fact that seemed to be mentioned, was the first assault at Mike's home. Mike, saving Bell from getting a bullet. It was decided, it was Chopper stopping the gang leader, while Mike, was lying on the ground, holding the leader's legs.

To some kids in Cheryl's group, the threat by the Atlanta gang, was not real. Her dad and Teddy Bear were killed for nothing. Cheryl slanted the truth. She was jealous of Mike's attention, by her dad. Cheryl's hate, went further. Her desire to exact revenge, was the fuel needed for her crusade against Mike.

"Look guys, he was the reason both my Dad and Teddy Bear were, killed. Our parents put their lives on the line to save that skinny butt of his. Still, the gang leaders got away. Do any of you seriously think, this has ended. There will be another fight. If there is, then you too might lose your dads." Cheryl looked at each face. every face had the same expression. Every face saw the truth to what she was saying.

"Even if that happens Cheryl, what can we five do about stopping it," asked Liddea?

"Well, Liddea, the first thing we can do, is to make that weak, skinny kid, regret the day he ever arrived. We can make him feel not wanted. Make fun at him. Encourage our friends, to help us. Make them see, what we see. He is a threat to us all. Next, we shun him out of all the get togethers we have. Make him feel unwanted, anytime we get together with the club or among ourselves. Write on walls calling him names, throw objects at him, you know the routine?"

"Cheryl, from what we all heard, Mike is a great fighter. He could take us all apart."

"Lou seriously, you really believe a kid his size, can do all the stuff we been hearing? Come on."

Lou responded," well, from what my dad said, and he as practiced fighting with Mike, he is very powerful."

"If you are afraid, then, you hide and throw rocks at him. Anybody who feels that way can hide in fear with Lou."

Bobby stood up, "I'm not," defiantly speaking to his friends. Bobby was the tallest and strongest of the boys. His words were respected and followed, unless Cheryl counter manned his words. He never challenged her in anything.

Liddea retorted, "you only say that, because you have a crush on Cheryl." Bobby's face reddens.

Cheryl stopped the arguing. "Quiet, we don't need that kind of talk." She glances at Bobby, flashing him a tiny. Bobby felt better and sat down.

"Well, all this might or might not be true," Macy took his turn to speak up. "We do know, Mike has over developed senses and we need to be very careful approaching him."

"Why Macy, Bobby asked? What is he going to do? If, for any reason, we get in a fight with him, whether we beat him, or he stomps us, we win." A curiosity crossed all the faces. Cheryl was amazed hearing Bobby's remark. It just dawned on her, he was correct.

Cheryl takes over. "Yes, yes Bobby has a good point. If we get him to fight us and any of us gets hurt, he will be blamed."

"How," asked Liddea?

"Don't you all see it? Mike will be a loose cannon, around us. He will be thought as a kid, being trained a deadly art, too young to be taught by Cho. He could hurt the kids in the group. Even if we teased him, he should have the discipline Cho's training instills in him to reframe from a fight. Especially with kids. Cho's training is supposed to make him a responsible person to possess this great knowledge."

"Wow, your right." Liddea finally understood her and Bobby's logic.

Cheryl stood putting her hand out. "Do all agree to this plan? If you do this, give me your hands. All hands stacked on her hand. Good, a pact, we all agreed to."

Everyone got up walking out of the neighborhood park. Liddea spoke to the group, while walking. "Cheryl, my mom said, Mike runs from the club driveway and down the road, every day. Sometimes, he turns and runs down this street. He always makes a round trip back to the clubhouse early, every morn."

"Yeah, your right," Lou said.

Then, Bobby spoke, "we do know where he is staying. We can go to his camp and mess it up while he's running."

"Cool," replied Lou.

"Hey, he should be beginning a second run, by two. Mom said, "she sees him running at least twice, past the house. We got maybe an hour to get over to his camp and surprise him with a ransacked camp," Skip speaking up.

"Skip, Cheryl turns, you can surely surprise me, sometimes."

"Let's go," two kids shouted out with glee.

"Wait, we need to stop at my house to pick up a few items," replied Cheryl, before starting to the camp.

"What you got planned Cheryl," Liddea asked?

"If we are going to do this to his camp, let's do it right. Wait here, I will be back soon." Down the street, around a corner, Cheryl dashes home. Going into her garage, she finds what she was searching for. Upon her return, she holds up the item, for all to see.

"Way to go, Cheryl. With that axe, we can really do some damage." Bobby reached for the axe. "Here, let me have the honor." Cheryl gladly complied.

Down the road, a small band of friends came to the clubhouse turn off. It was the same dirt road, Cho and Mike road down going to the clubhouse. Halfway up the road, the small band of kids spotted a lone figure running in the opposite direction.

"Quickly, everyone dashed to the side of the road into the trees, announced Cheryl.

Even though Mike was running in the opposite direction, his abilities still provoked respect by the kid conspirators. Once Mike was clear from view, the small band of saboteurs ran up the road turning into the driveway. Within minutes, they reached the campground. Bobby removed his axe from his belt. Cheryl looked around the area.

Liddea quipped, "he ain't got much of a camp."

"Yea, Lou followed, he doesn't look to have many things to make a proper camp?"

Over to one side, Cheryl spotted a bag hanging from a tree. Quickly Cheryl called Skip over. Skip was short and wiry. He could shimmy up a tree, pretty good. "Quick Skip, shimmy up the tree and cut that pack down."

Swiftly, Skip was up the tree, cutting the bag loose. On the ground, Cheryl opened it. To her surprise, only one shirt, one pants, two pairs of socks, and small things to use around camp was in the bag. There was one problem, a smell accompanied opening the bag. Dumping the contents on the ground, a squirrel recently skinned fell on top of the items.

"Ick, cried Liddea watching the transgression to Mike belongings. It's dead."

"Really Liddea, "Cheryl replied, after hearing her remark.

"Cheryl why would anyone put a dead, skinned, squirrel in their back pact and hang it in a tree?"

"Liddea, you never been camping much, have you?"

"Liddea shook her head, no not much."

"Well, with fresh meat, you skinned, you need to place it up high, to keep other animals from getting to it."

"Really, you mean he plans on eating that thing?" Liddea face contorted, contemplating the idea, "Mike must be bad off, to eat that thing."

"Hey, that's gives me a great idea, guys, Cheryl cries out. We can destroy his camp and with this squirrel laying on the ground, Mike would figure, a wild animal did this to his camp."

"Good idea, Cheryl, except for one thing," Lou said.

"What is that, Lou?"

"Well, an animal would eat the meat or take it off with him."

Skip agrees, nodding his head.

"Yes, you are correct, Cheryl answered, but not if Mike showed up, before the wild animal had a chance to do that."

Bobby calls them over to where Mike's sleeping bag laid, opened by him. "Look at this bag. It seen better days. He really is roughing it, with this old worn-out bag."

Liddea spoke. "Hey guys, from the looks of all he owns, he hasn't got much to tear up. Maybe, we shouldn't do this. He looks like he is living without anyone giving him anything. My parents said he was poor; his parent didn't have much."

"Yeah, I was told the same thing. I was told, he was trying to live out here and didn't want anybody to help him. He felt, it would be a burden on the club. They had done so much for him. He kind of has an attitude, he feels responsible for the battle, at the warehouse, and doesn't want anyone to aid him. He felt blame for the battle and the people hurt or killed. Lou continued to say, I remember my mom wanting to offer him our place to stay."

"Yeah, my mom did too," Liddea announced.

"Well, we all agreed to do this, and it is too late. We pledged an oath. Besides, he should be returning soon," Cheryl rebutted her girlfriend.

Bobby picks up the axe coming down on the bed roll, with a whack. A hole was placed in the center. Then, he ripped the axe down the hole. Looking up at the group, Bobby replies. "This will make it look more like an animal tore his bed roll. All agreed?"

Cheryl waves to them, "let's get out of here, before he comes back."

Mike, ran up the drive and unto the road. He saw the six kids approaching down the road, away from where he was beginning his second run. He pretended not to see them continuing run down the road. After giving them the time to make their way to the driveway, Mike turns, sneaking back through the woods. Quickly, Mike returns to watch the small band turn to enter his camp. Silently, he crept up to a tree, watching them go through his gear. They tore all his belongings. He decided, they would do that, whether he was there to prevent it or some other time, coming back and try again. Maybe, it will do them some good, taking out their anger on my things, Mike pondered watching them destroy what few belongings, he owned. Listening to what they were saying, Mike could hear them beginning to doubt what they did; was it a right thing to do? He was right not to intervene and stop them. Mike sensed this might happen, after Cheryl blamed him for her dad's death.

Mike heard a remark made by one of the kids; "maybe we shouldn't shun him or make fun at him. He seems to be sorry, for your dad's death, Cheryl?"

Mike's heart was gladdened upon hearing those caring words. He thought, "there is hope, for these kids. They really ware good kids, just being misled by Cheryl, filled with her dad's death, looking to blame someone, me."

When they left, Mike came out of hiding. Over at his bed roll, he saw the extent of the tear. "Hmm, not too bad, he thought. I got a needle and thread, soon, it will be good enough to sleep in."

A squirrel laid in the dirt. Mike lifted it up, brushing off the dirt. "Well, it should still be edible. Picking up his gear to examined, not much damage, "good. I'll put the squirrel back in my pack." After tying the rope around the bag tight, retying the cut part of the rope, he hoisted it back into the tree.

Mike began his run, anew. By the time he restarted his run, the kids had run back to their street. They started to walk back into the park area, when Mike rounded the corner.

Mike neared them, calling out, "hi." Then, without another word passed them by. All six of the kids turned, amazed Mike he was upon them, without them seeing or hearing his approach. Each kid watched Mike run down the street. Bobby felt the need to shoot a finger at him. Lou quickly spoke up.

"Hey, you think he's been to his camp?"

"No way," replied Bobby.

"Yeah, Bobby's right, Skip counter. If he saw his camp, he surely would have said something to us."

"Maybe, Cheryl replied, maybe."

Mike continued down the road thinking, "hopefully, that will give them something to ponder on, before they act again."

That night, Bone breaker stopped by the camp. He saw Mike sewing his bed roll. Mike greeted him, as he neared. "Hey, what happened to your bed roll, came Bone's remarks first before Mike said a word?"

"I think, a wild animal got into my camp."

"Really Mike. All the years we had this camp, and all the stuff left out, I don't believe we had wild animals, ripped stuff up." Bone places a bag on the table.

"Well, Bone Breaker, I guess some animal smelled my squirrel, up in the tree and wandered in."

"Maybe Mike." Bone breaker examines the earth around Mike's camp, while wandering over to the tree Mike had his backpack hanging. Looking up, he asked Mike, "did they get the squirrel, you got hanging inside this bag up the tree?"

Mike, not looking at Bone, knowing he suspected otherwise replied, "maybe. I hadn't checked the area for any animal signs." Mike wasn't lying to him. He knew no animal was there and didn't check for animal signs. Kids did that."

Bone Breaker saw no tracks, but noticed the footsteps of more than one person. About five of six people, other than Mike's footprints, where the bag hung.

Mike felt Bone Breakers thoughts watching closely, Bone looking around the bag and the ground. He scraped away the footprints with a subtle swipe of his bigfoot. Mike sensed Bone didn't want him to know, he knew the foot prints were there. Why, was in Mike's thoughts?"

The reason Bone Breaker made this special trip, came from what a kid said at the store. He happened to be in the store buying some food, snack foods to take over to Mike's camp. Bobby was talking to two boys about a conspirators group forming. They apparently planned to make Mike's stay, as short as possible. They wanted to turn the club against him. Bone breaker waited inside, until the three boys left. Then, made a bee line ride back to Mike's camp. It was still daylight; Cho was to show up at dusk. It was his nightly chore, to check on Mike, before the night came. Bone breaker suspected; Cho was worrying over him.

"Hey kid, I have a present for you. Put that sewing down and take a look in the bag"

"Gee Bone breaker, thanks, what is it?"

"Kid, it's a surprise. Open the bag and look."

Mike takes the bag, opening it without a thought of preserving it. Inside, was a large bag of barbecue potato chips and soda. "Dang, I was sure missing that. I was just savoring the thought of them. You learn to mind read, Bone?"

"Nah kid, I jist figure eating all that good, wild game, that's been fatting you up, you might just be hankering for some junk food, to put in that fat belly, you got hanging over your belt. He, he, he."

"Ha, ha, Mike chuckled, trying to grab belly skin with little success. You really think, I look fat?" Bone Breaker gives Mike a smirky grind. That was all the answer Bone gave Mike.

Mike spoke, "I guess, I have gotten a bit, thin."

"You think kid. Soon as all the ladies see you, they be after Cho and then the rest of us. It's been a week. Cho's been busting your ass, with all his training. Them women, be making our lives miserable, they think, we've been starving you. Much less, making you stay outside in the cold and wet, like this. Do us a favor, go inside and get a real meal, once in a while. Bone said, pondering why Mike was outside, alone, then replied; Yea, I understand how you feel. Just think about it. Okay kid?"

Sitting beside Mike chomping down on his chips, Bone breaker puts his hand in the bag of chips. Mike pulls it away.

"Hey Kid."

Mike retorts back, "if I let you eat my chips, I won't get any. You eat the whole bag. Besides, didn't you say, you brought them, to me. I need to fatten up."

"Yea, I did. But you be all greedy like that, I might not feel so dang soft hearted, to fetch you more."

"Good point, Bone breaker, take some." Mike holds the bag for him to take some chips out of the bag.

"Nah, I changed my mind. Your right, I would eat all of them. Besides, I will stop at the store and load up for me. So, eat them. Gots to get some weight on that skinny body. No girl, would ever look at you."

Cho's bike was heard, stopping at the entrance to the camp. Cho came walking down the path with a hand full. A large bag was placed on the table. Mike and Bone breaker looked at the bag. Bone breaker spoke first. "Ha, I see you got the same message, I got from the ladies." Cho nodded.

"Yes, but not just the ladies, but the one lady, Bell. The last time she saw Mike, she made me aware of how thin, he was looking."

"Heck, it's only been a week, since he arrived. How can some-one get as skinny as they think, he is, so quickly? Cho, it will be your fault and not mine, when Bell sees Mike looking like a bag of bones," Bone quickly pointed out to Cho.

"I know, I know. Looking at Mike, Cho speaks. Mike, tonight you are going to stuff that belly. I got enough food in this bag, to fill the three of us, plus two more."

"You ain't talking to me, Cho, you know how much I can devour?"

"When you told me, you were coming tonight, I made sure to git extra, Bone. Cho reached into the bag and began emptying the contents. Ten burgers laid on the table with four fries and four shakes. Bone breaker quickly took five burgers, two fries and two shakes.

"See Bone, as I said, I considered your needs."

You're the master," Bone answered Cho, stuffing his mouth with two burgers at one time.

Soon, both Cho and Mike's belly were stuffed. Bone breaker saw the sixth burger left on the table and without asking, "decided it was too late now, for them to eat it. It was his. They should have been quicker."

After several hours of friendly talk and not one word of the inci-dent Bone over-heard at the store, both him and Cho stood bidding Mike a good night. Bone was about to speak walking down the path, concerning what he overheard at the store. Cho stopped him, before a word escaped his mouth. Quietly they got on their bikes and rode to the house.

Inside the house, the whole leadership was waiting for them to return. First, on the agender, was the Atlanta gang. Cho was to head that event, after the services for Stephen and Teddy bear. They were still loose and needed to be taken care of, once and forever.

Chopper explain, "this needed done, before they had a chance of re-organizing to strike at them."

Cho spoke. "Chopper, Mike will need on this."

Chopper agrees. "This time, he will take part. We act as a team. He is now part of the team. But for now, everyone, Mike is to be left in the dark, until he completes his training." Cho agreed.

"Next Cho, Chopper paused, I have some news, you are not going to like, and neither is Mike. Apparently, some of our children decided that Mike was to blame for Stephens and Bear's death. They are going to react with some nasty tricks played on him. Also, I fear, maybe some other things, besides tricks. Mike will be tested. I hope Cho, your training can prepare him for this? If he should react wrong and our kids get hurt, they 'll be bad consequences to follow. I will have no choice in the matter. You know how women can be, even if it wasn't Mike's fault. All they will care about, is that their child has been injured."

"Chopper, I am responsible, and I will deal with that matter, as I see fit. Thanks for the head's up. Mike, he is aware of their attitude toward him. He was first, to bring that to my attention. He felt, they would find a way to provoke him. He was concerned for them. He told me, "not to worry for their health. He had known kids will say and do hurtful things at him. He has been through many examples of what they, intend to try."

"Well, Bone breaker speaks up. I was at the store tonight, to take Mike some food."

"Good Bone, Chopper said, Bell's been on me about the way Mike been looking, so thin."

"Yea, me too," Razor retorted. "Same with me," Jack knife replied. "Apparently, she spoke to everyone," replied Chopper. Cho spoke, yes and so has some of the other ladies, as well."

"Seems, we have another problem to address, Chopper answered back. Everyone nodded. Cho, Mike is ahead of this, is what I gather from you?"

Cho replied, "he has been, since the outburst, Chopper."

"That's a find kid, Cho. I'm glad we all made the wise choice. He will make us proud."

Bone spoke again to the leaders, "as I started to tell you at the store, I overheard three kids talking about, what they plan for Mike. They figured no matter what they do to him, he will get blamed.

This kid, Bobby went on to say, Cheryl and him, agreed, if they cause a fight and Mike beats them up, they win. They win because Cho chose the wrong person to train. He cannot he trusted with Cho's knowledge."

Cho hearing this turned to Chopper. "I will deal with them."

Chopper replied no to Cho. I will, when the time comes. Just keep a close eye on the kids. Let this play out, for a while."

Razor agreed. "Mike will need to deal with this problem. Many times, to come, he will need to deal with problems arising. Let us watch him and see how well, he can work through this."

"Yes, there is wisdom in what you say Chopper, Razor, Mike will be tested, and my training will be tested. This problem will not resolve itself, due to the nature of it. When the time comes, as Chopper says, we will intervene."

"Okay, unless there is further business, I contend we drink to success. Anyone here thinks otherwise, get the hell out. We are drinking men. Here, here, shouts called out" Beers passed out, everyone was sitting at a table or at the pool tables. Outside, rain pounded on the roof top. Chopper along with Razor, and Cho thought about Mike. Bone worried more, after recalling Mike's torn sleeping bag.

Night came and went. Mike was under the table and a good thing it was. When the rain came, it came hard. Mike's bedroll was quickly soaked. Water was trying to pry inside. Mike spent most of the night, trying to prevent getting any wetter.

"Tomorrow, I got to take care of this, thinking trying to keep the holes squeeze tightly closed."

Morning rose and Mike with the sun rise. If not for some firewood stashed away, Mike would be sitting on a cold bench, wet through and through to the bone. He started to make a fire, then a car drove up. Inside, was Bell. She made her way through the wet-soaked-muddy ground, squirting mud out with a squishing sound from each tire.

Thinking out loud, Mike could hear her thoughts. "Who in the hell thought this was okay, for a child, to spend the night in this storm last night. What is wrong with those men"?

Soon, she spotted Mike. He was bent over attempting to start a fire at a table. He was as wet, as the ground. He looked pale. "Definitely, was cold. He must be freezing, because I sure am walking down this road," Bell assumed. Coming up to him, "Mike looked better, than she figured. Pondering Mike's appearance, what he looks like and what he feels like, is a different matter. He may look fine, but I know, he trying to hide that from me. Men, who can figure?"

"My, my, it sure poured last night. You looked like you didn't sleep any last night." Mike nodded. "How you get so wet, I thought you had shelter." Bell looked under the table where his bed roll was left laying opened to dry. Quickly, her eyes spotted the seam, sloppily sewn. Reaching down inside the roll, she felt the wetness.

Bell turned looking up at Mike. "You mean, you stayed out in this, all night long. Even a dog, has sense to get out of the rain. Why didn't you go to the house? The door was opened."

Mike knew she was right and thought of that. "My pride kept me from doing it. The way I was thinking, I wasn't going to let the rain beat me. It did. Now, I'm paying the price, Bell's bantering at me driving her point home."

"Okay, you want to act all manly, now you're soaking wet. Most likely catch your death, in this cold. You're coming to the house," demanded Bell.

Cho walks up from the house seeing Bell with Mike in tow. He knew from the words she was throwing out at Mike. "I want none of that. Mike got himself into this. I figure, he might come to the house, when it rained. His pride needs a bit of humiliation. Bell is perfect, for that lesson."

Cho turns silently walking away. Mike noticed Cho silently turn, proceeding to the house. Bell was to intent, making him see the error of his ways to notice Cho. At the clubhouse, Bell had Mike strip. She grabbed hold of his wet clothes from the other side of the bathroom door.

"Now, take a hot bath, while I wash and dry these nasty clothes. Bell sees Cho sitting at the table watching. She started to comment about Mike's condition, but changed her mind, after seeing smirky smile on his face.

Two men was making their way from a car, walking into the park. For nearly three hours, the two strange men stood in the park. Several older kids came and talked to them and quickly as they arrive to talk, just as quickly, left. This happened two more times. For several weeks, prior to Mike arriving at the house, these two men were commonly seen hanging around the park.

Some of the wives talked to other wives about the two men hanging around. Few of those women mentioned their concerns, to the Biker wives. Many of them, wanted to move to another sub-division. "Them bikers being there, gave their area a bad name." In some ways it did, what those ladies never realized, the bikers living in the sub, prevented that kind of people coming into their area. Most of the time, the biker wives made it a point to spot bad people hanging around. The current problems from the battle, had kept their vigilance less alerted.

After a good twenty minutes, allowing the hot shower to clean the dirt and smell away, Mike dried off. He was glad for the shower. Bell stood at the door, waiting to hear the shower turn off. When it did, she called out to Mike.

"Mike your clothes are still in the wash. I got some clothes from the lost and found room." She cracked opened the door, handing Mike some used clothes.

"Okay Mike, we are going to supper. You be waiting by the road, when we come by. We will pick you up by the road."

Yes, Miss Bell, responded Mike coming out of the bathroom wearing baggy clothes. They were dry and clean, just two sizes larger than his size.

FIRE EATERS DELIGHT

Standing by the road, a car and several bikes came to a halt. The car door opened; Mike got in. Cho said, "I need to go out and eat supper with Bell and Chopper. It was not a request."

Mike squeezed beside Bell in the front seat. Her arm quickly wrapped across his shoulder. Chopper drove. Razor went ahead, to fletch his wife. Jack knife called ahead to his wife and kids, to meet them at the diner. Mandy sat in the back with Pretty boy, in Razor's car.

Arriving at the diner, waiting out front, was nearly twelve bikes and several riders. Bone Breaker came to the car, to open the door. He was at the funeral home, along with Mandy. Mandy drove back to the house, when the two bikers bringing Susan, showed up.

Susan often went to the funeral home every night. Cheryl accompanied her. Bone Breaker stay behind, to wait for Cheryl on this night. Cheryl left the house with Susan after her display toward Mike, a few days ago. That was the last time Mike saw Cheryl, until the camp incident and this night. Susan told Cheryl to ride with Bone breaker. He toted her on the rear of his bike. Susan wanted to stay. It was agreed, someone would deliver her a meal, later.

When the contents of the car emptied, Cheryl saw Mike. It took everything she had to remain quiet. Her mom made her promise to be polite or quiet. She remained quiet.

Everyone piled through the double doors into the diner. Razor was waiting. He made sure there were plenty of tables arranged for his troops. A circle was formed, each biker chose a place beside either their spouse or friends. Bone Breaker made sure his seat was next to Mike. Besides Bone, a thin red headed woman sat. Bell took the other side with Chopper next to Mike. Cheryl chose a seat near some kids, farthest away from Mike.

Many of the biker children knew each other and usually lived nearby. So, it was common and natural for them to make bonds. Cheryl wasted no time to express her opinion about Mike to her friends. Many heard stories about Mike from their parents. Many wanted to see this wonder kid. Like Cheryl, Mike's appearance gave them little to be awed. Cheryl's remarks soon found a new home. Most accepted her remarks about Mike, without even trying to make their own assessments. They went to his camp, destroying what few belonging he own. Now, they sat at the far end staring at Mike, with eyes filled with hate. Mike watched Cheryl and her friends, seeing quickly what she was up to. It proved correct, when all of them turned to look his way.

"Not many smiles on their faces," Mike thought?

A waiter took orders from each biker, Bell asked Mike what he would like to eat. Mike never ate Chinese food and had no idea what, he should order.

"Here Mike, let me order for you. Bell takes the menu from Mike's hand. She peruses the list. Mike do you like chicken or pork?"

"Chicken," Mike responded.

"You want something spicy or sweet?"

"Spicy would be okay, Bell."

"Good, see not hard at all, Mike."

"Hey Mike, what you have Bell order for you," asked Bone Breaker.

"I don't know, ask her. Bell heard Bone Breaker's question answering, sesames chicken."

"Good, I'll order the same. Then, Bone slaps Mike on his back and begins a long spell of non-stop questions and storytelling. It was good, it took Mike's mind off everything.

Cheryl and her friends started to gaggle among themselves. Mike could make out the noise and many of their words. They were making puns at him.

"Bell has to order his food. He can't even to do that. What a deweeb."

Cho overheard the same remarks meant for Mike. It hurt, that his son had to endure this torment, alone. Cho knew this was for his own good. "This will give him strength." Still, it wounded him hearing those mean, taunting words.

Plates of hot food arrived quick. Bone breaker asked for the yellow hot mustard. A big glob was placed on his plate. Quickly, the first egg roll was covered from one end to the other end with the hot savory goo. It disappeared with three bites, followed by a huge gulp of iced tea. A slight pause, to allow the burn to subside, then on to the second egg roll. Only after the third roll followed the same path, did Bone breaker asked Mike to try the mustard.

"Hey Mike, me lad, try some of this. It's a bit on the hot side, but good. You like hot stuff?"

"Yes, I eat a lot of barbecue chips. I usually get the hottest brand they make, Bone."

"Good, then you going to like this mustard."

Bell listening to what was being said between Bone breaker and Mike interrupted. "What, you trying to get Mike hurt, that mustard is too hot for a young kid, to try?"

Cheryl caught the remark made by Bell and giggled. Mike heard the giggle and replied to Bell. "Bell, I like hot food, thanks for your concern, but I will be fine."

"Really now, Bell retorted. Go ahead and have some." A smirky grind crept across her lips. Cheryl and friends watched with a sense of glee. She tried the mustard once; it was way too hot and never had it again. The same was true with her friends, it was too hot.

Mike dipped his egg roll into the mustard and took a big bite. The mustard seemed okay after two chews. Then, suddenly a volcanic explosion erupted in his mouth. The heat quickly burned his tongue rising up into his nose.

"They were right, this is hot," Mike realized with a terrible regret.

Mike reached for anything to drink. He grabbed the glass of cold iced tea. It offered little relief. Not helping him, he takes hold of a cup of hot tea. He sipped at it. To his surprise, the hot tea stopped the burn, instantly.

Mike continued to sip the hot tea looking around Cheryl and her friends were laughing and pointing at him. Bone Breaker spoke.

"They laughed at you, but you don't see them eating the mustard."

Bone was right. Mike realized he could eat the mustard without the full affects being felt, if he drank the hot tea.

"Mike you okay, asked Bell? I did try to warn you."

Mike answered, "you sure did, Bell. But I was caught off guard and surprised. I think I can handle it, now." Mike placed his egg roll back in the mustard, to test his theory. After each bite, he took a sip of hot tea. The burn quickly went away with little effects felt. "Good," he thought to himself.

Everyone across the table with Cheryl, sat watching, Mike dipping the egg roll into the hot mustard. Each expected to see him scramble for water. What they expected, was not what they saw. With each dip of the egg roll in the mustard, Mike took a little sip of tea. Not a gulp or a stop to allow the heat to pass. He just dipped his eggroll taking another bite. Each dip, Mike purposely put more mustard on the egg roll. Even Bone was amazed, seeing him putting as mustard on his rolls, as he did.

Bone had great pleasure watching his fellow bikers watch him eat the mustard. He was a champ at devouring hot food. Many tried their metal against Bone in the past. Not one, unseated him from his throne.

Mike constantly looked around the table. Chopper, Razor, even Bone Breaker sat, staring at him. Cho was the only person to know what Mike was doing. He learned that trick years ago and knew Mike had discovered the same fact he did.

Mike addressed the bikers around the table. "I challenge any and all to a mustard eat off." Looking at the kids around Cheryl, he nodded to them, daring them to take on this challenge.

Several bikers looked at Mike. "Okay kid, I'll take you up on that dare. Me too," came another, then ten bikers were at the ready.

Bone Breaker looked at Mike. "Hey, these guys eat this stuff like candy, Mike."

"You scared, Bone Breaker, retorted Mike?

"Hey kiddo, you just made your first mistake. I happened to be the winner eating hot stuff. You just made a terrible mistake. I was going to let you off easy and not enter in this contest, but no one challenges me, to a hot eat off. You'll going down, kiddo. Get plenty of water ready, kid."

Bell and Chopper stared hard at Mike. Mike could see Bell's concern. Mike leaned over and softly whispered into Bell's ear. "I will be okay, this hot tea I drank, keeps the mustard from burning. They'll going down. Mike looks up at Bell smiling, she returns the smile. Bell turns to Chopper whispering the message into his ear. Chopper chuckles. He saw Cho do the same thing and forgotten about it, until Bell told him Mike's plan.

Only one of the kids took the challenge, Mike offered. Of course, Cheryl made it known, one of them better take the dare. One boy had a crush on Cheryl, this dare was his chance to try to win her love. Maybe, hoping a date. That is what Bobby confided to his buds raising his hand to accept the challenge.

"Here's the rules, Bone Breaker stands and announces to all. Everyone got up. We are going to sit at another table. This way, you can't fake it. Chopper, Razor, Bell, and Jack knife will judge. To keep it fair, we will have one of the younger kids, also judge. Cheryl quickly raises her hand. Bone Breaker heard about her outburst and silently hoped she would volunteer to judge. Something inside him said, Mike wanted her too, as well.

Everyone found a seat. In front of each seat was a bowl of the hot mustard. All bowls in the diner was grabbed off every table. Few patrons made any protest. In fact, they stood and walked over or turned around in their seats to watch the event.

Everyone watching silently, chose their champion to win. Only three seemed to think Mike, had a chance. Money was flashed, bets were made. Money was now at stake.

"Here's how this is going down, Bone Breaker commanded. Each person will take a spoon full of mustard, to eat any way you can, within one minute. You can drink all the water or whatever you preferred to drink, within that time. No food or antacids! Once everyone finished, another spoon full will be giving to each of you still in the contest. You cannot eat the mustard, until everyone's spoon has been inspected for volume. We will do this, until only one person is still alive. Got that!" Everyone nodded.

Large glasses of soda, tea, water, and milk was poured into each person glass as requested. Mike was the only one requesting hot tea from among the group. All eyes looked at Mike's choice, with curiosity. Seeing them look at what he chose to drink, Mike quickly tells them, he likes hot tea and didn't drink cold tea. All thought that was a good excuse excepting his explanation. Besides, a large glass of water was placed next to his hot tea.

"Okay, you fire eaters, get ready, set, go, called Chopper. Bone Breaker quickly licked his spoon dry and held back from drinking anything. Many of the others took a good lick. Those that did, quickly were gulping their chosen drinks.

That first spoon full of mustard was nothing, compared to the little dips they made with their egg rolls before entering the contest. All that mustard alone, was more than too much for five of the ten enrolled in the contest.

Only five of the bikers were left willing to go on, with the dare. Mike held back, until he saw most of the bikers taking their first lick. Looking across the table, down two seats, sat the kid Cheryl prodded to enter. He held back seeing if Mike was going to back out and he wouldn't have to wimp out, first. Mike seeing his hesitation, smile at him. The kid spoke up.

"Hey, I see Bone Breaker ain't afraid of some mustard, he just licked his spoon clean all at once. Well, I ain't no wimp, either. Let me show you how a man does it." The kid held the spoon to his mouth, then with one quick lick, cleaned his spoon.

"Well done, I'm not that big of a hurry friend, I have plenty of time to clean my spoon," responded Mike. Mike took a good lick and sipped his hot tea. Then another lick, followed with another sip of tea. Mike continued, until he finally lick cleaned his spoon.

The kid drank his glass of water and scrambled for more water. Tears filled his eyes. He screamed out it, I'm burning inside, help, help. Bell and several ladies rushed over to his aid. One lady said, "drink milk, it will counter the acid." He drank milk. Didn't help much.

Finally, Sifu Cho came from the kitchen, with hot salty water in a glass. Cho hands the glass to one lady, asking her to have him drink it. It was helpful, but a little too late for easing the fire burning in his mouth and down his throat.

The contest halted, until the kid finally called it quits, getting up from the table with two women aiding him. He went directly to the bathroom. One of the ladies followed. Five men pulled back from the table. Five bikers remained. Four were on the verge of quitting. Nothing to eat with the mustard, was a requirement. The amount was not what many expected. That much mustard at once, was an eye opener. Mike noticed Bone Breaker had a slight grimace on his face, with a hopeful look, seeing the first five drop out, Mike felt encouraged.

Thinking, Mike figured, the next spoon will end the contest. The hot tea helped a lot and like Bone breaker, the amount was hard, even with the hot tea dissolving the mustard. It occurred to Mike of the lesson taught him in school. His teacher said, "hot causes particles to speed up and spread apart. Heat when applied to an object, loosens a tight hold on objects. It causes the substance to spread away, releasing its hold. Conversely, cold brings things together. Cold slows the particles down and compacts them". That is why, the hot tea helps preventing his tongue from burning. Hot separates the mustard and disperses it," Mike recalled.

Once the tables were cleared, the remaining players received their second spoon. Mike noticed two men were deciding not to try. Their spoons full and the ordeal each went through moments ago, reappeared in their minds. A second thought crept into their minds. They looked at Bone Breaker and Mike.

"The two bikers realized after their first spoon; it had little on effect Bone or Mike. If they made it through this second round; that was it. A third round was out of the question. Why go through all that and lose?"

Before Chopper had a chance to begin the second-round, both of the men talked themselves into quitting. They pulled back from the table. Now only three remained.

The second round went about the same; Bone Breaker licking his spoon clean. This time, he drank a glass of water. The others slowly licked at each spoon. Two quit, before the mustard was licked clean from their spoons. Mike continued to lick and sip hot tea. Nearly fifty seconds elapsed, before Mike finished off his last lick, cleaning his spoon. Two of the three men had backed out. Now, there was three still in the contest, Bone, Mike, and a third rider, red face, gulping water by the gallons.

Three remained. Cheryl was amazed seeing Mike make it, as long as he did. After his first attempt at eating hot mustard, she felt certain, he was going out with the first lick.

Bell walked over to Mike, asking if he was okay. "Mike, you made your point, it will be fine to back out, now. Then, Bell bends down to whispered in Mike's ear. Mike, by the looks of it, you might win. This has always been Bone Breaker pride, to be the best fire eater in our club. You might consider that, as you and he fight for the championship."

Mike looked up at Bell giving her a nod of understanding. Chopper calls everybody to attention. "Okay people, we are down to the last three. Mike, a little applause accompanied, Bone Breaker, the floor erupted with applause, and our final contestant, Music man followed with less applause. It clearly showed Bone Breaker was the favorite. Most of the applause seemed to come from the kids rooting for Bone, to Mike's ears.

Chopper waits until the third spoon is dipped in the mustard. Okay, to the best fire eater amongst us. Bone raises his spoon, then licks the spoon clean.

Music man made a huge lick like Bone Breaker had done, realizing his mistake and horror, it was too much for him. He quickly pulled away from the table, running to the bathroom. Chopper calls out.

"Two left now. Mike, the kid and Bone Breaker, our current champ, for now."

Bone Breaker wasn't taking his usual big lick on this third spoon. He opted for a slower pace, like Mike.

Mike looked at Bone Breaker, sweat was beading on his brow. Mike felt, he was going to quit, soon. There was no glass of water by Bone Breaker bowl of mustard. Mike slid his hot tea over to Bone's spoon.

Mike said, "you might want to try this hot tea. It can help you. It's better than water. Try it."

Bone Breaker at first, hesitated, then, slowly gave way to the temptation to drink. Lifting the hot tea to his lips, slowly sipping at it. Suddenly, his mouth stopped burning. A subtle surprise and a realization came to him; he had been had, comes over his face.

Mike spoke first, before Bone had a chance to make a comment. Everyone, I quit, Bone Breaker is the best and still the greatest fire eater here. Mike threw in a cough or two, to add to his capitulation. Bell gave Mike a nod with a smile.

Everyone crowded around the two of them. Each received their share of back slapping and great job. Once all the fuss ended and Bone Breaker was returned his title, and all bets paid off, they returned to their tables. Their meals were still warm. The contest lasted less than five minutes.

At the table, Bone Breaker told Mike, we two need to have a conversation later, about this. Mike knew what he meant. Cheryl sat with a frown on her face. A little cheer wailed inside; "Mike didn't win."

After the meal, everyone was in a happier mood. The challenge had the effect of taking their minds off the loss each felt for Stephen and Teddy Bear. Soon, their feeling came back while making their way out the front door. Cheryl and her group waited for Mike, to pass through the door. Each made their move passing, shoving him. Even when he was clearly out of their path, somehow, they managed to shove him passing to leave. It hadn't gone un-notice by the leaders or Cho.

Mike stood stoically, allowing each to have a turn at him. It wasn't any good complaining or reacting to their petty attempts to mock him. They made up their minds and hopefully in time, maybe they will see him differently, Mike thought.

Cheryl had to make one last comment passing Mike. "Look at the way he is dressed? We need to leave here quick, before anyone spots us with this vagabond. His clothes are too large and wrinkled."

Bell nearly hit the ceiling. Chopper grabbed her arm, pulling her toward the rear, away from the front door of the restaurant. The trip back to the clubhouse was quiet. Cho sat next to Mike in the rear seat, Chopper, and Bell in the front seat. They stopped long enough, dropping off Cho and Mike by his camp site.

"Good night," Bell yelled driving away.

"Tomorrow Mike, we will rest, Bell will take you to a store for an outfit. You did well, tonight. That was nice of you, to let Bone Breaker win and unto your little secret," replied Cho.

"Secret Sifu, what secret?"

"Mike, don't conceal anything from me," answered Cho.

"I'm not Sifu, hot tea dissolved the mustard's burn, I saw you knew this, when you gave the hot salty water to that boy, crying out for help."

"You saw me?"

"Yes Sifu. When the boy stopped his screaming, I realized you were giving him something to stop the burn. It had to be something similar to what I was drinking."

"Very good, very good indeed, you are way ahead of our training. Within a few days, I will change your training. It will be the hardest thing to get through to date, Mike. Your mind must be ready. There will be great pain. Rest assure, I believe in you and you will prove me right."

"I will not fail you, Sifu."

"I know you will not, Mike. Now, would you mind, if I stay here with you this night. I feel like some fresh air and the nightly star-lit sky is soothing. A fire was quickly started. Both Sifu and Mike sat by the fire, looking up at the starry sky.

SHOPPING SPREE

The morning day came with birds singing wake-up songs. Mike remembered waking every morning, while on the road, to their songs. It seemed to make the day's journey begin on the right foot. So to was this, on this day. Sifu Cho was up and about. Mike was soon up and began his chores gathering wood for a fire.

"Well, what's for breakfast," Sifu Cho inquired?

"I haven't caught it yet; I saw a stream yesterday through the trees. I figured to make my way to it and try my luck, Sifu."

"Well, all I can say is good luck to that." Cho was a master of his art but not much a master to survival skills, as Stephen or Mike.

"Sifu Cho, have you been fishing at that stream and know something that will aid me to catch our breakfast?"

"No Mike. I never had much luck and neither did many who attempted the chance to catch a meal in that river."

"Well, I will give it a try. If I don't come back, let's say, an hour, we will just go hungry, Sifu."

"I've been hungry before, Mike."

"Me too, Sifu," chuckled Mike.

After several minutes walking through the under-brush, Mike came to the stream. He unraveled his line with several hooks, then attached worms to each. He quickly located bait making his way through the shrubs. After placing the lines in the water, with several hooks, ties the lines to a branch. Mike removes his shirt and pants entering into the cold stream. The water came up to his waist and remained at that waist along the edge of the stream. Slowly, Mike made his way down stream, poking his foot into any hole. Once a hole was found, Mike reached down under the water, shoving his hand into the hole. On the second hole, pay dirt. A fish head was felt. From the feel of it, Mike realized, it was going to be Cho and his breakfast.

Mike slid his hand into the catfish's mouth. Its jaws clamp down on his arm. Mike grabbed hold and a fight was on. Slowly, Mike began his tug-a-war battle. The fish was giving way. Defiantly, the catfish held his own for several minutes. Mike thanked God he could poke his head out of the stream long enough, to catch a breath of air. This fish was locked in good. In the end, Mike won out. The fish emerged from the hole. Mike raises it up out the water.

Cho was watching from behind a bush. To his dismay, Mike caught a fish, not by a hook and line. "This young man has some secrets of his own," Cho thought. Cho left the bush concealing his presence, walking over to where Mike had a line in the water.

Again, to his amazement, the line was jerking. Cho reached down gently touching the line, a fish was clearly on it. In fact, maybe two. Cho couldn't help himself, he had to draw one line in. Cho felt like a child catching his first fish. To be honest, it was maybe his second time he ever tried to fish.

Mike left the stream, picked up his fish tossed on the banks. He walked to where he left his clothes and fishing line. Cho was there, pulling one of his lines. Cho hadn't noticed Mike's approach. The fish on the line clearly kept him, inattentive. Mike stood there watching the fun Cho was having pulling at the fish. When he had his fish on the ground, out of the water, Cho sensed his protégé presence, standing behind him.

"Well done," Mike called to him. Cho, slightly embarrassed being caught unaware and for catching Mike's fish, started to apologize.

Mike was now, the master and the teacher, he stopped Sifu Cho from what he was going to say. "Glad you were here to bring them in, we might have lost them. It took me longer than I expected, to catch this fish." Mike fell up his single fish for Cho to see. Cho realized Mike's attempt to ease his embarrassment, just nodded.

"Well, I see Mike, we are going to have a fine breakfast. I'll help in cleaning them. Back at camp, it was plain, Cho knew little about how to clean a catfish. He could clean a scaly fish, doing so quickly.

With a knife in one hand and a tight grip on the catfish head, Mike makes a clean circular cut around the neck. Then, grabbing the skin, pulls the skin down and off the tail.

"Sifu, with catfish, we can skin them or eat them with their skin on. I see you have the other fish skewed and hanging over the fire. With cat, we need to pan fry them."

Mike pulls out a frying pan from his backpack, after gutting the fish. Removing some of the squirrel meat-fat he had from the nights hunt before, placed it in his pan. It was a lucky catch, the squirrel happened to make a silly mistake, eating nuts off the bench. With a quick toss of Mike's pole with the Knife attached, ended the squirrel's lack of awareness, providing him a meal. Mike had time to quickly skin and toast it up before leaving to the diner. He placed the squirrel in his knack sack hanging it on a tree before leaving to eat Chinese.

Mike put some of the squirrel meat in the pan, to warmed it. "Squirrel is lean meat having little fat, Mike explained to Sifu Cho. Cooking releases some of the fat. We can fry our cat in that, Sifu." Within minutes, three fish were cooked. Soon, both bellies were satisfied with their meal.

Mike just finished extinguishing the fire, when Bell and another lady appeared. It was about ten in the morning. Both ladies were dress nicely. Bell was wearing a dress. Unusual for her, to Mike, it looked like she was poured into it. She was a very attractive woman, when she was dressed, thought Mike. The other lady wore a dress, it never looked as good, as the way Bell wore her dress. Each lady said, good morning, first to Sifu Cho, then to Mike. The lady with Bell, was Razor's wife.

"Well Mike, we have a long day today. We come to take you out for breakfast and shopping."

Mike wasn't sure whether he should tell them, he and Cho just ate. The choice was made by Cho, for him.

"Mike is starving. We were just talking about, where we were going to go to eat. Turning to Mike, Cho looked at him and said, right Mike."

"Sure, yes, we were talking about food, not to long before you showed up," Mike stumbled to say.

"Cho, no offense, but we hadn't planned on you accompanying us."

"No, no, please feel free to go without me, Cho quickly answers. Mike looks at Cho with a, "hey what the heck, you put me into this, and you ain't going, stare." Cho returned his look with, "sorry," then quickly leaves Mike with the two ladies.

Both ladies walk over to Mike, grabbing hold of an arm. Quickly, both let go, stepping back. "My, my, Razor's wife spoke first. What is that smell. You take a bath in the creek? You smell like fish."

Bell responded; "you can't go with us, smelling like that. Come with us." Both led the way back to the clubhouse.

"Okay young man, in there is a shower, remove your clothes and take a bath. Mike walked inside the bathroom, stripped down to his under shorts. Bell yelled for him, to give her his clothes through the door. Mike handed them to her. Both ladies inspected the clothes, both came to the same conclusions, they smelled worse, than Mike.

Calling back to Mike, before he entered the shower," do you have any other clothes to wear?"

Mike returned her answer, with a yes, but added, they might not smell too good. Mike grabbed hold of a shirt and another pair of pants when he left home. Both were not yet washed. Each was worn, like the other for many days training.

"That won't do young man. We haven't time to wash these. We will get you some clothes from our lost and found. They will have to do."

Mike stayed in the shower up to a point, the ladies were getting a bit antsy. "Hey, Bell shouted, you drowned in there? Finish up. We have some clothes for you to try on. Mike dreaded what they had for him to wear. The last time he wore clothes from the locker were two sizes bigger, than what he wore. Then, the remarks and laugher from the kids, made that worse.

Both Bell and Razor's wife opened the door to the bathroom, just as Mike wrapped a towel about his waist. Both ladies stood staring at Mike. Both heard stories about his encounter with a bear and beaten with a whip. Bell saw them before, when she first met Mike. That was when her heart melted and began her attachment for him. She had forgotten how they looked. Her first seeing them, was almost a shock. See saw wounds before, nothing like them and never on a boy.

Razors wife saw them for the first time. The shock, caused her to step back and almost faint. Bell grabbed her. "Oh my, my, my, dear God," came a reaction from her mouth. Mike wanted to cover up looking at saw her face. He couldn't and besides, it was too late to try.

"Do they hurt," Razors wife asked Mike?

Mike replied, "the bear claws do on occasions, the whip marks have healed and give me little trouble. Truth being told, Mike always have some difficulty with stretching, those scars kept his skintight. Even during training, the pain often followed every stretching session. "What really hurts and never healed properly is this snake bite, on my arm." Mike held his arm out right for Razor's wife to inspect.

Razors wife looked to where Mike pointed to twisted muscles with a dark, almost dead, ashen appearance across the skin, on his arm. Again, Bell had to take hold of her. Bell handed Mike clothes, freshly ironed, while he was in the shower. Mike took the clothes, while Bell escorted Razors wife out of the room.

Outside, Bell explained to Razors wife, Miriam, how she first reacted to seeing his scars. She made it known to Miriam, his scars were far worse, when she saw them. Miriam just cringed, thinking of the pain, the dear boy must have been through. Now, Miriam understood Bell motherly attachment to him. Tears came to her eyes.

Bell spoke, "Miriam, clear them tears away, before Mike comes out."

Mike walks out wearing his freshly iron pants and shirt. The shirt was loose fitting and the pants, a size to big. Mike had to hold unto the pants, to keep them up.

"Hey ladies, can I have my belt, I can't go around holding these pants up all day."

"Why Mike, it makes you look dashing holding your pants, up. Miriam smile, Mike frowned, and Bell giggled. Miriam left to retrieve the belt off of Mike's pants. They hung the belt across the doorknob, while they put his clothes in a washer, forgetting the belt, finishing their ironing.

While Miriam was away, Mike inquired about her shocked looked. Bell answered, "Mike, she and everyone knew about your scars, but only the few of us at the inn, we first met, saw them. It was a shock to her. And to be honest, it shocked me when I first saw them. Today, when I saw them a second time, I had forgotten, and it shocked me some. I'm sorry, so sorry."

"Why Bell, it happened, and I have learned to deal with it."

"I know Mike, I'm sorry I was so shocked, again."

"Don't think about it Bell, to me, it shows how much you care about me. That means a lot to me." Mike reaches over and hugs Bell this time.

Miriam returns seeing them hugging. She recovered from her shock handing Mike his belt. The way she handed the belt to Mike, made Bell curious.

Turning to Miriam, Bell asked, "why are you suddenly afraid to touch Mike?"

"I'm not," Miriam quickly replied back to Bell.

"That's not what it looked like, Miriam."

Mike confronts Miriam, after hearing what Bell asked her. "Miriam, it's okay to feel that way, about my scars. It's okay to touch me. I won't cry. I'm fine, it touches me, you worry about not causing me any pain." Mike reaches over to her. Looking at her, before taking her hands, Mike asked, "may I give you a hug?"

Miriam looking at this handsome young boy look at her, with his brown eyes and sweet smile eases her fears. She nodded to Mike, It's okay, to give me a hug. She squeezed Mike as hard as Bell did and a bit longer. She was hiding her tears formed in the corner of her eyes. She stopped hugging Mike, when she was able to stop her tears. Bell handed her a rag during the embraces, before she let go of her hug.

"Now, let's go eat," Bell shouted. All three were walking out the door, when Bone Breaker and several other bikers were entering. Bone Breaker inquired about where they were off to. He hinted; he would like to accompany them. Bell got the hint nixing it, before he could say anything further.

"Bone Breaker, this is for us girls and Mike. We are going shopping and that is not a man thing. Do you agree?" Bone Breaker agreed and waved Mike off. Also, lipped Mike his blessing.

Bone turned entering the bar with his comrades, making a quick jest. "I like that kid a lot. I wouldn't wish that on my worst enemy. I wish I could help him?"

"He's beyond any of our help," one of the other men quipped. All three laughed walking to the bar.

"Three beers, I got first dibs on the pool table," boasted Bone Breaker.

"You know the rules Bone, you got to shoot for the play. Get your stick and wait your turn, after Mechanic and I start."

"You're that sure, you going to win the shoot, Peanut? Yep, just as you were, with the mustard. You're good at that and we are good at this. So, take your shot and have a seat, until it is your turn, buddy."

Both ladies sit in the front seat, while Mike takes the back seat. Ten minutes and they were in town. Soon, they came to a diner. In the parking lot, they got out of the car. To their surprise, Susan and Cheryl were at the same diner. Bell went over to Susan, asking her if she would join them. She accepted. Again, Mike had to deal with Cheryl. The same smirk was on her mouth.

"Thank God, Mike thought, walking side by side into the restaurant, she said nothing to him."

Once everyone was seated, Susan got up to go to the restroom. Miriam followed. Bell was going to do the same, but remembers the first encounter Cheryl had with Mike. She felt, leaving them alone, they might return to see two people fighting. The way Cheryl stared at Mike and Mike trying to avoid her stare, only proved to her, she was right to remain at the table with them.

Inside the restroom, Susan asked why they were with Mike and what was up?"

"Oh, we decided, Mike should look nice for the services tomorrow, Susan. His family has little money and from what we saw, his clothes are in bad shape. They smelled so bad, we had him change and take a bath, before we took him out."

"Is that why his clothes look to big for him, Miriam?"

"Yes, we found some clothes in the lost clothes closet. We got as close to his size, as we could. We put his clothes in the wash and ironed these." A tear formed in Miriam's eyes. Susan quickly noticed the tear, before Miriam had a chance to wipe it away.

"What's wrong," Susan asked?

"Please don't make me tell you, Susan. I'm afraid, I might start to sob uncontrollable again."

"Again, why, what is it, please tell me. I'm your friend, am I not?"

"Susan, you have enough pain right now, you don't need any more coming from me."

"Hush now, I can handle my pain, just fine. Besides, your pain may help me deal with mine."

Miriam had little strength, when it came to this kind of horror. She never wanted to talk or have shop talk around her. It always upset her. Men fighting and dying and all the bloody details men speak about drinking.

"Susan, if I tell you, please don't tell Bell, I told you, not now."

"Okay, I promise, Miriam.

"Well Susan, when Mike was taking a bath, we walked in on him. He was finish drying off. His towel was around his waist. We saw, saw, we saw, those scars everyone had spoken about. They were bad Susan, really bad. I almost fainted. It took all my will power not to get sick. That poor boy, my God Susan, the pain must have been horrible. Mike says, they don't hurt much. The ones the bear made."

"Bear, what bear? I don't remember anyone saying bear scars. Stephen mentioned to me he had some bad scars on his body, but never said anything about a bear attack."

"Oh yes, he had three deep cuts going from one side of his chest to the other side. Miriam mimicked the arc across her chest to make the point to Susan the extent and length of the scars. That wasn't the worse scar he had. He was bit by a snake."

"A snake too, Miriam."

"Oh yes, Susan, on his arm. His arm Susan, the muscle was all twisted and almost black. He said he tried to tend to it in the woods the best he could. He told us the story of how he got bitten in the car over here. He used some moss and an old cigarette butt to draw the poison out. He managed to walk or crawl to a lady's home that lived by herself in the forest. She took care of him for weeks."

"That is not the only scars he showed me. Susan, his backside looks like shredded wheat. Bell said, an old man found him in his barn. Mike was sick with pneumonia having a high fever. The man tied him to a post and wailed him with a bullwhip. He stopped, when his wife heard Mike scream running to the barn to investigate. Mike escaped, running through the fields. Somewhere in the night, a farmer heard his dog barking. He found Mike in a field. Him and his wife tended to his wounds for days."

"My god, I see why you are so upset. Now calm yourself, Miriam. Thanks for telling me. I will not mention this to Bell at the table. But us girls need to see how we can help Mike, while he is here."

"Yes, yes, that is a wonderful idea, Susan." Both left the restroom returning to their table. Nasty comments were heard across the diner.

Back at the table, Cheryl was belaying Mike with mean and ugly comments. Bell had enough of Cheryl nasty leers at Mike and made it known to her.

"Young lady, this is going to end your ugly display around Mike. This will end now, or I will assure you, your mom and you will be receiving guests appearance from Chopper, Razor, and Jack Knife at your home. I will have this discussion with your mom, after the services. Furthermore girlie, you will keep this conversation private until after the services. Rest assure, one word of this to your mom and there will be serious consequences for it. Your mom has enough worries without you adding to it. I know full well the hurt you have and your need to find someone to blame. Believe this, Mike is not to blame in any way. We will have a sit down and you will come to understand how foolish you have been. Now keep your mouth shut, or so help me. Bell almost raised her hand to slap Cheryl. She didn't, but was seriously tempted."

Mike raises his hand to stop Bell. Please Bell, she is hurting and me being present, isn't helping her to deal with her pain. Turning to Cheryl, Mike asked her if she would step outside to have a short talk. Bell started to interrupt but Mike looked at her, asking with a please to let him and her have a moment.

Cheryl stood up with a snap. She was waiting for this moment to dump everything she had pent up on the killer of her dad. She was going to take full measure of it, while she had the opportunity. Both stood quickly stepping outside the restaurant. Both turned preceding to the rear of the building.

Behind the building, out of visible sight, Cheryl unleashed a devasting thrust kick to Mike belly. Mike knew ahead it was coming and allowed her to make contact. Cheryl quickly followed that kick, squarely making a hard impact to Mike belly with him showing little effects from it followed with a punch to his face. Again, Mike took the full blow without offering a hint of blocking the punch.

Mike made a subtle movement twisting his body at the time of impact to glance away most of Cheryl's power. Exhaling allowed him to prevent her kick from knocking the air out of his lungs. Cheryl perceived her impact made its mark. Now, without a correction to her awkward stance, caused by Mike feint, any strike at Mike was made less powerful. That little feint caused Cheryl her balance while leveling a series of punches at Mike. The first punch hit Mike's face. Again, not unexpectantly to him. He turned his face just at the moment of the hit. What would have been a jaw loosen strike, felt more like playful slap by a kitten to him.

Seeing her punch had little effect, Cheryl began a barrage of punches aimed at Mike guts. After a slew of punches, she began to tire. She spent her anger punching his belly. She nearly dropped to the ground from exhaustion. Mike caught hold helping her to her feet. Then, Mike quickly turned to walked back to the front of the diner. Cheryl was going to tell him she didn't want his help. She never got the chance before he walked away.

Once inside the diner both Cheryl and Mike sat quiet. Susan and Miriam returned to a quiet table. The waiter came over and took their orders. Bell told Mike to eat all he wanted. Mike looked at the menu. It had been a while, since eating eggs and bacon. He turned to Bell asking, would it be okay to order more than two eggs and three strips of bacon that came with his order."

Bell replied, "of course, order as many eggs you want."

Mike responded, "I haven't any money Bell, I will do any work for you, to pay for this meal."

Hearing this, Cheryl quickly makes a snide remark. "So now, you want someone to pay for your keep." Bell, Miriam, and Susan sat shocked. Mike quickly asked to change his order.

He said to Bell, "I decided I am not that hungry." Then rose out of his seat, thanked Bell and excused himself and preceded to walk to the front door.

Mike got to the outside when Susan took hold of his shoulder. She stopped Bell from chasing after Mike, before she had a chance to get up out of her seat. Outside, she apologized for her daughter's cruel remarks toward him. Mike accepted the apology, but insisted, he rather take a long walk and would return after they had their meal. He mentioned to Susan, he caught Cho and himself their breakfast. Cho had him accept this meal out of good manners. Susan was about to argue, she felt Mike was trying to make an excuse. Mike stopped her.

"Remember Bell mentioned to you, I smelled pretty bad."

"Yes, Mike."

"Well, the reason why was due to my fishing in the river. I caught our fish wading in the water with my hands." Mike showed her the fresh teeth marks left by the catfish. Besides Miss Susan, Cheryl will most likely make a scene. She has much hurt inside. That much hurt is hard to hold in. I know, you think you can cope with her. You may well be able to prevent another outburst from her. Why take a chance and have her upset everyone sitting at the table? I am fine."

Susan watched Mike walk down the street. Her last thoughts was of the catfish bite mark on his arm and thinking, he went fishing this time of year in an icy, cold river.

Returning inside, Susan sits at the table. Mike walks down the street. Susan tells the group Mike had already ate earlier and needed to take a walk. Cheryl quickly made a short nasty reply.

"Good, now we can eat in peace. Bell's eyes lit up. Miriam nearly, but held back what she wanted to say, for Susan benefit. Susan just slapped her daughter. Cheryl started to rise and leave. Susan grabbed her arm. Then, commanded her to sit. She sat.

"Now not, I mean not one word better come from that mouth, young lady!" Susan never struck Cheryl before. She was clearly upset with her bad attitude.

Everyone's order came out. The waiter took Mike's order and left before it was cancelled. It sat getting cold. So, did Bell's meal. Also, Miriam ate some but left most. Susan ate little of her meal. Cheryl cleaned her plate.

The meal ended quick. Everyone said their goodbyes. Bell reminded Cheryl of their conversation. Each group road off. Bell drove around the block, then another block before seeing Mike. Mike was sitting on a bus stop bench. He saw her car approaching, standing when Bell pulled up to him.

Soon, Bell, Miriam, and Mike were at a clothing store. Mike got out asking them to not spend too much on his clothes. Mike explains to them, why. "I don't mean to be ungrateful to you and for helping me dress correctly for this sad event. But I have no place to keep the clothes I will be wearing. They may get ruined outside by my campsite."

Bell looks at Mike and realized he was trying to allow them an excuse to not spend much on his clothes. Bell quickly got over her madness toward Cheryl behavior and rebutted Mike's excuse. "Don't be silly, Mike."

Miriam followed, "there is no way you are attending this service, not looking good. I be damn if you are going to look like a bum around us. We told everyone we are going to dress you nice. So be it."

Bell replied, "so be it then. Mike shut up, not another word about cost. Your family, we take care of our own. You are going to be the best dressed man there. You represent the two of us. You will look good. Got that?"

"Yes madam," replied Mike following them into the store. Inside was a man greeting both ladies. He apparently knew them, from his familiar address to both women, Mike surmised.

"We want this young man looking good. He will need to be dressed head to toe. We have three hours to get this done. You have him ready when we return, we will expect him to set the standard in this town."

"Yes madam," the elder man replied.

Mike stood on a stand while the man took various measurements. Several jackets were brought for Mike to try on. Then pants and shirts. Mike had a large neck and every shirt was baggy. Another man appeared taking two shirts into another room. Mike kept one shirt on to aid the fitter to assess a selection of ties for Mike's outfit. Socks and shoes were next. Several styles were brought out. Mike was offered little choice in the selection. Everything was chosen by the fitter. Two shirts were brought out from the room, they disappeared into. Mike tried on the shirts. They fit perfectly. The final articles were his under clothes. Mike was handed his clothes then asked to enter a room and change into them. A man entered the room and tried to assist Mike. It was no use trying to stop the man. Mike did stop him from aiding him with his under clothes.

Two hours elapsed. Bell and Miriam walked in the store just as Mike walked out of the dressing room. Mike stood facing the two ladies fully dressed. Both ladies walked around Mike, inspecting every aspect of his dress. The fitter handed Bell a second shirt fitted for Mike exact size, a second pair of pants, two pairs of socks, two packs of under clothes and several ties. The final item was a small can of shoe wax.

"Wonderful, he looks like a million dollars."

"Miriam remarks to Bell, "all the young girls will swoon over him, like bees to honey. Bell agreed.

Now, one more stop, Mike. After paying the bill with cash, all three loaded into the car driving to another store. Inside was not only men's clothing. It was stocked with women, men, and children clothes. It had it all. Over at the men's side, Miriam was blousing through jeans. Bell was at the casual shirts. Soon, both had several selections for Mike to try on. They knew the size he wore after talking to the fitter at the first store.

Once they chosen Mike play clothes, they had him try on sneakers. Then another belt and finally a raincoat and winter coat. "There now, you won't be needing much in the clothes and shoe category for some time."

Mike was dumb founded. Holding his head with his hands, asked both ladies, "where am I going to keep all of this stuff?"

"Oh, you silly young man, Miriam replied. You don't think you will be sleeping outside, while you are here?"

"Well, yes, Mike answered back. It is part of my training."

"Well, you can train outside all you want to. We have you a place to stay. I'm sure, Sifu Cho will not argue with us on this," Miriam rebutted Mike's answer.

"I don't know what to say, I am overwhelmed by your generosity given to me. You must allow me some way to repay this gift."

Bell broke in, "Mike, I told you no talk of cost, I mean it. You are family and we take care of family. Now drop it."

"Yes madam."

"You call me madam a third time Mike and I will have Bone Breaker give you an attitude adjustment."

"Yes Bell."

THE MEETING

That night, Susan and Cheryl received visitors. True to what Bell said, they came. Susan welcomed them inside. Susan was pretty sure, she knew the reasons for the visit.

"Please come in. Can I get any one a drink?"

"No thank you, Susan. This is not a friendly visit but a visit that has to take place, before the services. I feel this is more important to discuss now, than later. The problems are just beginning, we need to find a solution before our club is dangerously torn or fractured," Chopper said with a heavy heart.

"Yes, Chopper, I saw this coming and I am glad to have this out, now. Please feel that I to want this to stop. I know why, and I can't resolve this without your assistance. I am in full support. Cheryl stood by her mom listening to Chopper and her mom's words.

Cheryl realized once all eyes turned to her, this was about her. She felt scared and sick inside. Standing before her were the leadership, Chopper, Bell, Razor, his wife, Jack knife, Bone breaker, and Cho.

As each guest took a seat and before anything was said, the bell rang sharply again. Susan rose to answer the doorbell. Standing in front of her was every kid Cheryl knew and been talking to. Their parents were left at home. None of the kid's parents were informed of this meeting. It was not necessary to have them informed, unless this meeting resulted in the wrong solution to get solved.

Each of the four boys and one girl entered the house. All came to a sudden halt. They stood still, staring at who was also invited. No one was expecting all the leadership to be present. All Bell said, "be at Cheryl's home and be there exactly on time."

Bell after shopping with Mike reported what she heard from Cheryl at the table. Chopper asked her to inform all the kids Cheryl associated with, to be at Susan's home by four this day.

"Bell, this needs to be dealt with quickly. I sense some unease rising among our children, starting the night Cheryl met Mike. After some small talk from parents in the house, I realized we were going to have a problem. I didn't expect it to flare up this quick. This can fracture our group, if we allow this to fester."

"I agree. I will immediately get in touch with all the kids Cheryl hangs with. I know where they usually hang out," responded Bell."

"Good, I will inform the other leaders to meet at Susan's home arriving at the clubhouse. This ends tonight, Bell."

There weren't enough chairs for all the kids to be seated. Susan told them to sit on the floor. Several wanted to find a place less visible to the assembled leaders. Bell quickly put a halt to that.

"Where do you three think you are going? There is plenty of space sitting in front of us. One boy attempted to make an excuse.

"Miss Bell, we were just going to."

"That enough, the boy did not finish his explanation, just sit down here!" Bell pointed to the spot for the three to sit. They got lucky. Bell gave them center stage facing the leaders.

Each kid sat quietly. Each felt the menacing eyes from the assembled leaders. Not one smile or hint of why they were asked to come to Cheryl's home was revealed. A sense of judgement day had come to each kid.

Bell turned to Cheryl requesting her to stand amongst her friends sitting. She found solace sitting between them. That quickly changed. Bell asked her to remain standing. Every kid never raised an eye to look at her. All kept their eyes glued to the assembled group.

Bell spoke first. "You were called here for a very important reason. The Riders was founded by these men sitting before you. It was a group based on shared values; brotherhood, friendship, respect, and honor won by each member. A bond sworn, never to break. Each pledged their life to the others. Whatever the fight, not one person would be faulted or blamed, should a life be taken. All knew the risk and accepted this pledge."

"You sit there among the best of the best. All served this country and continue to this day. Each person is well-aware, they may die one day. Their wives were all part of this pledge and accepted their duty to their men. Every one of you were trained for a reason. It was to protect and prepare you, if the need rose."

"Every man is a specialist, uniquely, extremely, highly qualified, and met standards proposed for membership before joining. This wasn't a biker gang for anyone. It was for America, we serve. We cannot allow our group to fracture, especially by people who have little idea of our values. Childish behavior and stupidly is not a requirement ask of our children. What we expect is a strong moral value with respect for others and fairness to each person."

"All are given a fair and honest chance to justify their actions. If any questions asked, we hoped you would come to your parents, or any one of us. The door is always opened to enter. This day, one person did not enter that door. That person took the loss of a love one and replaced it with scorn and hate. That person did not want hear the truth or allow that person an opportunity to plead his case. He was viciously scorned. To make matters worse, that person brought others into her hate and scorn for this person. Each of you are just as guilty as that person. There is no excuse for your actions. You chose secretly to scorn this person. No one approached a parent nor this assembly for an answer. You, Bell pointed her finger at each kid sitting, not Cheryl alone. Yes you," followed by a short pause.

"Each one sitting here has betrayed their family, friends, and this club. You forgot your pledge allowing yourselves be dictated by a vile hate filled child. You think you were wiser. The rules were okay to break. You place yourself above our laws. You are hypocrites, you say and pledge one thing, then betray those things when they don't agree with you. What's was so bad, all you had to do was asked."

Every eye of the leadership assembled stared at each child sitting on the floor. Chopper rose.

"Thank you, Bell. What you said, could not have been put any better. Before me are six young people bringing shame to their families and this group. You, all of you. Chopper paused staring hard at the kids. Then, with a fierce, loud, yell, commanded, don't you dare look down at me when I speak." All eyes quickly shot up at Chopper's eyes filled with anger peering back.

"You have the guts to scorn a boy, a boy this group, and yes, your fathers sworn to protect. Protect, meaning sacrifice, if need be. Some loss their lives doing so. We mourn each loss greatly. It saddens me during this time of great loss, our children replaced their sacrifices, with hate in their hearts and not mourn with us."

Every kid sat shocked hearing Chopper words. "One of us. Who? Chopper continued his reproach. Yes, one of us. Mike was made a member this year. In fact, he is the youngest member given this honor. The honor, you six betrayed and shamed our group. We all earned our place in this club, and so did Mike."

"Yes, I can see your faces, he never served in the military. What he lacked, he more than made up and demonstrated to everyone in our family. He was deserving. A vote, every one of you are aware, has to be taken. It had to be unanimous, it was for Mike. In facts, many cheered this vote for his induction into our club."

"Mike never spoke one word against any of you six. In fact, when we brought this to his attention, he plead with us, not to do anything. He said it will work itself out. He went on to say, he would leave soon, and this matter will be done with. When does a member leave our group? We all pledged ourselves to each other. Leave us, just the thought, galls me to no end."

Chopper was mad, he worked himself into a place, he rarely wanted to be. Let me explain something to you all. I rarely need to explain my actions to our group. They trust me and any decisions I make. Apparently, you six don't. One of the kids rose his hand to speak. Razor stops him.

"You are here to listen and not to speak. I hope this is the last time, I tell you all sitting and standing before us."

Chopper takes a breath before continuing. Less than a year ago, a boy entered our mountain inn. He was cold and hungry. He saw big mean bikers drinking and raising hell. He showed no fear. He walked over to the bar asking Mac for some food. He told Mac, he had not eaten for several days and would gladly work for a meal. Mac, being Mac told the kid to scram. Mike turned walking to the door. Before walking out, an opportunity to hide in a corner between two crates presented itself. He was cold from the rain. It was always cold at night in the mountains. Mike had no coat; his shoes were nearly worn through to the soles. Plus, he was wet to the bone."

"Let me make this clear to you, he didn't come begging for food. It was clear, he was starving. His body was thin; you could see his bones, yet, he wanted to work for his food. I can guarantee not one of you ever been that hungry."

One of the girls started to cry. Chopper continued. When Bell, Razor, Jack knife, Bone Breaker, and I entered, we sat in a corner. On the table some magazines laid. Once we drank our beers and finished off at least two more, I picked up one of those magazines. I read several articles. One article was about a giant alligator caught in the swamps. The largest ever found. The article credited the kill and the lives of the owner of the boat to a young boy, going by the name, Mike. There was a picture with Mike's face inside the magazine."

"I read the article; Mike was tossed into the river and nearly got bit in half. The boat was damaged and sinking. The old man was hurt bad from the alligator ramming the boat. The son was handling the boat. If not for Mike courage, they were sure, they would be gator supper."

"Mike didn't whine like a baby after nearly bit in half. That gator charged several times. The son almost went into the river on one of those charges. Mike put his life on the line. The gator charged the boat. Mike hauled the son in the boat, the gator jaws snapping at him. The gator charge was where Mike sat. He had stretched across the boat, half in the water holding unto the son. Mike saw the gator coming, he held unto the son, the gator came down with his jaws on the boat. The teeth nipping at Mike guts stretched across the rim. Mike didn't let go. One bite, then another, still, Mike held on to the son."

"I don't know about the courage it required to not let go and save yourself. I don't know if I could have that courage, to hold on. I think about what he did sometimes, knowing each gator chomp Mike might his guts, ripped out. He held on to the son with a gun in his hand, never before having held a gun, shot the gator after pulling the son back into the safety of the sinking boat."

"Mike shot the gator. The article read, Mike said, looked right into the gator's eyes. Hate, hate was there. Mike done not one thing to make that gator hate him. But there it was, hate for no reason. That gator hated Mike, because he was in a boat with men, who killed gators for a living. Mike was abducted by the gator men to find the giant gator. He was simply in their boat and that dumb beast figured Mike was just as bad, as the gator killers."

"You know about your fathers and their courage in battle. They have medals for their courage. What courage did it take to fight someone who didn't fight back? Another article was in that mag, I read." Chopper paused for a second allowing each person time to think, ponder on his words.

"There are many kinds of bravery, not just the kind facing an enemy. In the second article, Mike was also mentioned. Mike assisted a team of scientist locate a haunted house. The story read; Mike spent the night in the house. Many frightening things occurred. Mike profess to seeing ghosts and fire coming from the chimney causing burns to his arm. He went on to express, the doors actual breathed in and out, like someone breathing strongly. Not to mention, the scientists were quick to believe the young kid had an over imaginative dream. After some investigations, each of Mike's claim seemed to be true. Mike went ahead to the college to assist with picking up instruments. He disappeared at the college. That night many strange things happened to the team of scientist in the house. Two were injured. One was out of her mind with fear. The house was skirted off to prevent any trespassers. This story described the young kid. It fitted with Mike's picture. The house was several miles from where the gator was shot. Mike stayed the night alone, alone in a dangerous swamp for days. Then, ventured back to the house, to help the scientist."

"I looked up from my table to tell my friends and to my surprise that kid in the magazine, his face was staring at me from a corner in the mountain inn. I recognized the face immediately. I called him over to me. He didn't respond at first. He figured I wasn't calling him. I sent Bone Breaker to fetch him." Bone Breaker interrupts Chopper.

"Yeah Chopper, that kid, he fought me all the way over to your table. Bone Breaker looks down at the kids sitting. Mike told me to take my hands off him, me, he told me that, no commanded me. I gave him a friendly tap, his response to me, "do that again and he was going to kick by butt." How many of you would dare think, they could tell me that?"

Bone Breaker points to the biggest boy sitting in the room. "You, Bobby, stand up and tell me that. Bobby declined. What's wrong, you scared. No response came back. Bone breaker took a step toward him. Again, he told the kid to stand. Again, the kid declined. Then Bone breaker said, you are a shitless sissy. I know your dad, Bobby. He wouldn't back down to any man how big or bad-ass he was. You, you are his son. How you think your dad would feel knowing some kid half your size, stood his ground with me and even threaten me? You ask your dad if any man ever did that to me. If they did, you ask your dad Bobby, go on ask him what happened, or, are you a sissy around him? By the way, your dad was there that night."

"All this talking to these kids was to provoke respect and to make them see what it is to have honor and the definition of what courage is," Bell whispered into Susan's ear. She nodded back her understanding.

Bone Breaker sat down. Chopper paused to allow the kids to digest Bone's words. Chopper continued; "well, with some friendly persuasion by Bone Breaker, Mike was gently place in a chair." Bone Breaker made a slight correction to Choppers gentle seating of Mike.

"You actual mean Chopper, I nearly crushed the chair from the impact on Mike butt being gently placed in the chair."

"Ahem, Chopper replies, I was simple trying to keep from hurting your feeling and not making it seemed frightening to these sweet kids. I didn't want to frighten them anymore than, they are now." Chopper returns staring at the kids sitting.

"I was saying, Mike was seated, quickly looking back at Bone Breaker, smiling, turning back to the kids continues his story. I questioned Mike on the truth in the stories I read, asking if it was him in the picture. I had him why he was traveling the roads alone. Now, you brave caring young fair-minded kids listen to me carefully. Mike told us all, he saw his mother run over by a car thinking her dead. He and his sister were walking their mom back to a friend's house. She was drinking. She stumbled falling in the street. A car hit and ran over her. Mike saw this just a foot away, he lost his grip when she stumbled. He tried to grab her. A second car ran over his mom again. If not for a waitress watching and quickly reacting, he would have been a second victim in the street. She grabbed him just as a third car ran over his mom. Him and his sisters thought their mom was dead after the second hit. Mike told us, he thought his mom would live but not after the third car ran over her. His heart gave in. To him and his sisters losing their dad several years ago serving our country, and this happening. Mike stopped. I saw him holding back tears. I stop asking about the accident."

Mike went on to tell us, they were once placed in a foster home. When they got home, they had to break in. They couldn't find the keys to the house. Neighbors found out about him and his sisters living in their house alone after several day. Both sisters were taken in by friends. Mike was with one friend for a day. No one offered to take Mike in. He stayed at the house alone. His sisters came checking on him. Mike said he feared they were going to place them in a foster home. Then, tells them, he was going away."

For months this kid lived on the beach. Sleeping under the sand, bridges, piers, and sewer drains to keep warm. He had only the clothes on his back. Some carnie people let him work for food. Up until then, his food came by making friends on the beach and invited to share lunch with those friends. Most times it was finding left over food thrown away. He did some fishing along the inlet, with some success. He started to learn karate from a school passed in the city looking in trash cans for food. He practiced on the street looking in the window. Most times at the beach."

"One day, the teacher caught him practicing across the street. He let Mike learn but had him work around the dojo to pay for his lessons. Mike quickly excelled. A misunderstanding happened. Mike saw the police at the school thinking his Sensei called the police to get him. Later, he learned, the police were just inquiring about lessons. That is when Mike began his long year long trek. Living and learning to survive from people aiding him. What you heard about Mike and the bear, is true. He was bitten and nearly killed by a snake. He was threatened and attached by town kids. Made fun at. Some played cruel jokes on him. Mike told me one. Bell almost got sick when he told all of us."

"He was foraging behind a chicken joint for food in trash cans, hoping to find some fresh food recently tossed inside. A man walked up to the trash can, while Mike was pulling out a box. The man stopped Mike, asking why he was going through the trash can. Mike explained then asked if he could work for a meal. The man agreed to left Mike work for a meal. Mike work hard for several hours with an empty belly. After completing dumping the grease from the fryers, washing the walkways and inside the kitchen area, and cleaning the bathrooms. You get the picture, doing all the nasty work most didn't want to do. The man told Mike to wait out back, he would send boy his meal. Several boys came out with Mike's meal. Inside the box stuffed with chicken to Mike's surprise. Another bag had fries and biscuits. Mike immediately took out a piece of chicken with the boys urging him. He normally would walk to a private place to eat. He was hungry. He ate three pieces before the man came outside. The boys were giggling."

Chopper looks down at the kids. "Do you know why those kids were giggling? They saved all the chicken falling on the floor. Some person thought it would be a hoot, sprinkled toilet water in the box. The man came out after seeing the box on a countertop, he filled for the boys to give to Mike. Quickly, the man realizes what the boys were up too. He tell Mike, "hey kid, these boys are having fun with you, that chicken is bad, it's been on the floor and god knows where else. Throw it away. Here is the food I made for you." He turns disgusted telling the boys to leave. Mike, continued to eat the chicken. "Why you still eating the chicken after I just told you what they done," asked the man to Mike.

"Mike looked at him, you know what he said to that man? Bell got sick at the inn listening to what Mike eating. Then, she began to cry after what Mike said. He told the man those kids had done, happened many times. When you are hungry and not eaten for days, even weeks, and eating crickets, worms, fruit, and seeds, anything tasted good. I been sick from some of the things I ate. I knew it was going to make me sick. But the taste of food, any food, was worth the chance of getting sick, that is what Mike told him."

"So, you see kids, you sweet, well fed kids with loving parent, money to spend, is why Mike plead not to say a word to you. He has had people scorn, call him names, throw rocks at him, and beat him up to the point he could barely walk. Now, the part I was holding back. We sat in the bar discussing our adventures. Soon, a contest began between us at the table. Each person bragged about his war wounds. Mike got into the bragging. Sometimes we, you know, a might over exaggerate how bad our wounds are and the circumstances that caused our wounds."

"I began with my first scar, then Razor. We both showed Mike our scars. Mike, every time, countered showing his scars. The first was a bear claws across his chest. Three long and deep scars barely healed. One scratch was bleeding. It never healed all the way. You could see and feel the pain he was feeling."

Bone Breaker interjected, "I didn't know Chopper, God, I didn't know they were there. He said nothing to me, slapping him on his chest."

"I know Chopper. Looking at the kids, Chopper explains why Bone Breaker is upset. Mike, you see was still a bit feisty after gently placed in his seat. He smarted off to me. Breaker made a slight attitude adjustment on him. He slapped Mike on the chest. Knowing how gently he can sometime be, it was loud and hard. Mike made the corrected attitude adjustment, without a word or expression of pain. As the contest went on, Mike showed his whipping scars on his back. It Kris-crossed on his back like a checkerboard. A farmer found him sleeping in his barn. He wouldn't let Mike explain, he was sick, wet, and looking to find a dry place to spend the night. The farmer had some things stolen from him and incorrectly assumed Mike was the thief. The whipping stopped with his wife hearing the screams running to the barn. Mike found his way to another home that day. He passed out on their door step. He had pneumonia."

"Yes, the farmer believed the worst and acted upon that. Mike suffered for the farmer's mistake. He simply was sick, wet, hungry, and alone. He spent five days under a lean-to, he built during a hurricane sweeping across the area."

"Mike been through a lot of suffering, still his story wasn't over. You see, I made a promise to Mike the next day. I promised we would find him and check on his well-being. We respected his journey and wished him well."

"We located Mike's home through a newspaper article. It told of the awesome journey a kid made to get back home. The picture in the paper was of Mike. We got on our rides that same day. We saw Mike coming home from school. After an encounter with the local law, we gave him a lift home. Mike's mom had lived. The hospital bills cost so much, she had to sale their home. With what they could carry, moved to Georgia where the mom had family. For Mike, they waited as long as they could. With no information coming from the police and having to vacate their home, they left word with neighbors taking a train to Georgia. After months on the beach, Mike went home and found his mom was alive. Not wanting to go to the police, feeling they would place him in a home for run away, he decided to make the walk."

"Just before we got to his house, Mike saw three men trying to break in. They had weapons. The gang we attack resulted in our two brave and honorable friends death. Mike had saved the life of the newspaper man, later printed the story of Mike's journey home. Those gang members attacked the newspaper man. They chased Mike all throughout Atlanta. Mike had a badly injure leg at the time. Finally, Mike couldn't evade their doggedly pursuit. He made his way up a river leaving a trail for the gang to follow. By the night, they arrived. Mike had prepared a party for them. The path prepared by Mike led the three men chasing through briars, poison ivy, and up a steep hill. Sifu Stephen would be proud of Mike, and was. Cheryl, your father heard all this from Cho and Mike, he knew what he endured."

"At the top of the hill, Mike set up a small fire. The gang approached in the thick of the night, Mike threw wet leaves over the fire. You see, that fire led the gang straight through the briars and such. It was dark. The smoke flowed down the hill filling their eyes and noses. Coughing and wiping tears from their eyes, they heard horrific animal sounds. Mike had the bear hide given him by the people doctoring him back to health. He saved their preacher man from the bear. Mike attacked a six-foot bear with only a knife. A knife and killed it."

"You called him afraid, Cheryl. He stood up to a bear twice his size. He stabbed the bear several times with a knife, forged for him by the family who cared for him after his whipping from the farmer. Good caring people they were. They asked no questions and cared only to help him. The bear swiped Mike off him with a force sending Mike flying through the air. He stopped his flight when a tree trunk got in the way. The bear approached him. Mike was passing out from the sudden stop of the tree trunk. But, but, that kid fought to stay awake. You know why he fought to stay awake, it would have been so easy to blank out as the bear was about to maul his face off? No, you probably wouldn't know." Chopper looked at their faces.

"A man, a preacher man, he was black and told Mike to run while he had the bear chase after him. Mike turned to see if his friend, got away. The bear had the man cornered. That is why Mike ran back, to save his friend. Mike kept awoke long enough to feel the bear claw tear at his skin. Like three knives cutting a path across your skin. Before the bear had a second chance to bite Mike's face off, the opportunity came for Mike to drive his knife up the throat and into the brain of the bear. All the while looking at the mouth of the bear with large teeth about to bite down on his face. Mike came too in his friend's arms carrying a limp body to his house, barely breathing. Three words Mike spoke. Sam, your alive."

"Those gang members were getting really scared hearing bear screams coming from Mike. Mike said, they wanted to leave. The leader man kept them there. Mike crawled down the hill on his belly. Once he was within arm length, stood and growled. Two gang members ran, the leader man stayed punching Mike in the face. What Mike did next, shows you, this kid had no quit in him. He didn't run, instead got back up. He swung his bear claws gloves at the leader.

Blood covered leader man's face. He screamed. Mike chased after the other two. After some punching and kicking delivered to them, they laid on the ground screaming in fear. Mike stood making a final bear scream. They got off the ground running through them briars like they weren't there. The police responded to a call heard screaming. Three men came running out of the woods all bloody. They told the police wild animals attacked them. They never reached the police station. They got away before the police could arrest them."

"Mike saw the same men with tattoos trying to break into his home. He ran jumping on the back of the main man. He drove his knife into his upper back. Bone Breaker saw the second man turn to aid the leader. Bone Breaker got to him first."

"Yeah Chopper, he made a good hole puncher in that metal shed."

"Me and Bell went after the third man going to the front of the house. I hit him first. Bell second. Bell left me hearing a man going to blow Mike's brains out with his gun. Bell ran around the corner. The man saw her. Mike was holding onto the man's legs. Mike removed his knife from the shoulder before the tattoo leader threw him off his back. Mike jabbed his knife into his foot. The gun was pointed at Bell when Mike stuck him in the foot. Mike saw Bell and the gun pointing at her. I caught up to Bell. She stopped seeing the gun."

"Leader man had the gun pointed at Mike's head when Bell stopped coming at him. He wanted Mike dead, more than he wanted Bell. He was about to squeeze the trigger. Mike was willing to take the bullet. The man shot his gun. Mike jerked at his legs just enough for the man to miss his head. Then, the fool saw me. He had just enough time to point the gun at me. Mike jerked his legs again and I got to him, the gun went off. The bullet missed but found another. It hit Bell."

'Twice, Mike save us. Once for Bell and the second time for me." Bell made a remark.

"Mike saved our lives; he asked us to stay on our bikes. We heard the screams and went to help."

"Thanks Bell. Mike asked us not to kill the men. I didn't. Some of our men decided to teach them a lesson; make them realize what will happen the next time they decided to come back for revenge. So, you see, this battle began our involvement in this fight after we interfered with Mike business. He saved two lives in the process."

"Mike was severely injured in the last fight we had before the Atlanta battle. Some of you may have heard of the five men attacking Mike and his friends at a haunted house. Mike protected his friends with his life. What Mike did that night, left a lot of people shocked with awe? He locked himself in a room after making sure his friends escaped. Then, with a bad knife cut across his arm received stopping it from gutting a friend, Mike bled badly. He took on the five in the dark. We know what happened, because a film crew had videos covering the whole house, inside and out."

"The leader took four shots at Mike, during the fray. Mike dodged each shot while fending off the other four. One man hit Mike on leg, nearly breaking it with a crowbar. He received a second knife cut after Mike fell to the ground from the crowbar hit to his leg. Getting up, the man cut Mike. He stabbed Mike in his midside. Mike felt the knife and twisted just in time to prevent the blade entering deep into his guts. It sliced opened his belly. A lot of blood, little damage. It was a nasty cut. With each attack, Mike ended a man's life, the third shot came. Mike was able to see the gun and the finger on the trigger. Cho's training saved Mike's life the third time that night. Mike saw the finger squeeze the trigger and dodged the bullet. By that time, Mike was on the fourth man. The fourth man's life ended. I will not go into the gory details of what Mike done to each of his attackers that Mike. What I will tell you every crew member of the movie team were amazed. They praised this kid stopping those men single-handedly."

"Mike went after the fifth man. He got hold of him, a fifth shot was heard, Mike tore the gun from the man hands. The bullet, again missed it's intended target. The man got afraid quick, seeing what his men had been dealt. He tore from Mike's grip reaching down to retrieve his empty pistol. Mike had lost a lot of blood. He struggled to keep on his feet. He was trying to get to the man before he got Mike's friends. Cho training alerted Mike; they had not yet driven away."

"We found Mike on the floor crying. He was crying for two reasons. One, he was afraid for his friends, he was scared he had cost them their lives. Second, that he was weak. He had embarrassed his teachers, Cho and Stephen. He feared the cuts he received was not up to their standards and failed them."

"So, I hope you six understand the fight in Atlanta was caused by us. Mike had been a member. We were protecting him, as he would have done with no complaint for any of us. Mike never knew about the battle. He was half dead, when we finally got him to the doctors. The battle happened several days later in Atlanta."

"Mike couldn't have been there. God knows, he blames this on himself. He believes Stephen and Teddy Bear, both friends and to some extent father images, their deaths was his causing. So, you think your name calling, bad mouthing is harming him. Maybe, but nowhere as much as he blames himself and hurts inside."

Cho stands, Chopper steps to one side. "Mike is my protégé, Stephen was too old. This was both our decisions. Stephen was worthy of being next in line. With Mike, we saw in him potential a master next in line. Mike's good heart and strong spirit was the main reason Stephen and I chose him. Yes, Mike has a tendency to look at Stephen and myself as father figures. He lost his when he was very young. Yes, both Stephen and I regarded Mike as our son. That didn't mean we replaced Mike with our family love ones. It meant we adopted him. Susan was aware of this. We decided in time, Mike will be brought here to meet all of you. We hoped you would accept this fine, wonderful person as one of our own. We saw in Mike a great love, caring, compassion, willingness to help, and this great untapped person with amazing abilities. This young man would bring us greatness. He has no selfish bone in him. He offers aid, without being thanked. He asked for nothing and feels embarrassed when he receives it. Who among you can say that?"

"We shared but a few of the trials this young man has gone through. There is much more not spoken to you about. This should suffice. If not, time will tell, and we can assure you, it will be dealt with in the most extreme way if this course, you find yourself on does, not end tonight."

Chopper stands, "Cho please go and get Mike."

All eyes flashed opened. Mike name was silently whispered. After the lecture, Mike was the last person any of the six wanted to see at the moment. Cho returns suddenly; Mike following behind. Mike was surprise seeing the kids sitting. Chopper waves for Mike to come and stand by him. Chopper asks Mike to remove his shirt. Mike hesitated. Turning to Chopper, asks why?

"Mike, this is important; I would never ask this of you or anyone. This is a difficult time and we need to make some concessions to resolve this. Please do as I ask." Bell stands placing her hands on Mike shoulders.

"Please Chopper this, this is." Bell stopped Mike from speaking.

"Mike," Bell in her sweetest voice. Mike could never resist her sweetness ways. "Do this for our group" Mike nods his head. Slowly he unbuttons one button, then another. All buttons opened, his shirt sprays apart. Not so much as to reveal anything. All eyes were staring at Mike. Mike felt he was doing a strip tease act.

Bell grabs hold of Mike's shirt aiding him in with the final removal. Mike stood there looking at all the eyes focus on his nakedness. Mike's body had transformed over the course of all the training Cho put him through. No longer was Mike skin and bones. His muscle grew and were sinewy. His tummy rippled from all the sit ups. The scars remains on him.

All eyes stayed glued to Mike's scars. Some slight uneasiness was seen in their eyes. Bell held Mike's arm out. Then a few, oh my came from the kids. It was everything Chopper told them, and others said. It looked worse than what was told them. His arm was nasty to look at. Cheryl was the closest to Mike. She saw the gut wound from the knife. See saw the still swollen leg from the crowbar strike. After seeing them, she looked at the other scars. First the bear, then the arm. She almost wanted to beg Mike to forgive her. Her pride was too strong. She held back the impulse. Mike was asked to turn around. That's when the Ahs, dear God remarks were heard.

Cheryl felt a great shame for all the things she said and conspired against him. She thought, "how in the world could anyone endures so much hurt. Then, suddenly it came to her. Her pain was so much less than what Mike had lived through. And now, he has to endure more of what she caused him, thinking to herself. Yet, I cannot yield to my desire to ask Mike, to forgive me."

All the kids stood and one by one gave Mike a hug. Each asked him to forgive them. Each was ashamed. Mike thanked each one and lovingly said everything is good, no harm done. Cheryl gave Mike a hug after all five had finished. Cheryl said she was sorry.

Susan stared at the young man, stuck how masculine he appeared. Bell saw, heard, and realized what she was thinking. Bell turned to look at Mike, again. With a sudden awareness, she began to see Mike differently. Not a young kid but a young man, a good looking, well-developed body of a man.

Susan walked over to Cheryl. "I want you to look close at those scars. I want you to touch them. Feel them, that's all you can do is feel the scars. You never had anything like that done to you."

"Mom please, I don't want to touch his scars."

"Do it Cheryl, or so help me you won't see outside your room for months. Do it. You were brave boasting how weak he looked. Now who is weak? Touch those scars."

Cheryl slowly reached out to touch Mike's skin. Then, Susan grabbed her hand quickly pressing it to his skin. Cheryl turned away. She could feel the unevenness of the skin. She felt repulsed by the feel, she tried hard to pull her hands away from Mike's skin. Her mom held them tight to the scars. Cheryl began to heave. Susan released her hands.

All the kids were told to go home. Cheryl was sent to her room. All the leaders stood, patted Mike on the back. "Well done." Chopper gave Mike his explanation for the show.

"Mike, our group was being divided by Cheryl harmful actions and words about you. It was getting out of hand. Our team was founded on trust, friendship, courage, and honor. You know these truths, because you belong to our group. We needed." Mike stops Chopper.

"Chopper, I understand, I truly do. No need to explain further. I am part of this group and want it to be strong. You are the leader because of your strength, and wisdom, and above all else courage and love you have in your heart."

Bell hearing these words coming from Mike had to hug him. Feeling Mike's warm skin against her own aroused something other than a motherly yearn to hold him. Before the leadership departed, Susan asked Bell about what should be done with her daughter?"

Bell reply," wait until she comes to her. That will be the right time. Now, Cheryl has some soul searching to do."

That night, Cheryl had little sleep. The thought of Mike's skin and what Chopper said haunted the long night. She tried to fill her heart with hate, but not after what she heard about her dad. Not after the talks she remember having with her dad. Not after the stories she recalled from some of his minor missions for the club. And not after he spoke to her about honor, courage, and commitment. She felt shame. She wanted this whole thing to just go away. She woke early in the morning. Mom was still sleeping. Cheryl wanted to avoid her for a while. She was glad her mom was still sleeping.

Cheryl got dressed and decided to walk to the small store from the subdivision to get something for breakfast. The walk would allow her to prepare for dad's services today. Thought she quietly got dressed and stealthily walked through the house and out the door. Susan was awake and heard her leave. Susan had little sleep that night.

Mike was up early. He decided not to make a fire. He had little sleep. He constantly was reminded of all his training spent with Stephen. Every day and every experience were clearly recalled. He decided to walk up the road for a while. Along his walk picking up soda bottles. It was a habit required over the course from his homeward bound travels leaving Virginia. After the third bottle, he earnestly looked for others to pick up. He found a bag capable of holding his bottles. Mike had a bag full and could buy himself breakfast.

Around the corner at the end of the dirt road was a small store. With his bottle jingling, he swiftly walks to the store. From a distance Mike spotted five older boys lingering on the corner of the store. He continued his walk to the store. The boys saw him approaching. All five turned to watch this skinny kid toting a bag their way.

SLAP HAPPY

Inside a store at the counter, Mike finished paying for his items. Suddenly, a noise was heard. Outside the store, the appearance of a young girl was trying to enter the same store Mike was leaving. It was Cheryl.

Five older boys lined up in front of the store door blocking her entrance. It was the same five Mike notices at the end of the store, he entered. Immediately, Mike strolled toward the five boys blocking the store entrance. All five cast a glance toward him. An attempt was made by several to confront Mike. Two boys stepped toward Mike attempting to halt his progress out the store. They were stopped by another, shorter boy. He was more intent on something else and seemed not to want his lads to be distracted by Mike. Not looking to see where the leader boy's attention was keyed on and not showing interest was Mike's way of not drawing any attention. Mike continued through the front door without hesitation.

Outside, the attraction came up the parking lot walking toward the store's entrance. The five boys made a move off the corner wall they were glued to. Slowly, with little attempt to hide their reasons from the girl watched her walk to the door. She quickly recognized what their attentions were. It was too late to alter her plan. To show fear was not an option. This was taught early in her life from her parents. Instead, she increased her effort to show no fear. The five boys stopped directly in front of her.

A palm shot out at Cheryl's chest. The impact caused Cheryl to stop. It was strong enough of a blow to cause most people to be thrown off balance and back step to regain their balance. Not Cheryl.

She stood before them, stoic and brave. Mike watched Cheryl showed no fear. Mike began to move toward the door to assist but recalled his last encounter with Cheryl. "She was most adamant about my inabilities making jest about how pathetic I appeared. Her fuming remarks to friends about her dad's dying for a skinny kid on my prowess, still stung."

Cheryl's display of angered toward Mike unsettled him. This was before he was properly introduced to her, by Bell. Still, the reason for the disrespect and angered was unfounded. Sifu Stephen was his mentor next to Sifu Cho most favored becoming a father figure to Mike.

Still, Mike allowed the thoughts to pass. He stood vigilance on Cheryl and the five older, larger boys standing in her path. The palm thrust to her chest almost made Mike react and dart from the store. He waited just long enough to see why he need not react to quickly.

The leader remained blocking Cheryl's entrance into the store. The impact from the palm thrust to her chest and a slight grimness on her face, worried Mike. The pain went unnoticed to leader but not by Mike. All leader boy noticed was a quick block on his arm lying upon her chest, then the sudden slap across his right cheek. She said nothing to the leader. His head turned slowly facing a defiant girl rubbing his redden cheek. Anger filled his eyes.

Cheryl's eyes darted up meeting his eyes with his palm on her chest. A fire was building in her eyes. Cheryl knew them, it was apparent, to Mike. Also apparent, her dislike for them. The glare was mutually returned from the leader boy attempting to return a slap at Cheryl. Cheryl laughed at his attempt. She simply brushed the pathetic attempted slap with a chuckle mocking leader boy.

"Ha, ha, is that all you got Jeremey, I mean jerk? Here, let me demonstrate the proper way to slap a lady. In your case, little girlie."

Mike listened, watching the banter back and forth confronting each other. "Cheryl surely has a way to infuriate a person, with her mouth. Definitely a gift of the tongue," Mike thought.

"You ain't calling yourself a man, girlie, because you ain't big enough too."

Then came a swift slapped to the other side of leader boy's cheek. Quickly the five youths surrounded Cheryl. One grabbed her from behind. He felt the heel of her foot to his groin. Another tried to grab the arm slapping the leader boy. She swung the arm holding hers in an upward loop, twisting his wrist. His hold weakened; his arm was left dangling in the air. Not for long, it floated in the air before meeting with another arm. Cheryl quickly made a path through the dangling arm with her free arm connecting both to his nose. Blood droplets created a mist in the air, he fell to the ground holding onto his nose.

Cheryl had skill, that apparent to Mike. He realized her skilled was no match for the five boys standing in front of her. Mike quickly picked up his bag and walked to the door. Outside, Cheryl just receive a punch in her guts by a third boy while the leader was recovering from his second slap. Mike stepped out the door.

Cheryl regained her composure from the gut-wrenching hit. Looking up, saw Mike. The leader stopped and turned to face Mike. Mike asked the leader a simply question.

"Hey mister, does it normally take five guys to beat up a girl around here?" Cheryl hearing Mike's remarks and before any response to his question was forthcoming, Cheryl shouted to Mike.

"Stay out of my business! The day I need help from a scrawny kid like you, is the day I will kiss your ass." Leader boy laughed and laugher erupted from his friends. Cheryl was clearly annoyed by Mike's interference.

"Yeah, you best git along kid or I will need to spank your butt after I'm finish with this bitch."

Leader boy turned back toward Cheryl and received a third slap on his cheek. His cheek still hurt from the first slap, even more from the second slap on the same cheek. Leader boy grew angry from that slap. With a quick punch, hit Cheryl in her belly. She bent down in pain. Mike walked past turning the corner around the building. It took every ounce of his will power to not intercede to assist Cheryl. She would only yell at him later with more ridicule. Mike was told of the impending mission to attack the Atlanta gang by the club. If he assisted Cheryl, his life would be a living hell from her constant berating. Even though a meeting took place at her home with the leadership, Cheryl still held unto her hurt. She was having a hard time not blaming Mike for her dad' death.

Cheryl was in need of help. Mike knew there was another way to provide her aid. This way, he can keep her safe and unaware of his help. "Yeah, a win, win, either way I put it," thinking Mike walking to the end of the store. The small seven-eleven store was isolated from the surrounding neighborhood. Trees blocked any viewing a run-down building located across the street. A two-lane road separated the store from the subdivision.

Around the corner of the building, Mike set his package down and picked up a rock. Peering around the corner, Cheryl was out of the fight. She was at their mercy. One boy had her from behind with both arms held tightly. Leader boy was laughing at her. A third boy reached over to cop a feel on her tits.

"Hey little girlie, you ain't so tough now. Now, I am going to teach you some manners." He slapped Cheryl's cheek, then another slap. Blood dripped from her mouth. Cheryl made one comment.

"You still hit like a little girl, jerk."

"Still feisty," Mike thought stepping away from the corner of the store. Quickly unleased the rock. A flick of his wrist was followed with a snap of his fingertips, the stone flew at leader boy. The rock flung, had the force of a bullet. The impact nearly ruptured the guts of the leader boy. One boy noticed the skinny kid snapping his fingers. He thought nothing of it. The stone went unnoticed.

The boy pondered seeing Mike snap his fingers, "if that kid intends to hurt someone with a rock, he would have tossed it like a baseball. Instead, he simply snapped his fingers. The little stone seemed insignificant." He laughed at Mike futile attempt to throw a rock. He pointed at Mike to his compatriots standing by his side. The same boy copping a feel on Cheryl tits.

Cheryl was quickly released from the boy holding unto her. She fell to the ground next to leader boy. Leader boy felt a sharp sting to his belly from the tiny stone. It was enough to drop him to the ground releasing his hold on Cheryl.

"Git him," cried leader boy lying prone next to Cheryl. All four boys took chase at Mike.

Mike stepped back around the corner of the store waiting the boys approach. Their speed flung them wide of the corner. Each boy stopped turning to face Mike. Only until they stopped had they realized Mike's position. None of the four had the chance to gather into a consolidated unit. Their assault came sporadically giving Mike the advantage. Mike decided not to take the opportunity to take each one down. Instead, decided it would be best to demonstrate their mistake attacking him and the girl. They assumed wrongly, because they were many, Cheryl was a girl and he looked skinny, they could prey on them. All four boys stood facing Mike. Mike raised his hand stopping them from making the first move at him. It worked. They were stood motionless, stunned seeing his hand holding them back. Mike spoke clear and plain to them.

"You boys seem to think it is okay to slap around people. I am going to teach you to respect others. Now, which one of you would like to learn first. Which one of you has the guts to punch me out?"

Before Mike could complete the last syllable in the last word he spoke, one of the boys shot out a punch to his face. Before the blow got close, Mike blocked the punch and with the same arm, struck the boy across his face with a backhand slap. The boy was startled grabbing hold of his slapped redden cheek.

Mike chastised the boy, he slapped. "Just one punch. Maybe I should have slapped you harder. Can't you at least try with several punches. You might get lucky with more than one punch, unless you are too afraid to try more than one punch at a time."

"Hey runt, I'm going to hit you so many times, you think rain was falling on your face."

Mike smiled. A flurry of blows followed. With the same arm, Mike quickly blocked each blow, following each block with a slap to the boy's face. It looked more like a game of slap box played by kids. First, the boy right hand was blocked, then countered with a slap, then a left hand blocked, countered with a second slap by Mike's same hand to the opposite cheek. All the slaps on the kids face caused him to see stars. He staggered backwards only to be replaced by the second boy.

The second boy boasted as the first had done. "You is a little one, you ain't as big or strong as me. Let's see if you can keep that silly grin on your face, now asshole."

Quickly a furry of blows assaulted Mike. Again, each was blocked and followed by a slap to the boy's face. He lasted a bit longer than the first boy. The third boy replaced him and again came the same results. Before the third boy was out, the leader boy stepped around the building. Seeing what one of his boys was attempting, unsuccessfully, dropping to the ground after repeated slaps. The fourth boy took his place and began his burgage of throwing fists. Same results as with the others. The fourth boy laid at Mike's feet.

Watching his boys laying on the ground, leader boy turns to Mike. "Hey, them were easy, if that all you can do is slap someone, try slapping me?"

"If you wish," Mike replies.

The leader boys stands facing Mike. Instead of throwing a punch, he started with a low kick to Mike's groin. Mike shot a punch down on leader boy's kneecap at the same time, twisting his body to prevent the kick from reaching his groin. The force of the blow halted the kick. Mike felt the kneecap shift.

The leader boy hadn't time to feel the pain. He had committed to a second blow and well on to a third follow up punch in his mind. Mike finished the strike to the knee. His arm quickly moved up in an arc meeting with the first punch. After the blocking the punch, Mike delivered a devastating slap to leader boy's face. The second punch following was weak. It was merely following the first punch. It lacked any power or purpose. The slap totally disarmed leader boy, sapping any power or strength from the second punch that followed. Then came a furry of fore hands open palm slaps followed by back hands slap. Mike whistled a tune in beat to his slapping.

Leader boy stood idle watching and waiting for the next hit. "Enough, fight me like a man," shouting at Mike. Before leader boy ended his last word, Mike obliged deciding to drop him like a rock. Leader boy fell like a rock. He hit the ground like a rock. He sprawled out like a rock shattering, spewing on the ground. Mike stepped over the sprawled leader boy retrieving his bag and walked behind the store into a growth of trees. He sat under a shade tree, out of sight. He sensed Cheryl was on her feet groggy walking to the side of the store.

Cheryl spotted the leader boy fly from the side of the store, hitting the ground. Holding her stomach, walks over to the fallen leader. Around the corner, was all five boys laying on the ground. Each had a strange, red blister on the side of their cheeks. Cheryl saw no one.

"What in the hell?" Mike heard Cheryl shouting before she turned going into the store? "Dam," Cheryl thought walking back to the door. "I must have been doing better than I thought? I sure don't remember doing all that to them? Must have done that in my dazed condition. Hell, I don't know my own power. I'm better than I think I was."

Several went by, Cheryl came out of the store with a bag of chips, sipping on a soda. No one was there. All the boys gathered themselves off the dirt, leaving with their pride wounded.

Mike sat under a bush eating peanut butter soda crackers out of his bag. He watched Cheryl walk down the street toward her home. Later that morning, Mike followed the same path to his home.

THE DAY OF SERVICE

Mike was returning from the store stopping at his camp. The birds were singing, their songs were a good sign. Not to soon returning to camp, the soft footsteps from a person exiting a car was heard at the entrance to his camp. It was Bell.

Before Bell could see Mike at camp, he stood beginning a slow-paced walk up the dirt path to meet her. Bell was already dress in a black outfit. She was very lovely. Her long red hair went wonderful with the black dress. Mike greeted her before she walked far from the car. As usual, Bell greeted him with a hug. Both turned to walk to the car.

"Mike, we are going to my house. Chopper left early to meet with his team. You can take a shower and change into your new clothes. Rhonda, Jack's wife, and I argued who was going to keep the clothes and pick you up. I told her, she had three to prepare and a fourth might be too much. So, I won taking your clothes to my home.

Within several minutes, the car entered a driveway. A tall two-story house appeared. It was brick with four white columns on either side of the front door. Very little shrubs decorated the yard. The grass was freshly cut. Compared to Stephen's home, it was plain but larger.

Stephen's home was a single-story brick house. Much longer than Bell's home. Bell's home may have been shorter but made up for it in height. Mike was told Stephen's home was called a ranch style house. The yard had many shrubs and flowers adorning the front. A fence was on the sides and continued to surround the entire back yard. He recalled sitting in the car waiting to be asked to enter when the kids pass by. None noticed Mike sitting in the car entering Susan's home. They knew nothing about why they were asked to go to Susan's home. It was that discussion concerning him. It was the first time meeting the five kids taunting him. Bell and Chopper made it perfectly clear what he was going to do. Mike was to wait in the car until notified. His thoughts ended wandering as the car entered Bell's driveway.

Bell stepped out of the car. Mike followed her to the front door. Inside Bell's home was a large living room, nicely furnished with a stairway to one side of the entrance.

"Mike, upstairs is a room to the right and at the end of the hall is the bath. You go up there and clean up. Your clothes are laid out on the bed for you to change into. I will be down here taking care of some planning chores," Bell commanded.

Mike walked up the stairs turning down the hall. To one side of the hallway his room's door was opened. Bell placed his clothes on the bed. After showering, he walked to the room wearing a towel. He closed the door and began the long dressing up.

After fitting a tie around his shirt, he realized he had no idea how to properly tie it. Walking down the stairs with a tie knotted like a rope, a wonderful smell caught his nose. Apparently, Bell was finishing cooking a meal for them to eat. She made breakfast for Chopper. He ate alone while she got dressed. Bell told Mike during their meal.

"Welcome, come sit down, Mike. Entering the kitchen, Bell spotted the tie in a knot. "Oh my, that will simply not do. You look fabulous Mike, but that tie really takes away from that look."

"Well Bell, that fitter man spent a lot of time doing all the dressing for me. Guess it never occurred to him, I didn't know how to tie, a tie properly."

"Here Mike, let me tie this tie. Bell takes the knot out of his tie. Chopper taught me this knot," explained Bell in a motherly tone. You start with the proper length measured. Now watch me, take the longer, wider part of this tie, wrap across the thinner side of the tie. Then, pass up through the hole and to the opposite side, then back down through the hole. To finish, simply pass it through the looped you made. Now pull down to tighten, then slide the knot up to your neck. There, a perfectly even looking tie. I do hate those lopped sided knots most men use for a knot. This makes a perfect triangle."

Stepping back, Bell examined her handiwork. Both hands sat on her hips as her eyes peruse the outfit Mike donned. "Now young man, you are one handsome person. Now let's sit and enjoy this meal."

On the table Mike was amazed. "How you cook all this food, so quick, Bell?"

"Well Mike, the bacon and sausage I had cook earlier for Chopper. He loves a lot of meat for breakfast. I cook more than he usually eats. The eggs and toast take little time to cook. The potatoes were also prepared earlier and all I needed to do, was warm them. So, you see, I just cooked the eggs when I heard the shower turned off. Now eat all you want and enjoy."

After they finishing their meal, Mike assisted washing the dishes. Bell put away the food, wiped the table, and cleaned the stove.

"Okay Mike, every one of the leaders will be meeting at the clubhouse. We will need to meet with them." After a short drive, they arrived at the house. Parked in a neat row were many bikes. Bell parked the car and before they could enter the house, three large limos arrived.

The limos come to a stop, neither Bell or Mike halted their progress to the house. Inside was a complete surprise to Mike's eyes. Every one of the leaders were not dressed in their club jackets as Mike expected; instead, each wore his own branch of the service uniform. Mike saw all branches represented. Bell explained what each branch a Rider served in to Mike.

"Mike, Razor is a Navy seal. That emblem is given to all seals. You will notice many have a purple heart received from being wounded in action. Also, everyone has several bronze and silver stars on their chest."

This medal around Razor's neck is the highest medal this country offers to our men in service. This is for heroism up and above the call of duty. Mike looked at the medal, then scanned the assembled group. Four others wore the same medal. Besides Razor was Chopper, he had the second one around his neck. The third one was

OZ

arounds Bone breaker's neck. All three were Navy Seal except for Bone Breaker. He was an Airborne Ranger. Among the Riders were Marines and Army. Both Army men were green Berets. Jack knife was the sole Marine. He had two Silver stars and two Bronze medals. Chopper was the only officer present. Mike recognized the chief chevrons on Razors arm. It was like his dads all gold.

Each wife was dressed in black. Miriam stood next to her man, Razor. Bone Breaker had a girlfriend beside him.

"Mike, this is my gal, Penny. Penny smiled at Mike offering her hand. Mike shook it.

"Hey Mike, you better say she is pretty."

Mike replied, after Bone Breaker delivered a sharp punch to his shoulder. "You don't have to tell me that, Bone Breaker. Anyone with eyes can see how beautiful she is. Penny smiled. Her cheeks redden. Why is she with you Bone Breaker?" He stuck his fist at Mike, grinning.

"Jack Knife's wife, Rhoda, wasn't present. Bell said she was going to be at Susan's home aiding her with two other wives. Bell has Mike step back for the leaders to examine him.

"Well done, Chopper cited to her. Razor and Jack knife agreed. Bone Breaker simple nodded, his girlfriend turned to Miriam to whispered into her ear. "He is quit the dashing young man."

Miriam nodded her reply. "Yes, he is."

Mike heard the remark; his training it enabled him, like Cho to hear things most people would not. Others seemed to have only heard a whisper. Cho wasn't present but suddenly came walking through the front door. Cho was wearing an Army uniform, two medals hung from his neck, one was the Medal of Honor and another was a similar medal from another country. He also had pinned to his chest several of the same medals, but very different medals not like the ones the other leaders shared.

Bell softly said, "Cho was in the CIA serving secretly for America in different countries." She said nothing more.

Cho walks over to Mike. "You look good my son. I came by this morning to take you out for breakfast."

81

Bell speaks up, "Cho, I picked Mike up early to take him to get cleaned up at our house. I'm sorry if I messed up your plans."

"Quite alright, Bell. I was going to bring him to your home once we ate. We both had the same idea and you beat me to the punch."

Cho pulls Mike to one side. "Excuse me while you gentlemen and ladies go to the limos parked outside. I need to have a chat with Mike, please." Bell was about to ask Cho; Chopper knew his reasons for the talk and took Bell's arm. She allowed Chopper to lead her out the door.

Mike, I will be part of an honor guard for Stephen. You were requested to take hold of the casket, by Susan. Chopper, myself, Razor, and Jack knife felt this was just. Please understand, Stephen had wanted you to sit with his family, if it went wrong. It you want, you may sit with me. I will be sitting with the family as well. Susan and Cheryl considered Stephen and me, brothers. We served on many adventures in the service and in this group. He too was a special service member. He earned many of same medals I have."

Mike said nothing, just nodded. Privately Mike had some reservations considering Cheryl attitude toward him. All were seated in the limos. One stop was to Razor's home. All the children were gathered there from the leaders. The oldest girl at Susan's home was left in charge. When the cars arrived, all the children entered the third limo.

It was a short drive to the end of the neighborhood most lived. Waiting at the intersection was several police motor bike officers. One officer directed the traffic. Both police bikes led the way. All three limos turned to follow. Behind the third limo was a long line of bikers following in two rows. Every biker was in uniform of his service. One more stop was needed. It was at the funeral home.

At the funeral home several bikers were waiting for the main group to arrive. Another limo was parked to one side. All parked in the lot. Everyone walked to a spot and collected into a formal formation, then walked to the entrance.

Inside Susan and Cheryl was sitting in the parlor. Every man and woman waited to give their condolences to both of them. To one side was the two coffins. Cho informed Mike, Teddy bear was a bachelor. He had no family living, Mike believed, but the bikers. Teddy Bear has a child. Cho stunned Mike with that revelation. We could not locate her. Many years went by between Teddy Bear's daughter and him. She was part of the hippie scene, My son."

Mike waited his turn to see Susan and Cheryl. Seeing Mike standing in front of her, Susan spoke first. You certainly look a lot different, now. Wow, you look good, Mike.

"Thank you, Miss Susan."

Mike barely held back his tears. Susan stands to take Mike into her arms. Mike lost it with tears flowing down his cheeks. Cheryl watched his tears and felt the hurt he was feeling. She finally understood Mike's regret and his pain for her dad's death.

Mike let go of Susan wiping his tears away with a handkerchief taken from his coat pocket. Then Cheryl stood, giving him a hug. Mike hugged her back, no words said. The meaning was clear to him.

Mike walked over to Stephen's coffin. Behind him Cheryl followed. Both stood their looking down at him. Cheryl reached for Mike's hand. Then both of them walked over to Teddy Bear's coffin. He was dressed in his dress uniform. Mike recognized it belonging to the Marine Corp.

Many things were spoken that day. Chopper, Razor, Jack knife each recited the many deeds Stephen and Teddy Bear done. One concerned the group and their duties. Another, Razor, described their military records. Jack Knife commented on their final fight. This also included the incident at the haunted house prior to the Atlanta battle.

Bone breaker stood. Several words he attempted to say and couldn't. He stood there looking with a long pause. That pause helped steady him, waiting for his words to come. Mike heard a slight gut churning tone in Bone's voice, as did Cho. "They was my friends." Those words brought tears to everyone sitting. Just four words had more meaning and understanding than anything one could say. Cho rose.

Standing by his chair, Cho turns to face his friends and speaks softly. "Bone Breaker said it all. Any words I speak, cannot match what he said. I need to say these things about my friends, comrades, and brothers. We served. Our memories are our legacies for others to follow. Our deeds are in the past and soon forgotten. What we done, was out of love for family, friends, country, and God. Each of us here today, bears the scars of our duty. Each family member present here is our family. We bear the same life Stephen and Teddy Bear shared with us. Only family can feel the pain, we feel. Stephen and Teddy Bear will forever be part of us, all our lives, until we die. No one will be able to have these moments we shared with them. They will have the words and not the life we shared. Our lives were linked in ways others will never have a chance to experience. I pray our family will remain strong and preserve the legacy each and every one present here shares. We are strong and will remain strong if we never forget the sacrifices our fallen have given to us this day and days to come."

Many words were spoken that day by friends and by the preacher, giving prayers to all. Six bikers folded two flags. Chopper carried one flag to Susan, Razor to Bell, for Teddy Bear. Each leader spoke the words Mike recalled his mom received at his father's grave site. A memory Mike had forgotten until this day.

Every man stood, forming a line for the coffins to pass through carried out the church. The line led outside and to the hearse. All the bikers stood erect in their uniforms. Swords were raised forming an arch outside the church.

Susan and Cheryl stood leading the line. Cho, Chopper, Bell, then Razor, Jack knife, and Bone Breaker followed the daughter and wife of Stephen. Stephen's mother was rolled in her chair by his only brother's son. Then, one uncle and the family of Susan. Mike was last of the main party to fall behind. All the family members of the biker group made up the remaining party. Finally, neighbors and local people who showed up, finished the mourners.

Everyone entered the limos waiting. Cho entered the car with Susan and Cheryl, Mike sat next to Cho. The police were waiting. At the grave site all the honor guard lined the path. It was a huge guard, each Rider sharply dressed in his uniform carrying a saber. All sabers held at an arc for all to walk under. To one side was a rifle team, ready for a final salute. The hearses arrived; all the pall bearers assembled along the rear doors. First; Chopper opposite of him Bell. After them was Bone Breaker and Mandy. Finally, Cho and Mike. Slowly each took hold of the handle to the casket pulled from the hearse. Teddy Bear's pall bearers consisted of, Razor, Jack Knife, Tallman, Cowboy, Magic, Pretty Boy, Mechanic, and Marcus. They made their way to the site. After placing the casket down, the flag was draped over each with a large wreath on top.

Once seated, the preacher gave a short prayer, the rifle team offered a salute and taps was played. The seal members stamped their emblem on Stephen's coffin. Then, it was over.

Chopper stood announcing to all an invitation to attend the supper for Stephen and Teddy Bear, located at a restaurant a short distance from the cemetery.

The restaurant had been reserved to accommodate the entire party. Plans for nearly one hundred were made days before the services by Bell, Miriam, and Rhoda, "Jack Knife's wife," and Penny volunteering as often the case.

Bone Breaker asked if Penny could assist and was gladly accepted by the ladies. They knew Penny a year after Bone introduced her to them. They figured Bone Breaker was going to ask her for her hand. They figured all he needed to pop the question was for the group to give him a little prodding. Penny agreed. Plans were put in motions, then and there. There was little hope for Bone Breaker after that.

SCHOOL BEGAN

After the funeral dinner, everyone parted going their separate ways. All but the leadership. They remained behind. Everyone entered the limos. One limo with the children was taken back to Miriam's home. The rest of the Riders went to the inn. Susan, Bell, Miriam, Rhoda, and Penny went into the kitchen. They returned carrying cold beers. The men formed a row of tables into a circle. Cheryl asked Mike to one side. Over in a corner, Cheryl gave her reason to be alone from the group.

"Mike, the other day at the store, you tried to offer help against five boys. I thought you left me alone, as I demanded. When I got off the ground from that leader boy's gut punch, I saw one boy flying away from the side of the store. I walked over to him lying on the ground. I presumed; I had done that."

"Yes, I was watching you come around the corner, replies Mike. Cheryl said with astonishment. "You were, I didn't see a soul."

"I was sitting under a tree eating crackers for breakfast."

"Mike, I thought you hadn't any money."

"I didn't Cheryl. I found some soda bottles and cashed them in for the crackers. I learned to do that on my journey back to Georgia from Virginia."

"I thought after the speech we got the other day; you lived off worms and bugs? Also, out of trash cans. So, you actually got food looking for soda bottles?"

"Yes, Cheryl. Those things, the worms and bugs take a while to learn to eat. I really never liked to eat them. But hunger can drive you to try anything."

"Well, that's not why I called you over to this corner to discuss the taste of worms and bug, Cheryl replied with a grimace of disgust on her face. On the way back home, I ran into those five boys. They told me if not for you, they would take up what they begun. Then, they explained what you did and were awe stuck. Even afraid, they were waiting to see me. They told me to tell you, they were never going to cause me any more harm. Then apologized to me. What I want to know, where they got those blistered cheeks? They didn't go into details about what happened."

Mike hesitated, trying to pass off the incident as nothing to really say much about. Cheryl was insistent and kept Mike in the corner, until he confessed to what he done to them.

"Mike, you are going to stay right here, until I get my answers," demanded Cheryl.

"Okay Cheryl, if you must know, all I did was slap their cheeks."

"Okay Mike, when I went around the corner, I found everyone laying on the ground. Slapping someone on their cheeks don't knock them to the ground."

"Well Cheryl, I slapped them several times. That's all, I swear it." Mike raises his arms attempting to express to Cheryl, it was all I did. "It was all, except when I slap someone, it's like being hit with a two-by-four board, Cheryl."

Cheryl stood looking at Mike. After convinced about what he told her, she allowed him to pass. Both walked over to the table. Cheryl was given a soda and Mike a beer.

"Hey, why does he get a beer? Mike is not any older than me."

"Well, for your information, replies Chopper, we got him drunk back in the mountains. After all he's been through, becoming the youngest member we got, he can drink a beer. Besides, who's going to stop us?"

Razor speaks, "no cop will dare walk in this place. You going to tell, Cheryl?"

"No Razor, just asking.

"Good, now all raise a glass or bottle to Stephen. Here, here another for Teddy Bear, shouted other."

Ten to twenty beers later or three for some and two sodas with one tittering on the blink of falling off his chair, the women decided it was time to head their men home. Chopper and Bell took Susan and Cheryl home. Mike was trying to stand to say goodbye. Cho assisted him to his feet. He took Mike and got on his bike. Bell suggested Mike ride in their car. Cho insisted the fresh air would do him better.

"We meet you at your house, Chopper." Chopper tosses Cho the keys.

Chopper called to Cho, "we might be a while. Get him changed there. Then to bed, Cho." At the house, Mike sobered enough that any assistance from Cho was not necessary. Mike staggered upstairs changing into his regular clothes. He left the suit on the bed. He met with Cho outside. Cho took him to his camp site. Mike thanked him sliding off the rear of the bike. Cho reminded Mike to be up early. His new routine will begin tomorrow.

Mike's head was spinning making his way down the path. He felt like falling down on the ground and sleep spying the table appearing miles away. "The heck with the sleeping bag, rolled up under the table." Recalling Bell's last visit seeing him soaking wet, he decided it was best to unfurrow the dang thing. It didn't take long to get tucked inside his bag, then out like a light, he went. Next morning, Mike woke to the presence of Cho sitting on the bench above him.

"Good morning my son. I trust you had a pleasant sleep?"

Mike heard the tiny bit of laughter hidden in his voice. Also, quickly became aware of four others. Then, before he acknowledged Sifu Cho address, it became obvious to Mike the word son, Cho said. Son was never a word ever used to refer to him before. Something has definitely changed. Mike felt a sense of having been consider a son to Sifu Cho. He had hope this deep inside. The desire for a father was growing strong over the year. After making him Cho's heir, Mike finally found a belonging.

Cho immediately sensed Mike's reactions. He had strong feeling for Mike. Now, no words were needed saying, both shared the same sentiments.

Mike sat up, scanning the area. True enough, four men were standing behind Cho's bench. Mike recognized three of the four.

"Good morning sleepy head, replied Mandy. I saw the way you walked out of the house, last night. I been there many a time. Welcome to a morning hang over."

Sifu Cho stood watching Mike crawling out from under the table. Cho turns to the four men and begins his introductions.

"Mike, you know several of these men standing across from you. What you don't know is why, they are here? Mandy, you know is an expert in firearms. Pilot, you met arriving at the house. He is our resident flyer. He can fly just about any aircraft there is. Next to him is Magic man, his specialty is communications, also, he has a talent for escape and magic tricks. Finally, Mike, this is Sensei Marcus."

Sensei Marcus bowed, "thank you Master Cho."

"He is an expert in various forms of Japanese martial arts. Ju-jitsu and aikido, and the use of the sword. Each one of these men will be training you. Later, you will be introduced to several more persons added to your training roster. I made a schedule for your training. Beginning with your morning run, followed by two hours with Sensei Marcus three days a week. A one-hour rest then breakfast. Next, Pilot's training on the same days you will receive training from Marcus. He will begin with classroom lessons before actual flying. Then lunch and more lessons for several hours. Finally, after supper, you will be with me. Mainly at night. Mandy will have you for a whole morning between Marcus's training days. Magic will take over after lunch. Then, with me after supper." Mike stood stunned listening to all the training; he was going to get.

"This schedule will continue until all instructors are satisfied with your skills. This will begin tomorrow. Today, I will be with you the whole day." Each instructor bowed to Cho and Mike bowed to each one leaving.

"Good, now that the introductions are over, Mike, my son, prepare for the day's ordeal. It will be such." Cho had already prepared a special fire pit with a huge bowl sitting on a four-legged stand. The metal bowl sat over a hole cut in the table allowing the fire to heat the bowl. Inside the bowl was sand.

"Come Mike. Cho stood in front of the bowl of hot sand. Watch Mike, commanded Cho. Cho, with both hands amazingly slid them palms up through the burning sands. Now Mike, do as I have done. You will continue this until I have decided enough. The training will be done every day, until we have the intended results.

Mike did as he was told. The initial pain searing his hands was difficult. His hands felt on fire. Still, he slid his hands through the hot sands. Cho rubbed both hands with an ointment after the session; then to another place. Mike knew this exercise well. It was a wooden dummy. This dummy was made of metal. All the dummies before, Mike destroyed.

"This one won't be as easy to break," Cho told Mike with a chuckle.

After each session, Mike rested, then on to the next. Practice punching, blocking, and kicking while standing on one leg and one arm behind his back. He was to strike at a tree six inches away. To add to the training, Mike was required to always wear weights on both leg ankles and wrist and a twenty-five-pound backpack containing rocks all day and night when practicing. Sleeping, he could remove the backpack.

Every time Mike did not strike the tree with the force Cho required, he was given ten more minutes on each leg. After practice, Mike faced, Cho. He would attack him without mercy. All Mike was allowed to do was block, twist and move to avoid each blow. He had to evade every attempt made by Cho striking him. One hit and Mike had to do twenty-five sit-ups, push-up, and chin-ups.

To make matter worst, Cho would cool Mike down, throwing cold water over him. As daytime ended, the exercises changed with the night. Special in the dark sparring was not new to Mike. Fighting with Cho was always done in the dark. Cho would throw object at him, also strike at him.

Mike's hands and feet became hard. They looked horrible to the unknowing eyes. The training made him hard. When Mike was not practiced fighting, Cho had him during resting practice exact finger strikes at target points on a wood dummy. These were median acupuncture points. Mike had to dip his finger in water before he struck the dummy. Each strike left a tiny print where his finger hit. Any misses, resulted in more practice time.

Mike never complained. The next day was with Marcus. They practiced on various joint locking moves and throws. Mike thought he was in good shape and was. This training was totally different, he felt the effects by the end of the day. After lunch, Pilot took over. This was a blessing from all the fighting. Mike enjoyed the lessons and quickly his skill became evident.

The first few days in class was learning how to read instruments, radio, and mapping techniques. Learning to read a map was easy. Mike learned similar skills from the men in the mountains on his journey home. Later, he was taken to an airport. Mike was handed over to Tech, he worked on the club's aircraft. Mike learned to make repairs to plane engines. Also, how to maintain proper maintenance for the aircraft he wasn't going to fly.

Several weeks elapsed. Mike was ready for his first solo flight. Cho and Pilot watched him take off and land several times. Pilot cited to Cho; Mike has done an excellent job mastering the controls with a top rating. Pilot was impressed. Cho was filled with pride.

Marcus was very pleased with Mike. He was a quick learner. Magic man taught Mike various tricks with a deck of cards and how to play several games of poker. One of the tricks Mike practiced over and over, was the deal. Magic taught Mike how shuffle the deck of cards learning the secret of pulling any card he desired. Magic told Cho; he will teach him escape tricks soon.

Mandy said Mike took to guns as if he was born with one in his hands. He quickly learned to dismantle all the guns given him with great speed and reassembled them. His clock repair training gave Mike a good mechanical knowledge aiding his learning with most devices. Mike could shoot the eyes out of potato spuds a hundred yards away, without a telescope.

Cho had contests with the other bikers for Mike. One contest was to see who could shimmy up a rope the fastest. Mike held the record. Soon, many of the bikers sat around the camp site watching Mike go through his training. Many were asked to aid in his training. Cho's training was the only time no one was allowed to watch.

One day, Mike was doing his morning run carrying his rock sack and weights. By now the added weight felt normal. Down the road running he heard noise off to one side. Mike stopped turning into the wooded section. Making his way silently through the thick growth of shrubs, vines, and trees, he stopped short of an open field. In the clearing were several men sitting around a fire. From the looks of them, they were men of the road. Mike first encounter their kind on a train, passing through Atlanta.

Slowly, Mike appeared from the cover of trees into the open. He approached the three men around the fire startled by his presence. He appeared suddenly without the hint to anyone becoming aware.

One man stood instantly to face Mike. Mike held his hand up conveying he was a friend to the men of the road. They saw the hand sign Mike's companion on the train taught him.

"Hello, Mike said. Each replied back. I see from your empty fire you have little to eat. Are you aware of the river, behind where you sit?" One man spoke.

"Yes, we tried fishing last night. There don't seemed to be any fish to catch."

Mike replied, "I always found success fishing in the river. It you like, I would catch fish for your meal." No one objected.

Mike pulled his backpack of rocks off laying it near the fire. "Please tend to it. I will be back in about fifteen minutes."

Each one of the men giggled saying, "good luck young man". They sat watching Mike make his way toward the river. Mike could feel them attempting to check out the contents of his back pack. He knew they would after lying it near the fire.

At the river, Mike quickly removed his shirt, pants, kicking his shoes off, before jumping into the river. Working his way along the river ledge, Mike found a hole. Removing his foot from the hole, dives under the water. The hole had a catfish inside. One fish laid on the bank. Within a short time, Mike located a second hole, again, inside was a catfish. It was big. Two fish on the banks.

Mike crawled out of the river making his way back to where he entered. Once fully clothed, he walked back to camp caring two large catfish. All three men were awed, seeing the fish. Mike handed them the fish. Enjoy.

One man asked Mike to accept their apology. He said, "we looked inside your pack."

Mike replied, "I knew your ways and no apology is required. I will be on my way." Two of the men tried to stop Mike, wanting him to stay and share the fish. Mike thanked them but said he had to be off.

One man, the same person to greet Mike, asked Mike to answer a question the group pondered on." Seeing your bag by the fire and how lumpy it appeared to us, made us curious. When I grabbed hold of your bag, it was extremely heavy. Looking inside, we were amazed and struck with intense curiosity. Why are you toting a bag full of rocks?"

"It's simple, I am in training, replied Mike, turned, flipped his bag over one shoulder, as if it was empty running down the path back to the road.

For the next several days, Mike stopped to check on the men. Often, he would catch them fish. At night, he would bring them squirrels caught for his supper between his resting time periods or left over from a meal Cho brought to camp. Cho knew what Mike was doing and never once inquired. Mike often put extra food they shared into his pack.

Cho and Mike rarely ate at the house. One day Cho spoke to Mike. "Mike, I need to go off to tend to club business. Mike asked Cho to go with him. Not now Mike, your training is far more important, now. Soon, very soon you will be with me, when I am on a job."

TO MANY MOTHERS

One day after Cho left on club business, Mike was by himself practicing, a car stopped. Footsteps were heard coming down the trail. It wasn't Bell's, but definitely a woman. Bell often stopped along with Chopper or most often Bone Breaker, to see him. To Mike's surprise, it was Susan.

The day came with the warming sun, the night's chilly darkness was yet to replace the light. Susan walked over to where Mike stopped punching at a tree. The second tree. The first was clearly beginning to show the effects from all the pounding Mike laid on it. To spare the tree's life, a new one was selected.

Susan watched Mike walk toward her. When he stopped punching a tree, she looked at him with, "what in the world are they doing to you, Mike look." Mike saw her look at his hands. Both hands looked blacken with blisters, plus he looked thinner than the last time he went to her home to eat a meal. Mike realized what Susan was about to say to him and waited until she said it.

"My God, Mike, what is happening out here? You look half starved. Your hands, what, I mean how, don't they hurt?"

"I am doing fine Miss Susan, but it is nice to hear your concerns for me."

"Well, stop what you are doing. You are coming home with me for a meal and to tend to those hands. "But Susan," Mike attempted to say, but quickly realized, like Bell, there was no arguing with her or any woman.

Hearing those words, a meal; Mike gave up any attempt to do otherwise. It had been many weeks, since he last ate a meal, he didn't catch. Some of those days were spent with the men of the road's camp site. What he caught in the river was shared among the four of them.

"Susan, I need to clean up before I go." Mike pointed the camp site hose.

"That won't be necessary, Mike. Just get some clean clothes. You can take a bath at my house.

Mike went to his bedroll. Unwrapping the roll was several jeans wrinkled. The same was for the shirts. Neither of them had seen the inside of a washer for some time. That was apparent to Susan, smelling, spotting the clothes dirty appearance.

In the car, Susan rolled the windows down. Quickly arriving at her home, Cheryl opened the door seeing both walked up the driveway. "Hello Mike." Mike forgotten her kindness at the services and was preparing himself for a reception other than what he received, by Cheryl.

"Mom told me, she was going to ask you to come for supper. We were told by Bell and others; you and Cho rarely came to the clubhouse to eat. We figured since Cho was off, it would be good to feed you a home cooked meal. We were the first to have you over. The other ladies will be stopping by, while Cho is off."

"Thanks, but I was doing fairly well living off what I caught."

"Really Mike, replied Cheryl, you mean worms and bugs." Mike saw no point debating her or Susan, he just committed to their request.

Cheryl showed Mike to the restroom. After a ten-minutes shower, Mike emerged with clean clothes on, after realizing his other clothes were removed from the place, he laid them. Cheryl heard the bathroom door opened and met him rounding the corner to the living room.

"Your clothes, I guess you are wondering, smelled bad. I put them in the washer. Don't tell me you never change your clothes, either." No comment was returned, Mike kept quiet. She was correct.

At the table was a plate of meat loaf, assorted vegetables, and a big bowl of mashed potatoes to his delight. After a prayer of thanks, each plate was handed to Mike. His plate was half loaded with mashed potatoes.

Susan said," if I had known how much you liked potatoes, I would have made two bowls." Everyone laughed.

"So Mike, how is your training going, was the first question asked him, by Cheryl?

Susan responded with bluntness, "Cheryl, those training sessions are private and not to be spoken of."

Mike quickly said to Susan, "it was alright. He could answer her. I can tell you about my other teachers training, but Cho wants his training kept private."

"Oh," Cheryl replied with some trepidation in her voice.

Mike answered each question Cheryl posed to him while eyeing the food on his plate. He was so busy answering her questions, he couldn't take a bite. Susan watched Mike with amusement. She noticed watching Mike eyeing his plate of food, being polite, answering Cheryl's questions, he was hungry.

"Well, besides Cho martial arts, Sensei Marcus is teaching me ju-jitsu, aikido, and sword. Then, I have Mandy for firearms, I start explosive this week with Madd. Pilot is training me to fly. I took my solo flight last week. Then, there is Magic, card tricks and some useful sleight of hand. Currently, I have been learning how to tie knots and untie them with one hand. Yesterday was my first attempt of freeing myself tied up. Magic is teaching me how to escape from many tied methods."

"Oh, is there a trick of getting out of being tied," Cheryl half-jokingly asked?

"One thing I can tell you, when you are being tied, inhale and expand your body while they are tying you. "Why?" Well Cheryl, when you are all inflated holding your breath, then exhaling, you become smaller and the ropes loosen. There are many ways but that is one method I am taught. The last lesson will be to learn locksmithing and unlocking various cuffs and locking devices."

"Wow, they sure have you busy. I can see why you look so gaunt. Seriously Mike, where have you been eating." Susan stared at Cheryl asking questions. Susan kept giving Cheryl a please shut up smirk. Cheryl continued to ignore her mom's smirks. She wanted answers. It was plain to see Cheryl becoming interested in Mikes' doings, to her mom.

Mike was a tad hesitant to answer, because Cheryl was pretty close to the truth. Many days, he was so tired, sleep and eating eluded him. The days with Pilot, Mandy, or Marcus fed him. Sometimes, one schedule was too close to the following sessions, meals were missed. Mike answered the question, his teachers usually brought lunch.

Susan looked at Mike with trepidation, as had Cheryl. Mike felt the truth was sadly not accepted by them. It was the truth; they did bring lunch most of the times. The other meals, well maybe, not so, but only said lunch to Susan's question.

Susan and the other ladies made inquiries with his trainers, quickly learned the truth. Susan realized Mike didn't want their sympathy, so said nothing. "Mike, eat before your meal get cold, requested Susan before Cheryl asks more questions. Cheryl got the hint.

Mike stuffed, then expressed delight for a wonderful meal. Cheryl and Susan suggested a car ride back to camp. Mike declined. He asked for his clothes. Susan replied, "they were not finished washing. We will bring them to your camp tomorrow."

"Thank you, Miss Susan." Mike was escorted outside by Cheryl. Thanking Cheryl, a second time, Mike lit off running fast own the driveway. Cheryl stood watching Mike fade into the dark of night. Her heart was filling something for him.

Mike turned down the road to the long driveway leading to the clubhouse and his camp. A yell came across the street. It was coming from the three men of the road's camp. Quickly, Mike turned following the path to the sound's source. To his amazement, two of the four boys at Cheryl's home on the night of Mike's strip tease exposition were making the screams.

Two men, not anyone he recognized was beating on the boys. They were trying to rob them, it looked to Mike. When they spotted Mike coming toward them, they let the two boys fall to the ground. Both boys were badly beaten and not moving.

"What's going on here," Mike yelled.

One man said, "well, well, well, look what we have here?"

The other man responded, "yeah, your right, we got us a hero.""

Boy, the first man called at Mike, this is the wrong night to be in the wrong place." Quickly both men charge at Mike. To their surprise the boy didn't turn and run off. To their surprise, the boy stepped aside eluding their grasps. The first man felt the lift under his arm, next air born, and finally a hard impact on the ground.

"That was curtsey of Sensei Marcus, you may thank him when you meet him."

The second man turned to face a block to his wrist. He grabbed hold of Mike's arm. A sudden grasp to his hand followed by a twist. The twist swiftly took him to the ground. A snap quickly followed.

"You can also thank Sensei Marcus for his fine training I received and gladly taught you this night."

The first man rose, Mike responded with a short snip remark. "Sorry mister, Sensei Marcus is not here tonight. It is not necessary to rise to thank him." Mister didn't get the chance to answer. Mike made a looping high kick bringing the heel down sharply on his back. He laid beside his friend.

Both boys could barely stand. They got up slowly thanking Mike. Mike had one question to asked them.

"Why were you two in these woods, tonight?"

Both boys started to speak. One answered the question, "we were going over to see Cheryl. We took this short cut. We always went this way. We ran into to these two men. They were with someone. I guess we bumped into them selling dope?"

"Dope, what is dope?" Mike had never heard of dope.

Each boy looked puzzled about Mike's ignorance about LSD. After a short explanation, Mike realized a new problem was happening near the clubhouse. This needed Chopper's attention immediately. Mike helped the boys back home. Neither wanted Mike to walk them to their door. He did so, anyway. The first house Mike met the mother at the door. She recognized Mike right off. Seeing her boy beaten and her hearing stories about Mike, she came to wrong conclusion, "Mike was the reason."

Mike sensed her fears and explained to her what happened. Her son was quick to support Mike explanation. Mike realized for the second time this night, another problem rising. At the next house,

Mike escorted the younger boy to his front door. This time, the door opened before he knocked on it. A tall man stood facing Mike. He grabbed his son thanking Mike for helping his son To Mike's surprise; he asked Mike to come in. Mike declined thanking him, turned, and left.

The first boy's mom called ahead to the second boy's home. Mike assumed, "the mother had phoned ahead explaining the story concerning their two boys. The father of the younger boy wanted answers; Mike had none. He needed to find out what was occurring in the area. Any answers provided to the dad would only give him reasons to ask for more questions.

The next day, the story of Mike saving the boys likely killed ran, through the club faster than a wildfire. Soon, Mike had followers at every training session. Meals were given to him and his instructors. So much food, Mike felt bad not eating all the food on his plate. All his instructors not married, never complained. In fact, they told Mike to keep quiet. They enjoyed the home cooked meals.

AN OLD GUARD ENDED

In the subdivision, one of the biker's wives overheard two women, not associated with the club talking about two strange men hanging around the park. Hearing them discuss two strangers walks over asking a few questions concerning their knowledge. She was quickly shunned. Both women turned and walked away. Not chasing after them, she decided to meet with her Rider group of moms. A meeting was set up within an hour. Every woman showed up. All arrived, sitting waiting for Bell and Miriam.

Considering the events that occurred to their own recently, this was serious. Action was required and immediately. At the park, every woman waited for Bell and Miriam to call an order to their meeting. Bell commanded the women to follow her. Every woman walked over to one of the snotty women's homes. Arriving at the main trouble-maker in the neighborhood's home, Bell rang the doorbell. The lady answered her door, then immediately attempted to slam the door shut. That did not happen. One biker wife grabbed snotty woman yanking her out of her house. Next, tossing with enough force to end up on her butt. After making two complete spins, like a ballerina, her chubby legs gave way with an awesome smack on her ass to the hard-concrete patio porch.

Slowly getting back to her feet, the over weigh, middle-age snotty woman attempted to speak. Another biker's wife stuck her finger in her face. "One word out of that fat mouth and I swear to you, the next words will come from a mouth with no teeth." Snotty woman kept her mouth shut. "Our leader has something to say and you will listen!"

Bell steps up introducing herself. My name is Bell. I am the leader of our organization of biker wives. Beside me is my second

Miriam, and third, Susan. We lived in this area for years, during that time, we were aware of your displeasures about us, living among you. During that time, we accepted your unwillingness to associate with us. That was fine. We also had little desire to relate to you." The snotty woman stood quiet holding onto her ass.

"I am going to tell you this, one time. I suggest you listen carefully to every word I say. When you repeat this message, it is best not to misinterpreted it the wrong way. We kept a vigilance in this community, we and you live in. We kept the wrong kind of people from entering this place. By that, I mean gangs, drugs, hookers, etc. This has been a safe place, do you agree?"

"Well, you done a fine job of that I see. We got some men hanging around here, we think might be dealing drugs."

The biker wife told said to keep her mouth shut laid a loud and hard slap across the woman face. She yelled, turned attempting to say something. She decided to keep her mouth and opinion to herself, seeing the woman preparing to slap her again.

Bell continues, "we had some terrible things occur recently and been in mourning. I must apologize to you and our community our lack of vigilance. When two of our children were attacked and nearly killed, it was upsetting to us. Especially, when these men have been hanging around the park and not one of you bother to inform us. We provided safety for your children and in return you allowed ours to be harmed. It is your responsibility to help us protect our children. You seemed to not think this so and left the protection solely on our backs. You will gather the other ladies in the park within one hour. Trust me, you better be there. You don't want us to come and get you, miss."

"To make sure you comply, your new friend will remain with you escorting you to the park," demanded Bell. The biker lady smiled at her new chubby friend. Snotty mother was aided back to her feet by her new friend. Quickly, both made their way to every home. At every home, the mother was told to make a call to the other mothers. "Tell them to be in the park by noon."

One hour and every lady was seen walking to the park. "It sound like a gaggle of geese," Miriam snipped to Susan. The four biker women leaders were waiting on the women walking into the park. Seeing the biker babes made every woman, gaggle more. Bell had requested the biker ladies to get their bikes before the gaggle group assembled in the park. She gave them specific directions when they returned.

Before the whole group had a chance to voice their displeasure of meeting in the park, a loud roar was heard. Every woman biker rode their bikes around the subdivision women, herding them into a circle. Bell wait until the neighborhood mothers arrived before giving the signal; encircling the mass of women. They were given little option surrounded and trapped in a ring of bikes. Once everyone calmed down, Bell wave for the bikes to turn their engines off.

Bell, Miriam, and Susan stood atop of a table. All three were imposing. Bell spoke, two of our children were attacked the other day. Nearly killed if not for one of our own boys happening to be nearby. He easily defeated them, saving our sons from a terrible beating or worse. We currently been mourning a loss in our membership. We have not been keeping vigilance, maintaining a safe, secure area for all to live in."

"As I have said to one of your big mouths earlier, we desired to have little contact with you. We are of two different worlds. The one fact we all agree upon is our children, are the most important thing in our lives. We have, to your lack of knowledge, been safeguarding this area for years. Another thing, you can agree upon is this place, albeit our presence is a nice neighborhood. We kept you and your family safe, away from the wrong kind of persons. No drugs, or gangs except present company. We have for the most part, you can agree, been very easy to live with. No parties or riding our bikes through the streets at all hours of the night. No guns and shooting. Never once were police called here, concerning us. For some of you, well, let's say, we got our problems and you got yours."

"This has now changed; you allowed our children to come to harm. Our protection ends, this day. Some of your children were spotted buying drugs and we were about to deal with that. You chose this, you will be the bane for what happens to your families. Those night rides, parties, shooting pistols, well, will be changed, enjoy.

Any complaints from you will be dealt by us. You want our animos-ity; you got our animosity. We will not intervene in your behalf. Now get the hell out of our presence, bitches. Our husbands will have a talk with any husbands who don't like our little discussion. Or please, feel free to discuss with us your displeasures. Any ladies here among our group is itching to have a discussion group with you."

Bell waved for the Bikes to start their engines. An opening appeared among the circled bikes allowing the women to leave. Bell gathered her girls together after the other ladies left for home. Engines turned off. By the table, she informed the girls what was occurring in the area. The drug dealer's assault on their kids. Some had not heard the complete story of the two boy's ordeal. A meeting was to take place to inform all. This was as good a place as any. Later, other business will be discussed.

Bell spoke," listen all, do not get involved with any of the other people's children activities. If they are doing harmful things, call the police. Either way, we will keep these bad activities away from our children. We will let the police deal with theirs. One thing will be made clear this day, our children will be banned from being with theirs."

At each subdivision lady's home, phones buzzed. Every sub wife was commenting about the biker kids getting beat up. Big mouth hadn't confided with all her neighbors, only the ones she thought needed to know. Soon, all realized their area was now at jeopardy. Some knew what the biker ladies had been doing. Some were even thankful for their involvement. Few said, thank you. Now, they were left without a valuable defense for their children. Some women were becoming suspicious and concerned for their children. Questions arose, whose kids were involved with these drug dealers?"

UNLIKELY HEROES

After the biker mom's confrontation with the neighborhood mothers, their new focus was centered on their children. Every child was told to report any person new to the area, quickly. Do not have any contact with them nor contact with the other children. This included any friends they have with the locals. Few of the kids had any contact with them anyway, but now, it is an order. Every child will be watched by others, so if the orders have been disregarded, it would make its way back to their mom and Chopper or Bell.

Local moms soon felt the effects of the lack of patrols and several unfriendly and unknown faces begun appearing. Fears increased. Big mouth was constantly receiving phone calls concerning the unknown strangers.

"Mike, since Cho was off on a mission would venture down the path checking on his new friends, men of the road. At the camp site frequently visited they were in the preparations of picking up camp.

"Hey, I see you intend to leave. One of the men stopped, hearing Mike call out, to answer Mike coming inside camp.

"Hi there, glad we got a chance to say goodbye. Reaching out he shakes hands. Hey Mike, some kids dropped by this morning. Three boys and a girl. They walked in on us asking why we were out here? We told them, we stayed here on our way through the area. We kind of mentioned that you came by and caught us fish and bringing us some food. We thought you were very kind. Since you were nearby, you hadn't said to us to go, we figured it was okay to stay a few days. We are leaving, we explained to those kids. When we told them about you, they acted strange?"

"Yep, their attitude turned, hearing your name mentioned. They were a tad upset, telling us to git out of here, then, offered to assist us, after hearing your name said. Let us show you another place far better than this area," replied another hobo.

"They explained two kids were attacked by some men. They thought we might belong to the same group. When you were mentioned, they offered to help us out. We followed them along the river, not far from here. Over to one side was a large cabin. They said it was owned by an old man. He died years ago. They thought about using it as a club house until spending a night. They kept hearing strange sounds, thinking, the cabin was haunted."

"Really, haunted," Mike replied?

"Yes, well, we all been in a lot of old homes having strange and eerie things happening. Nothing that caused any us harm."

"Maybe just a fright or two," replied the first hobo welcoming Mike to their camp.

Hearing the cabin was haunted took Mike back to the old two-story house, he spent the night in the swamp. A fire soared from the fireplace burning his arms. Then, the double doors began breathing in and out. A creepy chill ran up his spine recalling those memories.

"We asked the three kids, if they knew you. They told us you lived under a table at the club's camp. You slept and lived there alone. We thought maybe you might want to move to this place, instead of living under a table. From what's we heard it seems you been gitting a bit of unwanted company, of late."

"Yea, you might say that. My Sifu, teacher, prefers a private place to instruct me. He would probably prefer this place, instead of where I have been staying. Thanks for keeping me in mind."

After Mike aided his friends cleaning their camp, he followed them along the river to the cabin. There, they parted ways. Mike entered the old cabin. It detected a strong mossy odor lingering in the stale air. The fireplace looked good. Some furniture made from logs, still solid. The table and two chairs were covered with dirt. One good thing was a working intact stove and wood stacked outside. Most of the stack of logs were rotted. Mike had an axe.

Mike remained cleaning the cabin for the rest of the day. After several hours passed, the cabin was fit to live in. Mike closed the door and began his run. Back at camp, Bell stopped by. She was about to leave then spotted him coming down the path. In her arm was a basket of hot food.

Mike could smell the chicken. "Mm, that smells really good, Bell. Mike gazed the basket. Bell, you going to a party or picnic with Chopper?"

"Picnic, with Chopper, never happens. No, this is for you."

"Me, thanks, Mike hoped she would say that. Bell, are you going to stay and eat with me?"

"Yes, silly."

Both were about to sit then Bone Breaker arrives along with pilot. "Something surely smells good, Bell." Before he was asked, Bone had one hand in the basket. Pilot had the second hand, in.

Bell quickly covers the basket. "This is for Mike and Me."

"Mike speaks up, it's okay for them join us, Bell."

Bell replies back with a snap, "it would be, if I had known they were coming. It just enough for us and some left over for you to eat tonight, Mike."

"Bell now, Mike, he always shares his food with us, whenever those fine women brings him food," Bone answering her snappy retort.

"Yeah, I know Bone, and I also know he gits little from their description of you pigs. He just a kid and no money." Mike started to say he gets along fine, but Bell stopped him from speaking.

"I won't have you grown men take this poor kid's food. You got plenty and he has so little. He never asked for anything and always is willing to share his food with you. Even if it means, he goes hungry."

Bone and Pilot look at Mike. Mike replies," hey guys, I am not starving, it is fine by me. I enjoy the company and I can fine food anywhere."

"See Bell," Bone looked back to her as Mike is explaining, Pilot agrees with a nod. Then Pilot said, "Yes, he always asked us to dine with him."

Bell gives both of the men a nasty snarl. Then Bone puts down his half-eaten chicken, or bone followed by Pilots bone. "Sorry Bell, we thought it was the polite thing to do, when he offered us his food."

"Really, why are you two here, by the way," quipped Bell?

"Well, I come to pick him up for parachute training. I will be flying Bone and Mike up for his first buddy drop," shyly replied Pilot.

"Well, it can wait. Go sit at the house. I want to be with Mike without the two of you buzzards staring at this food." Shortly, both were in the clubhouse downing beers.

Mike decided he better inform her about his new house. "You don't need to worry about me in the rain, anymore. These men, I met a weeks ago camping near the river told me about a cabin. They walked me to the cabin, before parting to go. I spent the day cleaning it. It will be a great place to stay. Cho should be pleased. It is far from prying eyes."

Bell answered, "I know of that cabin. I will tell Cho and the others."

Mike quickly asked Bell, "please keep it somewhat private. Cho has been upset lately with all the visitors coming by watching me train. Bell, besides, I really don't want all them folks coming by. I don't mind them at this camp site training from Pilot, Magic, Tech, or Marcus. That is in the day. At night is Cho and my time."

"Okay Mike, between us, that hurts a tad."

"I don't mean, you can't visit Bell, just all the others," Mike counters trying to ease her hurt.

"Oh, then that is a fine idea." After they finished their chicken, Bell assists Mike packing.

"I'll leave this here, until I finish with Bone," Mike tells Bell.

"No need Mike, I'll get Susan and Miriam to help; we will move it for you. Bell, Mike began to repeat what he requested. Bell stops him. I know, just a few people. Besides, I need to inform the leadership of this move, they are the leaders, Mike."

Mike decided there was no point arguing with her. He simply walks up to the clubhouse and enters. Bone and Pilot finishing their third beers was just getting up to fetch him.

"Good to see you Mike, save us a walk and besides, I don't need Bell giving me the riot act," quipped Bone.

"Hey guys, you know Bell. I was fine with it."

"Yeah, don't need to say a word, kid. We know her. It's fine."

On the way to the airstrip, Mike informs Bone of his new home. "Hey, that sounds pretty good, kid. We be by later to check out your new digs. Cho, he be liking the seclusion."

"Hey, you hear from him lately, Bone?"

"Nah kid, he should be back in a day, maybe two. Hey Mike, you aren't going to go all weeping on us about Cho being gone." Mike knew it was Bone's sense of humor, quickly replied back.

"No, unless it was you, you, I would bawl my eyes out."

"Go on, Kid. Cut the mushy stuff out." Then, bone firmly plants a slap on Mike's back.

Two flights and two drops from the plane with Mike landing on the ground safely. "Bone, you prepared Mike good. No broken bones," Pilot said watching Mike wandering over dragging two parachutes after landing his plane.

"Okay, here is your backpack, now go and finish your run, we be seeing you later, Bone tells Mike. Mike waves bye, then flew down the road. Twenty minutes later, Mike was turning down the road leading to the subdivision. No one was outside playing. It was weird. Usually, Mike saw children playing at the park. Upon entering the road to the clubhouse, he came to the path where the men of the road were camped, Mike turned. Making his way through the camp coming upon five men. Two boys and a girl were with them. Mike halted just in time for either party to spot him.

One of the men wore a t-shirt and sporting a bandana around his head. Both arms covered with tattoos. Mike quickly realized one man was part of the gang causing all the trouble and the death of Stephen and Bear. The others did not appeared to be in the same gang. Mike could feel his blood pressure rise. It shot up even more knowing the kids with them. Cheryl and her two boyfriends.

Cho had been instructing Mike on Chi power. Quickly, his mind became flooded with those lessons. Cho said, "everyone at birth has Chi entering into their bodies and departing it at birth. This Chi always flowed in a continuous pattern. When disrupted, the yin-yang becomes imbalance. This life force flows along a system of meridians or channels into my arms, legs, then the torso just below the skin's surface. The chart Cho had me study from Nei-Ching, showed those meridians," Mike thought.

"Cho told me treating one part of the body, affects the other parts, this is true of yin-yang internal organs. The conditions of these organs can be diagnosed when taking one's pulse. In the east, the pulse is not simply observed at the radial artery on the arms and legs, but in Chinese medicine, there are twenty-eight grades of pulses describing not just the rhythm and frequency of heart beats or the conditions of the aortic valves."

"Mike, this is why proper breath should be learned and mastered. Breathe out the old and breathe in the new is one of yin-yang principles. Cho went on to tell me, Mike thought, but was interrupted watching the five men begin a not so nice of a greeting and definitely a not so friendly welcoming displayed toward the three kids. In fact, down-right nasty manners. Maybe even very bad, nasty, rude, down-right ugly, with intent to harm, Mike thought building his rage."

Mike held back. He wanted to allow the scene to unfold, maybe allow them to say more about the reasons for accosting the kids. Plus, why their presence here, again. The same site he found the two boys getting beat up. He gave each of those men a beating that should have deterred others. His mind wandered back to Cho's lesson watching intently at the five men. Cho mentioned five elements that made up concepts pertaining to the tsang and fu organs. Breathing exercises aim to produce Chi. All illness was caused by either bad Chi circulation or the lack of Chi in the body. Both yin-yang, yin being equated with negative, dark, cold, feminine forces and yang equated to positive, light, warm, masculine forces. This principle is where the five elements arise, earth, fire, water, metal, and wood, a physical manifestation of all creation. Certain organs are related to each of the five elements."

"Cho continued explaining each element relations too; wood-eyes, sinew, gall bladder, liver, and anger. With fire; the tongue, blood vessels, small intestines, heart, and joy. For earth, it was the mouth, muscles, stomach, spleen, and anxiety. Metal, Mike thought was earth, but Cho differed on that, explaining it concerned the nose, hair, large intestines, lungs, and sadness. Finally water, had the ears, bones, bladder, kidney, and fear. Fear, Mike knew that element well."

"It is why exercising these internal organs through proper breathing is essential and why Cho said he stresses breathing. Remember all four elements are unified through the fifth element earth with the mind-mediative exercises. These exercises need doing, exhaling on certain movements, and inhaling on other moves filling your lungs in different ways, enable the proper flow of Chi. Mike, your Chi begins drawing up through your spine and through your body. It starts at the kidney, then back to the head, and finally back down the front of your body to the beginning, increasing your internal energies, strength to your body, your punches, kicks, blocks, etc."

Talking to himself, Mike begins his breath," I need to slowly, and calmly prepares for what will come next." Tattoo man made the first move. Good, Mike thought. This isn't some drug meeting. Mike prayed inside it was not so. It for another reason was his concerns. Thinking, Mike arrived at what he hoped was not what was in his thoughts, drugs. All three kids were now in danger. That was clear. Cheryl attempted to fight. She stopped once a knife was held to the throat to one of the boys. Then, a gun appeared, That is going to alter my attack, dang," thought Mike

Mike couldn't hold back, he had to react. In the dark and wooded area, the shots and their deaths could go un-noticed. He realized his first target. He wanted the tattoo man but the safety of the three kids was foremost, now. Mike began exercising his Chi breathing. He could feel the power surge inside of him. Then swiftly ran behind the gun man. Slowly, Mike relaxed, ending his sense of self and fears. Nothing to alert the one man holding the gun to take the shot. Mike was easing swiftly behind that man. The gun man never sensed another behind him. Quietly, with speed no one saw, the gun was grabbed. Mike took the gun twisting it in the man's hand. The gun came out quick. Within a flash, the gun man went down. To everyone present, the first man went down. Mike had enwrapped his other arm around the gun toting man's neck. With a quick un-noticed move, snapped his neck. No one saw the neck snap. It was as if, the man fainted.

The second man received a kick to his knee followed by a, what appeared a light slap to his neck by Cheryl and one of the two boys watching. The head tilted to one side. Before the second man fell, Mike was on the third man. Tattoo man was holding onto the second boy. He held the knife at the boy's throat.

Cheryl was free along with the first boy the gun was pointed at. The knife hand of Tattoo man jerked down, then made a funny twirling spin in the air in front of the tattoo man's face. He had a funny expression on his face, watching in awe, his knife twirling. What caught his eye, the knife had a hand attacked to it. The hand had no arm. Mike took the knife hand, then used it to sever tattoo's hand from his wrist. The act of doing that put a wickedly bend to the tattoo's man arm. Mike had to contort the arm to get the correct angle to sever the man's hand off holding the knife.

Number four guy felt the fist to his nose followed by Cheryl's foot to his groin. The second boy grabbed hold of the fifth man. Cheryl stopped Mike from doing what he wanted, asking him for the pleasure. Mike allowed her to give the last man a token of her displeasure. She picked up the knife with the hand attached, off the ground. Then returned the knife across the fifth man's throat Bobby was holding. The tattoo man missing a hand, finally connected the knife seen twirling in the air, was his hand. That realization came to him lying face down in the ground.

The three kids stood wondering how Mike done what he did to the first three men. Cheryl spoke up, "Mike, you killed two men, why not the third guy."

Mike looked at all three, standing, staring at him. Mike had to repeat two more times before it was understood. He realized they were in shock.

"Listen, this guy, I didn't kill is part of the Atlanta gang. You must not tell anyone what happened here. If this gang finds out it was me, this whole place could be a war zone. You got to keep this quiet. When it comes out, you three did this."

"Hey, Mike you saved our lives, you deserve the credit. It ain't fair we be looking the heroes for what you did."

Mike replied, "I do what I have to, not for glory, but to help others. This is Cho's and my code or way. We cannot continue this with everybody knowing. We would have our faces plastered over the papers. Everybody bad, will come at us. We need to keep in the dark. Please try and understand. Please do as I ask."

"It is not fair, replied Bobby. That man with the gun was going to kill me."

Mike responded, "life is not fair, and I lived with that a lot. People treat me wrong. If I attempted to get revenge every time someone destroys my property, call me names, throws things at me, well, you get the drift, what will that make me?"

Bobby suddenly felt shame. What Mike said made him reflect, could he know about what happened at his camp?" Bobby was hoping he didn't.

Mike picked up the tattoo man and quickly tied off the severed hand to stop the bleeding. Now, looking up at the three, commands them to follow him to the house. Mike lifted the man onto his shoulders. He was twice the size of Mike. Lou and Bobby both stared at the ease Mike lifted the guy onto his back.

The gun man was found later, by a biker. The gun, nowhere to be found. One biker noticed a funny lump in the gun's man throat after attempting to pick him up, along with the other three to quietly dispose of the bodies. Upon examination of the man with the missing hand, a gun was located halfway down his throat. The second man was quickly killed, his neck snapped. The third body was easy to determine the cause of death. His throat was sliced in half. The fourth man was told by the kids, Cheryl punched out. Cheryl hit him in his nose followed by a kick to the groin. They attempted revive him, they noticed his throat was caved in. Later, the caused was cleared up by Mike. Mike said, "he accidently stepped on the guy's throat beginning his run to the clubhouse."

Chopper suspected, "to keep Cheryl from realizing the truth, she killed the man."

Without a word, Mike ran, not walked carrying the big man. All three of the kids could barely keep pace with him. Mike slowed for them to keep alongside of him. Neither asked to relieve Mike of the burden on his back. Didn't matter, Mike thought. It would take too long if they tried carrying tattoo man.

Within minutes, they arrived at the clubhouse. Chopper just arrived with Bell. Bone and Pilot was outside chatting with them. Razor was inside along with Jack knife. Penny had entered with Miriam. Susan sat with Magic. Magic was showing her one of the card-tricks, he taught Mike. He told Susan, after her asking, Mike was good at getting out of cuffs and ropes.

Bell heard Cheryl's screams first. Then, all turned. What they saw was unsettling. Mike stopped short of them with a man on his back. It was noticed by the leaders Mike's burden. He had a man with tattoos and a missing hand on his back.

Quickly, they escorted the three kids and Mike toting a one-handed man into the house. Over to the first table Mike flopped the man down. Most of the people in the house were sitting at the bar and little to see Mike flop the man down. Susan almost screamed noticing Cheryl coming inside along with two of her friends. She was to be at home.

"Cheryl, why are you not home, while looking at Bobby and Lou?" All three didn't have a chance to say a word when Bell told someone to fetch the first aid kit. Susan turned looking to see, who needed first aid. Quickly she imagined it was one of the children. Then seeing all the kids were fine, imagined it was from one of the kids not in their club. "Could there have been a fight among the kids, this soon?" Then, spotted the arms with the tattoos. He was not one of the subdivision children. Next, came a realization to what happened, seeing blood dripping to the floor from tattooed arm. The arm was a missing a hand. Where, what happened, was a better question needed asking?"

Cheryl, then Bobby along with Lou spoke at once. "Mike cut his hand off. He stopped me from being shot, Lou had a knife to his throat, Mom they were going to kill us. Mike, he saved us all. Bobby said, Cheryl did pretty good herself Mrs. Stephens. His knife was floating in the air, the first man fainted, or we thought he did. Cheryl spoke, Mike took him out, first. He had the gun on Bobby."

"What, slow down, repeat that again, no, stop, we will discuss it when we get home."

"Mom, we can't tell anyone about Mike doing this," Cheryl anxiously replied.

Chopper walks over to Cheryl. Explain Cheryl, why Mike cannot be mentioned to anyone."

"Mike, Mr. Chopper told us this is one of those Tattoo men gang member from Atlanta."

Quickly Chopper gathers the kids into a corner together calming them. "Listen to me. Mike is correct. This must not be mentioned outside this group. If you value the life of your families, keep this quiet." Everyone could see Chopper's eyes nearly exploding out of his face, demanding them to keep quiet about this incident.

"Mr. Chopper, Bobby said, Mike told us we are to take credit for this. He wants us to be praised for saving our lives. Chopper looks at Mike. Mike looks back. Chopper realizes the truth of Mike statement to the kids. He is correct."

The one-handed tattoo man laid on his back, while Bell tended to the arm. Mike tied a tourniquet before hauling him down the road. Razor put a blade in the fire. Bell removed the tourniquet from the tattoo man, blood began to leak out quickly.

Bell screamed to Razor; you got that blade hot. Better bring it quick, if you don't want this man to bleed out." The tattooed man looked at Bell in terror. He was dying. She removed the tourniquet.

"On my way Bell."

Bone held the man's arm down. Bell placed a rag in his mouth. Razor did the honors. A red-hot blade touched the arm. A crackling sound could be heard from blood crusting from the searing heat. An odor filled the house. The children in the back corner sheltered from the leader's conversation could hear and smell the tattoo man's yell. Each child, including Cheryl, got sick. The smell made them sicker. Back on the table, the tattoo man passed out. Jack knife brought a cold bucket of water to the table. Approximately fifteen minutes elapsed.

Chopper gave the order. He had enough sleep, wake him. The cold water was dumped over his head. He woke. Looking up and before remembering why he was there, the pain came. He tried to grit his teeth.

Razor said loudly, "he got guts, not trying to scream. I'll give him that."

Again, Chopper gave a command. Asked him where his gang's hang out, is. Razor asked, the tattoo man heard something, the pain kept his mind clouded with pain. Then a hard slap on his face made him aware of a man standing over him. A second slap made him hear, what was asked. A third slap came, when he did not answer the question.

Bone knew this guy wanted to keep secrets. Bone squeezed the wrist to the hand missing. To the tattoo man, the hand felt like it was still there. It wasn't after Bone squeezed his hand. Bone kept squeezing his hand. The man said three words to Chopper. "Kiss my ass, then fainted."

Cold water was dumped on his face. He awoke. Chopper got into his face. "Let me tell you one thing, tough guy. You ain't that tough. Before this night is over, you will tell us where your hideout is? We can let you leave here alive or make your life, as long as it lasts, be one living hell. Think about it?"

Bell walked up to the table holding a knife. Jack Knife pulled tattoo man's pant down. Bell took hold of his man hood; nuts to be exact. One slice over his nut sack and he talked.

"Okay, okay it is in a warehouse near the last attack. We kept the old place secure, to return back. We been hold up there."

"Is that where Leader man and repeater man are?" "Who?" Your two leaders that survived the fight at the kid's home." "Oh, them, yeah, they're there."

Chopper heard the children scream and throwing up. He walks over to them. "Come with me," he commands. He led the three into the back room away from the ugly scene.

"Look, Chopper said; see how everyone is trying to help Mike. All your moms want to bring him food or have him stay in your homes. They heard about him saving your two friends. Mike is a wanted man by this gang. They want revenge on him and us. We took care of most of them. Two of their leaders are the ones that hate

Mike the most. They blame him. Like I explained days ago, it was our fault, more so than Mikes'. Mike declined your parent's offer to stay in your homes. Why, because he was protecting them. He knew one day, they would come for him. He did not want you or your parents involved. He would rather get killed, than see anyone in this club come to harm."

"You keep your mouths shut. If word gets out, which it might, then you will be the heroes. Also, remember the police will want on this. We definitely don't want the police on this. No one outside this club, better not hear of this. Got that. So, live with it."

Quickly the kids were sent home. Miriam and two bikers escorting drove them home. What was to be said, was for the leader's ears only. Any more the kids heard might be leaked. The little they know, the less chance of discovery, was decided among the leaders.

Chopper turns to Mike. "Where are the bodies? Mike replies at the camp site where the men of the road stayed, it was along a path to an old cabin. Bell spoke up. I know where that is, so did Bone and the others.

Chopper quickly turns to several bikers playing pool to go and remove the bodies. Make sure they are secured. This was not needed said. The point that Chopper said it made the reason that much more of a serious threat. The job was to be done with the up most care. No trace, period was implied.

"Mike, Cho will be back tomorrow. You and Cho will see me, after he gets settled. Bell take Mike to his camp. You men, take this garbage out to dump with the others."

Bone asked if he could go. Bone said, "Chopper, they may be others Mike hadn't seen."

Mike hearing what Bone said to himself, there wasn't. If there were, he would have been aware of their presence. Mike said nothing. All three left for the cabin.

At the bar, Chopper sent out messages to inform all the members and families of this new threat. Words went forth quickly. Before the hour ended, all were aware of this new and serious threat. The men were told to be at the clubhouse early the next day.

MISTER CASPER

Bell, Bone, and Mike quickly arrived at the cabin. Mike entered a cabin with little inside after he left, then returning shocked what the ladies done. A fire was lit in the stove. A carpet laid on the floor. Everything was clean. It looked as if some painting was evident, also was the faint smell of fresh paint. His bed roll was across a bed having a mattress with supports slats needed for a mattress. Mike now had a bed. He welcomed the change of not sleeping on the cold and sometimes wet ground. A pot, some glasses, and plates were neatly stacked on the only shelf. Towels and such other items made it homely. There was no bathroom. In its place was an outdoor house and a camp site shower bag hung on the eave next to the cabin door. It could be filled with river water used to wash after a hot sweaty workout.

"Well Mike, how do you like the cabin?"

"Wow, you ladies did a bang-up job. This beats that cold, wet, ground any day. Thank you so much, Bell."

Bell was clearly happy. After showing Mike about the cabin, Bone came inside. He took the opportunity to scout the cabin after Bell and Mike entered. Coming inside, he was as flabbergasted as Mike. Turning to Bell, he cites, "Bell you aim to spoil the kid with all this homey fixing up?"

Bell did not reply to his usual banter. On the table was a basket with Mike's supper. Bell pointed at the basket before Bone saw or smelled the contents. She quickly escorted Bone to the door with both saying good night to Mike.

Mike sat in the cabin by a small kerosene lamp lit, eating his supper. It was a slice of meat loaf. To be exact, it was Susan's meatloaf with some assorted vegetables and a big heap of mash potatoes.

Night was darker in the wood around the cabin. Mike quickly noticed the difference at the campground and at the cabin far into the woods. He laid on his new bed in the total darkness. It felt nice to lay on a bed other than a hard, cold ground. He was gladdened the men of the road told him about this cabin. Sometime during the night Mike felt the need to awake. His eyes quickly adjusted to the darkness. Before his bed stood a figure of a man. Mike sensed nothing of any stranger entering his cabin. There he was quietly standing at the end of the bed.

"Hello, Mike asked. Nothing came back. Mike reached for the kerosene lamp near his bed. Once the wick was lit and flame adjusted flame, he turned back to get a better look at his visitor. He was gone.

Morning came, Mike was up. With a fast dress, he took to the path for his first run. Returning to the cabin, Mike saw two words written on his tabletop, in dust. It read Mister Casper. The same was written on the wall above his bed.

Later that day at the clubhouse, Mike met every biker. "Wow, Mike thought. Chopper had a well-oiled team. Last night Chopper called them together and less than a night, everyone was here, except Cho."

Everyone took a seat. Once seated and before the first cups of coffee delivered and their several wives and the older children present, roll call was taken. Cheryl and Bobby was here, Mike spotted. Cho walks in. His first glance around the room was to see his son, Mike. Seeing Mike, he gave him a nod.

The room quickly filled with cigarette smoke. All leaders sat at one end of the room reserved for them. Chopper stood. He had Cheryl, then Bobby recant their stories from last night. Each explained how silently Mike appeared. His attack was blinding fast and deadly. The fight ended before anyone had a chance to take a second breath.

Cho appeared unphased from hearing them recant of what happen. Inside, he was filled with pride. Mike saw the subtle change in his breathing. Bobby went on to say, "Mike begged us to never revealed, it was him. He wanted us to take the credit." Chopper stood to explained why Mike asked that of them.

Mike was not focus on the talk. He was remembering a lesson about the way. The way or do, said there is no gate on the way or do, of life, refusing your entrance, if you want to enter through. It sounded odd to Mike. Then, Cho continued, there are thousands of paths to travel to succeed in your way. When you succeed in your way, it will disappear, and you will become the way. The ways are many to choose your life path, because your mind is the way. This is Zen."

"Cho, no Marcus, once told me a story when he was in the orient. He came upon an old man sitting on the ground, in a lotus position, naked above his waist. His body was covered with mosquitoes sucking his blood. Funny thing Marcus said, no one standing watching this sight was bothered by any mosquitoes. Around the old man laid hundreds of fallen mosquitoes. Everyone assumed the mosquitoes were so sated, full of the blood, drained from the old man and could not rise to fly. Marcus remained behind after all departed. He was curious, he asked the old man noticing all the mosquitoes were dead; the real reason none could fly, how they had died. The old man replied, 'they were poisoned." The man confessed it was balance, a circle is the key to balance. All movement stems about the circle. Keep your body upright with your trunk position central is mastery of any art. Without balance, you have nothing. With every movement reflecting readiness."

Mike recalled looking at Marcus with confusion. How is that related to the circle, Sensei? That was my same reaction, responded Marcus to me. The lesson of the circle stuck with me. Maybe, that was the sole purpose of the story, to teach me the meaning of the circle. This story was similar to one of Cho stories. Mike reflected, "it was a poem, "When the moon of your mind becomes clouded with confusion, you are seeking around for the light outside." It was a story first told to me once I thought I mastered a certain skill. It seemed no matter how hard I practiced, it was never good enough for Cho. He always found fault in my mastery."

"Cho seeing how I was unsettled by my lack of reaching this mastery expected of me, I wanted to change my approach, so he told me this story. An old lady lost her pin in her bedroom. She went to look for her lost pin outside. She looked and looked. A friend stopped by; she asked her for assistance in locating her pin lost in her bedroom. To the friend's astonishment, she asked her why she was looking for her pin outside, when she lost the pin in her bedroom? Her answer made sense, it was because there was no light in her bedroom, I am searching for my pin where I have light outside with the sun high overhead."

Mike just realized what Cho meant, Mike beamed a smile on his face. "Changing my approach would not improve my skill. Improper way, leads to an improper way, and a loss of the way. The way must be found from the inside and not trying to find a way that is not true to my path or the correct path. In my mind, I was trying to find a way, while the light was the way, I was looking in the dark and not the true light where the solution was to be found. Through hard work and diligence, one will fine the way. It is the entrance to the way, I refused to enter." Chopper began assigning every man to a task.

Plans were set, each had their commands. Each group had a leader. Cho and Mike were given a specific task. Mike was to walk on the path of greatest threat. He was to enter the den of wolves. Cho was his shadow. Each group was to prevent escape. This time, we will have them all, Chopper decreed.

Every mom was told to prepare for the worse. By the noon hour, Cho and Mike were well on their way to the big city. Their clubhouse bordered the city limits and their ride took less time than Mike thought.

THE BIG CITY

Entering the city, Mike asked Cho to stop at a tall building. Inside was the office of the newspaper man, he befriended at the river in Macon. The same person who printed his story and the one, the movie man contacted to locate the boy to make a movie about. Cho escorted Mike into the building. They made little progress to the elevator. A man dressed in a security uniform halted their entrance at the elevator. He took one look at the way the two were dressed and immediately assumed they were the wrong type. Cho explained to the man with little result, then Mike gave the guard the name of the paper man. "He is a very important man," responded the guard.

Mike insisted the guard call the very important man; they would leave without any further trouble. The guard was about to explain to Cho, the two of them were leaving, whether he called or not. The guard was quickly tapped on his shoulder, the pain sped ran down his spine. He could barely move. Cho politely explained to the guard, "they will leave after seeing the important man. The pain will ease. Most likely cease, after a week."

The guard called the office of the very important man. Soon, a secretary came out of the elevator. She hurried over to Cho and Mike. "Right this way, sirs. Cho and Mike walked with her. Mike quickly noted the pretty secretary the paperman had. It seemed to Mike; every man of power had a pretty secretary.

The guard was told, when they returned back to the lobby, Cho would ease his agony. It was two hours sitting and rehashing Mike and his first meeting before the true cause was revealed to the paperman.

"Mike, I will offer any news you require. I have my team on it, now. Paperman picked up a phone. Later, a man asked to enter the office. When he entered, Mike recognized him right off. It was dark glasses, the man who tailed him from Atlanta to his aunt's home. He had Boo with him. The first question asked Mike, was of Boo.

"I had to leave Boo back home. I was not sure what was going to transpire on this new journey, I am on. I feared for his well-being. I miss him more every day," responded Mike.

Turning to his boss, Dark glasses inquires what services he was need to do. Quickly, the paperman explains the visit of Mike. "Oh," responded Dark Glasses, "I know of these members to that gang. Just several months ago, there was a war and many of their members were killed. The leaders got away."

"Do you know where they are," Cho asked?

Dark Glasses was about to asked who the Asian man was, then decided if he was with Mike, it was fine. "I been keeping tabs on this gang, after learning of the fight at your home. We were very glad Mike; your family was safe."

"Thanks a lot. I appreciate your caring about me and my family. Now, they are after me again and I intend to end this. If you have any known information where they are, please tell Mr. Cho. Mr. Cho is a friend and has many resources at his disposal," Mike plead.

Newspaperman asked Mike, "Mike you don't intend to go after them yourself?"

Mike answered, "this is Cho, he is a very good friend to my family and has been there from the beginning." Mike noticed, Dark Glasses still wore his shades, that green coat, and the hat listening to Newspaper man.

"Mike, from all the sources at my disposal, I learned they are hiding out in the east end of the warehouse section. Not far from their old haunts. I think it is the same building, they first occupied before moving to the place most of them were killed. Kind of smart, if you ask me," replied Dark Glasses.

"How so, paperman inquired of Dark Glasses?"

"Well who would think they had the smarts to go back there?"

"I see your point, replied newspaper man. Cho said, it is logical. Mike shakes Paperman's hand. He stands escorting Cho and Mike out of his office. Dark Glasses received a hug from Mike. Both Cho and Mike enter the elevator. The pretty secretary led the way down.

Outside, the lobby guard stood by the elevator. He was sweating and looked to be having a heart attack. On lookers kept to their own business passing without wanting to offer any assistance to the security guard. No one attempted to asked him, if he needed assistance. "Funny, Mike thought, how the way people enter the entrance to find their path and along that path, they receive their reward one way or another." Mike pondered each person path leading them too. They had little concern for the well-being of the guard, clearly in stress. What will their path's journey be like. Clearly not filled with the light.

Cho saw the agony, the guard was surely in. Cho felt pity for this man trying to do his job. With another tap on the guard, the pain quickly left. The pain still had a hold on the guard. Cho desired the guard to contemplate his actions for the next time they meet. "That little pain remaining will wear off in two days," Cho told the guard

Quickly, Cho drives to the warehouse section. Mike gets off the bike walking through a gate. Cho send a message to the other bikers; Mike continues down a road between two building. Soon, Mike came upon several men with tattoos standing at a building. One man walks over to Mike, the other man lingered slowly creeping behind, keeping his eyes glued to this kid.

"Hey you, why are you walking around here." The tattooed gang member stopped within an arm's distance of running into the short scrawny kid. A hand slammed into Mike's chest. It was expected to knock the kid to the ground. To the tattoo man's surprise, his intended blow felt like a brick wall.

Mike responded, "that ain't your business." He knew that answer would draw their anger to him. It's what Cho told him, he needed to do. Make sure their quarry was indeed, inside the building. To attack without this knowledge, could allow the leaders to flee again."

One man, the one that Mike responded too, tried shoving him, continued with his banter. His hand planted on Mike's chest, attempted to renew his shove. It was a futile attempt to make. Mike twisted as the tattoo man renewed his shove. He pushed air almost falling to the ground. Mike giggled at him. A second man advance closer to Mike. He attempted to grab Mike from behind. Cho told Mike to resist but not so much to reveal his skills.

The second man landed on his back, attempting to grab Mike from behind. The flight over Mike's back was quick. Mike needed not to touch the man, simply waited until the attacker was at the end of his grasp. The momentum his back sneaker upper was all that was needed for him to fly over Mike's back side. The third man was flattened by the impact from the second man landing on him. He came out of the door not knowing what transpired with the two guards. A surprise greeted his ignorance. It didn't matter much; he was out cold and could not contemplate the situation.

Mike assisted both men to their feet. The first man assisted the third bracing himself on Mike. The second man slowly getting up. Mike explained, "I heard a gang with a good ref was here. We are tired of belonging to a loser gang. We wanted to change to a better quality, gang." The first man was about to punch Mike, then stopped after hearing what he said.

"I guess I made a mistake, if it takes three guys to take me on. You guys must all be losers. Let me go, I will leave this dump. Their got to be a gang with some creds around this city, who has the real creds," Mike told them?

One of the leaders happened to be at a window watching what occurred below him. Watching his men being thrown about by a young kid caught his noticed. Calling out to others in the warehouse, "hey, you guys it looks as if we might have a new man. We are down to a handful and sure could use some replacements. This kid below, has some talent."

"What you talking about? What new man?"

"Over here at the doors. Three of our guys nearly got their butts handed to them." Two of the leaders still alive and the two Mike knew well, stood at the window peering down at the scene unfold. The damage their gang received from the bikers, neither leader got a good look at that gang. They did remember the bikers. Mike had grown and changed from a skinny kid to a much more, healthy lad. His hair was grown out.

Several raps pounded on the windows above was heard below by three guards. One of the men looked up seeing his leader waving. "It seemed, they wanted to see this guy."

"Guys," the boss wants us to take this kid up to see him. The big bellied guard commanded the second man to open the doors. He awoke from dreamland faster than Mike thought he would. Next, big bellied guard pointed to the first guy, "me and you will take the kid up. The first man did what big belly told him to do.

Cho was watching the scene unfold from another roof top. "Good, Mike has succeeded gaining entrance."

Mike was shoved forward by the big man. Then pushed through the doors. Inside, was a big empty warehouse. Mike remembered what Magic Jack said he had done to the building. "He wondered if they had discovered all the surprises Magic had placed inside. The bikers planned on them returning here. They disappeared for several weeks prior to the battle, then returned to their first warehouse unexpected. Wont they be surprise, when we return Them tricks Magic installed, is going to be a hoot to watch. After several more shoves assisting Mike walking to the leaders; Mike was getting a tad upset with the two guards. He was about to teach them to stop shoving him. The leaders met Mike at the foot of the stairs.

Mike thought, "well, I guess I won't be needing to teach them to stop pushing."

The stairs led to an office room on top. Mike saw a light on. "The hangar room to this warehouse was huge, only about ten to fifteen men occupied vast empty. If Mike included the ones outside, this gang might total twenty men. Cho and I can take this group ourselves. Only thing wrong with that idea, some men could get away," Mike debated on the idea.

"Hey kid, the One Eye leader said to Mike, I was a watching outside. You got's some grit. I saw you don't take a ton of crap from my boys. They are pretty tough dudes. You gots some good moves. So why you here?"

Looking at the One Eye leader, it took all Mike could muster not to take him out, right there. Thinking, "Be damn the others." Mike contemplated on that notion for a second. "Our group wanted all of them. They deserve their share of this gang hides. Besides, if I did that, it would throw a monkey wrench in the plans. One stupid act now and the whole plan can fall apart," Mike realized.

"Mike, Mike calm yourself," to himself. Mike decided to allow his needs to be put aside for the better of the bikers. One Eye stood waiting for Mike's reply. The same man Mike had stabbed in the shoulder and foot. Prior to that in the park, he bear clawed One Eye on that not so pretty face, he was wearing, now.

"Well, Mike said to the leader man, whoever you are, I was thinking of asking to join up with your gang. From the way your so-called tough guys were flown around by me, I think I might try some other group?"

"Look kid, there is no better than this gang. We have been through some tough times me and my gang. You want in on the best, we are the best. Why else you show up at our doors, if you didn't think so, Huh?"

"Okay, you got me, Mike said hoping Leader man would say that to him. I heard about how bad ass you were and thought I would check you out. My gang ain't much. We joined up with this local group. Our group was done in by this biker gang."

"Yeah kid, what is the name of this gang you belonged to. Mike thought quickly, he hadn't figured on being invited into the warehouse. Mike figured along with Cho, just take a walk around to check out the place. Later, they would plan a way to get in with this gang."

Mike responded with the name of the group Stephen mentioned the bikers took out, prior to the battle in Atlanta accumulating in Bears and Stephens deaths.

"We thought another gang eliminated that so call group trying to squeeze into their territory," answered One Eye.

Before One Eye could evaluate Mike's words, Mike responded, some of us were away doing scouting. When we got back, we found the place being swept clean. My buddies and I watched every one of our friends being buried. We watched them clean our place up real pretty. They was professionals. Our place looked like no one ever was there. It plum looked like a new Building. They were some bad asses. If me and my buds join any other gang, they are going to be pretty bad asses themselves."

"You mean to tell me; you got some others wanting in along with you? Well kid if they are half as good as you talk, then, we can sure use some new blood. You go and gits them."

"Now Mister One Eye, they might have found someone better and decided they don't want in with your gang. I'll go and tell them about your invite. We will talk about it. Maybe in a week, I get back to you with our decision."

"You do that kid. Also, tells them we got money and weapons to boot."

"Yeah, you do, huh, Mike said in an unbelieving manner. I don't see much of that. I guess you scared of letting anyone see them. You think someone will come and take them away. I can git that." Maybe they be rusty, single shot, old as hades guns." That remark was what Mike figured would make One Eye show him their weapons.

"Nobody was carrying a weapon when Mike first met the three gang guards outside. Inside, it appeared no one was carrying a gun among the others surrounding him. Most of the tattoo gang guys wore very loose-fitting shirts with another shirt overlaying the first one. To Mike's thinking, they all had the same clothes designer. If they are carrying, then all them shirts might conceal what they got," Mike figured.

One Eye reached behind his raised shirt. So, did all the other gang members standing around Mike. Each man removed a pistol. Most were 9 mm handguns of different models. The second man in charged, not talking, walked over to a metal door by the stair wall. The door was locked. Mike was waved over to the locked metal door by the second leader man.

One Eye pointed Mike to go over. Mike walked over to the door. The second leader man opened the door. Inside, Mike gasped at the total number of various rifles, mainly M-16 and shot guns on racks. On a table was a huge stack of pistols. Along the walls was stacks of ammo on shelves about ten boxes high. Ammo cans were in a clustered under the shelves.

"Well kid, still think we ain't got any guns?"

"Damn, Mike responded. Me and my friends had a gun, but never had we ever saw so many guns. Mike looks up to One Eye, if we come in, we git to choose our guns we want to carry."

One Eye looked at Mike, "kid you carry as many guns you want too. We got more. We also got plenty of other benefits to go with that stash of guns. We takes care of our men. That's why we are the best. We want the best. You bring your friends. If they check out, you as good as in."

"Hey, with what you got, I don't know why they won't want to join."

"One thing kid, replied Leader man with a serious threatening tone, keep your mouth shut about what you saw. We don't like to advertise what we have. When we want buyers, we put the word out."

"Hey One Eye, that is one problem you ain't got to worry about. We know how to keep our mouths shut, also, to follow orders."

Leader man seemed satisfied nodding his head. He turned to see what his second man thought. He nodded back. Both men bought his story. Mike turned to leave. Leader man had the two guards escorting Mike in, allow him to leave by himself. Outside, Cho was still at his perch spying on the entrance.

One eyed turned to his second man after Mike made a comment. "Why you let that kid git away calling you One Eye?"

"That name, the kid called me, I like it. One Eye suits me. You got a problem with my new name?"

"Nah, just asking is all."

Mike is taking too long, Cho was thinking. He didn't see anything crazy happenings in or out of the warehouse, so sat still waiting. Seeing Mike leave the warehouse alone gave Cho a good feeling. He was correct about Mike. He is ready to travel with me on some of my trips. Still, Mike needs to complete his training," Cho thought.

Cho went to the ledge to scrambled down off the roof. At the corner of the warehouse, he leaps off the edge. Quickly, extending his legs. Each foot made contact to one side of the adjacent wall where the two building came together forming a right angle. Then, laid his palms on the walls. Cho descend slowly. He was slightly leaning away from the wall. His descent went faster than expected. It prevented him from making a correction with his body angle between the two corners. Halfway down, he flipped off into a somersault softly landing on both feet.

Mike made his way up along the building, keeping his senses tuned for any who may be watching or attempting to follow. Mike felt the eyes on him up to that point. When all eyes were off, he turned down the adjourning side street leading to the outside fence, surrounding this section of the warehouse district.

Cho spotted Mike the same time Mike sensed Cho coming. Both met outside the fence, further down the road. Cho jumped onto the ten-foot fence, only touching the link about mid-way up. From that link, he swung his body up into a back flip over the fence. Again, Cho landed softly. Mike watched Cho hoping one day, he could achieve that kind of skill.

Both Cho and Mike ran two miles down the old broken paved road littered with potholes. It was apparent, this part of the warehouse district was seldom used or traveled. Both thought that was good. It will keep the damage clean, no collateral harm when the attack comes.

GOOD NIGHT

Cho, those guys are loaded with all kinds of guns, excitedly Mike explained. They have a room with wall-to-wall rifles on racks. A table Cho, as big as the clubhouse's pool table stacked this high with pistols. Mike held his arms out to demonstrated how high the guns were laying on top of the table. Then Cho, you won't believe all the boxes of ammo they got. They got enough to arm an army."

Mike, first thing to remember. You can't shoot a gun, unless you have a gun in your hand to shoot. Those guns are in a locked room. Is that correct?"

"Yes, then Mike caught hold of Cho's wisdom. I see your point, Sifu."

"Good, Cho answered. One more thing Mike, a gun can only kill you if the aim is true. A bullet can kill, only if it hit's it marks. Mike, do you agree?"

"Yes, Sifu."

"Mike, do you believe a man firing at another has a good chance of hitting his target, when the target is still?"

"Yes, Sifu."

"To many targets moving can be difficult to hit. Also, Mike, when one person has fear residing in him, his aim and his mind is not focus. A steady hand and mind will usually succeed over an unsteady hand and mind. We are trained to keep our hand and mind focus, thus steady. We train to make our foes, be filled with fear and to be unsteady. Mike, do you agree?"

"Yes, Sifu."

Good Mike, no more talk of this foolishness. Our path will be clear. The way we chose, will prepare you. Trust in the way."

Their bike ride went past the building in the city Cho and Mike stopped to talk with Paper man. Not stopping this time, both continued down the road up to the turn off. The same cloud of dust was still trying to enshroud Cho's bike at the driveway to the house. The cloud never had a chance, Mike thought turning his head to watch it fall to the ground, as before. "Somethings never changed, he contemplated."

At the clubhouse, Cho and Mike walked through the door, aloud roar was heard as the door closed. Other bikers were coming down the driveway. Those that remained in the city, stayed on their post, only the ones with families rode back. Inside, after all were seated, Razor address the group. Chopper and Bell was at a women's meeting. Bell set up to discuss the incident with the local moms.

Mike quickly went through the facts. "Razor, about twenty men were at the warehouse. Both Leader man and Repeater man was there. It was the same warehouse Magic Jack had staged all them spook traps."

Razor stared at Mike, then spoke, "first Mike, how do you know about Magic's trick he placed inside the building? That was a secret, before you arrived."

"Well you see er, Cho interrupted Mike's attempts to explain how he was aware of them. "I told him about the tricks on the way there, Razor."

Mike and Cho did talk about the tricks, Mike mentioned he looked to see if he could spot where Magic had placed them. Cho turned to Mike softly saying, "we need to work on how to frame your assessments and what to say when asked lessons". Mike nodded, then began his recap.

"Mr. Razor, over in the corner, facing the street I came down to the warehouse, was a locked room. It was a single steel door with a key lock. The second Leader man had a chain with many keys attached. He fumbled through the keys trying several, before he got the right key to unlock the lock. The doorknob turned easily, but the door was sticking. The Second man had to really pull on the door to make it opened. Inside was a table stacked eye level with various makes of automatic pistols. From what I could tell, everyone one of the pistols visible didn't have a magazine in them. All the ammo was on shelves opposite of the racks of rifles. The ammo was not stacked in any order. To find the ammo to a pistol or rifle was going to take time. Those guys were not orderly. All the rifles in two racks had mostly M-16 rifles. The only other rifles not shot guns mixed with the rifles, I believe carbines. I did not see any single shot guns or revolvers. The only light in the room came from an overhead uncovered light bulb. The switch was on the right side of the door. Second man had to reach his whole arm, nearly up the elbow reaching for the switch."

Entering the warehouse building, it was dark having little light. Most of the light came from the windows. Not many guards and what guards that were posted was only on one side of the warehouse. Several of the windows were left opened. My guess, to provide clean air. Only one stairwell leading to an office. The office was surrounded by a fence. One door. Didn't appear to have another door, other that the main door to the cage."

Cho listens to Mike unbelievable detailed report. Mike continues his description. "I noticed walking inside, most of the men sat to the left of the stairs centered and forefront of the two sliding doors. The only rear exit I spotted was in that corner. Several tables and many chairs were strewn about the corner. Between on either side of the stairs were two bathrooms. Overall, the space was quite bare. Little to hide behind for cover. On every man present, not one wore body protection."

Mike was about to finish when he remembered one more fact. "Razor, there was no oven to prepare meals. Nothing. Only several large trash cans. I saw a lot of take out."

"Well Mike, then to Cho, that was some report. Cho, you train well. Mike replied, "thanks". Mike why don't you take off and we will see you later? I think the ladies would like to speak with you. I hear you moved to the old Cabin," Razor said?

Cho looked at Mike with a queer stare. Mike saw the stare remembering he forgotten to tell him about the cabin. Both walked out of the house. Mike quickly explains to Cho about the cabin and why he moved. Cho was satisfied telling Mike, I was planning to change our location due to the high amounts of spectators recently showing up. Okay Mike, I will see you in the morning. From what Razor said, you will soon have company." Mike turned and ran down the driveway. Wasn't long before coming to the riverbanks nearing the cabin. Inside, he hadn't time to enjoy the niceness of his new abode. Quickly, Mike removed his clothes then wrapped a towel around his waist. Outside, he stood under the camp shower. The water was icy cold. Mike' s baths were always in cold water. Drying off, Mike entered the cabin.

Out of nowhere stood the stranger from the night before. The next day a name was written on the wall. Mister Casper. Mike stood still watching this stranger. He slowly turned to face, Mike. He was clad in old clothes. No color to the clothes appeared to Mike. For several minutes, Mike stood watching him. Mike figures someone had to make the first move. He made the first move taking a small step toward his bed. The strange man constantly turned keeping his face at Mike. At the bed, Mike dropped his towel and donned clean pants and the shirt he worn yesterday. It had not developed a strong odor, yet.

With Mike's back turned to the stranger, he asked him a question. "Twice you have come here. Is this your home? Am I intruding, and do you want me gone?"

Mike heard the steps of two people coming to the cabin's door. Mike turns toward the door. Then turned back, the strange man was gone, the door received a hard rasp to it.

Mike slid his shirt on just as the front door opened. The first woman to enter, saw Mike finish dressing then swiftly stepped back out the door. Mike called to her, "it's okay, I am finished dressing". The lady walked back in. It was Penny, Bone's girlfriend. Next to come inside was familiar footsteps to Mike' s ears. Susan entered and stood next to Penny.

"Hello, glad for the visit," responded Mike with a pleasant smile. He was half expecting the ladies to arrive. He wasn't sure when or who was coming. It was the main reason he decided to take an early bath. Good thing, he thought as both ladies suddenly entered his cabin quickly. This might have been somewhat more embarrassing."

"Mike, you remember Penny?"

"Yes, Miss Susan. Hello," Mike offers his hand. Penny was a red head, with long flowing straight hair. She had a perfect nose to Mike's way of thinking. A pretty sweet, but shy-like smile against a very pale complexion. The only blemish to her attractiveness was her freckles. She had just enough to take notice but not enough to distract from her beauty. Bone chose well," Mike thought to himself.

Susan was as tall as Bell with black hair tied into a bun behind her head. She wore jean pants, as most of the biker wives had done with a short shirt exposing her thin belly. Both ladies stood looking about the room.

"Bell told me, she and some ladies came here and found a pig's stie. They added some items and cleaned the place. From what I see, it looks nice."

"Yes Mike, we saw where you been staying, this is far better. Don't you think?"

"Yes, I do Penny, I plan on thanking the ladies for doing this for me. Cho and I got back about an hour ago. Razor told me to get back to my cabin. I was told some ladies were stopping by. How can I be of service?"

"Mike, you were to stay at a few homes each night. We are here to bring you to my house, replied Susan. Penny came to make sure I knew the way. Bone had brought Penny out here many times."

"Miss Susan, as you can see, this cabin looks fine."

"Mike this stay overs we have arranged, is more of our way of saying thanks to you. You will stay the night at all the mother's home. Besides, this place still needs some work. Also Mike, it will help the mothers feel much better having you near their children. Everyone is buzzing how you took on five men. It will be good for everyone to get a chance to know you."

"Yes, I see your point. Wait a second, I will grab some things."

"Mike, I think you might make those things, something not so dirty."

"Huh, Mike was turning red face. He thought he looked nice and smelled clean."

Susan saw Mike's face redden. She felt his embarrassment, wishing she could take back what she just said. Mike grabbed his dirty pants and the shirt he changed out of walking over to the ladies trying hard to shield his face, from their gaze. Each lady felt they should be the ones to hide their faces.

Penny was about to take Mike's dirty clothes, then noticed three words mysteriously had appear over the bed. When they first entered the room, she could have sworn, the wall was empty.

"Look," exclaimed Penny pointing at the wall over the bed. Both Mike and Susan turned, both saw the same three words over the bed.

Over the bed written in large letters "Yes, No, No." "This room was just painted. How did those words get there," Susan said with a stunned tone to her words?

Mike quickly realized where those words came from. It was the strange man called Mister Casper. He left a message on his wall last night. This was his answer to my questions, I asked him," Mike thought out loud.

Penny said, "who is Mister Casper," followed by the same sentiments from Susan?

Mike realized he was talking out loud. It was a habit he understood needed to be corrected. "Well, I met this strange man in the middle of the night standing at the foot of my bed. He stood there, looking at me sleeping. I never once felt his presence. I awoke for no reason seeing him standing there." Penny looked frightened hearing Mike's story.

Mike saw her expression and tried to explain, "he offered no harm. Penny, he just stood there. When I got to my feet to on my light, he was gone. The next morning after my run, there was this name written on my wall, in the same place."

"Mike, what did it say? She said it, as if ready to bolt out of the of the room.

Penny, I asked the stranger for his name. It was his name written on the wall.

"Where is it then," Susan responded?

"Susan, the name written on the wall was gone, when I came in this day. The stranger reappeared after I took a shower. Just before you two walked in." Penny was turning a tad whiter. Her eyes widened; her breath quicken.

"What was his name Mike," Susan asked again.

"His name was Mister Casper, Susan. The three words on the wall are his answers to my questions I had asked him, before you two entered. He disappeared when Penny walked in." Penny was backing out of the cabin. Susan's arm behind her, stopped Penny's backward march out the door.

"The first word was his answer to, is this your home? Yes. The second question was, am I intruding? Which he answered, No. The third word was for the final question, I asked him. Do you want me to leave? He responded, No."

"Mike, are you telling me a ghost was here and, and, the writing on the wall, when I came in was him answering your questions? The writing appeared, just appeared, as I, we were standing here;" Penny managed to say?"

Susan spoke up, "there was nothing on the walls."

"I saw nothing written on the walls. Now, right there are three words. There is a ghost in this cabin, trembling in fear," exclaimed Penny.

"Don't be silly, Penny. Mike turned to see an opened cabin door begin a slow creeping swing closing. It was left open by Susan, when they entered. The door was closed, now. Susan turned to tell Mike it was open. All three looked at the door being closed. Penny wanted badly to bolt out the door. Both Mike and Susan turned back to the bed. Penny eyed the door for any signs of it opening.

The wall was clean. The three words disappeared. Susan told Penny to meet them outside. The door re-opened. Penny did as told and never once looked back. Susan followed Penny walking backward, to the opened door. Mike simply walked out, saying good night before he closed the cabin door.

Mike had to go back inside to turn off the lantern. On the wall, another message was written. It read, "good night, Mike." Mike walked over to the table turning his lamp wick down, until the flame went out. He was decided, the ladies might not want to hear about this last message."

Penny was already sitting in the car. All doors were closed. Susan drove, Mike was invited to sit in the front seat with Penny between Susan and him. Penny insisted. Mike's arm was held tight by Penny. Any tighter, her breast would poke a hole into Mike's side," he thought.

The first stop was at Bone and Penny's home. Penny said good night. It was apparent, she didn't feel the need for any company, except for Bone waiting at the front door. With a leap, she was out the door running to Bone. She jumped on him before he had a chance to spread his arms. "Quick, get me inside, please Bone".

Bone and Penny's home was on the opposite end of Susan's neighborhood. Their home was the same type with a different color scheme. Penny loved to work in the yard. During the day, Mike saw a well-manicured yard. He was informed, Penny was trying to create a yard similar to an English home. To Mike, that was still a mystery, it explained little for him to visualize her theme.

"Penny, why didn't you asked them in," Bone inquired as she got to the open front door.

"I will explain when I get inside and you pour me a glass of the strongest stuff you got in a bottle." Bone looked perplexed. He went and got a bottle and two glasses. "This was going to take a while," he figured.

A short drive across the street and around the corner, was Susan's home. Once Susan was out of the car, the first words coming out of her mouth to Mike was, you are not going back to that cabin."

Before they got to the front door of her house, Mike answered, "this is my home now, he means me no harm." Susan was agape. Mike explained what he saw written on the wall reentering the cabin, to put out the lantern.

"Susan, he wrote," good night, Mike," above my bed. Now, do you really think he means me any harm, after writing that on the wall? I think he is lonely and welcomes a visitor in his cabin," Mike explained.

Susan just stared at Mike. "You got weird notions. Once this gets around, there is a ghost in the cabin, in the woods. Well, I don't know. Maybe no one will dare come out there ever again. I know that it is scary to me."

"Well, maybe that will be a good thing. Cho wants more privacy, while training me."

"I see," Susan was upset hearing Mike's reply.

Mike got the message, loud and clear. Susan, that didn't mean I don't want visitors. I do. I value yours, Bells, and Miriam's friendship a lot. Lately, any training I get from Cho is at night. He wants me to practice in the most extreme measures."

"Really, what is so extreme of fighting in the dark, Mike?"

"Well for one thing, try practicing while balancing on a wire or a ball? Susan, everything he teaches, is to prepare me. To protect me. When I run through the woods at night or whether I run down roads, there are always surprises waiting around every corner, every tree, every place, and everything I come upon can be a potential for great harm. I need to be ever vigilant."

"Mike, is that how you been living, scared every time you are awake? Always prepared for an attack? My God, what is so important for any child, person to live in that extreme." Susan realized Mike was no child, hoping her remark went unnoticed by him. She was beginning to see Mike as a young man, not much younger than her. She married Stephen at a young age.

"Susan, I know that may sound hard, but I chose this. I knew full well what this choice I took, meant. I do this to protect my love ones. Susan, you, and the people here, I care a great deal about. This is a little sacrifice to make, to keep everyone I care about out of harm's way. Have you forgotten already the three lives I stopped from being harm. Also, the two others before them? What if I hadn't been there, if I was there and Cho not prepared me, what then?"

After a pause, Mike finished, "I feel so honored, that you care so much about me, I hope you see my choices and deeds, how much I care for you, Susan?"

Susan takes Mike in hand, hugging him. "I know, I just care about you. You have become part of my life and I want what's best." A tear fell down her cheek. Cheryl opened the door as both separated. Cheryl saw her mom's tears she tried to wipe away.

Entering the house, Mike got hold of the aroma her meal was permeating the room. "Okay Mike, Cheryl said. You know the routine. Upstairs is the bathroom, now hand over those smelly clothes. Be off now, leave the other clothes on the floor outside the bath," she commanded.

"Cheryl, I do believe you enjoy bossing me around."

"Mike, whatever gave you that impression." Cheryl said with a grin, followed by a gentle shove toward the stairs.

Once the bath was done, Mike cracked the door to reach for some clean clothes. To his surprise, there was none to be worn. Mike called down to the ladies. "Hey, where are my clothes?"

Cheryl walked to the stairs shouting up to Mike. Them clothes are still in the washer. Mom is bringing you some of dad's clothes to wear." Stephen, Mike remembered, was a foot taller than him. After waiting several minutes with only a damp towel wrapped around him, Mike heard Susan coming up the stairs.

"Here you go," Susan handing Stephen's clothes through a partly opened door to Mike's waiting hands. The clothes were what Mike expected, several sizes too large. Mike tighten his belt, then rolled the pant cusps up. The shirt didn't much matter, he let it hang. Down stairs, both women were sitting at the table. A roast with potatoes and carrots waited for him. After the meal, Mike insisted washing the dishes, his clothes were finally dried.

Mike excuse himself to walk out to the park. The dishes were washed, he had changed into his clean clothes. Out the side door, he turned toward the park.

Cheryl yelled to Mike, "hey, wait up." Cheryl ran up to Mike crossing the street. Both walked over to the seesaw. Cheryl sat on one side opposite Mike. She sat there watching him. Mike said nothing, just looked at the sky.

"Why are you so quiet looking up at the sky." Silently, Cheryl hoped he would say something nice, concerning her. Mike looked at her smiling at him.

"Cheryl, rarely do I get a chance to breathe the freshness of the night air. The night air seems to be cleaned of the day smell with the coming of night. It seems the stars are pushing the sun-down just to clean away the old day, to welcome the new day to come. I keep busy with all my training. I rarely get a chance to experience the night. When I was walking home on my journey to be with my family, I spent many a night under the shelter of the stars. Cheryl, in a way, those stars kept me on the path home. Many a time, I felt them comforting me. I could hear them say, sleep, we will watch over you. Under the clear night sky, one can see clearer, here more, smell the new, feel the cool on your skin soothing the blistering heat, and taste what food I had little of, so much better." Cheryl swooned hearing Mike's poetic words describing what he was feeling.

"I sit here with you and for the first time Cheryl, I really see you. I must say you are very pretty to look at. That first day we met obscured this fact from me, for a while. Now, sitting here those memories of anger on your face have faded away, I see the real Cheryl under the stars. You are a star among the stars, Cheryl."

Cheryl was stunned and thrill to hear those words Mike was saying, up until the other words that soon followed.

"Cheryl, I see your smile and how you feel the way I do toward you, but there is a but to this. Cheryl, all I can say, my way will be dangerous. I will suffer and may be the cause of suffering. My course is set. For me to contemplate any close ties to anyone, can court danger for them. Now, my mom and sisters are in danger. I have to save them. Being here has put all of you in danger. Chopper said, it was the clubs doing, but that doesn't change the fact, I have enemies." Cheryl's smiles soured.

"Cho is passing down to me a great gift, with many responsibilities. I have accepted his way and together we are ever bonded. Those bonds will never be severed. Anyone who cares for me, needs to totally understand what that means. I certainly wouldn't want any person to live this kind of a life I have to offer. No real home or roots. Forever be on my guard, wary of everything. What person would want to live life with me, knowing that is all there will be?"

Cheryl wanted to take Mike in her arms and tell him, she would. Something inside her made her hold back. So, she sat there with Mike in quiet.

The next day, Mike was up and through the door without breakfast. Susan watched Mike run down the road. Cheryl walked over to her mom. "Mom, I care about him, a lot."

Standing by her daughter hearing her say that, came with little surprise. Susan tensed hearing those words coming out of her child. "Her little girl is becoming a young woman."

"Cheryl, is that what you two were talking about in the park? Cheryl nodded in compliance. "Cheryl my love, Mike can only bring you pain. You will suffer, when he is away. You will constantly worry about him. Is he alive or hurt, lying near death in some remote woods? Mike's path is not yours. If you continue to try to harbor feeling for him, I will not interfere. Know this, with your father, it was the same. I have felt as you do for Mike. It will sustain you for many years. Then, one day a child will come from you two. The world will look different. Mike being away, in danger, you alone with a child to tend to by yourself, you will begin to feel about his way of life cannot be that for you and your child. You will remember this day and what I told you." Cheryl shook her head denying that would happen to her.

"Please consider what I say, before this grows stronger. This strong feeling will make reason leave you, being replace by your heart's desire. Our heart is not always right. It wants what it's wants, regardless of the soundness or wisdom we know comes with that decision. Secretly Susan hoped her stepchild would heed her words. She knew the pain to come but also was having the same feeling for Mike.

IT'S A MAD, MAD, MAD WORLD

Mike ran to the firing range for further field stripping of weapons and practice firing. Later, he finished his training with Magic Jack. Mike got pretty good at getting out of most of his ensnarement's Magic put him in. Today, Magic equipped him with a utility kit to keep on his body to use if captured. Mike learned to improvise many of the tools in the kit. Later, he decided not to carry the belt.

Once leaving Magic, Mike went to spend extra time with Tech. He got to enjoy working on aircrafts. Tech was helping him build a single seat motorized glider. This was the day; they finished the build. Mike will finally get to fly his home-made flyer. Bone was there to watch him fly. He remained waiting when Mike landed. Bone had finished Mike's parachuting drills and came to take him to the mad bomber.

Madd had his own shop, off from everyone. His skills could really screw everyone's day, if he made a boo-boo. Bone left Mike quickly, after dropping him off. Madd was inside. Madd heard and saw the kid enter his building watching on surveillance cameras. Mike spotted the cameras right off.

"Hello Mike." "Hello Madd," Mike replied. "Good, come over here." Mike walked over to the bench. "Here, take hold of this." Mike did as he was told. "Now, whatever you do, don't let go? What you got in your hands, is called a bouncing Betty or flying Betty. What it does is, when you step on it, it shoots up in the air and explodes in your face. The shrapnel will fly and take out everyone in its range."

"Okay Madd, anything I should know, while I am holding unto it?"

"No, just, if you let it go, it will go boom." Mike takes the device placing it on the table. Then steps away from the bomb.

Madd was an older man, sporting a beard with white streaks. Most of his hair on his head mainly covering the sides had a similar streak of white. Later, he removed his dirty ballcap having a baseball insignia, Mike saw a bald spot it was covering. Madd looked old and held himself in a state of ease. Almost a peaceful resolution for everything he did, this demeanor he kept at all times.

"Mike, didn't you hear what I just said? It will go boom." Madd went nearly crazy grabbing the bomb. That demeanor rapidly disappeared, when Mike did the most unexpectantly thing. Madd fumbled inserting the pin back into the device. When he finally looked up, Mike was out of the room.

Madd walked outside. "What in the hell were you thinking? That bomb could have killed both of us."

"Yes, Mad, I knew that. I also knew, I didn't know a thing on how to disarm it. I knew you did. I figured you would leave me standing for a while, to watch how I acted. I figured it was real. I knew if you didn't test me with a real device, you would never know how I would react under that kind of threat. Since you were the only who knew how to disarm it, I figured you would do so. So, you see, you disarmed the bomb."

"Dam kid, they told me you had smarts and guts. You'll do. Now come back inside. Your training, just begun."

That day, later when Cho was with Mike at the cabin, he told Mike what Madd said.

"Madd said you nearly scared ten years off his hide with that stunt."

"Yeah, he got even with some demo we set up in the bomb yard. After showing me the results of different kinds of explosives, my ears are still ringing. The sound almost did my ears in. One of his demos, he said, the shock wave from a blast can do a lot of internal body damage. Then, he went and gave me a small taste of how a shock wave felt. I laid on the ground and quickly felt the impact of the explosion. I learned a ton today about how to keep from being hurt from blast shrapnel, shockwave, fire, light, etc. He was pleased learning I knew how to repair clocks. Timing devices and things should be a snap with me," he said.

"Good, Bone has a treat for you, tomorrow So, I will give you the time off for him and you. The next day begins your Spanish lessons."

Dang Sifu, this is just like school with all the things you have me learning."

"Mike, my son, life is always learning new things. Better be prepared, than find yourself wanting when in need. Madd's wife, Rita will be your tutor."

"Okay, sound like a plan." After practicing for three hours with Cho, a car drove up and Cho departed. Cho finished telling Mike at the end of the week, he will be staying at the cabin. All his duties have been completed. Besides, he said to Mike, "you will need to drop back at the warehouse. Chopper and Razor have started with the plan. Things are being put into place before we go back to the warehouse."

Rita and Miriam drove up stopping their car just as Cho rode off. Miriam gets out of her two-door red car. It looked new. Rita was shorter than Miriam with short brown hair. She had darker skin. She appeared to Mike to be the older of the two approaching the cabin. Rita was introduced by Miriam.

"Good evening, Mike." Miriam spoke in her usually soft-spoken southern way.

"Hello Miriam and to you Miss Rita," replied Mike. Miriam continued her talking.

"This is Rita, she will be teaching you Spanish. I brought her along to have you two, meet. I don't think you two have met. She is Madd's wife."

"Well, it is certainly a pleasure to meet one of my husband's students. He told me about you getting home on the first day. You certainly left an impression upon him, Mike."

"I hope it was a good one. I sure don't want to have an accident out there in the field."

Rita looked a bit confused with Mike's response. After a second or two, she got the drift of his pun and giggled.

"Oh no, Madd would never have an accident like that. He would certainly make it happened, if he didn't like you." Mike had a slight confused looked, until Rita smiled. He smiled back.

"Well Mike, you ready for my house and supper tonight?

"Miriam, I am sad to say, I have not cleaned up yet from Cho's workout."

"No matter, get in the car. Miriam points to her new car with the motor running. In the car, Miriam asked Mike, I hope you like smoked ham and yams."

"I'm so hungry, I could eat an old shoe. Not that I am calling your food an old shoe. Ham sounds wonderful to me, Miriam."

"Mike, how old are you, may I ask," Rita inquired.

"I got my driver license Miss Rita," Mike returned.

"Well, I hadn't wanted to be nosey and put my nose in your business. Seeing you for the first time I was struck how young you appear, especially after all the words being bantering about. I have two children with Madd, and an older girl from a prior husband. I am a widower and Madd found his way into my heart. We been together for twelve years, now."

This small chit chat continued to Rita's house. Rita was constantly trying to get as many answers from Mike as she could find out. "How is your family, what did your dad and mom do for a living, any sisters, and brothers? Are you from this area?" When the car finally stopped, Mike was pleased the questions ended.

After several minutes, Miriam arrives at Rita's home. To Mike's surprise, she lived two houses down from Miriam and several homes from Bell's and Chopper's home. After letting Rita out, Miriam drove around the corner to her home on the other side of the park. Susan's home was opposite of hers.

Leaving the car, Mike caught scent of the ham cooking. His mouth salivated from the smell. "Hmm, that does smell wonderful, Miriam."

"Well get inside, Razor should be home by now. Usually he is in the back, playing ball with the boys. Cindy is most likely in the kitchen tending to the meal."

"I wished you allowed me to clean up, I might smell a tad ripe to everyone."

Don't think you will have any trouble in our home. Between Razor and the two boys working on Bikes all the time, we kind of used to smelly men in the house. You'll fit right in, Mike."

Miriam was right. Cindy was one of the oldest girls in the club. She and Pretty boy had dated for some time, until he was seen with one of the other girls. That put an end to their dating. It hadn't stopped Pretty boy from constantly calling her.

At the table Mike, was assigned a seat between the two boys. Razor sat at the head of the table. Grace was given and the food past around. Miriam was again correct. Both her sons did smell of motors and gasoline.

For the second time Mike had millions of questions shoot at him from each of the two boys. Most of the questions centered on the two encounters he had with the drug dealers. They wanted to know everything about the fight. Miriam had to interrupt them prodding Mike for more graphic details on each fight. After supper, Razor pulled Mike aside to speak with him.

"Mike, Mad is impressed with you. I told him to hurry you through certain bomb making skills. You will need to master when you and Cho return to the warehouse. Everybody has real confidence in you. Cho speaks very highly of you, as do all your instructors. I want you to know, you are under no pressure to go through with this. Some of the wives made it their business to comment on your involvement. So, please be careful and not get hurt. For our sakes."

"I will Mr. Razor. Thanks for telling me about this."

"Mike, what is this I hear about a ghost?" The question was sudden and unexpected. It always impressed Mike how fast word got around, in this group. No wonder Cho keeps his ears glue to every word spoken near him."

"Oh, he is friendly. He has written my name on the wall and wrote his name. Razor seemed curious about the spirit's name." He eagerly leered at Mike to listen for the name.

"His name is Mister Casper, Razor."

"Do you two talk much, Mike?"

"No, not much. He mainly writes responses to my questions on the wall over my bed. Sometimes, I awake at night, he would be standing at the foot of my bed. The first few times he done that, did unnerve me a bit, but I have gotten over it. Many times, I welcome the company. If you don't have any more questions I'll be on my way, Mister Razor."

"Okay Mike, you wait, I'll go get my bike and zip you over to the cabin."

"Thanks Mister Razor, Cho prefers that I do most of my traveling by running. Besides, the fresh night air is great for running."

Two women stood by the kitchen window watching Razor and Mike talk. They couldn't hear much, that wasn't the purpose of their vigilance at the kitchen looking at the two men.

"Mom, he is very handsome. Some of the girls said he was cute. He is much cuter than that. You think Pretty boy will get jealous, if I mention to him, how cute Mike is?" Miriam listening to her daughter's plans quickly made it known to her.

"Cindy, you will do no such thing. That boy has enough worries, without you adding to them. Leave Mike out of your schemes."

"Yes mom, just thinking."

"That's all it better be, missy!"

THE CAVE

The sky was partly clouded when Mike began his run. Leaving Razor's family gave him some relief from all the questions, his two boys pounded at him. Another thing that caused Mike some grief was Cindy, his daughter. Cindy was constantly fixated on him. Her stare was annoying and made him feel like a side show freak.

Through the park Mike could see Susan and Cheryl's home. The kitchen light was on. To the opposite side of the park, two strange persons with three kids hanging near the swings was spotted. Mike watched them looking toward him. Something seemed funny about their behavior. Mike didn't recognize the kids or the other men.

Across the park, Mike continued to running to the road leading out of the subdivision. He ran down the road turning off the path, normally taken.

This night, Mike decided to run further along the road until coming to a small unused path. Before turning down the trail there were three men approaching up the road. Thinking to himself, "it sure seems to be a lot of traffic around here this night?"

The darkness made seeing any distance difficult. Mike learned to see well at night with Cho's training. The three men approaching down the road clearly were not able to see him, much less, sense his presence. Mike turned onto the path running until coming to a clearing. At the clearing, his cabin emerged from the darkness, like a lighthouse beacon. The starlight percolated through the trees onto his cabin. Still, the cabin's glow was not emancipate by the little moonlight making it visible in the darkness. Mike sensed the glow surrounding the cabin came from another source. At his cabin door a fire was burning in his fireplace. It was just enough to keep the dampness out with little light. The one lantern he lit from embers removed from the fireplace.

"Hello Mister Casper." No return call was given. Again, Mike called out, "any new thing happening tonight, Mister Casper?" Again, no reply was given. He gave up trying to get an answer and began to strip down to take a shower. Outside naked, a chill bit at his exposed skin. Usually Mike ignored the chilly nights reaching for the cord to release the water. No water came out. Then he remembered not refilling the shower bag with water. Picking up the bucket, he makes his way to the river flowing in front of the cabin.

"Ah, what the heck? Mike put down the bucket. He decided the river would do for his bath and jumped in. The river was cold. Just as his head poked out of the water, three men were heard approaching the cabin.

Meanwhile, Cho on this night, decided to stop by to see Mike. He parked his bike near the road. Three men had turned down the path leading to the cabin. Cho quietly pulled off the road. He saw the men turn. Swiftly, he ran through the shrubs and trees without disturbing a single twig. Cho was a wisp of air in his movements arriving at the edge of the cabin, the same time Mike entered the river. Watching the three men walking toward the cabin suspiciously. Each man kept to the shadows, kneeing low to not be seen. Cho knew Mike was unable to sense their presence under the water. He stood hidden watching the men approach. Two men separated from a third man. The third man was attempting to cross the river farther down from the cabin. It was plain to Cho; their reasons were not a friendly get to know you visit.

Both men arrived at the cabin, one placed himself across the entrance in front of the cabin nearest the river, not knowing Mike was taking a bath. The other man on the side not heavily covered with shrubs. Cho suspected they did not need to conceal themselves due to the darkness. They did not know it mattered not to his son.

The light in the cabin slowly ebbed dimmer. Neither of the two men saw the light grow fainter. They both faced the river after hearing splashing Mike made entering. Cho saw the light fade, assumed it was Mike's doing. That was before he sensed Mike was in the river.

Mike arose from the water, his senses suddenly tingled. There was someone present. Suddenly, two men appeared, one in front of his cabin and the other stationed on the side with no shrubs. They basically blocked any escape on all sides. Mike realized from their position, his only way out was through them. There was another way, it laid on the other side of the river. Turning to view the opposite side, Mike not seeing the man waiting, peering in the blackness to spot him. He knew a man was there, unseen by him, but felt by his senses.

The third man coming down the road Mike turned off, was one of the three on the opposite bank. He figured, if he got past the two on the cabin side, the third man could forge the river quickly to help his comrades. Either that or take a shot at him with a night scope. That probability seemed unlikely. The third man would have spotted him in the water with the scope and end him here and now.

"Hey, you two men, I see you thought of everything. Two in front and I am pretty sure one across the river waiting. Lest I forget, the one across the river belongs to you as well, he would wait there, if needed is what you planned."

"Kid, you are quick to get the point," the first man of the two men standing in front of Mike replied with a snarly answer.

"The point, Mike answers back, is you thinking you got me trapped."

"Yes, you sure do catch on quick, doesn't he boys?" "Yep Don, he does seem to catch on quick. I bet he figured we going to kill him, too." The two men quickly drew their pistol from under their shirts. The third man already had his drawn.

Mike silently was working himself into a position to improve his chances to get out of this fix, he been caught in. A third option was to duck under the water swimming downstream. Thinking, Mike realized they would follow him on the dry land. Still, it may offer an opportunity, which from his position now, offered little chance for survival.

Cho watched Mike and the three on both sides of the river. Even if he acted, the man on the opposite side of the river could drop Mike and him. Cho was about to panic, until the most amazing thing occurred.

The cabin door swung open with a bang. A light, as bright as the sun appeared in the door. Then, without any sound, the light swiftly charged at the two men. The man across the river watched the light engulf his two comrades in a ball of brilliant light and froze with fear. Cho wasted no time, neither did Mike.

Mike saw Cho leap from his hidden spot. He sensed Cho just before the cabin door burst open. Mike changed his course, turning to swim at the third man also engulfed in the mysterious glow. He was out of the water with a huge splash. Water flew into the third man's face. His gun never had the opportunity to level a bead on Mike. Mike dove back in the river speedily swimming across to the cabin side, then exiting with a little splash. Cho arrived taking out the first man enshrouded by the glowing mysterious light.

Cho pointed to the second man running down the path. The darkness made seeing him impossible without the cabin's light. Second man took off the second his comrade was enshrouded with this mysterious light, then suddenly lose his head. Blood spurted everywhere. Blood from his friend sprayed on his face thawing him from his frozen state of fear. He took off back down the path they had come.

The light engulfed the two would be killers on Mike and Cho's side of the river. The glow had swiftly floated across the river to the other side. Cho signaled Mike to get across the river just as he leaped from his hide-away. Mike was already swimming in that direction, quickly reaching the other side climbing out of the water.

Mike was unaware of the mysterious ball of light rapidly floating across the river to his aid. From Mike's perspective, it was a sudden flash, he believed caused by his lamp falling off the table hitting the floor bursting into a fire.

Mike had the third man down. It was easy, the man did not move, stricken with fear, a glow had enshrouded him. One punch to the lower jaw to his man; teeth littered the ground like snow. The head snapped; his body followed the downward descent. The light had drifted rapidly across the river's in front of Mike. The light was bright, the third man could not see anything approach. All he could possibly know, or feel, was his teeth and lower jaws shattering from an unknown impact.

Cho didn't have the need of the light blinding his man. He didn't need help. Cho appeared and disappeared into the bush, after quietly ending the life of the first man on his side. Cho preferred to strike with his fingertip. It had the effect of an arrow striking the core of his intended target. The mysterious light quickly faded, once Cho struck his man.

Cho was deadlier than Mike. Years of dealing with this type of people taught him, leaving them alive will only provide another opportunity for them to try again and maybe succeed. "Mike will learn this as time goes by," Cho thought after dropping the first man near the river's edge. Cho disappeared into the shrubs chasing the second man attempting to flee down the road. The glowing light was upon the second man. He halted, terrified. Cho reached him. He left the man lying on the road, then quickly made his way back to the cabin.

Returning back across the water, Mike spotted Cho coming up the road, while drying off. Mike filled his bucket with water. Both Cho and him walked back to the cabin. Mike thought after defeating his man across the river, the cabin would be blazing on fire. The ball of light was seen by Cho and Mike floating across the river returning to its place of origin. Returning to the cabin, the glowing light faded, the lantern was still on the table, lit.

Inside, Cho turned to Mike. Mike perceiving the question Cho was about to ask, turned to the wall over his bed and spoke." Thank you, Mister Casper, then turns back to Cho. Mister Casper is a spirit living in this cabin, Cho."

Hearing this, Cho replies, "thank you Mister Casper, for your assistance saving the life of my son."

Cho sit at the table while Mike begins to walk over to the bed to get dressed. On the wall was written, "your welcome Sifu Cho." Mike saw the words donning his shirt.

Cho saw the writing and asks Mike, "is this how Mister Casper and you talk?"

"Yes."

"Do you talk to him every day, my son?"

"Most of the time. Sometimes he will answer my questions immediately after I asked them. It took some time before that happened. I guess, he needed to trust me. I see he trust you, Cho. Otherwise, he wouldn't answered you so quickly in the cabin."

"Mike, you mean to tell me, you can see him writing on the wall."

"No sir, he will reply only after I look away."

"Hmmm, thanks again for your most kindly trust in me, Mr. Casper." Cho waited staring at the wall for a reply.

"See Cho, he will not answer while you are watching. Believe you me, I tried to sneak a peek. He is weary. By the way Cho, why the visit this night? You said you would see me in the morning."

"Yes, I did, my son, for some strange feeling, a notion came over me to check on you. I think Mister Casper has become your guardian angel."

Cho turned, on the wall was two words. He was amazed seeing words that quick. Mike, "He only done so after he got to trust in you. The first word was welcome, the second word was yes. Your right Mike, I never saw the writing being written. Yes, he says he is your guardian." Mike was awe struck from that word written on the wall. Mike slowly bows at the wall. Cho stands and bows.

"Mike, those bodies need tending too. Chopper told me he is running out of places to bury all these men; we been ridding the area of. Now, I got to go and tell him there are three additional bodies needing fresh holes dug."

Mike calls to Cho walking out the door. "Wait Cho, look on the wall." On the wall was written, cave at river's bend.

Cho speaks, "Mike you go and check out this cave at the river's bend, I will go get the club to assist us taking the bodies to the cave. Be back in twenty."

"Be waiting, Cho. By the way, I'll go and take one of them with me. Better go and get ahead of the work, while I'm at it. Cho yells to Mister Casper, "thanks again."

Before Mike leaves the cabin, he tells Mister Casper, "you are certainly full of surprises."

"Yes," appeared on the wall. Mike turned before leaving the cabin. It had become a habit, double checking the wall. "Never know when something is going to appear written on it." Mike realized he asked question and immediately turned around to see if he received an answer. "Yes appeared." "See, Mike thought to himself. I was right, always check the wall."

Swiftly, Mike placed one man under an arm effortlessly toting him down the river to a bend. Mike placed the dead man down and began to search through the brush. The riverbank abruptly ended along a high rising cliff. Searching along the ledge was becoming increasingly difficult, without entering the water. Mike re-enter the water a third time.

"No point drying off this night, Mike pondered to himself making his way along the cliff wall in the water. Soon, he came to a hole on the down river flow of the water. Unless you were traveling upstream, it seemed very unlikely you would spot this cave. Besides, Mike thought, the river is down and it was barely visible, now."

Mike Entered the cave and immediately saw the hugeness of the interior. Several small branch portals led off in different directions. Mike took the first opening. It was a tight fit entering but quickly gained in girth and height. He could tell it went on for a while. Exiting the first, opening he went into the second opening. It was easier to get in, than the first. It too went on and on. Mike decided, he might as well check out the third opening.

In the third opening, Mike made his way through the main entrance for nearly fifty feet before reaching a third hole in the wall. It twisted off to one side. His first thoughts were, it went nowhere. He entered the hole, anyway. After a few more convoluted turns, he was in another large chamber. It had several holes in the wall. The chamber was too dark for Mike to scout out the interior. Thinking out loud; "this chambered offers the best hiding possibilities." Returning back to the original entrance to the cave; Mike brought his companion inside, placing him near the first opening. Then, left preceding back to his cabin. Cho had not yet return.

Mike decided to wait. Several minutes passed. Mike went down the road, lifting the lifeless body began toting it back to the cabin.

OZ

The leaped into the river again swimming to the other side; fetching body three. He was nearly completed with both men laid out in a neat row on the cabin side, when Cho returned.

Chopper, Razor, Jack knife, Bone, Mandy, Marcus, and Bell were the main group to first appear. Several others Mike knew by their faces but not personally had met, a short time later, arriving. Chopper was the first to react to the two dead men.

"My God, he turns to Cho, Mike was now alongside of Cho, you two got to stop this. We ain't got the places to stick them in." Bell rushes to Mike. She started to give her typical hug, until her hands touched Mike soaking wet clothes.

"Mike, you, okay?"

"Yes Bell, I'm fine. Lucky for me, Cho was here." Mike left out mentioning Mister Casper. He felt Mister Casper wanted his privacy. Mike wanted to give him credit for his action this night, but realized, it wasn't necessary for a spirit. It wasn't like they were going to pin a medal on him or give him an award. "Mr. Chopper, there is a cave a short walk down the river's bank. I checked it out. I have one of our guests waiting for the rest of their party to arrive. That cave is huge, sir."

"Hell kid, that's dang fine work done tonight," said Bone. Mandy walks over to Mike patting him on his back, "glad to see you learned a few things from me, kiddo."

"Your welcome Mandy. You doing well," Mike asked him?

"Hey, I'm better than I ever been. Nice to see you too, Mike. I heard all about that night at the haunted house. Cho filled me in on the other things with the producer. Wish I was here earlier, to greet you. Been in therapy most of the time. Was going to talk to you at that supper. Got feeling pretty bad, heard all about you eating that hot mustard. Sorry, I had to leave. Bone won. Kind of thought you might win, before I left. He always wins."

"That okay Mandy, I'm just glad you are okay." Mike hugs Mandy finishing his greeting.

Chopper turned to Jack knife. Jack knife was getting the bikers moving. Bone one man under his arm. What was left, the other bikers shared toting. One man was twice the size of his comrades. He needed two bikers to lift him. Along the way, they needed a rest and two other bikers replaced them, before they got to the cave. Soon, all the bodies laid at the entrance. Like a conveyor belt, a body was handed to the next in line through the cave opening. A stack laid piled as a cord of fresh cut logs inside.

Meanwhile, Razor was in the cave with Mike. "There are three openings you can see, Mister Razor. At the third opening, farthest away, is a meandering tight passageway. When you get to the end, it opens back into a large chamber. Then, in that chamber, there are three additional openings. The one on the left is the best place to plant our bodies."

Razor waited for his men to return from each of the three openings. All six men returned. "The third hole is the best. It is as Mike said it to be," replied Bone exiting last. Within minutes, all the bodies were inside the third hole of the first chamber. Next decision, which of the other holes in the next chamber should they place the bodies inside?"

Bell replied with a solution. "Men, men, can't seem to see the solution to the simplest task. Look, put all the bodies in the smallest hole and take these rocks to fill around the hole, making it appear as a cave in had happened."

Chopper, Razor, Jack knife smiles. "Your right, Chopper said, it's takes a woman to see the obvious. Soon, all the bodies were neatly tuck inside the small hole. Rocks strewn about. Chopper wraps his arm around Bell and follows the team walking out the cave.

Cho and Mike part ways with the other bikers. Mandy called back asking, can I with stay the night at the cabin with the two of you. Got some catching up, we should make.

"Sure," Mike replied. All three walked back to the cabin.

BONEBREAKER'S SURPRISE

Morning came late. The night was long. Still, all three were up early at the usual time, five a.m. This time Cho ran along with Mike. Mandy remained behind making coffee. On the wall was written, "good morning, Mandy." Mandy woke after Cho and Mike arose and dressed. Mandy saw the words on the wall thinking Mike wrote them.

When Cho and Mike ran together, it was not an ordinary run. Cho took great pleasure in making a simple thing more difficult. After several obstacles, tree climbs, wall walking, flipping, jumping, and crawling in a crouching position through a wooded area, it was back to a normal run. Arriving at the clubhouse, they walked in.

Not one-word was mentioned of the fight or who those men were attacking Mike. Inside the clubhouse, two men were waiting for their arrival. Chopper and Jack knife sat behind the pool table drinking a cup of black coffee.

"Welcome Cho, Mike, spoke Jack knife, as soon as they walked inside. Motioning to both, "come, sit down." After sitting, Chopper quickly got to business.

"Cho, those men happened to be from the same group attacking the two boys and the other three several nights past. It seems we have a new gang to deal with. This time we deal with them, there will be no more of this follow-up we have with this Atlanta gang." All around the table nodded in agreement.

"I sent men to find out everything on these men. Once the Atlanta gang is ended, will take care of this matter. Hopefully, a rest after all this action. Mike, how is your Spanish lessons coming?"

"Good Chopper, I seemed to pick it up quick."

"Mad says you learned much. Training will continue with him. Now, you go to the airport while we talk, to Cho."

"Yes sir, Mike replies scooting out the door redonning the weighted backpack."

"Cho, when do you believe, we will return to the warehouse?"

"Soon, Mike said we would return within a week, Chopper."

A loud explosion was heard down the road. Mike was nearly halfway to the airport. Nearby was Madd's lad. The explosion came from neither direction Mike senses revealed to him, it came from the clubhouse. Quickly, Mike turned on his heels dashing back to the clubhouse. Nearing the house, plumes of smoke were rising over the building. Ahead, revealed what was left of the house. Mike stopped long enough to allow his mind to comprehend what he feared was in his heart. Half the house was burning. The other half remained intact.

Mike ran to where the door was located. It was gone. He brushed aside the smoldering, burning wood debris littering about him. A small fire was burning near the bar. In the corner laid three bodies. Mike's heart raced. Three men, he came to love, laid covered with shattered remanence of the house. Without a thought of the searing pain, he lifted the burning shattered wood lifting off his friends. He was aware spinal damages may result removing the large ceiling beams the bodies. It didn't matter, he had to know, if they were still alive.

Soon, several legs appeared. Then an arm, finally a head. The back of it was slightly singed from the burning beam. That beam could have decapitated the head from the shoulders easily, if the beam was just slightly lower. Each person uncovered was gently rolled over. The first man revealed was Cho. His shirt was burnt and torn. Cho looked unharmed, just knocked out from the overhead beam. His chair was nowhere near him as was with the others.

Mike quickly realized, Cho detected the bomb, stood to shield his two friends. Knowing the explosion was coming, Cho prepared his body for the blast. He bent with the blast, like a willow tree. This

Mike realized saved the lives of all three men. Cho was coming conscious while Mike tended to the other two.

"Cho, you saved Jack knife and Chopper, Mike called back to him. Mike looked at Chopper, his eyes opened. Lay still Chopper. Chopper wanted up. Lay still, Mike commanded. Jack knife and you are fine. Thanks to Cho quick actions, the house was the only thing damaged."

Mike making sure Chopper remained down, tended to Jack knife. He was facing the same direction as Chopper, on his back. He was less shielded from the blast, compared to Chopper. Shards of glass and wood were littered across his face. One shard just missed his right eye. One piece of wood was poking out of his right side. From the shard placement, it appeared to have missed any vital places. Mike prayed, thanking God.

Cho quickly shook off the effects of the blast, with a quick assessment, determined the extent of Jack's wounds. Cho gently pushed Mike away. Mike watched Cho remove the splinter, replacing it with a compression bandage. Cho had developed many skills in the service. He signaled Mike to remove Chopper from the building. Cho lifted Jack carefully following Mike. He laid Jack along side Chopper outside the clubhouse, far away from the fires burning. Mike quickly went back into the building. Inside the sea-bag closet, he grabbed blankets. Returning outside, handed Cho the blankets to cover the leaders.

Swiftly, the road to the house was crowded with bikes and cars. Bell and Jack's wife were the first to arrive. Both were enjoying a morning get together with Susan and Miriam their custom. The blast shook the house. Some plates fell, most pictures made crooked hanging on the wall. None fell to the floor. Cheryl was upstairs. She bounced from her bed. At the window, she observed children stopped swinging, two were clinging to each other on top of the snake slide at the park. Moms came running out of their homes. Cheryl ran down the stairs. All the ladies stood wondering what or where the blast came from.

Everyone went outside, a plume of smoke rose up over the trees. The trees were in the direction of the clubhouse. Miriam screamed realizing Razor was there. He had a morning meet with some of the leaders. Her fear made Bell gasp. Chopper was at that meeting.

Cheryl came running down the stairs and out the front door. "Wasn't Cho and Mike going to meet Chopper and Razor this morning, mom?" Then, she realized Miriam and Bell was standing beside her mom. The car was quickly filled racing out of the subdivision heading to the clubhouse. Out the car both women ran over to where Cho was kneeling. Cheryl and Miriam quickly followed.

Mike saw Jack wife at the super, he introduced his wife, Rhoda. She was a stay-at-home type mom. Rarely, did she come to the clubhouse. She waited in their car outside the clubhouse. Mike noticed her remaining in the car watching them. She was frozen at the sight unfolding in front of her. Slowly, she exited the car walking tenderly to where Cho was caring for two men.

Rhoda was the first to scream, seeing her man's face. Cho was laying a cover over him. Rhoda's first thoughts, she was looking at her dead husband. Tears ran down her face. Cho quickly stands taking her in his arms.

"Rhoda, he is fine, some minor cuts and a small wound on his side. Other than that, he will be up on his feet in days."

Miriam spotted Razor up the road; running to him, the first words were, I thought you were at the house? You were supposed to be here. Thank God you weren't. Where the hell were you? That blast scared the hell out of me. When I saw three people hurt and neither of them was you, the first thing to enter my mind was, you were blown up. Don't you ever do that again," she commanded. Then punched him hard in the gut.

"So, let me get this straight, next time, be on time to get blown up. That would make you happy?"

Miriam looked perplexed; "you know full well what I meant. Dam you, scared me awful bad, dear."

"Sorry Honey, I thought a little humor would ease the scare. I love you too, Miriam."

"You better, Razor."

Susan walks over to Razor informing him the good news. All three lived.

Bell sat by her man beaming a huge smile, seeing her. Bell looks at Mike and silently thanked him.

Cho commands one of the bikers to call an ambulance for the two men. Mandy left the cabin and was standing at the river's edge, when the explosion happened. Seeing the smoke rise in the direction of their clubhouse, he quickly jumped on his bike. He was the second biker to arrive.

Mike and Cho stood to one side, watching the women tend to their men. Mike whispered to Cho. "It is too early for any retaliation from this new gang. Could it be from the Atlanta gang. Maybe, they located the house, this could be part of their plan, they mentioned to me concerning a."

Cho turns to Mike; "shh, no more of this right now, you are becoming quite the tactical expert. I do believe, you hit the nail on the head. Mike, we need to act before any further attacks come."

Mike replied, "right. When?"

"Before the next night. Get ready. I will inform everyone to prepare for the fight." Susan was standing near Mike over-hearing the plans, they were discussing. Susan places her hand on Mike's shoulder, gently.

"You okay Mike?"

"Yes, thank you Susan. Cho noticed her listening.

"Susan, please keep what you heard quiet for now." Susan nodded back to Cho's request. Mike saved our lives today. Susan looked at Mike noticing his charred hands.

Mike replied, "Cho is giving me too much credit. The hero was Cho. Cho used himself as a shield, Susan. Using his body, kept the others safe. Sifu Cho over states my actions."

Mike was beginning his errand, running to inform everyone about Cho's plan, Susan stood in his way. Mike sensed, she was expecting some kind of a reward for being there or showing her concern for him. Before he left, he hugged Susan, then went over to Jack's wife. She sat by her man. Mike placed his hand on her shoulder. Over to Chopper, Bell rose. He greeted her with a hug. "Bell, I need to get going, Cho has me on a mission to tend to."

Cho walks to Razor, he said one word, "Atlanta." Razor nods back. "I'm on it. Cho, gets ready." Cho replied, "preparing now. Tonight, or early tomorrow."

Before arriving to the cabin, Bobby and Cheryl had decided to drop by, while their parents went to the clubhouse to inspect the fire. Everyone heard the explosion in the subdivision. Most people were standing outside their homes looking toward the column of smoke. Only the bikers knew where the smoke originated from.

At the cabin, Bobby looked about. "Hey Cheryl, isn't this the spooky place, we stayed one-night last year on a dare?"

"Yes, the very same Bobby." Looking around, Cheryl saw the bag hanging from the hook, then called out. No answer was returned. Bobby replied, "he might have been at the clubhouse, you think Cheryl?"

"I hope not, Bobby."

"Well, he wasn't riding with Mandy on his bike flying past us, Cheryl."

"Bobby, he takes a morning run and could still be running. We will wait inside for a while."

"Fine with me, Cheryl."

Inside the cabin was a table with a coffee cup half full by an empty chair. "Hey, that smells like coffee. Must be Mandy's before he left?"

"Yes Bobby, I believe you are correct."

"Hey look Cheryl, Bobby points to the wall over Mike's bed. Written above the bed was, "welcome Bob and Cheryl". "Mike must have been expecting us and left us a note."

Cheryl had noticed the wall being blank entering the cabin. "That note appeared after they came in," thinking quietly to herself.

Up the road, Mike came running. Just before reaching his cabin heard the roar of two bikes catching up to him. Mike immediately recognized Bone's bike. The other was not a chopper, like most bikers rode.

Mike reached his cabin; two riders met up with him. The other rider was Tech. He was riding a smaller bike, Mike thought it might be a Honda, definitely not a chopper.

"Hey kid, saw the smoke, rushed over here, figured it was an attack. Wanted to make sure you were okay, first."

"Thanks Bone. It was. Someone set off a bomb. Bone was about to turn his bike about to ride over to the house. Mike's comment stopped him. Turning back, "how you know that, Mike?"

"Well, I was there and left to run to the airport. Chopper told me to get over there. I never made it that far." Cheryl and Bobby heard the last few words standing in the door. "When the blast occurred, I ran back. I found Cho and the others lying in the debris. Cho looked as if he tried to block the blast with his body. He is okay. Gonna need a new shirt. After pulling him free from the burning wood pile, I checked on the others. Chopper was fine, Cho stopped most of what would have hit him. Jack knife took a lot of shards in the face. He got a splinter in the side. Cho removed it. He told me and his wife, it was minor. One good thing Bone, the bar is still intact."

"Well Mike, thanks for the update. I still need to check on them. Before I leave, this bike Tech's riding, it's yours. He and I fixed it up. I'll, teach you later how to ride it."

"A bike for me, why the present Bone?"

"Tired of seeing you run so much. Besides, in this club everyone rides a bike."

"Thanks Bone and you too Tech." Mike walks over to the Honda. Tech straddled on the back of Bones bike.

Cheryl called over to Bone, "hey that won't be necessary, I can teach Mike how to ride it."

Tech called back to Mike, "that airplane engine you thought you were working on, it was this bike. So kid, enjoy, you fixed it."

Bone waves, then both him and Tech sped down the dirt path. Mike walks around his new bike. Cheryl and Bobby meet with him. "She sure is a beaut," Mike said.

"She is a fine bike. My dad taught me how to ride one just like this one. It was to be a birthday present for me, next month."

"Oh, I'm sorry Cheryl," Mike quickly said.

"Don't be. I hope you won't mind if a girl shows you how to ride?"

"No way, it would be an honor."

Bobby watched the expressions on both Cheryl and Mike's faces. Bobby realized Cheryl had feeling for Mike. It hurt, but Mike was a good kid. In a way, that seemed to help ease the pain of losing her. Cheryl got on the bike and began to demonstrate to Mike, the mechanics. Mike had to stop her.

"Cheryl this is not the time, right now. I need to prepare for a trip. Cho and I have a mission."

"A mission with Cho, Bobby spoken out with astonishment. Cheryl looked at Mike, also with the same curiosity Bobby was having. "Cho usually went on missions alone. Mike going with Cho meant something real special was going down," Cheryl realized. Cheryl could not hold back a question gnawing inside her.

"Mike, this mission would it be concerning the explosion, we just heard?"

"Cheryl, I shouldn't tell you this, nor you Bobby. But, if you promise not to say a word to anyone, I will tell you one thing."

Both promised Mike. "Yes."

"That's it, yes."

"Yes, that doesn't tell me anything."

Bobby caught the clue. "Yes, was Mike's answer the explosion was related to their mission."

Cheryl balked. "I want to come along."

"Cheryl, this is not a game we are going on. You haven't the experience, nor the skill."

"Well, I been training with Marcus and you for weeks."

"Cheryl, Cho works alone, I am his protégé and been in training a long time. This discussion has ended for now. It is out of my hands. Remember, you said you two would keep this quiet. I will hold you accountable, if this info gets out."

"It won't, Mike."

"Good, now you two want to come inside while I get ready. When I am ready, we can head out together."

Bobby replied, I want to go to the clubhouse." Mike reminded him, the leaders want no one around there. Fire and police will be in an out. The cause will be due to a kitchen fire, is what Cho told me. So, for the whole day I am going to be busy."

"Okay, we get the message, Mike."

Cheryl, Mike asks starting down the path. Would you be so kind to take my brand-new bike with you? I hate to leave it here. I am not sure when I will get back. You and Bobby enjoy using it. You know, break it in for me."

The frown covering Bobby's face quickly disappeared. "I got dibs on driving it back, Cheryl."

Mike tosses the keys to Bobby. Whatever the reasons, Bobby seemed so sad quickly went away. Both scrambled for the keys. Bobby got them. Cheryl climbed on the back of the black Honda behind Bobby.

Mike stood watching his brand-new Honda bike speed down the path. "Good. Love the bike, but I do believe Cho might have other thoughts for me, than for this kid riding on a bike. Still in training."

THE DAY AFTER

Before the day ended, Cho was stopping at the cabin front door. There was signs Bone left. Mike walked out the door hearing another bike's roar. Cho calls out to Mike, "where's the present Bone gave you?"

"Cheryl and Bobby stopped by to see me. I gave the bike to Cheryl for safe keeping. I didn't want to leave it here in the woods."

"I talked to Bone about the bike, you would love it."

"You mean to tell me Cho, it was okay for me to have a bike? I figured my training came first."

"It does Mike, but that doesn't mean you can't learn to ride a bike. In fact, learning to operate different vehicles is one of the skills you going to get taught. But you are correct, the bike needed to be safely stowed away until we return. Well, did you like the present?"

Mike smiled at Cho, "what do you think?"

"Get your stuff, Mike."

"Got it and waiting inside. Returning back outside with his bag, Mike straddles the bike with one hand holding unto a small bag. "I am going to drop you off at Madd's lab. You will need to pick up a few items. Get checked out before I come back."

"Yes sir, Cho."

At the lab, Mad was waiting. Mike was off the bike and both of them went into the lab, Cho left. Cho stopped at Chopper's home. Bell answered the door.

"Come in Cho," Bell greeted him. Inside Cho, Bell, and Chopper discussed the plan. It was simple.

"Mike is to infiltrate the warehouse and check on the playthings left behind by Magic Jack earlier this year. Timers were to be set before Mike left. When Mike is ready to have our Riders arrive, all the devices should be set to go off before we get there. Now Cho, while they are preoccupied with all our tricks, the boys will get in position to prevent any escapes. We need to keep this quick and neat. I want those two leaders, when this ends."

"My sentiments as well, Chopper."

"Me too, Bell said. Bone arrives along with Razor. Bell let the two in. Chopper quickly tell Bone; you will take Jack knife's place as leader for this raid. Any questions, Razor asked Bone?"

"No sir."

"Cho, we discussed this earlier when they arrived back from their excursion at the warehouses. Didn't mean to leave you out of this."

"I understand fully, Chopper. Mike and I will be ready in the morning. We leave tonight."

Cho leaves the rest to discuss the details. Razor looking at Bone asks, "where are you positioning your team?" Bone wearing his jacket and several pieces of hardware was biting at the bit to start.

"We will take the west side and the rear."

"Good, I got the roof and the front and east side."

"Sounds good Razor, I will be on the road leading in and out of the warehouse area. This place will be sewed up as tight as your ass hole," Chopper said wrapping up.

"I'm coming on this raid, Chopper, Bell sternly told he husband."

"Okay, then you will be with me. We go in together and we go out together."

Back at Madd's lab, Mike was finishing some last-minute practicing. Madd gave Mike special timers with explosives to plant around the building. Madd carefully explained where to plant the devices to Mike.

Outside, Cho returned remaining on his bike. Once Mike came out of Madd's lab, he quickly informed him, "we are stopping at Susan's home for a meal. She was very demanding about that."

Quickly arriving at Susan's home, both were greeted by Susan at the door. Susan looked like a model. She was a stunningly beautiful young woman. Mike couldn't help but see her in a different light. Inside was a large table beautifully dressed out with her finest china.

The glasses were crystal. Each napkin had a silver ring holding the napkin in a carefully folded sprayed design. It looked like a royal setting to Mike's eyes.

Cheryl came down the stairs simply stunning. Mike gasped at the metamorphic she had undergone. Oh my, Cheryl you and your mom are beautiful. You two look like a princess and queen and we looked like two peasants. We probably smell like one two," Mike shyly said.

Cho simply said, "we are very appreciative of this fine meal you have created for us. We are proud to have been asked to attend."

Susan said in a polite way, "I will hear none of that this night. We did not do this for any flattery from you, nor expected you to dress for the occasion. Now, come in and enjoy our meal made for you two."

Cheryl led the way, sitting Cho on one side and Mike on the opposite side. Susan sat near Cho while Cheryl sat near Mike. After the meal Cho and Mike thanks Susan and Cheryl for their wonderful meal, then began to leave.

Cho stood for a moment to reflect on some words for Susan and Cheryl. He recalled an old Chinese passage, said to him long ago. "The goodness of a house does not consist in its lofty halls, but in its excluding the weather. The fitness of clothes does not consist in their costliness, but in their make and warmth. The use of food does not consist in its rarity, but in its satisfying the appetite. The excellence of a wife consists not in her beauty, but in her virtue."

Both women listened to the remarks Cho made. Cho quickly asked permission to leave. Both ladies stood, dazed from the suddenness of Cho request to leave soon after their meal.

Susan asked Cho, "you are leaving, can't you two stay, awhile?" Cho was adamant with his reply.

"We would dearly love to remain, but this has to be a short diner. Maybe when we return, we can all gather again and definitely stay longer?"

Cho grabs Mike arm escorting him from the table. Cheryl and Mike seemed to have been somewhere else. Outside, Cho knew what was in Mike's mind. He quickly explained the rush.

OZ

"Mike, to remain in the company of those two lovely ladies would make the parting later, much more difficult. I see that you and Cheryl are on good terms."

"Yes, Cho, we have settled our differences."

Both ladies walked to the door watching Cho and Mike get on his bike. All four waved a departing goodbye. Susan felt the same as her daughter. She said nothing until Cheryl spoke. "Mom, I have a funny feeling about this mission. Was it this way with dad? Susan held her daughter's hands. She felt Cheryl's on her hand. Susan softly said to her daughter, "yes."

By the time they reached Atlanta it was mid night. In another hour they would reach the warehouses. Bikers were keeping a surveillance steadily for a week. Cho parked his bike a mile from the warehouses behind a road sign covering it with branches. Both him and Mike ran the rest of the way. Cho separated from Mike for a short period. Marcus met with Cho and Mike. Several bikers left the clubhouse early, once the command was given. They waited at their arrange stations arriving at the warehouses.

"Marcus will be with you. You told them there was more than you. The rest decided not to join; is what you will explain to that gang. Marcus will do most of the talking Mike," Cho said. Mike, while Marcus is talking, you need to make yourself scarce. Try to find good places to plant our surprises. Set the timers. We will be waiting until you two are set. When we hear the signal, we will be coming. So, don't hesitate." Mike looks at Cho, "what signal." "Marcus will explain, Mike."

Before Mike turned to receive the answer, to what signal, Cho disappeared into the dark. Marcus says to Mike, "I wish I knew how he does that?" Mike knew and sensed his departure. In fact, Mike knew exactly where Cho was.

It was nearing three in the morning, when Mike and Marcus decided to knock on the door of the warehouse. It took nearly thirty minutes before either heard an answer to their knock on the door. One man inside awoken by the constant rapping slowly made his way to the door. The door cracked open. Marcus explain to the man answering the door, their reasons for being there. Not one guard was

169

awake, Mike sensed scanning the warehouse. The last time he was here, he had three guards stop him.

The guard explained, "we been pretty busy for the last two days. Most of them was tired. The trip back from the old house took a long time. We stayed up most of the night making sure there was no one present, when set their surprise for this biker gang."

"We understand," Marcus replied. You okay we come in or would you rather we stay out here, till morning?"

"Yeah, that's a good idea, you stay outside here. In the morning, you can come in."

Marcus and Mike walk over to a patch of grass and sat down. The door man watched them sit, then closed the door. Around nine the next day, the door re-opened. Marcus said to Mike, "we should have attacked last night. Mike reminded him, we aren't sure if all the leaders were still there. If they attack and they miss the leaders, Chopper will not be please. Besides, what's a few hours. Don't we got the whole area surrounded, Marcus?"

"You'll right Mike, I get impatient waiting. It never was my strong suit." Mike was about to reply to his remarks recalling Cho requiring him to be patient, always. "Allow your opponents to get nervous and make the mistakes. There will never be time to make the corrections, then wished you had waited, when you are dead." Mike decided it wasn't his place to make a remark to his Sensei. He felt it might seem improper to rebuke him.

Sitting on the grass waiting for morning sunrise, Marcus had time to fill Mike in on the plan. "Listen, while I have the leaders occupied, you go to the bathroom. Set a timer. In the first stall behind the toilet is a small box. Open it and throw the switch. That switch will begin a sequence of tricks. Sensors are set all around the building. If any of those men walk by one, it will set off the spooky scares tricks Magic planted. That is when you set the rest of the timers, five minutes later with that remote Madd had you practice with. We meet at the doors."

In the morning all was clear. Three men walked from the warehouse door. It was apparent, they were not informed of the two people present, sitting on the grass. The suddenness of seeing two strange men made them anxious and foremost weary. One of the guards recognized Mike. He had the other two lower their weapons. Walking over to Marcus and Mike, he asked aren't you the one around here nearly a week past?"

"Yes, I was, answered Mike. I told the Leader man I would return later, with anyone who wanted to join your gang. This is Marcus, one of our gang's leaders. He wanted to check things out." Marcus extends his hand to the door guard. The guard shakes Marcus hand. Then invited both of them inside.

Once inside the warehouse during his first visit, Mike was searched, this time around, he was left alone. This was a concern Mike had with the timers he was carrying. As soon as they were inside, Mike asked if he could use the restroom. I was about to look for a private place to take a dump outside, then you guards came out." This was Mike's excuse to separate from Marcus and the welcoming committee.

The guard pointed to the stairs. "Behind them is the restroom." Mike nodded back walking over to the stairs. Behind the stairs, Mike could inspect the rest of the warehouse. Most of the members were sleeping. Marcus was led upstairs by the welcome group leaving Mike alone. Mike quickly place his first device under the stairwell, then silently moved near the closet door where the weapons were stored. Mike heard a rustling sound; two men were lying near the door. Mike assumed they were guards asleep, on duty, good," Mike thought.

Near the corner of the door was a nook. In the nook was paper bags someone threw. That is where Mike placed the second device. A third device Mike planted near the two front doors then casually made his way back to the foot of the stairs. He stood silent waiting for Marcus to come down. Each device, Mike set the timers. He decided not to use the remote-control hand-held device. It might be spotted.

Marcus came down the stairs, along with two committee members and the lone guard, came one of the Leader men. All three made their way to where Mike stood. Mike reached out his hand to shake the Leader man's hand. It was not the main leader, but Repeater man.

"Thanks for returning, Mike."

"You're welcome. I see your alone, this time. Is the leader with the patch, here?"

"Yes, he's here, upstairs. He will be down a little later. Marcus tells me you two decided to join our team. As I was about to tell him and now you, we just put an end to a major problem we acquired. Wish you were here. You would have seen our gang in action."

"Wish we were too," Marcus replied. His thoughts quickly went to the clubhouse explosion as the major problem, Repeater man was speaking about.

"Yea, this gang of ours got the best rep around. We had this biker gang try and mess with us. They attacked us, we kicked their asses. Some of them got away. We found where they been hiding. They was still shaking. We thought they was done in, until we heard about some old house, they were hiding in. Last night, we snuck in around the house planting a bomb. We waited at the road. It went off with a huge bang. We laughed all the way back here. We all had a good night's sleep."

"Dang, wish I was there to see that bomb go off. I never saw no bomb go off. I bet it scared everybody living nearby?"

"It should and maybe the whole state. It was big. No body will try anything like that against us, now. Now, they knows how bad ass, we be." Repeater man began to laugh. Soon, everyone was awake by his laughing Mike, was told by Magic, there was a hidden switch near the door to turn the second set of gadgets on. Mike found the switch quickly after planting his bomb by the door. Magic said, All it will take, was anyone to get near the beams of light."

Everyone was up and walking about. Some went straight to the bathroom; others went to a corner to pee. The two sleeping guards stood and reassumed their pacing near the armory door. In the opposite corner of the warehouse, another guard found a seat to sit on. One man ventured into a small kitchenet and started the coffee maker. A refrigerator was sitting center near the stair well.

Mike watched close at the men waking and there various traveling about the large open space. A loud yell or scream was heard. One man came running from the stair well. He kept saying there was a ghost by the refrigerator. Several men walked over to the area to investigate what the yelling man saw. A cold mist descended from the roof. An eerie aberration appeared at the top of the stairs. Everyone stared at the ghost floating there. Then, came a woman moaning, heard throughout the building. Something jumped up, it looked like a giant rat or lizard. It quickly disappeared once it landed on the floor. Six men stood where it leapt up. None notice where it came down. All members in the gang were too busy running from the creature to see what it was, much less, see where it landed. It happened to quick.

Three men came running out of the bathroom. One man was trying hard to pull his pants up. The other two left their pants on the floor. One of the two men that left his pants behind, gave off a most horrible odor. A large brown gooey smear was dripping down his leg.

Mike grabbed Marcus's arm tugging at it. Marcus understood immediately. Several men were making their way to the main door. Mike reached the door first. He quickly sensed the fuse had ignited. Hurriedly shoved Marcus away from the door.

Other men were trying to make their way to the doors. Somehow, Mike lost sight of Marcus watching the men approach. He worried his timers were ready to blow any second. Where did Marcus go? Mike leapt away from the doors just as the bomb went off. Two, maybe three men behind Mike caught the fullness of the blast. Mike was flung backwards.

The shove Mike gave Marcus actually propelled him out the door, to one side. It was difficult for him to see into the warehouse from the angle he was tossed. Marcus was on his feet fast. He looked around for Mike. The smoke was thick. A second explosion went off. Marcus knew Mike planted three. The armory was not yet exploded.

Marcus called out to Mike over and over. Many of the remaining gang started a rush to get out. Marcus was caught in the stampede. Soon, he found himself shoved out the door, again. Smoke followed. Then, the third bomb went off. Marcus was within the doors. He attempted to re-enter looking for Mike. The blast hurled Marcus through the doors and across to the grassy area they had spent the night.

Cho was waiting, snipers on another roof was shooting gang members like floating ducks at a carnival. There was plenty to shoot at.

Bone watched several men coming out the back door. Smoke followed them. Bone was glad to welcome them with open arms. He popped two like a pimple with his palms. The other two met with Pretty boy's knives and Pilot's navigational aid, a large pole once toting a flag to gage wind direction.

Cho dealt out his own justice. The first to feel his nose departing his face was the guard that escorted Mike inside. A second man near the guard was trying to resist the present Cho was handing him. The gift was just too wonderful for him not to take. As Cho was relieving the guard of a sinus condition, he also ripped off his hand from his wrist handed it to the third man. When the third man opened his mouth to thank Cho for his present, the hand got stuck inside it. Third man was in a hurry to accept his gift and ended up shoving the hand down his throat, thinking it was a box of sweets. He stopped breathing. Cho assume it was because he was so choke-up from his gift.

Cho spotted Marcus in the grassy patch of ground after giving a fourth man a lift to town. The fourth man never thanked Cho for his airplane ticket or was it the hitchhikers map that poked out of his back. Either way, he went flying down the alley. Cho rushed to Marcus lying on the ground unmoving. Quickly, Marcus was cradled in Cho's arms. One man slowly made his way over to Cho tending to Marcus. Marcus was dead. Half of him laid next to the half not attached. A glass pane sliced him in half.

As the lone figure got close, Cho turned to confront him. Cho recognized the man. It was one of the three men at Mike's home. Cho met him the night Bone brought them to their camp waiting for Bell and Chopper to return. Bell was shot, Bone announced to everyone. It was when Cho learned a small skinny kid saved Bell's life and possibly Chopper nearly getting killed doing it. This same man was holding a gun. Cho smiled. The gun found its holster. Cho shoved the pistol through Repeater man's pants and up his rectum. Repeater man had a most queer expression across his face for nearly an hour. Several bikers noted that to others when telling their stories later back at the newly built clubhouse.

Jack knife's wife spent the night at the hospital. The doctors said Jack was fine but wanted him to stay the night. If not for Jack Knife's wife, he would have left. She remained the night with him. His face was covered with bandages making him look like a mummy. As soon as Jack and his wife walked out of the hospital, the bandages were torn off.

Jack was too late to participate in the planning or in the battle. Both Chopper and him were grounded by their wives. They waited at the house for any news. Bell noticed Chopper was not up to the mission. The blast affected him more than he planned. "No way you'll going on that mission Mister," Bell cited to him. She made the executive decision for him to remain behind.

Marcus was politely laid back on the ground. Cho called for a man to come and see to the proper care and respect for him. Then, Cho realized Mike was missing. Quickly, he ran about checking the scene. It wasn't necessary for Cho to see Mike; he could sense him from afar. This time, he could not sense Mike's presence.

Nowhere outside could Cho locate Mike, a fear rose up inside him. He feared if Mike was in the warehouse at the time of the explosions, even with all his training, his young body may not withstand the power from the blast. For the first time since Cho father's death, he never felt this kind of fear. It sickened him to the depth of his being. For the first time, Cho doubted. He called out to Mike. Cho realized the blast and the sound could have caused Mike to lose his hearing temporary, but still, he called out his name.

Bone came around the warehouse and heard the shouts coming from Cho. Soon several bikers followed with shouts. Cho walked toward the warehouse opening. The door was totally obliterated. A gaping hole, nearly as wide as the whole front of the building was left.

Cho, along with Bone walked through the debris, smoke, and fire. Each body was charred or burning. Cho stopped. He couldn't go no further. Bone had to know. You stay here Cho; I will search for him. Cho sat on the heap of a man remains. A prayer passed his lips. Bone returned soon.

"If Mike is in here Cho, I cannot recognize him from all the damage each body received. Cho and Bone sat together, the whole day. Many of the bikers removed all the bodies from the warehouse. The police arrived after the scene was cleaned. The only things remaining, was Cho and Bone.

The police asked the usual questions. Bone did the answering. He told them they came to watch the fire after hearing an explosion. The police couldn't hold them. Back at the house, the bikers brought the fifteen dead bodies. Before the Repeater man died from holstering his gun, Cho persuaded him to tell him where the Leader man was. Repeater man was quick to answer when Cho made him a promised, he would end his terrible pain. Cho kept his promise just not what the Repeater man expected. Cho allowed him to die slowly. He had planned to finish his pain before night, if he lasted that long. He didn't.

Each body was completely gone over attempting to locate Mike's remains. Mike was shorter than most and carried a watched given him by Bone. He lost a bet to Mike. The watch was given to Mike. The question soon arose, where was Mike? Everyone turned to Chopper, when asked that question. One of the snipers on a warehouse roof top spotted Mike moments before the blast. He was in the warehouse. He never left, as far as anyone knew. One thing was sure, Mike had to be in the warehouse.

That night, Cho and Bone returned to the clubhouse, a party was sent back to scour the warehouse debris, again. The police were gone, the search could be done more thoroughly. By morning, the search ended. Susan heard the news Mike was caught in the blast. Marcus was dead. Cheryl was outside coming in the house. It was apparent, she got the news ahead of Susan telling her. Tears fell across her face.

Many mothers found their way to Susan's home. Bell received her share of visitors at her home. Even some of the other mothers not in the club was at Bells home. By now, all knew her and Susan's feeling for Mike. Chopper came to Bell, later that day. Razor went to Susan's home. Both were told the news concerning the missing of Mike remains. They both tried to make it seemed, he might have survived the blast.

Many of the bikers had witnessed the three blasts. The word got out how awesome the blast was. Some spoke of the terrible conditions all the gang members bodies were in. Needless to say, Susan and Bell both heard the stories, before they were told by Chopper or Razor. Hearing them talk about their hopes Mike survived the blast, seemed to have made the knowing much harder. Mike was dead.

WALKING IN A DAZE

The whole day kept ringing in Mike's ears. Nothing was familiar everywhere he looked. Still coughing from the smoke hanging in the air, he manages to scramble through the fire and littered debris all around him. Mike wipes his face seeing bleeding from his nose. One ear nothing could be heard. It was bleeding. He was able to lift one arm. The other arm felt broken. It looked fine except for the burns covering it. Mike wiped at his arm. Most of the blacken soot covering wiped off. The pain remained.

Slowly, Mike made his way out through what appeared to be a rear exit. Some people were running to the front of the building. Mike noticed this huge fellow squeezing two men between his massive hands. After dropping them to the ground, he followed the others running to the front of the burning debris. Not knowing who they were and the way the big guy done in two men, Mike decided it was a better idea to go in the opposite direction.

Mike struggled making his way to road. Luckily not one of the men fighting took notice of him. He had to lay down his lungs were filled with smoke. Walking from the burning building was made difficult attempting to keep from coughing not to attract the fighting men. Into the woods stumbling, he quickly found an old shack. Inside, he fell to the ground. It wasn't until a ray of light came poking through the cracks catching Mike' s eye, did he awake.

Still dazed, unsure of where he was or for that matter, who he was, sat up. The pain went through him like a hot poker. For some reason, Mike held the pain in. He wanted to yell but couldn't seem to do that. Quickly, he fumbled his fingers on his good arm then over his body. He had many cuts that formed scabs during the night. Two wounds were trying their darndest wanting to bleed. Mike found an old rag tearing it into strips. Then, with his good arm managed to tie off the bleeding wounds. Blood stained the dirty cloth but the blood stained stopped growing in size.

Mike laid back down, the effort tired him. After several minutes, he stood up, deciding to leave. Suddenly, a tattooed man appeared walking toward him. Mike seemed to have recognized the man. The man definitely recognized him.

"Hey kid, I see you made it through the bombs you set. I was watching you from the cage, at the top of the stairs. It dawned on me where I saw you before. You that kid, I been trying to kill." Mike heard the man say these things. It seemed unreal. "Why?"

"Now you don't worry one bit, kid. My friends are here with me." Mike slowly turns his head in the direction men were coming. Five men was walking through the trees to where they were standing. Several others were at the road. Then, before Mike could comprehend the danger, the One-Eyed man grabs hold of him.

Wrong move, Mike reacted instinctively, Marcus's training prevailed. One Eyed man quickly found himself flying through the air toward his five companions. The One-Eyed man struck three of the five men coming at him. One of the two remaining ducked before the flying man slammed into his companions. He ran straight at Mike. It appeared he was attempting to tackle him to the ground. With his one good arm, Mike side stepped the charging man. With his arm extended, the charging man ran into Mike's forearm. An upward thrust under the charging man chin made his feet fly forward with his head and body going upward. It was like the time Mike was playing peeping tom in windows attempting to scare people on Halloween. At one house, a woman screamed seeing Mike's face with makeup. Mike and Jon made their faces look scary with costume make-up. A man came running out of his house chasing after him and Jon. The two of them ran in the darkness behind an open field between houses. The clothesline was invisible in the dark. Mike ran smack into a clothesline across a yard. His feet flew up and his head nearly taken off his shoulders. It was the same for the first man, accept, he stayed down.

A second man escaping the flying One-Eyed man got to Mike. He grabbed his hurt arm. Suddenly without thought, Mike spun around with a flying fist. It connected across the man's face causing the man to spin in a complete circle before hitting the ground. After Mike hit him, he immediately grabbed his arm turning, ran off. He dashed through trees instinctively running under the brush with a crawling run. He outpaced and outdistanced those that tried to follow. Soon, his followers were entangled in the many vines crisscrossing their path. Mike deliberately found the most difficult path to take. They followed like blood hounds. He was in a daze, still not knowing his name emerging from the under-brush.

Mike knew one thing, "get his ass out of there. He was in no shape to deal with this many men, chasing him. They were bent for hell to get him. The One-Eyed man leading the group seemed to have a special hatred for him."

Mike quickly found a road, running as far as he could down it. He hid for a while behind some trees. Once he rested, Mike returned to the road. Not soon after, Mike heard the screams of the One-Eyed man telling his men, Mike was up there. A loud bang was heard. Mike kept on running, the sound made it easier for Mike to take his mind off of his arm.

Shortly, Mike came to old apartment buildings. They were abandoned. Some campfires were smoldering near, what looked like a place the homeless might be staying. With all the noise from the men chasing him, Mike figured who ever fires these belonged too, took to hiding.

Coming to an alley, Mike went down it. The alley ended in a dead in. He was trapped. Turning around to leave the dead-end alley, he got about halfway when three of the faster chasers caught up to him. One man charged at Mike. He attempted to tackle Mike down to the ground. Both arms wrapped around Mike's waist. With a twist and a rear step between his two legs, the man slid off Mike falling to the ground. Marcus, a name appearing in his mind said, "raise your arms while taking away their balance. Many times they would try to keep themselves from falling and let go. Raising your arms will make their grasp slip away." It worked; the man fell.

The second man swung his fist. Mike blocked the blow simultaneously returning a chop with the same hand to his neck. Before the second man dropped, Mike laid a kick deep inside his guts.

The third man made a front kick to Mike's body. Mike kicked his leg with a crescent kick. It caused the third man leg to fall forward carrying him forward. Mike with the same leg then with the opposite leg, delivered two kicks to the third man's head. The first kick rocked the head to one side toppling him. Before he fell, the second kick erected him upright. He fell hard on top of the first man coming back at Mike.

Mike turned before any of the three men could continue their attack. He ran back toward the alley's dead end. At the corner of two buildings, Mike jumped up kicking off the wall then spun back to the adjacent wall, landing higher up the wall, then repeated the stunt back to the first wall. After kicking-off the two walls, he was able to ascend the building high enough to crash through one of the windows with no glass. Within moments, Mike had scaled the building and disappeared into an open window, before any of the three men got a chance to recover long enough to see Mike's get away.

Mike watched One-Eyed man with the others. He caught up to the three men, he fought. The One-Eyed man was mad. He kicked and punched two of the three men. The third man was still lying on the ground. Mike sensed he was going to remain on the ground. Mike was getting good at his guesses. The man still on the ground did remain there. One-Eyed made another bang.

The One-Eyed man led the remaining seven down the street. Mike fell back against the wall he entered through the missing window, relaxing in a large empty room. After several minutes, he re-examined his side wound. It re-opened. The dirty rag applied to his waist, was all red with blood.

Mike looked about the dusty, empty room with paint chipping off the walls for any cloth. A door leading into the hall, half torn off its hinges, was spotted. In one corner, he spotted a cloth. Mike was too tired to stand, he slid to the corner. The cloth looked clean. It was an old sheet torn in shreds. Removing the old bloody rag around his waist, he examined the wound. It was mostly closed with a tiny hole, where the blood kept oozing out from. He made a patch using one strip, pressing it into the hole. With another strip, wrapped the patch around his waist. Then laid back against the wall shutting his eyes. Memories started to flood his mind.

Pictures and words formed in Mike's mind sleeping in that dusty room. "A finger pointed at various spots on the body can cause disabling injuries or relief. The body is divided into two equal lengths with twelve meridians, on either side of the two lengths. A total of three hundred and fifty-four pressure points on each of the sides and fifty-two on the central meridians. A face and a name kept echoing in his mind, Cho. Next, five methods using your fingers not needles could be used. A one finger pressure, a three finger, then thumb, pinch and palm," spoke the unknown face.

Again, the face appeared and a name, Cho. A stranger with intense pain across his face was with Cho. This Cho pressed a finger against one of those points and that man's face contoured with pain. He was a tall slender man carrying a cane. "Finger pressure at points can cause disabling, pain, or death. Some points were more sensitive than others. Each point had energy channel through them, like paths to follow. Applying pressure on points aided in control of desired disabling or healing effects. All that is based on a yin-yang balance in the body. Each point, when pressure was applied effected this flow of energy, causing an ebbing or increase in the flow."

Suddenly, Mike felt pain on his fingertips. A memory kept playing back in his mind. He was jabbing his fingertip into a board, then cement blocks. He was punching holes into each board or block. He experienced pain. Then, another memory watching his hands shoving through hot sands. "Funny, Mike thought, he was doing that on purpose. This man Cho required him to do it."

More images of himself practicing striking a dummy on those points over and over again. It seemed like hours Mike dreamed doing that. Then a face, another, not Cho. It was an older woman; she rode on a motor bike. She kept hugging him every time he saw her. Then Cheryl, the first girls name that came to him. She was pretty, he kissed her, why, it appeared he and her were enemies in another part of his dreams. What changed?" Mike awoke.

It estimated the time near three p.m. from the angle of the sun coming in through the window. Mike got to his feet. He remembered some of the main finger strikes, this Cho had him practice striking on the dummy over and over again. He closed his eyes visualizing the dummy on the wall. Then struck at the points seen in his mind. Opening his eyes, three small finger holes were in the wall where he struck the imagined dummy. The exact placement for each hole would have been the points located on the dummy.

Mike walked out of the room and down the hall. Soon, locating the stair well. He walked up the stairs clinging to a rail onto the roof. Better to travel up on the roof. Down on the streets, I could be cornered. This time, I remembered some useful things to help fight these men, trying to kill me," Mike thought.

Coming to the roof ledge of his building, Mike peered across to the adjourning building. The roof top for all the building on this street were stores with apartments above. Most of the stores were closed. It was too early for them to open. Little was stirring in other apartments. Some of the smokestacks coming up through the flat roofs weren't smoking.

"Hmm, I can leap across." Backing up, Mike runs to the ledge. Into the air he flew landing on the other roof with more than enough clearance, still standing. A sharp pain from his wound was all the reward he got, for such a daring leap.

Then, to the next building, Mike made the leap across. This time, the One-Eye leader decided to back track to the alley. One of his soldiers grabbed at his arm pointing up. Leader man saw the end of Mike's incredible leap unto the next building. Quick as a wink, he signaled his men to turn and run to the next building where Mike had to jump next.

Swiftly, leader man had three of his men go into the building Mike just leaped off. He took the others to the next building. Soon, all of his men were running up the stairs to the roof. Anyone that got in their way, was quickly shoved out of their way.

The first building three men emerged huffing and puffing coming out the door unto the roof. They saw Mike make the leap. All three men quietly thought to themselves, after the last encounter with the kid, thank God. Mike heard their panting. He landed on the roof and turned to see the men coming to the ledge of the building, he leapt from. They looked at each other. Neither had the desire to make the jump. Mike turned noticing them staring past him. Emerging from the door on his rooftop was the remaining men. One-Eye was not with them.

They were like the other three, panting to catch their breath. It was too bad for them. Mike realized, he needed to act fast. He did. He ran at the group of four, then leaped into the air, crouched like a spring ready to uncoil sailing toward the men. When Mike uncoiled, the throat of the first man flatten into the back of his neck. Upon landing, Mike quickly ducked down crouching on one leg, like a top spun whipping his other leg at two men's legs. That sweep took out two men. Both went into the air spinning before slamming down on the roof top. The fourth man tried to punch Mike rising to his feet. Mike extended his fore finger with a flash, then withdrew it from a point intended. The punch never got close to Mike.

All the evidences One-Eyed saw when he finally reached the roof, was three men half dead and no use to him. One man was left alive, he was knocked out. Two of his men injuries were easy to see the caused. The fourth man had a small puncture wound. Nothing serious, it seemed to One-Eye, yet, he was barely breathing. The man lying out became conscience. Slowly rising staggered to his feet. He looked down at the three men, desperately needing first aid. The three on the other roof witnessed the fight, they could only tell Leader man, "it happened so fast, the kid hitting one and sweeping the other two down on the roof. It looked like the kid different do anything to the two that got knock down."

What the three didn't see, Mike was standing, extended his finger to each fallen man. One man twisted in agony before he fainted. The other fallen man appeared to have a broken leg and arm from the fall. He did, but that wasn't the cause of his delirious state of agony. It came from the second finger Mike inflicted to him. He couldn't twist in agony as the other fallen man had done. He was already lying in pain with one leg and one arm broken. One-Eye merely assumed both suffered their injuries from the fall.

Mike jumped to the other roof and going down the stairs before One-Eye appeared coming through the roof top door, panting. Once he caught his breath and finish interrogating the three men on the other roof, he ordered everyone; "get to the street." Once on the street, each man looked to see where the kid was heading. Mike was spotted running down a street several blocks ahead of them. They were all panting watching Mike turn the corner.

One-Eye had only four men capable of following the kid. When reaching the corner Mike turned down, five men were standing in One Eye and his four men's way. Each man had tattoos on his neck. Each man sported a jacket, each jacket had a label, and each label read the same. One-Eye knew the gang. AC-72 was a small gang, maybe ten members all toll.

The leader knew One-Eye's gang. They had some small jobs given them on occasions. They heard noise on the street about their friends chasing a kid. That happened here in their part of town, and they just happened to be standing at this corner, when One-Eye's gang came around it. They figured to go and help their friends. Maybe grateful, the leader thought.

Seeing five men standing at the corner presented Leader man a brilliant idea. "You guys just happened to be here at the right time? It happens we could help you and you help us. How many men you got; One-Eye asked the leader of AC-72?"

"Well it so happens, we got eight totals, here today," AC-72 leader said with a curt smirk across his face. One-Eye took that smirk bad, thinking his smile will need removed after we is done with the kid.

"Good, then we have a deal. Get them here, now. Within a snap of two fingers, all thirteen men stood sizing each other up. One-Eye paired each group with one of his men. They knew what the kid looked like. From the way Mike appeared, it didn't matter much. He was going to be easy to track.

Three groups of four men were assembled. A lone fifth man came with One-Eye's group. Quickly, each parted, one grouped headed up the main street, the second group went up and turned unto the next block. The third group, One-Eyes followed the path the kid took around the corner. The objective was to cut the kid off from escape.

Mike had again, scaled two walls and watched the scene unfold at the corner. He was lucky the five men arrived after he entered a window. The crashing of the glass may have alerted anyone below.

Mike looked down at the street waiting for the gang to appear. Waiting and watching turned out to be a good idea. Five men soon appeared coming down the alley. From their jackets they were wearing, Mike knew realized they were a different gang. They stopped at the corner.

"This is curious," Mike thought. So, he stayed at the window waiting for what might transpire, when One-Eye got there.

Mike's curiosity soon went away, One-Eye with four members came to the corner. The second group gang leader halted One-Eyes' gang. What was said made Mike reconsider his previous plans. "This needs my attention."

Thinking, Mike determined, "if I was to get back home, wherever that was, I need to end as many of these guys from tailing me. I surely don't want to take them to see me mommy."

Mike waited until the One-Eye group went down the street. The other two groups left before One Eye's departed. Slowly, Mike lowered himself down to the sidewalk. Then, he raced back to the main street after one of the other smaller groups. Mike held back fearing they might hear him or someone in the group decide to turn around to look behind. He spotted the first group heading up the main street, quick. They never looked back, once. Mike figured, "it is too early in their search for him, to get suspicious enough to worry about being followed."

Mike ran silently along the building keeping a low profile. If anyone decided to turn, Mike could swiftly evade their gaze ducking behind one of the many things littered along the walk. Within moments, Mike reached the rear man. A quick chop to the base of his neck, followed by a two-handed shoulder grab pulling him back and straight down. The rear man's legs buckled at the knees, unconscienced from his chop, fell hard and fast.

Next, was the second man. This time, Mike only grabbed the rear man by his shoulders, his knees buckled. His head slam onto the sidewalk. It shattered like an egg falling from a roof top. The first two men went down so fast, there was little time for the other two remaining to take a second step in there strive.

Mike decided to give each man a different method of termination. The third man, Mike wrapped his good arm around the neck followed with a quick jerk back, lifted him, then with fluidity swung him around through the air. One watching would have seen a man lifted and flying around like a rock tied to a string being spun overhead. While he was swinging in the air, Mike twisted the neck. It snapped, he let him go. The man was alive. He would never walk again, but alive. The body hit the ground with a loud thump. The last man turned and saw Mike momentarily, before darkness came. Three men, out of four necks snapped or crippled by a hard slam on their butt cracking their tail bones.

"Dang," Mike thought. "Should have thought of this earlier. I could have had a complete set." The last man never saw again. He was left alive and conscience, just blindly wandering the street. A double finger strike into the orbits of his eyes either punctured the eyeball or drove it back into the socket.

Mike having disposed of one group decided he needed to determine where the other groups were. He knew the direction the last group was heading but the last team might surprise him. At this point the three groups were attempting to trap him between them.

Mike realized his injured arm almost caused him to get caught with a hit from one of the men, he disposed of. Mike took the hurt arm and tucked it into his pants. It no longer dangled, flopping around like a limb in the breeze. "Better take care of loose change, before someone hears the jingle," Mike mumbled. Mike ran up the main street and turned unto the next block. He believed he was walking parallel with the second group. "If I figured this correctly, they should turn and follow main street in the same direction, the other group took. We should run into each other up ahead," Mike's hoped.

Mike looked ahead on semi-empty streets. Rows of buildings lined both sides of the street. Many were abandoned store fronts.

Some were still opened. The businesses seen better times. Some people were beginning to troll around the street. Many looked like street people. Some were digging in thrash-cans. Mike felt for them, he lived that life for a while.

At the next block, Mike seen movement. Quickly ducking against the side of the building, he made his way up to the corner. "Silently and deadly was Cho way, Mike learned. Movement without being seen, the body moving in rhythm of his surroundings, bending like water through a rocky channel." Mike arrived at the intersection the same time the four men had.

Mike had the advantage, he saw them, they never saw him, until he attacked. A swift kick followed with a second spinning kick, followed by a flying wheel kick, ending in a sweeping kick. All four men were down. As each man attempted to rise, Mike greeted him with a warm sweet smile. Each man responded to that smile, out of reaction. Their smile was suddenly changed into, what the hell startled look, when his hand is offered. The first to shake Mike's hand soon learned he had one arm capable of moving. The other arm was twisted into a coil. Quickly the hand closed around the remaining hand. He felt getting turned and twisted twice. Mike hadn't allowed the hand to slip in his grasp, the man couldn't make it slip. The only other course was for the arm to twist. It did, the man barely had time to open his mouth. No sound came out. A finger jab struck the man near the base of his neck along a pressure point.

The second man rose, he too shook hands with Mike's hand offered to him. It seemed the natural thing to do at the time. He learned, with a gasp, he was sporting a new bow tie, both arms seemed to form a bow tie around his neck. He was unable to untie the knot Mike placed them in. He couldn't feel his fingers dangling from the knot both arms were tied in. He found his breathing was much, much harder. His face color changed from a cherry red to a pale blue.

The third man saw Mike hand extended for him to grasp. He was about to take the hand. He intended to grab hold and kick Mike as he rose off the ground. It was a good idea, if he succeeded. Mike had a similar thought. He took the third man hand without his permission. Third man went up, then back down. On the ground, Mike step over and across the body taking one leg then the other hog tying the man. Both legs were bent over the man's head and tied in front of his face. Mike stood above the man looking down, then made a comment.

"I bet you wished you had wash them feet, the last time you took a bath," Mike said to the third man's face turning blue.

The fourth man watched the action awe struck how easy kid tied his friend's legs around his neck. Mike could see how amazed fourth man was of his handy work. It almost made Mike make an exception. Exception that quickly went away, the fourth man decided to pull a knife.

Mike wanted to make a four of a kind statement display for the neighborhood, maybe a tourist attraction. With a knife pulled, his statement piece lost interest. Mike grabbed the knife hand, number four watched how Mike fed him his lunch the way a mother fed her baby. The knife left a nasty taste in number four's mouth. Mike figured he ruined the man's taste for knife ala mode lunches forever. Mike waited by the corner until seeding a five-man group appear down the street, three blocks off.

The group of five spotted Mike, partly because he was jumping up and down and waving his arm frantically. After having his appearance known, Mike took off in the direction, he left the first four.

"This way that third group will see what I done and maybe allow him to get home without them wanting to follow or simply so engrossed in his art piece statement, not wanting to leave." Mike hoped they were art lovers. He was correct, the two remaining AC-72 men decided they different want no part of that kid.

"Hey, that kid just took out six of my guys. You are crazy to chase him. We are leaving, our deal is over," shouted the leader to One-Eye.

One-Eye thought different. He wanted to continue the chase. The point was muted, when AC-72 leader decided to quit on his deal. Without more men, One-Eye had to leave. He knew, once the kid returned to his pals, they be after him. He needed to get far away for the time being as he can. Later, later when he has the men, he will return. The score will be settled.

The night came fast. Mike found a place to duck into. Rest and sleep were the two most important things on his mind. He was entering the main part of the city. By morning, he hoped to make his way home. He was still foggy about where that was. All he wanted for now, was rest. His belly hurt from the pain caused by his wounds but more so, out of hunger. Mike was thirsty and wanted water. Sleep had a harder tug on him.

HOPE CAME IN THE CABIN

Cho and Bone stopped by the cabin, before proceeding back to the city. Cho walked into the cabin hoping Mike was lying down, asleep. When he opened the door, Mike was not in his bed. Bone walks up behind Cho paused for a second, before entering. Bone went to the lantern on the table, lighting it with his trusty zippo lighter he carried everywhere. He never smoked but got the habit, when he was young. It looked cool having a lighter and a knife.

The lantern lit the room brightly. Cho stood at the door staring at the empty bed, Bone felt the same, looking back at Cho. Then, Bone turned seeing Cho staring at the wall over the bed. Over the bed on the wall was a message, "Mike is alive."

Cho turned, walked outside, immediately got back on his bike. Bone left the light burning rushing to the door and his bike. Both were roaring back to the city.

"Two days have passed since the explosion, Cho kept thinking riding hard and fast. Two days, Mike is injured lying somewhere bleeding. Two days I wasted feeling sorry for myself. Two days," and so it went all the way to Atlanta Cho constantly finding fault in his lack of actions.

It was night when the two entered the city. They parked their bikes in front of the Paperman building. Many people were walking out to go home. Another shift was coming in. The newspaper man was still in his office. They were escorted by the same doorman to the elevator. He was much politer, the second time.

The Newspaper man greeted them, as he done earlier. This time, he heard about the bomb explosions at the warehouse. He sent Green Jacket or Dark glasses, Mike referred calling him to check it out. Newspaper man spotted Cho just leaving his office, leaving for home.

"My man informed me, "he saw you leaving the site of the explosion." We kept that out of the paper. I hope you were successful with your problem," Paper man said.

Cho answered first, "we are. One of the two leaders is done for, the other one is a problem for the future. We are here, concerning a new problem."

"New problem, Newspaper man asked? Bone broke in before the Newspaper man had a chance to ask, further. "Mike, he is missing."

Several questions shot out of his mouth, typical of a newsman. "What, how, is he alive," followed Bone statement from Paper man?

Cho interrupted this time, "we thought he was blasted apart by the loudest of the three explosions. We searched and researched the area. We got men at the morgue and hospital waiting to find any evidence of Mike. I was, I mean, we were sure he was dead not finding his body."

Paperman felt Cho holding himself to blame. "He too was thinking this wouldn't have happened, if he remained out of this."

Bone, as usual saw the pity party begin and made one of his smart-ass remarks. "You two can blame yourself all day, if you wish. There is enough of the blame to share among us all. Mike wanted to go, we all believed he was ready, able, and most capable of doing the job. We let our feeling make us act silly. Enough of this silliness, that kid is out there, hurt. Maybe, hurt real, bad. I'm leaving, you two take care of the crying for us all."

Cho realized for the first time, Bone said what was needed saying.

Paperman asked, "how can I help?"

"Send out as many men you can. Mike will look like hell, probably cut with blood smeared on him. He may not know any of us." Paperman looked queerly at the last remark. Bone explained. "The explosion put him in shock or he can't remember much. His mind may be confused and disoriented. He won't trust anyone. He knows he is hurt and injured, not knowing why? Why will be on his mind. That will keep him alert to any strangers advancing toward him."

Cho breaks in, "he will be very dangerous to anyone approaching him. Do not try and approach him. Tell your people, this is no ordinary kid. He has special skills."

Paperman wanted to ask Cho, "what he meant? He remembered what Cho said referring to Mike a while back. "He was receiving special fighting skills. Could this be what he is referring about?" Paper man suddenly recalled the haunted house near Mike's home. "The children were attacked by some men, reported in a newspaper story. Later, Cho stopped by his office telling him what really happened. Ever since, Paper man had befriended Mike, he became a trusted friends to Chopper's bikers."

"Cho, I will make sure my people if spotting Mike, only report where his position is to this office. Keep contact with me. I too care about Mike, Cho, Bone."

"We will and thanks, Sir. Both Bone and Cho leave. They ride through town making their way back to the warehouse. This time, Cho wasn't in a daze with worry and dread. He knew what he had to do. He had a plan.

At the warehouse, Cho got off his Bike. Bone sat on his staying out of Cho way, until he got a fix on how to proceed. Cho paced back and forth in front of the warehouse door opening. Bone watched Cho pace and talk out loud trying to determine the sequences of events.

"What was my son doing, was he going toward the door? Marcus was outside. Surely, Marcus would have notified Mike, he was leaving. Mike would have told Marcus about the bombs and time settings. Mike must have been at the door. If the explosion went off, his training would have alerted him to find safety. He may have been too close to the door and could not to jump away. If he jumped, he would have gone in the opposite direction. That would have put him away from the door, maybe in a corner."

Cho walked inside, Bone was off his bike following. Constantly Cho walked through each step Mike may have taken walking to the far corner. Reaching down, Cho scratched away loose debris, there pointing. Bone, see, see that bare spot. Something was lying on that spot. Now, look here, see how the debris is leaving a path toward the back. Someone stood staggering, his feet pushed through the ash and debris of the blast. This happened after the blast. See, see, Cho points time and time again with each new discovery, look, there is a footprint. It is small."

Bone was now convinced, "Mike is alive. Cho you are correct, the footprint is that of a small person, a kid, Mike is a kid, he would have small feet, it's Mikes, Bone made the connections, it fits the signs, Cho."

Behind the warehouse, Bone was positioned prior to the battle. When him and Cho got to that place the footprints led, Bone gasped. "I was here. He was here, Cho. I must have just missed seeing him."

Cho responded, "maybe Bone, remember, he was dazed and if he saw you first, he would have avoided you."

"Yeah, your right, that's what he did. Okay, where to now, Cho?"

Crossing the street through the yellow tape, the police stretched around the crime scene, Bone and Cho entered a patch of trees. Night came without the moon or stars to light their way.

"Nothing Bone, I see nothing in this darkness, we have to stop for the night, Cho sadly stated. "It is too dark out. I don't want to take a chance of following the wrong trail. If Mike is hurt and we take the wrong path, it could take hours to back track. Mike knows how to treat wounds. He should be alright. Remember Bone what the cabin wall had written said, "Mike is alive." We need to have faith in Mike."

Both Bone and Cho lay near the last spot Mike was at. It was a shed. Some bloody rags were found by Bone. It was near two dead bodies. A third body was found off to one side, several feet from the first two.

"Mike definitely did not kill them. The third man was shot," responded Cho to Bone.

"Cho, there was fighting, how can you say Mike didn't kill the first two men? Mike was here and so were these men."

"Bone, open your eyes. Yes, Mike fought these men, he injured them, preventing them to follow. Look closer at their throats. Someone took a knife to them. Mike would never use a knife to kill, unless it was the only way he had left. Both men show some serious injuries, enough to disable them making it unnecessary to kill them. Leader man had his own men killed. He didn't want no one to slow him down. He has gotten to be a very dangerous person."

Mike found a nice spot to sleep for the night. After several hours, he was woke up. Thirst was burning his throat. Water was needed, Mike knew he needed to locate water. Standing, he was weak and fuzzy in the head. He slowly walked out of his shelter onto the street. Near a building, a faucet was extruding from the wall, quickly he made his way to the faucet. It lacked a wheel to turn. With all the training Mike endured, his body was hardening and strong. With his two fingers, he turned the threaded stub on the water faucet.

Water trickled out. With his mouth, Mike suckled the tap, sucking all the water remaining in the unused water pipe. It wasn't enough, but it satisfied the burning in his throat. Looking up wiping his dry mouth a store was across the street. He searched his pockets for money. Not one tiny jingle of coins was felt. He walked to the store with bars on the windows, peeking inside. He realized why the windows had bars. A lone man wearing a mask, was standing at a counter pointing a gun at the clerk. Mike pondered not to intervene but decided he could not walk away.

"There goes minding my own business," Mike thought entering the store.

The lone gun man heard the jingle of the entrance bell. Mike figured, "he could enter silently and take this fool out before his gun had a chance to point at him. Hearing the bell jingle, Mike silently thought, "that is my second mistake."

Gunman turned, his gun swinging toward Mike. Mike got within striking range before the gun halted in his face. Gunman started to squeeze his trigger. The hammer went back. Mike moved, twisting his body. The hammer was all the way back on the gun. Mike's arm spun around grasping the pistol. The pistol twisted upward pointing at the ceiling, then completed its twist entering the mouth of the gunman. The hammer fell forward. Its hammer struck the bullet. Gunman's lower jaw blew off. The wrist to the gunman was released. Mike removed the gun from the gun man's mouth returning it back to the man behind the counter.

The man behind the counter blinked. That was how fast the gunman lost his jaw from the time he pointed it at the young kid walking in his store. What was so amazing, the kid did that to the gunman without a second thought. Then, casually asked to work for some food.

Mike asked the clerk, "can I work for a drink and some food. I have no money to purchase them." Counterman turned and reached for a broom. He handed the broom to Mike.

"Thanks, Mike said beginning sweeping the mess up. Counter man handed Mike a dustpan. After the mess was placed into a trash can, counter man handed Mike some rags. Mike wiped the floor clean as best he could with his one working arm. Then, wiped the head of the gunman, placing some napkins inside the gaping hole on the side of his face. What was left of gunman jaw, Mike tied to his skull. Next, he lifted the man, placing him in a corner. Gently, took the duct tape counter man handed Mike and proceeds to wrapped both hands and feet of the gunman.

The counter man told Mike to take whatever he wanted. Mike walked through the store. He grabbed two bottles of water, took two sausages off a grill. Then placed both sausages in a bun, added some mustard and mayo. Then, finished with pickle placed in his mouth, turned, and walked out of the store.

Down the road, Mike walked several blocks. Police sirens were heard coming toward him. Two patrol cars, lights flashing, buzzed past. Mike was nearing the outskirts of the city.

"Maybe an hour, maybe two, I should reach home," Mike thought still not knowing where home was located. He only knew, he was traveling in the right direction.

Soon, Mike got to a two-lane road with many trees littering both sides of the road. Memories flooded his mind turning down the lonesome road. A day had come and gone. The sun was now high overhead. The few cars passing him honked their car horns.

Mike stepped off the road seeing a small stream. The stream brought back other memories. A snake in a bush. Walking waist deep in water, sticking his foot in holes along the banks. A hand was reaching down to aid him out of the water. It was a black man smiling at him. Sam seemed to fit the face. The memories faded as Mike wandered off road.

Bone called over to Cho. "Did you find a new track?"

"Yes, it leads to town. It looks like he is heading into the old part of town."

"Cho, ain't, that a seedy place, you know, lot of nasty kinds of folks." Cho only nods his head. Quickly Cho hopped on his bike, both of them rode to town.

It didn't take long for Cho to spot his first signs. Blood droplets, one, then two drops spattered near Cho's foot. Cho saw the red droplets stopping his bike. The trailed led toward an alley.

In the alley, laid dead men. Bone stopped, got off his bike, walked to the bodies. After examining one man, yells to Cho, it was Mike's doing. He won't be hard to track, with all these bodies he is dropping. It looks like he is leaving signs behind for us to follow, you think, Cho?"

Cho only nods, "maybe, Bone, maybe." Cho walks over to the bodies and quickly assessed; Mike did not kill them. Again, they were killed by the Leader man. Mike injured them severely, my friend."

Both Bone and Cho leave the bikes parked at the entrance to the alley, making their way on foot to the end.

"It's a dead end, Bone replied. If Mike went in here, he still must be here. Those Atlanta guys must have followed. There ain't no bodies lying around. They might have got him, Cho?" Bone scanned the walls, no exit.

Answering, Cho said, "maybe, maybe." Cho noticed the window two stories up. It was opened, the glass broken, no glass was on the ground, "Hmm."

With a quick burst of speed, Cho leaped up onto a wall, twisted his body once his foot made contact, then bounced off that wall to another and into the opened window. Inside the room, Cho spotted a rag with blood. "Mike changed his dressing. The rag was completely covered with blood. The wound is bad." By one wall, Cho saw a sign similar to those at the warehouse. A bare spot where someone laid. Scouring around, footprints led out the room. Following the steps, he realized Mike went to the rooftop. Returning to the window, shouts down to Bone.

"Bone, he went on the roof. You wait here, I will check how far and in what direction Mike is headed on the roof."

"You got it, Cho," shouted Bone.

Cho ran down the hall into the stairwell. On the roof, foots prints led north. Over the next two roofs, Cho jumped. On the third roof were signs of a fight. Several bodies laid in a small circle. "All of them are dead. Serious injuries to all but death came from a knife. All throats sliced from one ear to the next, the work of the leader. Cho followed the footsteps to the next building. From that building to the next, "this is the last steps Mike made to the edge of the building. Mike went back down to the ground."

Cho ran down the stairs. At the bottom, dashes outside. In the street, Cho looks around realizing he was not even a block from the alley. Cho ran down the street to his bike. Bone was walking up the alley. Seeing Cho, quipped,

"I thought you might figure Mike came off the roof and followed it down. Knowing you, it would be faster to run back to this alley, instead of climbing back up them stairs and back over the roof tops."

Cho spoke, "you guessed right, Bone. Come, Mike went this way," pointed Cho. He and Bone got quickly on their bikes. Soon, they caught sight of men carrying bodies. Stopping to observe several men carry a body around a corner into an old building; Bone turns to Cho, Mike?" Cho, nodded.

Setting their bikes down, they swiftly and quietly followed the men carrying a body into a building. Once inside, they were confronted with many more badly injured bodies lying in the center of a room. One man stood near the last body being place beside the others. He appeared to be praying. Bone wanted at him. Cho held his hand out stopping Bone.

Once the man rose his head, Cho removed his hand. Bone had him in a tight hold. Both his massive arms were squeezing the man in a vice like grip. Cho gave a finger wave for the man to keep quiet. The pain was too great. He opened his mouth to bellow out his pain.

With a speed not seen by Bone, Cho tapped the man on his favorite pressure points. He meant to teach that to Mike, during their next training section. Now, he wished he had sooner. The man stopped speaking; his face contorted. Cho asked one question. The other question came from Bone.

"Young man, I see seven men lying at my feet. Was the boy hurt?"

"No sir," the man barely spoke clearly from the searing pain he was feeling.

Next came Bone's questions. "Why were you chasing this kid?"

"We were being paid by One-Eye, to help him."

"Why?" Bone looked at Cho holding up two fingers.

"That is more than one question, Bone." The man could care less how many questions either asked. He just wanted the big guy to release his grip around his throat enough to breathe.

"He needed more men, that kid killed most of his."

"Where is One-eye?" Cho held three four fingers up to Bone.

"Don't know." "Why?" "We quit him. The kid nearly did in most of our gang. Every one of these men may die tonight. Why don't you get them to a doctor? Yeah, to many questions. I don't need that?"

"You may need that, before we leave. Think about that, when you are lying next to those seven barely alive men," Bone said increasing a little more squeeze. It wasn't necessary, Cho touched him. The extra squeeze was more for Bone's pleasure.

"Our leader wanted nothing more to do with that kid. We left him at the corner, several blocks down main street. Ask anyone outside. Most of the people saw the fight."

Soon, the man stopped talking. Bone let him fall to the ground. Cho was out the door on his bike. Bone got to his bike a little later. It was three blocks and Cho already off his bike, when Bone caught up to him.

Several People were mulling around a corner. Cho walked over placing his hand on one man's shoulder. The man turned around quickly. He had a frightening look on his face. Seeing Cho, his face relaxed. "Still, I have to asked what occurred on the street. Any tib bit of information is better than none at all," thought Cho.

"Why are you people standing around, looking at the ground," Cho asked curiously looking at the gawking onlookers? Cho stealth-ily pushed through the crowd of onlookers staring down at what looked like a squirming mangled person. Many onlookers presumed the man was dead, bent, and contorted lying on the street? One man looked at the Asian man staring down at the mangled man.

"Hey, you should have seen it. This kid, he looked battered or he been in a fire, whatever, these four men attacked him. The kid was bleeding. All that blood didn't come from the four men. In fact, there ain't no blood from any of them. Look at them men. That kid made pretzels out of each man. He did all that with one arm."

Bone walks up. The talking man stopped" just long enough to gasp. Cho pressured him to continue. Please, it is important that you tell me what happened here?"

The man stopped gawking when he heard the word, please. "Well, as I was a saying, this kid was hurt, it looked like they were going to finish the job. Bone interrupted the man with a question.

"You said the kid had one arm. Was the other arm missing?"

"No. It was tuck in his belt. I think his arm was broke. If that is all, now where was I, oh; most of us seeing the kid approached by these four men, assumed they done that to him. But, but after what he did to them. Heck, no way in hell would I have gone after that kid, if I saw him do that. Now, I realized they must have not seen him before. If they did, they would beat tail getting away from him."

"Go on," repeated Cho to the talking man.

He paused to think of the next thing to say. "Well that kid, I don't really know if I can say exactly, what he did. It just happened, just like that and it was over. These four men were all tied up with their own arms and legs. They were dead. Dead maybe, I sure hoped they are. The way they looked, I think if they be alive, them might wishes themselves to be dead. Not a drop of blood."

"Did anyone check to see if they were dead," inquired Bone?

Thinking about what the big guy asked, the man paused again, before returning his answer. "Well, come to think of it, No. These other guys showed up. I, we figured they must be their friends. They picked them up and walked off with three. This here man, I guess they be coming back for, soon enough." The man pointed in the direction Bone and Cho rode from.

Bone turns to Cho; we must be getting close. Bone turns to the talking man, "hey mister, about how long ago, was that?"

"Hmm, maybe an hour, maybe a little longer. Another person speaks up. "No, it was twenty-five minutes ago."

"See Cho, I said, we were getting closer," Bone quipped. Cho's only answer was, "maybe, just maybe."

Several blocks up the road, another similar scene was held at a corner. The same response was given to Cho and Bone. One thing was different at that corner. Mike had used a pressure point on these men with a finger strike. Cho said, "hmm."

Each man was lying on the ground in a ball of pain. Not a sound emanated from their mouths. "This is weird, one bystander saying to another. Look how they are twisted?"

Cho again questioned one man. "Excuse me, did anyone get a look at this person that done this."

"This kid, not bigger than my shoulder, had attacked these four men. They fell to the ground, like he commanded them to do."

"He only touched them. They went down all rolled up in a ball. They been this way for, maybe thirty minutes." replied another man.

Bone looked at them, said one word, "closer." Cho replied, "maybe, just maybe."

A FAMILIAR PLACE

Mike returned to the road slowly making his way a small town. The town looked familiar to him. Entering the main street, people were busy going from one store to another. Those that saw Mike, avoided him. What they saw was a dirty kid with torn bloody clothes. He had a slight limp. His face was darkened, half covered by a rag. One arm was tucked inside his pants.

Mike crossed the street barely making it to the other side when several motor bikes rode past him. He received a glimpse from a woman rider. Somehow, she looked familiar to him. The name Bell entered his mind. Mike quickly stopped pondering on the name Bell, when the bikers did not stop.

"They saw me cross the street. If they knew me, they surely would have stopped. They didn't stop, nor attempted to drive back," Mike reasoned.

Mike traveled through town until coming to a turn-off. "This road was the same the bikers turned from unto the main street of town. It feels like I know the road." Down the road he walked for thirty minutes. It was becoming more familiar. "I've seen these homes before. I ran down this street. Those homes had become a landmark to me. Every day I would pass by while doing my morning run."

Soon, Mike saw a subdivision on his right side. "I know the place." He walked through the entrance. A park was ahead of him. Over across the grass Mike walked. He sat on a seesaw. Suddenly a vision of the night sky appeared to him. I recall staring at the stars. Then, a pretty face, it's the same pretty face I dreamed about at the shed appearing again. Who is she," he thought to himself?"

Mike sat on the seesaw for a long time. Some children came to play on the swings. They saw him and ran off. Not long after the children ran away several women make their way over to him. Apparently, the children saw Mike got scared at his appearance. Instead of waiting to see what the women were up to, he decided to leave. The mothers watched Mike at a distance getting off the seesaw. He was out of the park before they had a chance to get near him. The person was injured, was apparent to all the women. One woman called out to him.

"Wait, can we help," she shouted. Mike ignored her pleas and kept walking. Swiftly Mike was out of the neighborhood heading down road leading to the house.

"That is where I need to go," repeating in Mike's head.

The woman calling to the injured man turned to her two friends. "That man, he looked like Mike."

The other lady spoke; "Susan, Mike is dead, how can that be him." She put her arm around Susan, "now, now you need to accept that."

"Oh, Miriam how can you say that. Didn't you see him. That kid was hurt. If it was Mike, wouldn't he be hurt?"

"Susan, if that was Mike, why didn't he recognize us? Why didn't he call back to us?"

"I'm telling you; I really believe that was Mike. Susan tore away from Miriam arms running to her home. Inside, was Cheryl. "Cheryl, I think I just saw Mike."

"Mike, mom, where?"

"In the park. He left, when I called to him."

"Why would he leave, mom?"

"Didn't Chopper and Bell once say, when you are in an explosion, you can get disoriented, maybe forget who you are."

"Mom, if that was so, he might not remember where he came from?"

"Maybe Cheryl, sometimes memories return a little at a time. Maybe he returned here, not really understanding why he came here. Cheryl, you know him best, where would he head to?"

Cheryl knew right off, she shouts out, "the cabin. Mom, he is going to the cabin. Come, I'll tell Miriam and Penny to let the others know. We will go in the car."

Mike made the turn on a dirt road. Within several minutes came to a small path instinctively went down the path. Along a river, a memory took him to a cabin. Not too soon, a cabin appeared ahead. Mike stopped and stared at the cabin.

"I knew this cabin. I know you. You are my cabin. Mister Casper are you in?" No answer came back. Mike walked up to the door. It was closed. The door opened as he neared. Inside a small lantern was lit, sitting on a table. In the corner was a bed. On the wall above the bed was a message. "Your home."

Mike walked over to the bed falling into it. He rolled over unto his back closing his eyes. For the first time, since the warehouse, Mike felt safe, he was home. The door closes, the lantern flickers out. Inside, laid a young man sleeping peacefully.

Susan quickly ran out the door where Miriam was standing with her. She caught her before getting across the street. "Miriam it was Mike, I'm certain."

Miriam didn't question her. The suggestion the hurt young stranger in the park was Mike lit a flame in her mind. She started to see similarities looking like Mike. Same height, weight, and clothes, burned and torn. It looked like the stranger was in a fire or an explosion.

"Quick Miriam, inform the house, Cheryl and I are driving to the cabin. We think, he is heading there." A loud rev was heard from Susan's home, a girl was leaving on a bike. "Cheryl left without her," Susan was stunned?

"Come Susan, you ride with me, Miriam said grabbing her hand. Penny, you inform the house."

Moments later, a car pulled out of her yard then turned on to a dirt road leading to the cabin. No sooner than Miriam and Susan car turned, three bike riders turned behind them. One rider was Bell.

Bell saw the kid with torn clothes and burns riding through town. She saw the bloody rag around the face. At first, she thought, "what mom would let her kid walk around town in that shape? They wouldn't have, she reasoned. Then, it struck her. It was Mike making his way home."

A loud noise outside the cabin made little dent inside to the sleeping occupant. Cheryl was the first to arrive. The door was closed. She jumps off her bike, rather Mike's bike, he asked her to keep safe while he was away. Before she reached the door, it opened. Inside, a lantern was beginning to light up.

Cheryl didn't require any light, just the same, thanked Mister Casper. Mike never told her his name. She had done some research on the cabin. The last man living in it, was an old man who built it. His whole family was killed in a robbery. He sold his home moving to this solitary, hidden place. Long before the bikers acquired the clubhouse built near the cabin. He kept to his own business rarely going to town. The bikers discovered the cabin and found a body of Mister Casper. They buried his remains around the back of the cabin.

Cheryl went poking around after Mike was presumed dead. She found the old marker. It was nearly rotten. She pulled the marker up taking it home. At home, she made a new marker and painted Mister Casper's name on it. That same day returned, replacing the old marker with the new one. Then, quietly said a prayer.

Inside the cabin, Cheryl saw a body lying on the bed. On the wall was a message. "Mike is back." Tears filled her eyes. She pulled the chair from the table and sat, watching Mike sleep. He looked peaceful. She knew Mike was fine, otherwise Mister Casper would have in his peculiar way let her know.

Cho stopped at a store. It was the only store on the way Mike was heading opened on that street. Entering, he walked over to the counter. A man stood there.

"Can I help you, sir?"

Cho responds, "Sir, did you see a kid come into your store earlier today? Just before noon?"

The counterman was about to say, no. He was grateful to the kid stopping a robbery and most likely, saved his life. On top of that, the stranger asked, "if he could work for food." He would have given him all the food he wanted, instead, he handed him a broom. For the oddest reason, he felt that was what the kid preferred him to do. The kid had, honor, or something. Either way, he owed the kid.

The counterman quickly changed his mind when Bone, a tall mountain of a man came inside. He stood by the Asian man asking him a polite question. A same feeling came over him. He felt it was the right thing to do, so, he told them what happened. Then telling the two men, "I handed the kid a broom to clean up the mess. Thinking it would be a good idea to explain why he gave the kid a broom. He quickly stated, "he asked to work for the food." I would have given him the food. He insisted on earning the food." The counterman was still telling Cho and Bone his story of what transpired as both men exited the store before he finished.

"Cho, Mike is definitely heading back to the house. We can catch up to him quick."

Cho simply said, "Maybe, just maybe Bone." Riding fast on their bikes, they reached the outskirts of the big city. Cho stops.

"What wrong, Cho?"

"Bone, what is wrong is that Mike is not going back home on the same road we rode on."

Bone looked befuddled. "Why you say that?"

"If you look at the road, instead of the end of the road, you would clearly see a bloody rag lying on the ground heading a different direction."

Looking down Bone scanned the ground. Sure enough, a bloody rag laid near the road, stuck to a branch. It waved in the air with the slightest breeze. "Sorry Cho, I guess I am in too big a hurry to notice things like that."

The road led to the same town they lived nearby. It was a way most bikers rarely rode. Cho took that road quickly arriving in their town. Both sped through town and onto the road leading to the clubhouse. They turned onto a dirt road and then onto the dirt road leading to the clubhouse. Parking in the front of the newly built wall of the clubhouse blown up before the warehouse mission, they walked inside. No one was in the house.

Bone said, "hey where is everyone?"

Cho realized Mike was at the cabin. "Come Bone, Mike is back." Outside both jumped on their bikes. Soon, were stopped at the small path. Many bikes and cars crowded the road. Cho and Bone got off their bikes running, weaving in and out of the jumbled pile of bikes. Quickly both made their way to the front of the cabin. Many bikers and family members were waiting outside. The cabin door was closed. Many people, mainly bikers called out to them worming through the growing crowd nearing the cabin.

"Hey Cho, Bone, Mike is alive." "Cho, he's in the cabin." "Bone, Cho, he walked back by himself." "Cho, Bone, did you hear the news?" The responses followed the two all the way to the front door. The door was shut. No one could get it open.

Cho and Bone walked up to one biker trying to pry the door open with a crowbar. Voices were heard inside. They couldn't open the door on their side. Cho reached for the knob. Before his hand touched the knob, the door opened.

Both Bone and Cho were permitted to enter. The door shut tight once they entered. Chopper, Bell, Susan, Miriam, Penny, Razor, and Cheryl stood near the bed Mike was lying in. On the wall, a message read. "Do not awake this boy!" It was written in very bold print; the meaning was clear. Everyone obeyed the message.

Cho neared the bed. On the wall the message mysteriously changed. No one saw the change. Everyone was watching Cho. Cho awaken Mike. Gently he put his hand on Mike. A soft and gentle shake was given him. Mike slowly opened his eyes. Cho looked down at his son. Tears filled his eyes. Mike started to cry seeing his father, Cho. Two arms rose to grab Cho. Cho bent down to receive the arms. For minutes they laid their holding unto the other.

Bell began to cry along with the other women. Chopper nearly did the same. Bone had a tear flow down his cheek. He quickly wiped it away. Cheryl saw Bone Breaker swipe at the tear. She grabbed hold of Bone's hand.

Cho broke loose of Mike hold. Mike my son, I need to check your wounds. We saw much blood. You left a lot of blood on rags, we found. We feared the worse, seeing the amount of blood.

"Father my arm is broken. It hurts so bad."

Cho gently removed the rag around Mike's face. A cut crossed his cheek with a scab. "It would heal without much of a scar to be seen," telling Mike. Then Cho pulled open the shirt. He saw the wound covered with a thick rag. It was blood red. Slowly, peeling the rag wrapped around Mike's waist securing a wad of dirty dark purplish sheet. Cho recalled seeing the torn sheet in the room Mike went into before going to the rooftop. Then, he slowly pulled the wad from Mike's wound. The rag was stuck to the wound. The blood hardened. Cho pulled at the rag. The skin stretched out from Mike's body. Cheryl couldn't watch. Watching the rag pulling Mike's skin outward, she feared the skin would tear away from his body.

The wad tore off, opening the wound. Blood oozed out. Bell told Cho to back away. Her and Susan took over. "Men," Bell said? Susan nodded, "yes men."

Jack knife heard about Mike's return arriving at the clubhouse. Several riders went back for a drink, to celebrate Mike's return.

"Where is Mike?"

"Jack knife, hey man, we didn't hear you come in?"

"Where is he?"

"Okay, he at the cabin," Jack knife, taking a shot of liquor.

"Do they have medical supplies for his injuries?"

"Hey man, we really don't know."

"Then, you better know and damn quick." Each rider put his drink down fast. One went into the back storeroom, quickly both riders were on their bikes riding back to the cabin. Jack knife followed.

At the cabin, Bell just told Cho to back away. Her and Susan began first aid to Mike. Soon as they cleaned the wounds, they realized there was no medical supplies in the cabin. Before either had a chance to tell one of the men inside, the front door opened.

In came two bikers with medical supplies. Jack knife came right behind them. "Thought you might need some things," retorted Jack entering the cabin. The door remained opened.

Susan looked at Chopper with serious concerns riding on her expression. Standing, while Bell tended to Mike, she motions to one side. Bone, Razor along with Jack knife read the expression on her face gathering into a small group away from the bed. Cho remained at the bed. It was not good.

Every word spoken, no matter how softly spoken, Cho heard. Rarely could anyone keep silent enough for Cho not to ear. He kept that to himself. In this way, he always was aware of all the things said. This was not done from the lack of trust, just training his father instilled into him. "Always be prepared. The surest way for preparedness, is to be aware of everything said and done around you, son." This was one of the first lessons Cho instilled into Mike.

Cho heard what Susan feared to say near Mike. Mike heard her words, as did Cho. Cho knew Mike was listening. It wasn't necessary for Susan to move away from him. She done so, thinking it would spare Mike the bad news she would tell the leaders.

Quietly, with a soft tone, she begins to tell the men the news. "Mike has a serious wound; it will not stop bleeding. There feels to be something deep inside the opening. Bell is probing the opening. When she put her fingers inside of the hole, she felt a sharp object. The object is lodged in deep and tight. Bell said, removing the object, without the proper tools will widen the wound, causing more harm. Mike lost a lot of blood. The object may tear an organ open. This is going to take a doctor. Bell is afraid to try it herself."

Susan pauses wiping sweat and tears from her face. "His pain must he awful. Bell and I cannot bear to attempt this delicate removal. The other wounds look fine. There was some stuff sticking out of the other wounds. Bell thinks warehouse debris. She pulled them out. She is now cleaning and bandaging those areas."

Cheryl stood just far enough away from the group her mother was talking too. She was still close enough to hear mom tell them the seriousness of Mike's wound.

Chopper told Razor to call the doctor. Razor left as soon as he was told. The doctor was the biker's call to a physician when the need rose. Most of the time, the biker's wives were trained to deal with most wounds. This was a wound; they were weary of. Also, they didn't want to attempt.

Mike laid in the bed quiet. Bell told him, "it is okay to yell out from the pain Mike, while I probed through the open wound." Mike remained quiet. Not even the slightest movement came from Mike. He laid perfectly still with Bell's fingers digging deep inside him. Once Bell finished her examination, she covered the hole with a clean compress. Mike took his hand to covered the compress, pressing down with his palm. Bell was shocked watching Mike apply pressure to the very painful wound. He did so without the slightest grimace of pain on his face. Mike was hurting bad.

Bone felt a warm arm encircle his. It was Penny. He entered the cabin without noticing anyone. His attention followed Cho to Mike's Bed. Everyone did as Bone had done. All eyes stared at Cho and Mike holding unto the other.

DOCTOR, DOCTOR

A phone call was made. A doctor answered the phone. Razor told him the situation. A biker driving a car was dispatched, before the phone call was made. When the phone called ended, a car was entering the doctor's driveway. The doctor was ready with his bag. Within a short time, the doctor was leaving the car and rushing to the cabin's door.

Susan was waiting at the door, along with Cheryl. Cheryl and Susan took the doctor's arm escorting him to Mike bedside. Bell stood, "doctor, he has a very high fever. Two wounds, one on each side of his abdomen, I cleaned them. His head showed burns, second degree, I believe. Most of his hair has been singe to the scalp. The other wounds looked superficial."

The doctor stood quietly listening to Bell's report. His eyes were studying Mike lying on the bed. Bending over, he removed the gauge covering the wound. It was partly bloodied.

Bell remarked, "I probed with my fingers into the open wound, doctor. There is a sharp object two inches in. I was afraid to remove it on the possibilities, I might tear it loose causing severe bleeding or worse."

"You did correctly, Bell. The doctor knew Bell. She was his nurse for many years. He lost her to Chopper, the first time he was brought in for a gunshot wound. She tended to him for a week. Sometime in that period, her heart was given to him. After that, he had to find another nurse.

"Bell, I know you know this is a serious wound. Why did you wait until now to call me here? This wound is infected. That metal should have been removed, quickly. Wasn't he in severe pain enough to make you see the seriousness of the injury?"

Chopper broke in after hearing the doctor reprimand Bell. "Doc, we didn't know where he was? He just showed up today. It has only been minutes before you got the call."

The doctor looked dumbfounded. "These injuries appeared to have been cause by a fire or blast."

Chopper spoke, "it was."

"Where was this blast? Then, the doctor remembered the news about an explosion at a warehouse in the city. Looking back at Chopper, said, "you mean he was in that explosion?"

"Yes."

"How did he get all the way back here," Doc asked? Cho spoke.

"For two days, we believed Mike had been killed in the explosion. We search the site thoroughly for two days. There was no body to be found. We thought, he caught the main blast at the door exiting the place. We lost a good man that day, Doc. He was coming out of the building, the blast nearly cut him in two. What was left, was barely recognizable. His funeral will be tomorrow."

"I'm sorry Cho," the doctor replied.

"Doctor, Bone, and I went back yesterday. We found evidence Mike survived the blast. We followed his trail through the city," Cho said.

"Wait, you telling me, this lad walked all the way here with this wound? That Mister Cho, is impossible. Someone aided him. This lad would have bled out to even attempt such a walk. You must be mistaken, thinking he walked that far?"

Cho looked a bit crossed that his word was not accepted. Knowing the Doc for all these years allowed him to forgive the Doc of his offense.

"Bell, get my bag and fetch that bottle of glucose. We need to get fluids in him, now."

Bell handed the Doc his bag. Susan hung the glucose onto Bone's outstretched arm. The Doc stuck the needle into Mike's arm. Then, with Bell's assistance holding the light, took the probe handed him. Slowly he peeled the wound open. Next, he felt his way into the cavity with the probe, quickly finding the shard. He gave the metal a tug. It resisted his first attempt. Bell had a scalpel in her hand. Doc took the scalpel and made an incision, widening the wound. The shard could clearly be seen.

This time, the Doc knew what needed to be done. He cut around the shard. It was slightly imbedded in the small intestines. Bell could see the danger watching Doc begin cutting around the area. She was ready with gauge. Once the Doc removed the shard, an odor rose from the belly permeating the cabin air. The intestines were leaking out. Bell quickly passed Doc a needle to sew the tear from the shard removed from Mike's intestines. After more gauge was applied and the area rinsed, the wound was ready to sew up.

Antibiotic powder was applied. The doctor took out of his bag medicine, handing it to Bell. "Bell, see to it he is closely watch. You know how to give the medicine you had done for others. This time Bell, be prepared for a hard road. That is one sick lad."

"Doc, Can we move him, asked Susan?

"Susan, normally I would say it was okay. He has been moving too much. He needs to stay rested for several days. After that, you can move him. To do so now only will further the damage. Turning to face Cho, doc said, "sorry Cho if it sounded, I didn't believe in what you were telling me. It was hard to believe anyone, even you couldn't have made a walk that far with those wounds."

The Doc turned to Chopper, then he noticed Mike's his arm was tucked into his pants. Bending down unbuckles his pants. Then, carefully pulled the arm out. Mike groaned. Doc pulled back the remaining part of his shirt. The shoulder was seriously bruise. Feeling around the bruise, he felt the dislocation.

"Bell, we all missed this." Bell came over to the Doc. Quickly she noticed the whole of the shoulder was blackened.

Bell took hold of the arm commanded by Doc. "Pull when I tell you to. Doc took hold at the shoulder joint. "Pull Bell. Bell pulled while the doc directed the ball joint back into its socket. A loud popping sound was heard throughout the cabin. Cheryl walked out of the cabin, found a corner not occupied by well-wishers, then puked her guts out. She wipes her mouth walking back inside.

Cheryl turned away before Bell pulled the arm. She looked down at his wound, that almost made her sick, again. She turns away, trying not look at Mike. Bell was holding Mike's bloody clothes. Cheryl ran outside a second time. Mike made a slight moan. He was out from the drug, after his moan.

Walking over to Chopper, the doctor asked him a few questions. He knew he wasn't going to get many answers back. He had to ask him, though. "Chopper why was this lad at the explosion?" He was right, Chopper did not respond with an answer.

Bell and Susan wanted one. One question they wanted from Cho, answered. Cho would not answer them, while in the cabin. Everyone walked out of the cabin. Cheryl remained by the bedside after returning back inside. She sat by Mike's bed applying a cold compress to his head. Mike felt the cold compress, awoke. He looked up to her and smiled. He tried to say something. Sleep over took him, once again. He heard Cheryl speak but his eyes wanted badly to close.

"Sleep Mike, I will be here. Sleep and get better, you are in my hands now," Cheryl softly said. On the wall above Mike's bed was a message to Cheryl.

"We will take care of him, Cheryl."

Outside all three women present stood around Cho. Chopper walked past at a fast pace. Not here, at the house we can all hear Cho and Bones report. That was the final say. When Chopper spoke, no arguing, it was the law.

Cho told Chopper that he and Bone will remain at the cabin for a while.

Cho, you two stay and if you feel it appropriate come to the clubhouse. We will meet at six. One of you should come at least, Chopper replied.

Both Cho and Bone went back inside the cabin. Razor told two bikers to stay and keep guard. "If anything is required, it was their duty to tend to it." The two were rookies and not fully earned their patches yet.

Everyone departed. Susan drove her car with Miriam. Bell asked to ride with them. All three were in the car. Before they left, Miriam asked a question. "Hey girls, hasn't Cho and Bone been gone for two days. Maybe we should send them something to eat?"

"Your right Miriam, replied Susan. Susan got out of her car going back inside. She forgotten Cheryl was there. Seeing her by Mike's side eased her fear of her daughter being distraught.

"Bone, I know you are hungry and Cho, you can go a long time between meals. Besides that, we will bring you two something to eat. Calling to Cheryl, honey Mike should be fine. Will you come home with us?"

Cheryl never looked up, simply said to her mom, "I am staying here for the time being."

Susan said nothing to Cheryl. "We will bring plenty for all, even the two men posted outside."

Back in the car, Susan sat staring out the front window. Miriam didn't see Cheryl follow her back. Miriam assumed Susan thought the men were hungry and went in to get Cheryl. She saw the concern on her face.

Bell was concerned, she never once took her eyes off of the cabin. Even after their car turned to drive away. Bell kept her head turned looking back at the cabin, until the cabin was hidden by the trees.

Cho walked over to Cheryl gently placing both hands on her shoulders. Cheryl reached up to take his hand into her. Bone stood at the foot of the bed watching Mike. Watching Mike lying on the bed, seemed strange to Bone. He kept thinking what the Doc said. No one could have made a walk that far and lived.

"If only the Doc knew the whole truth. That Doc would be shocked dead. If only he knew what that kid went through to get back home. It wasn't just a walk. It was a fight for his life the whole way home." He felt Penny take his hand. Bone had on many times expressed his relationship to Mike. She knew he was hurting inside. Bone kept much to himself. Penny was making head way into those hidden fears, as their relationship grew.

Cho momentarily let Cheryl's shoulders go. He walked back to the table grabbing two chairs. One for him, the other for Bone. All three sat by the bed. Cho never took his eyes off Mike, then, only when hearing a car approaching an hour later. All three ladies returned. The two guards met them at the car. Each guard was handed several hot bags of food. One bag had cold drinks. The door opened by Mister Casper for those, he allowed in. Once the three women entered, the door closed. Both guards stood looking at the closed door, each still carrying the hot food.

The suddenness of the closing of the door unnerved Miriam. Anytime Miriam was upset, her way of dealing with trouble was to not think about it. So was it about the door, she quickly put it out of her mind.

Susan and Bell were waiting at the door to open. The guards had the food. "Mister Casper, please open the door. The guards won't come in, they have the food for everyone." The opened, both bags handed to Susan and Bell then abruptly shut. Penny left shortly before Bell, Susan, and Miriam drove away. Telling Bone, she was going to their home. She wanted to get him some clean clothes. He had been off with Cho for several days.

Before the two guards had a chance to sit, the door opened again. Miriam handed them a bag of food and a liter of coke. No beer, it wasn't allowed on guard duty, unless instructed by a biker.

Inside Bone sat at the table plowing through the two bags. Nothing prevented him from eating. Nothing until Penny returned walking inside. Bone closed the bags standing to greet Penny. She quickly went to Bone, giving him a hug, then clean clothes to change into.

"Babe, I know this is hard. Is Mike doing well?" "Yes, yes," then Bone hugged her back. Penny walks over to the bed. She saw a young boy cut across his body. His face burned on one side. Cuts everywhere. He was wearing what was left of the clothes he survived from the explosion left on by Bell and Susan tending to him.

Penny remembered how strong Mike looked and the energy that seemed to extrude from him. Now lying on a bed, maybe near death, he looked so innocent, helpless, and frail.

Cho commanded everyone to eat. Both Susan and Bell remained at the bed. Miriam served everyone hot food. Cho picked at his as did Cheryl. Bone wasted no time. Miriam ate a small plate of food. Two plates were made ready for Bell and Susan. Cheryl and Cho took allowing them to eat.

After the meal, the routine began. Cho paced, Bone sat with Penny, Miriam kept busy with different choirs, seemingly found needed doing. The other three women sat by the bed. Occasional one would get up to stretch their legs or needing to go outside to the outhouse.

At around the time Chopper called for a meeting at the club-house, Bell and Susan had enough of Cho's pacing. "Go Cho. Go to the meeting, give the rest of us a break from your constant pacing."

Miriam wanted to go. Both Susan and Bell thought that was a good idea. She could report to the other ladies. Most of the meetings usually were for the men. Sometimes, the women would get the gist of what they were about, by their hubbies.

The whole neighborhood was buzzing, the word got out, Mike was alive. More questions about Mike's wounds rather than the bomb blast occurring a week ago was asked. Most of the women were preparing for Marcus's funeral services. He was divorce and had many girlfriends. Of late, he was stag. Some of his old flames were informed. He had no children close enough to arrive in time. Apparently, the ex-wife kept them from knowing much about their father.

Marcus was a good father and did his duty. Not once did he miss sending his monthly childcare payments. Every birthday, holi-day, or just to remind them, he kept them in mind, he would send a present to each child.

Marcus trained many of the biker family's children self-defense. There were others that offered other skills. When it came to the mar-tial arts, he had the gift. He was a born teacher. The kids loved being in his class. Many received a black belt from him.

Cheryl received her black belt, then quit training. When Mike arrived, she renewed her interest. Partly out of anger, a need to revenge her dad. Once she understood the true reasons for her dad's death, she began the see Mike as no longer her enemy.

Miriam and Cho arrived at the clubhouse. She never liked rid-ing on the back of a chopper. Much less the older she got. Getting off the bike, told Cho she would rather walk home, than ride on a bike home.

Inside the house, Razor met his wife. Before she said a word, he told her, the car is parked outside on the side of the house. He knew her getting off Cho's bike, what she was going say to him. He heard the same thing for years. He was glad, he thought to take the car to the clubhouse.

Chopper seeing Cho walk through the doors, called to order those assembled. Everyone was required to attend a meeting. Rarely did anyone miss a meeting. Meetings were important. It was a time to organize and plan. Nothing in the house was ever said outside the house. Certain situations were never spoken in the house. It kept things, the police might want to hear from being exposed to prying ears. Many things spoken were guarded with coded words.

Chopper called Cho to the front. Before Cho spoke, a few words had to be said of the funeral services held soon, for Marcus. "Everyone here has been informed of Marcus's death and the explanations how it occurred. We all will miss him greatly. We lost many of late. Marcus will have a ceremony at grave site, his wishes. Of course, there will be a military formal attire required. His branch of service will perform the salute. Some of you will be assigned to his honor guard. You can discuss that with Jack knife. All our wives will prepare a diner. All children will attend."

"Now, Cho will you take the floor." Cho walked over to Chopper. After a short period or relevance with his head lowered, Cho looked up. He was troubled, but like Cho, he was hard to read. This time, many could read what Cho was feeling. Cho spoke with coded words to prevent any ears listening.

"As of late, many thought the house was being spied upon. It was, but not by the law. Most of you know, there was an explosion at a warehouse in the city. Mike and Marcus were scouting for a place to set up a bike repair shop for our group. The old shop was too small. They heard a ruckus inside the warehouse, they were inspecting. A gang was having a battle when the two of them walked in at the wrong time. Before they could turn and run from the fight, an explosion happened. Then another and another. Marcus was killed. His body found outside the warehouse many yards from the door." All this was coded in a way to prevent nosey people listening.

"The police arrived and questioned me about the blast. I was waiting outside the house at the timed Mike and Marcus had entered. I was blown off my bike just and beginning to stand, when the police arrived. I did my best to explain what I saw. They kept me at the site for hours. Everyone presents at the scene, left. Many of the Atlanta gang members were killed. One, was one of the two leaders. Unfortunately, he was not the main leader the police told me. Seems like him and appropriately eight of his remaining members got away."

"A thorough search was performed by the police and all other parties involved. After the police departed, another search occurred later. Both Bone and I had to know if Mike survived the blast. The second search found nothing from the reports. The two of us returned to the city looking for clues."

"Two days after the blast, Chopper was informed on our desire to return to locate a body. Returning late that day, we stopped off at the Paperman's office. He informed us of his willingness to assist. After thanking him for his thoughts, we left, arriving at the warehouse before dark. We will contact him tomorrow about our good news."

We searched through the ashes. I reasoned Mike was not by the door and he sensed the danger, believing he jumped clear of the main blast. I found a bare spot a body laid among the debris. Footsteps led out of the warehouse."

"Bone and I found several men dead in a wooded area near the warehouse. Those men were in a tussle and badly hurt. They died not from other injuries. It was apparent, the gang escaping the blast was chasing after Mike. Those men in the wooded area got injured. The Leader man shot them dead. I assumed it was for a simple reason, he didn't want anything to slow him down getting to Mike. My assumption to why this leader man wanted Mike dead was possibly, he witnessed things he shouldn't have."

"We remained for the night in a shed Mike rested inside. It was Ludacris trying to follow tracks at night. A bloody rag was found in the shed by Bone. In the morning, we resumed our efforts tracking Mike. He left several bloody rags and drops of blood along his trail.

Once reaching the city, the trail led to an alley. Inside the alley, several men were found death. A fight occurred. Again, the men were killed by the same gun man."

"We hoped Mike was not involved. I noticed a windowpane was missing on the second floor in a building of the alley. Inside the room, more bloody rags. Someone changed a dressing. I followed the footprints leading out of the room leading to the roof top. I called down to Bone, to follow. Jumping across several roof tops, I saw dead bodies. Each body had a hole in them, a gunshot hole. The cause was from the same gun man."

Whoever was killing these men were leaving dead men behind. That made following Mike easy. Both Bone and I feared for Mike's life. The trailed ended on the fourth rooftop I jumped across. On another roof, men following Mike went to the street. Mike's trail finally led to the street several rooftops later."

"On the street his trail began to fade. Bone and I split up traveling on several streets parallel to the main street. We met up at a corner. Proceeding down that street, we came across a crowd of people. They were gathered around four very injured men. Each man had injuries in an unusually way. One man had both arms tied around his throat. Another, his legs tied into a knot around his throat. Whoever causing injuries to these men, was an artist. He meant to show whoever following him, it would end badly for them to continue following him."

"Not until we came to a second crowd of people, gathering on a corner with similar near deaths, did it become apparent, the message was not received with the intended affects. Four men badly injured, in four different ways. Each injury done to each man was artistly displayed. Many in the crowd spoke with a consensus, the person doing the injuries rid the area of some nasty folks. They pointed the direction that person went. The day was getting late, we fretted not be able to locate Mike."

If the man killing his men caught up to Mike, we feared the worst. We lost the trail again. We found a place to camp. The night came quick. In the morning, we stopped at a local store. Entering the store, a counter man told us, a person stopped a robbery. The gunman pointed the gun at that person. The gun went off in the gun man's mouth. The counter man was stunned, he thought the person was going to die watching the gunman turn pointing a gun into the person's face. Instead, the gun man shot in his own mouth."

"After the robbery was halted, the person, hungry, he told the counter man he had no money to buy some food. The counter man told me, he would have given him all the food he could carry."

"You know what counter man told us?" Cho paused for a second. All eyes were glued on him. "That person told the counter man to allow him to work for his food. He asked for a broom. The counter man handed him a broom, he requested. That person swept up the mess, then, mopped the blood off the floor. He gently placed a rag under the bloody skull to soak up what blood was coming a shattered jaw. Next, lifted the wounded man to a corner, tying his hands and feet. Without a word he collected two sausages and a drink, then left. The counter man was still talking, Bone and I walked out of the store. He pointed to the direction the person went. It led us to where we located the person we been following. He was lying in a bed, almost dead. We left him there."

Razor stood, "that is the most amazing thing I ever heard a person doing. The doc said, "that would have been impossible from your description of the events." What ever happened to the individual in this story; we are yet to know the outcome."

"Where did Mike go; has he been found," asked one of the female bikers, known as Lacey. Cho answered.

"Yes, he is doing better now. In a week or two, he should be up and about."

"How bad was he hurt," a biker inquired?

"The Doc said that Mike should be dead, how he was able to travel from the city back here, on foot, was unbelievable. Mike had half his face burned with most of the hair on that side singed off. There were two serious wounds to his body. One wound was deep, a metal shard impaled tightly against his small intestines. Removing the shard cause some damage. The Doc did some surgery at the cabin. Then noticed Mike's arm was dislocated. Bell and Doc reset the shoulder. Mike will remain there for several days. The Doc advised us not to move him. He can see visitors in a few days," Spoke Bone.

Cho added, "we hope to move Mike to another home. Then, anyone can visit him." Cho left out one key factor about the cabin. Thinking, "you can't see Mike at the cabin, because a spirit living there might not let you in. The cabin spirit seemed to be a guardian to Mike."

Miriam wanted to comment about the guards not able to enter the cabin. The door seemed not to open. Cho told her, "that should be kept private. He asked her to keep the cabin's peculiarities to herself, except for the leaders." She got the message. Razor made sure his wife understood the meaning. Miriam had the gift for gab. Many times, what she heard found a way into everyone's ears. Most times, Razor didn't mind. When he did, she knew to keep a lid on it. This was one of those times.

Chopper stood, asked if there was any new business. There was none. The meeting came to an end. Razor ordered drinks all around. It was a custom, after each called meeting.

That night at the cabin, after everyone ate the meal Miriam and Susan delivered, night came quick. Susan thought about what Bell said departing the cabin. The women were about to leave, Cheryl stated she will remain the night. Susan asked her to go home, but noticed her attentiveness to Mike. Every moan or sound coming from him sleeping, Cheryl quickly sought to soothe the pain. A good remedy was a soft whisper or a cold compress to his forehead. The pills the Doc administered to Mike quickly took effect.

Both women gently kissed Mike's forehead to bid goodnight before departing the cabin. Bell walked them to the door.

"Susan, have no concern for her. I will be with her, along with Cho through the night when he returns. Bone will leave soon. Remember, Chopper posted two guards to remain the night. They will have a relief at midnight."

"Okay Bell, I'm concerned she is becoming close to Mike. Considering Cho's lifestyle and Mike trained to that life, I worry for her future." Bell nodded.

Cheryl heard her mom's worries expressed to Bell at the door. They tried to speak soft but not soft enough. The cabin had a way of echoing sounds about the room. It was a one room cabin with a table, four chairs, bed, and shelves for food and nit-knacks. The only stove was the pot belly oven used for cooking and warming the cabin. Sound had no place to be drown out.

The car turned around in the front yard driving cautiously back down the path to the clubhouse road. Once the car turned onto the road, Bone reminded Bell, "keep the cabin locked. I decided to go to the house to make my report. Cho should be on his way back, soon." With that said, Bone walked out straddling his Bike. Before Bone revved his bike, he reminded the guards, you two make sure you stay alert. We still got those bombers to fret about. They might try again."

Both guards told Bone, "we got it covered." Bone waved bye and left. Thirty minutes past slowly with Bell and Cheryl tentatively standing vigilant by Mike's bed. Outside was a different matter. Two men silently watched a biker depart on a bike from the cabin. One man had a rifle, the other toted a pistol. Each was wearing night vision goggles. Slowly, they made their way down the path.

One of their bomber sentries was posted to keep watch on the clubhouse, he noticed all the traffic took this path both armed men were sneaking down. The leader commanded, "if that kid, who killed several of their men was there, take in out." Both assassins halted in the cover of trees spotting two guards in front of a cabin. The rifle man kept his sight aimed at both guards. The other man with the pistol had a world's series baseball bat in his empty hand. Silently, the bat man made his way up the path. Neither guard could see past the light the cabin emitted. Ten feet separated the guards from the bat man. Quickly, he slipped up to the side of the cabin. One guard thought he heard a sound.

The other guard reassured him, "it's the night playing tricks on you, either that or this spooky cabin with all the strange goings on was making them noises." It didn't matter much. One man fell from a bullet to his chest. No sound was heard. The rifle man had a silencer attached to the muzzle. The second guard heard his companion fall. He turned reaching down to a shadowy figure that was his friend, his lights went out. The bat made a soft thud connecting to the back of his head. Both guards were removed, no obstacles remained, both men thought. The rifle man came running up the path to the cabin.

One man jokingly bowed, offering the door to his partner to be the first to enter. "You may have the prize," he said softly. Bat man took the handle turning the knob attempting to open the door. It didn't turn. The sound from his third attempt alerted the women inside the cabin.

"Shh Cheryl," Bell motioned. The doorknob creaked a tiny bit. Bell heard the faint sound. Mister Casper wrote on the wall. Someone bad. Again, the knob turned. This time, both women could see the slow turn of the knob. Bell softly spoke, "Cheryl it not the guards. They were told, knock three times every time they want to speak to us. No knock, it meant they were not their guards."

Cheryl tensed to the prospects someone at the cabin, coming to attack them. Bell sensed the fear Cheryl was having.

"Cheryl remember your training," Bell whispered. Then took hold of her hand. To each other surprise, another messaged appeared over Mike's bed.

"No one will harm you."

Bell squeezed Cheryl's hand reading the words. Cheryl whispered to Bell, "the spirit in the cabin has been looking after Mike. Bone told me, Cho saw the spirit come charging out of the cabin the night Mike was here. Three men came to kill him."

Bell looked oddly at Cheryl. Thinking, I heard some things, but that, it was the first time I was am hearing about a spirit actually attacking that night Chopper took the bodies to the cave. No one was told about the spirit aiding Cho or Mike. All we knew, they took out three men at the cabin, they had to stash away. Mike told Cho about the cave. That is all Cho said, nothing more than a cave was near the cabin to dispose of the bodies."

On the fourth attempt to open the cabin door, the door swung open. Two men quickly entered. Bell had positioned herself on the opposite side of the door's swing. Cheryl remained by Mike, near the floor by the bed. That position Cheryl offered the best protection from the immediate sight of the two men. Bell and Cheryl hadn't counted on either of the interlopers wearing night vision goggles.

The house reacted. The lantern suddenly burst forth a bright light. The brightness of the light stung the men wearing the goggles. Both hesitated. Bell swung a pot at the head of the first man entering the cabin. It made contact but not enough to stop him. He staggered several feet awkwardly toward the bed. His friend came in behind pot slapped bat man. Bell struck him with a round house kick to his face. He went flying out the door. The first man recovered from the pot and quickly turned to face Bell.

Bell prepared for his attack. Cheryl stood kicking his lower back shoving him into Bell. The second man outside got to his feet rushing back in the cabin when the bat man slammed into Bell.

Bat man held his bat high, while grabbing hold of Bell's neck. Cheryl stopped suddenly. The pistol man, also referred to as bat man aimed his gun at her. Both ladies fought well. The pistol man aimed at Cheryl; his friend was about to finish Bell. Both of the intruders saw Mike lying on the bed. Their prize was asleep. From his appearance, the prize wouldn't offer any resistance. Rifle man slapped Bell with the butt end of his rifle then sighted on Mike. Bell laid on the cabin floor unable to stop either man. Both women knew, they were going to die and nothing could prevent the two assassins from killing them all.

Mister Casper acted. A faint light appeared between Cheryl and the pistol man. The light grew with intensity, quickly. A man floated in the light. He was old having a beard. Both men turned watching the spirit hold out his arms. The light kept growing brighter. Both assassins squinted their eyes, then shielded them with their free hands.

Pistol man aka, bat man, couldn't squeeze the trigger. Bat man's arm holding the bat, felt a strong tug. The bearded floating man grabbed him. His hands felt icy cold on Bat man's arm. The bat was pulled from his grip. It hovered over his head; then quickly came down splitting batman's face open. Blood spewed everywhere.

The rifle man pointed his gun at Mister Casper. That was all he could do, point the rifle. It too was torn from his grip, like the bat from his friend. A shiver of fear ran up the spine of rifle man. He saw what happened to his friend. He felt the blood spray across his face. Some of the blood went in his mouth. He had enough time to spit it out. Then, a most unexpected thing happened, he watched the bearded man drop his rifle.

Dropping the rifle stunned second assassin. That was not what he expected. Seeing his rifle on the floor gave him relief. He assumed the rifle was going to be aimed and fired at him. Suddenly, it dawned on him to pick it up.

The rifle laid several feet from Bell's. Bell was on her feet, then seeing an opportunity quickly jumped, tucked, and rolled on the ground. She grabbed the rifle on her way to her feet. Bell was seriously tempted to shoot the scoundrel but held her trigger finger in check. She realized; they had not found out who the bombers were. Now, they had someone to question.

Cheryl walked out the door to check on the guards. One guard appeared dead, the other was hurt, but not dead. Going back inside, reported to Bell her findings.

"Okay bud, you sit in the corner." Bell pointed the gun to the place for the man to sit. Just give me one reason and that ghost will come back. You saw what he can do."

No sooner than the man sat down, Cho walked in. He quickly assesses the situation. Then, walked over to the rifle man. Bending down, Cho put his face, nose to nose with him.

"Who sent you, commanded Cho?"

"Go to hell, replies pistol man's reply. He was impolite. It wasn't what he said to Cho, "go to hell," but the rude replied saying it to Cho. One thing Cho would not abide, was rudeness. With his fore finger, Cho taps the pistol man where he had Mr. Peabody, then his boss Mr. Howell, the movie man from Hollywood. Pistol man remain in intense pain until every question from the leaders were satisfied, several hours later.

Cho turned back to Bell, "I am impressed Bell. To take on two men with guns is difficult enough for most men but to do so fast, without them getting off one shot was amazing." Cho was about to continue to laud Bell with praise. Bell had to stop him.

"Cho all that praise, which I am thankful for was not all my doings. Cheryl told me about the spirit, the night you and Mike fought three men at the river in front of the cabin. She said, "a bright light came charging out the door surrounding the men. Well, that light did the same again. This time, the light had form. It looked like a man floating in the air. He took the bat from that man on the floor with the bleeding face, whacking him on his head.

Cho kneel down to inspect the Bat man's face. The bat was by his side. His face was busted open starting at the bridge of his nose or what was left of a nose. It was so flattened; his face had a smooth without any contour. The split ran both up and down from that point. It appeared similar to the scene in the Ten Commandments, when the Red Sea parted.

Bell observe Cho inspecting Bat man's face. Once he finished, she took up where she stopped. "The spirit took the pistol out of bat man pointing at the other man in the corner. I thought the spirit was going to shoot the man with the gun. Instead, the ghost dropped the gun on the ground. I dived for the gun and that is when, you entered the cabin."

"Hmm, still you did well this night, Bell. Looking at Cheryl he noticed the disheveled looked on her. You did well this night Cheryl. You, okay?"

"Yes, thank you, Master Cho."

Cho picked up the no contour face man without a nose and placed him beside the rifle man in the corner of the cabin. Cho went outside, lifted the guard still breathing into the cabin. Bell tended to him. Bell covered the guard with a spare blanket, then turned to Cho.

"He has a concussion. He will live. Leave him on the floor covered. It is a small bump to his noggin."

Cho went back outside to tend to the guard Cheryl said was dead. He wasn't dead. Cho felt for a pulse. He found one. Quickly called to Bell. Bell coming out the door saw Cho with the guard's head cradled in his hands. She knew the guard was still alive. Cho gave her a signal, he done in the past to indicate whether a person was dead or alive. Cheryl went to see what all the commotion was about. Bell quickly told Cheryl she was mistaken about the guard.

"Cheryl, the guard lives. Go back inside; get my first aid kit."

The kit was near the door. Returning outside, Cheryl handed the kit to Bell. With a skill learned through all the times tending to bikers injuries, she stopped the bleeding.

"Master Cho, the bullet went clean through. It missed every organ. He was lucky," Bell replied, amazed looking at the wounded biker guard.

Cheryl stood there holding her breath. She started to say to Bell and Cho how sorry, she was. He could have died out here, if Master Cho didn't come out to check on him. She kept silent.

Rifle man started to stand and take his chance at escaping. The strange light reappeared before he could get to both feet. He sat back down. The light dim slowly fading away.

Bell stood and walked over to Cheryl. She was upset. Cheryl saw the frown on her face. "Cheryl, this is not your fault. Holding her shoulders, Bell looked into her teary eyes. With a tenderly voice her mother uses told Cheryl, "I have made this mistake so many times, it sickens me today. When I make a determination on a wound; I fret making that mistake all the time."

Cheryl felt better, "this will always haunt me, Bell."

Bell replied," it should Cheryl, it is a horrible lesson to learn. You learned that lesson and the man lived." Bell lowers her head; a memory came into her mind. A memory of the first time a person died. When she made the wrong determination. It is a scar, she lived with every day."

Cho sent for help; he was hesitant to leave the women alone. The pistol man wasn't going to be any problem. He just hated to leave them alone. The guard was coming to. He was dizzy. Bell made him stay on the floor.

"Look someone needs to go and inform the house. I can go, but." Cheryl interrupted Cho. "I will go Master Cho. I need to do something."

"Okay Cheryl, can you drive a car, Bell asked, not waiting for Master Cho to get his answer from Cheryl.

OZ

Bell handed Cheryl the keys. Cho lifted the guard into his arms. Cheryl opened the car door and drove off with the wounded guard. Cho returned to the cabin. Soon, the whole area was flooded with bikers. Chopper came jumping off his bike running into the house. Seeing Bell relieved his fears but not his anger. Once his eyes spotted the pistol man, Cho had to stop him from ripping him to bits.

"Chopper, Chopper cool down, think," Cho said.

Chopper didn't care, all he wanted was that man's neck. Cho finally had to persuade him, the way he knew how too. Chopper was gently assisted out the door by Cho. Anyone seeing the two thought they were coming out to discuss a plan. Instead, Cho nerve pinched, forced Chopper out the door. He wanted Chopper to save face. Once outside, the two stared down at each other. He was mad at Cho for stopping him.

Cho gave Chopper his quirky grin. That grin always brought a smile to his face. Chopper was determined to not smile at Cho's silly grin. It was too hard not to. All the years Cho had done that stupid grin, it made him smile. It calmed Chopper and he smiled. Cho released his pinch.

"Chopper, you know I am right, think of the others and maybe this man can stop us being attacked. We can't afford to lose this opportunity. You are our leader, if you are so bent on tearing him up, I will not stop you. I just wanted to give you time to think, before you act in a way you wished someone would have stopped you."

"I know you are right, damn, this makes me mad. Cho, by hell and high water, we are getting back at these guys."

Inside, rifle man was lifted over a biker's shoulder, then placed on back of a bike. The bat smashed face man was tied to another biker. Both were taken to the clubhouse. Bone stayed the night with two new guards at the cabin.

Chopper discussed the situation with Cho. "Cho, the women, Susan has spoken to me. She and Miriam think Mike staying in the cabin is not the best way to care for him."

Cho answered, "yes, they are right, but considering what happened this night, the same might happen at their homes. Out here is secluded. I will remain along with Bone and maybe one guard."

"Yes, and Cheryl, Bell, Susan, and Miriam, not including any other woman wanting to care for him, Cho. This place will become a Mecca for all those mothers," Chopper remarked.

"Yes, that will have to be addressed. You are very good at those kinds of tasks, Chopper. When Mike is better, we need to continue his training at the cabin, until he is fully healed."

"That's your specialty, Cho."

"When Mike is ready, Rita will come to continue his Spanish lessons, survivalist Darwin will begin training, teaching Mike bow and arrows making, also to chip flint and other fire-starting skills. When he is on his feet, staff training will begin. First, with a wooden bo, then with a lead pipe, and finally with a weighted lead pipe. This will be a good time for him to practice weapons training. Stick fighting, archery, and most of all, further training of my art in private."

Chopper knew how important this was to Cho and gladly supported his privacy with Mike. No one was allowed anywhere near the cabin during that time.

SCHOOLDAYS

In the morning, Mike awoke and hungry. Bell arrived early. Susan and Cheryl soon followed Bell into the cabin. Most of the men were told to wait outside.

Quickly breakfast was warmed. The aroma filled the air around the cabin. All the guards were hungry and wanted a warm cup of coffee. That was the one thing Mike had none in his pantry. It made for a long night for the guards.

Coffee was the first serving distributed to everyone. Cheryl had that chore. Eagerly hands fought for the mugs of hot joe. One guard nearly decked the other for the first cup Cheryl handed out. A cold mist settled on the cabin as the sun rose. Most of the biker guards came ill prepared for the chilly night. When Cheryl walked out the door holding the cups of hot coffee that was the cause for the near fight between the guards.

After two trips to refill each guard's cups, they finally felt much warmer. Each guard requested permission to step inside to warm themselves and to see Mike. Truly Cheryl thought the latter was the main reason. It was a good excuse.

Breakfast went to the guards on duty first. Next, was Mike and Cho. Bone was asked to make the rounds outside before eating. The real reason was for everyone to get fed first. Penny came, she brought Bone his special breakfast. It was to be a surprise for him.

Penny called to Bone before entering the cabin. Upon hearing her shout, Bone made a bee line straight back to the cabin. His eyes met with hers, just for a short time, then his nose got a wisp of her basket's aroma. It was an extra-large basket filled with a pound of bacon, half a package of sausages, five fried eggs, six buttered biscuits with grape jelly. It was just enough to sate him until noon.

Bone reached for his goodies and just as quick, Penny pulled the basket away from his grasp. Bone looked like a sickly dog denied a bone. Penny was adamant, "you know the rule," she said with a commanding voice. Bone bent down, grabbed her in his massive arms, and gave her a loving kiss.

Breakfast ended, the new guards came, replacing the night guards. They too, were denied entry into the house. They attempted to open the door without permission from the persons inside. It wasn't their decision to give, it was Mister Casper choice, who was allowed in or not. Everyone inside became acutely aware of this fact new change to the cabin.

This ghost seemed perfectly willing to be known. Most ghost rarely were seen. You go to a supposedly haunted house and no ghost. Not in this cabin. Even the kids coming to the cabin never returned, because of the appearance of a ghost.

Most of the guards thought the people inside, didn't want them inside of the cabin. Quickly, that thought altered when left at the cabin alone, with Mike. They attempted to enter the cabin to check on Mike and the door wouldn't open. They were told, the door was unlocked. The door only opened, when it decided Mike needed checking.

It didn't take long for the word to get around. Every biker knew about the ghost. The guard in the house of the night two gunmen coming heard Bell discuss the actions of this ghost, with Cho. A bright glowing light appeared, there was a man floating within the light. Now, most bikers were satisfied to remain outside and reluctantly went inside, when the door opened.

On the second day back, Mike was already practicing early in the morn before the sun rose. By 7 A.M. he completed bo twirling drills with his one good arm. The other arm was sore, so he practiced for half the time with the good arm. Cho required Mike to do his drills even injures. Three hours pass, Mike felt t tiredness come upon him. It normally took the whole day hard practicing to make him sweat.

Pistol man came by the cabin dropping off weapons for Mike to clean. Mad man sent manuals to study. Chemistry of various explosives and how to make them. By breakfast, Rita showed with Cheryl and Bell. After eating his meal, Rita and had him practicing Spanish. Cheryl joined the class. Every day after Rita ended class, she would help Mike practice Spanish. Noon came and Cho followed. Everyone was required to leave, including Cheryl.

"Sifu Cho, would it be okay to teach Cheryl some skills I learned, not any of the special training, you and I share?"

Cho studied Mike for a minute, before answering his question. "Mike, she would be acceptable to me for you to train."

"Sifu, before you totally agree, I should tell you, the other kids Marcus was training, no longer have an instructor. Cheryl asked me if they could also attend my training with her?"

"Mike my son, you are aware of our skills and why would you ever think it is necessary to ask me for permission. My trust and faith in you is the upmost. You must promise me though your training will not be affected with this extra time for those kids."

"That goes unsaid, father Cho."

"Besides Mike, it might work out better than expected, training the kids. They do need training for protection, and can help you, as training partners. Many bikers are hesitant of late, practicing with you. After the stories heard, and all their injuries acquired, we are running out of people for you to practice with. For the time being, we will practice much together. There is one question needing answered."

"Yes, father Cho, what is it," Mike asked?

When Bone and I followed your tracks, searching for you, you left behind many men with contorted body racked in agony. I do believe from their expressions, you used one of the pressures points I have not taught you?

"Oh, I dreamed of this map of the body and you leaving the warehouse. I couldn't remember much at the time. I was in pain and felt my pursuers would catch up to me, in my weakened state. I saw you many times strike a man in my dreams at a particular point. At the first opportunity, I tried it. I am truly sorry if this offended you, Father. I was not myself."

"Mike, no explanation is required or an apology from you. You did what was needed. I am glad, you had the skill to properly use it. Your safety is far more important to me, than anything you did. Always remember, you are first in my heart."

"As are you in my heart always, father."

"Your training is progressing far ahead of schedule. Soon, you and I will be one. I do have one other thing needing doe. I feel this will not sit well with you."

Mike looked at Cho, "what could it be he thought? Considering all the things he been putting me through, nothing could be that bad?"

"Mike, I am afraid you will need to improve your diet. The training will require you to be in better shape. All that fried chicken, potatoes, pizzas, etc. will need to end."

Mike's mouth dropped open. It was worse than what he thought. "No fried chicken, ever?"

"Well not forever, but not too often."

"Cho, I'm afraid to ask, what will I be eating, then?"

"For starters Mike, eggs, fruits, nuts, vegetables, rice. Your meats will include fish and white meats. So, you see, you can still eat chicken. Just not fried for the time being. One more thing, not any sweets."

"Dang!"

Cho walked over picking up the bo with a sligh smile across his face. "Now, show me your skill with this bo;" throwing the bo to Mike. Mike started to twirl the bo; Cho tells Mike to strike at him. "If you can touch me, then your turn to evade my bo, will not be needed." A smirk crossed Mike's face. "Mike, why is there a strange look on your face?"

"Father, you know that will never happen, why tease me?"

"There is always that possibility, my son." Mike knew that wouldn't happen, at least not while Cho was still living. Mike just accepted the hurt coming when Cho used the bo on him.

By the setting the sun, Bell stopped by the cabin. She took from the car Mike's suit he wore at Stephen and Teddy Bears service.

"Mike, in the morning, after your breakfast please change. Oh, by the way, Cho informed me of your new diet."

"You mean, no bacon and fried eggs?"

"Why, how did you know? Oatmeal and boiled eggs, it will be good. Cho said, "it would go down better with cinnamon," Mike.

On this day Mike had full use of his bad arm. It was still black and blue but little to no pain. Doc dropped by to examine his wounds. "Bells been keeping the bandages changed." He was pleased with Mike progress. "Doc, about my face, Mike asked?"

"Mike, the burns are not permanent. They will take time to heal, be patient."

Morning came; Bell was at the cabin. Cheryl and Susan arrived with Penny in tow. Cho showed a little later, he and Bone riding their bikes. Bone came inside, Mike eating from a large bowl of oatmeal. Mike looked up at Bone; his eyes begging Bone to take the oatmeal for his breakfast.

Bone looked back at Mike, "with a no way in Hades little buddy. I wouldn't touch that gruel for all the bacon in Georgia." It sunk in; Bone's face twisted in a disgusted manner. Even Bone had limitations to what he would eat. Oatmeal was on that list, never to eat. Cho sat at the table watching Mike eat the oatmeal; with cinnamon added.

The ladies stepped outside for Mike to change into his formal attire. Entering, Cheryl and Bell spoke at the same time how handsome he looked. Cho was in his uniform quickly and Bone, nearly didn't complete his change when they ladies came back in.

Cho told Mike, he and Bone had to leave to be part of the honor guard. Mike had difficulties combing his hair. Little had grown back. Susan tie his tie. Bell brought over a compact. Once Susan ended tying the bow, she took Bell's compact applying a cosmetic layer over Mike's burns on his face. All the women giggled watching Mike get a make-over. The men couldn't wait until they were alone with Mike to tease him.

Mike rode with the women. The service was the same as for the others. The only exception, Marcus had no family present. Mike felt more alone, than ever since coming to Atlanta. Seeing Marcus without family brought home, the life Mike stepped into.

After the service, all attended the supper. Mike looked at the wonderful foods he could not eat. Thinking, only if Cho waited another day. Cho walked over to Mike, "you eat all you want today, remember, tomorrow this food will become a past pleasure."

Mike ate everything he saw. He left off the fried foods. No exception, when it came to the sweets. Sitting along Mike side was Cheryl. Mike told her, "Cho gave his permission for their training."

"Cheryl, I will teach you and the others, three days a week. Training will be the same time, at six in the morning."

"Why so early, Mike?"

"I figure, if any kid truly wants to learn, they would be here early in the morning. A time they rather be in bed sleeping. Also, Cheryl make sure they run to the cabin and not ride or walk. Any who show riding in a car or bike, whatever, will be turned around that day. I don't care if it is raining out. Run! If any miss three days, they will be dismissed and not allowed to return to training. I haven't the time, nor the inclination to baby sit them."

In the morning, Mike stood outside the cabin, after his own practicing ended. He ate his breakfast Bell and Cheryl brought for him. Every day, it was the same meal, except with different women arriving with Bell and Cheryl. Soon, seven kids arrived shortly after him finishing his meal.

Five kids Mike knew were Cheryl's friends. Lou, Liddea, Bobby, Macy, and Skip came running up the path. Each one was panting from their run. After several minutes, Mike figured they were all that were coming. Two approached the cabin trying to run, but made only a few steps and walked over to the others.

"Well, all that panting will soon be in the past. Now follow me. I have not had my run."

Twenty-five minutes later, Mike stood at the cabin waiting for the rest of the kids. Cheryl barely made the first of the three appearing by him. Fifteen minutes passed, all finally showed up. Mike looked at the faces, he saw seven kids not quitting.

Thinking, Mike said to himself, "tomorrow will tell the tale. Okay, your first lesson is learning to breath. After ten minutes of breathing exercises, Mike began their warmups. Stretching followed by sit-ups, push-ups, jumping jacks, etc.; the basic types of normal exercises. Then to kicking, punching, and blocking drills.

After Mike made his assessments, he had all of them sit in a circle around him. "What I teach you from now on, is not the same things you learned from Marcus. Marcus taught you the primary ways in most martial arts. I will be training you very differently. Your training will be hard, your bodies will be in pain, constantly. Some training will be the same thing over and over. I will prepare your bodies for what will come later. This is the opportunity you need to consider, before returning tomorrow. There will be no second chances after this day. You return, good, you don't, good. I will not waste my time on those lacking desire to endure training."

The next day, all seven returned. The same drill followed the first day, run, breathing, warmups, punches, kicks, and blocks. The next day all seven came back. Each had weights to wear on their arms and feet. Then, the drills began. Each day, the training drills got harder. Mike practiced with them. Everything he had them do, he did.

"Power for your strikes come from your breath, your stance, your mind and will. Each blow will be done, until it is the only blow necessary to stop your opponents. From this day forward, you will strike at the board with no more than ten inches away. All strikes against the board with the same distance. All kicks and blocks as well. I will assess your speed and power with your drills. Remember, when you punch, kick, block, each movement requires many smaller movements. A block is not simply a rotation of your arm in an arch. It requires many smaller movements of other muscles for effectiveness. Each other smaller movement adds to the total of the block. A block can be as deadly as a punch or kick."

"A punch is more than what you were trained to do. When you punch, use your hips stepping forward along with the shoulders, elbows, wrists of the fist. We practice slowly until each muscle can be used, you can feel every muscle do its part, in the punch. Breath out at impact. Your mind does the same as the muscles. Without your mind involved, then it is merely a punch, no more, no less."

"Preparation of the mind in battle will decide the outcome. You learn to control your body and then you learn to control your opponent's body. You learn to control your thoughts, and you will learn to control your opponent's thoughts. Focus your mind on your opponent. Feel, what he is feeling, breathe, as he is breathing, tense, as he tenses, this you will learn. Then, you will learn to control his actions and not him controlling yours."

"Movement makes for a hard target, standing still is an easy target. Seeing movement is better, than being seen moving by your opponent. Learn to be pliable in your movement every day, not just in practice. Flow and become fluid with each step, each breath, and each thought. To think, is wasted time, it should be natural in all things you do."

Mike has one of his kids stand next to him. Then Mike places his hand on the kid's shoulder telling the kid to punch him. The kid did so. Mike easily evaded the punch. Again, and again, Mike had the kid try and hit him. Each time Mike placed his hand on a different part of the kid's body. Each time, the kid could never touch Mike.

"Now, let me explain this thing I performed. When you touch a person and he tried to strike at you, you can feel his movement. My hand on one side of his body felt Bobby' shoulder pull away. When one part of the body pulls away, the other side is pushing at you. The same is true whether Bobby had punched, kicked, or attempted any other attack at me. I want everyone to pair off. Today, and until I tell you, this will be a part of your regular drills. Once you mastered this exercise, I will introduce how to do the same without touching your man."

By the end of the first week after services for Marcus, a meeting was called. Mike had healed quickly with his practicing and new diet. Cho noticed the changes. He noticed Mike's skill levels increased more so, with his instructing the kids.

At the meeting, Mike was invited. This was a rare thing for him. He never attended meetings. They were strictly for full pledged members. Mike knew he was a member, but didn't realized he was a full member until this meeting. Cho drove him on the back of his bike, to the house.

Chopper, Razor, Jack knife all met the two by the door entering the clubhouse. Both were asked to sit at the table with the other leaders. Mike felt this was fabulous, but feared it might offend others in the club longer than him.

Months ago, a vote was casted concerning Mike's roll in the club. Every man voted to make a special exceptions to his status. Mike was to be allowed a special status as a leader but without the full authority coming with the special status. He was to be obeyed, only on special operations his and Cho's talents were needed. Cho insisted on this. It was necessary to have this authority for Mike in those operations. After the Atlanta bombing and Mike's incredible journey, this was made apparent to all, what Cho requested Mike's status be given. Today, at the meeting, Mike's status was stated with his sitting at the table. The discussion concerned the house's bombing incident.

Cho stood and presented the facts. "This gang is called the Black Tigers, they run drugs in the city. They appear to be a powerful gang dealing drugs. Mike's interference weeks ago, prevented three of our children from being killed. Later, several other kids Mike happened to come across in a similar situation." What I learned, the original Atlanta gang, we encountered was their main rival. That ended, after we wasted them. Since that time, they been expanding their territories into the Atlanta Gang's territories. They happened to be near our house, as I speak. Bone and I went through their turf, trailing Mike back here from the city. We got several men watching, while they scout outside our house. Two of their scouts have been monitoring us for two weeks. We knew about the men watching our clubhouse. The attack at the cabin was something, we did not expect. This cabin is well hidden and from what I believe, was by accident, they discovered. Too many people were making their way on the path to the cabin. Apparently, the scout took notice. This led several men following our bikes. That night, they attacked Mike and both women."

"The two men captured that night happily informed us of this lucky opportunity they received. They acted quickly, not understanding the full implication of their actions. The leader of their gang figured, it would be a quick in and out kill before anyone became the wiser to their mission."

"The main man in the Black Tigers is surrounded by a dozen guards at his manor. The manor has tall concrete walls surrounding the fortress. One way in, it's through a double guarded gate with scanners. There are motion cameras lining the walls and in the trees. Large dogs are let lose at night. One of our scouts watched several men dig holes on three sides in the lawn. We believe them to be mines. It is apparent, they want no uninvited guest." One Rider spoke, that means we can't go in mass. No one answered. Cho continued his findings.

"The traffic entering the compound is set at a schedule. No unannounced visitors are let in. They got money and resources. Some of the sources are American law and politicians connected with some over sea big shots. We are ascertaining information on all of them. Currently, the situation is quickly deteriorating. I believe, they plan on a quick and deadly assault on this house and the neighborhood. Our family will be in danger, if we do not act soon."

"Thanks Cho," Jack Knife stood, facing all the bikers present saying, "the plan is in motion. Turning to Cho, he asked, "are Mike and you ready?" Mike was startled hearing he was involved. He kept a straight face, holding back his emotions. Cho saw the rise in his breathing.

Cho thinking, maybe I should have prepped him before coming here." Then Cho changed his mine. "No, Mike needs to be prepared on a moment's notice. On our trip to the compound, there be time enough to bring him in on my plan. His training will be enough for preparation."

The next day, Cho stopped at the cabin; his usual routine before breakfast. The women always prepared two meals for the two of them. Cheryl was there, along with Susan. Susan was aware of Mike's stipulation for his students to run to the cabin. Cheryl always followed her mom running behind the car. Even on the days there was no class.

Bobby's mom came with Susan to ask Mike over for supper. Her real reason was to check on how Mike was training her son. She noticed his hands were bruised and sometimes bloody, as were all Mike's students.

Cho asked the ladies for some privacy after breakfast. Most of them cleaned and left in the car. Cheryl came on Mike's bike and stayed behind, outside by the door. This was one of the few days she rode the bike to the cabin.

"Mike, this night we will leave for the compound. This is the plan Jack knife spoke at the meeting. You and I will sneak into the compound. Our job is simple. We are to take out as many of the guards and disable all cameras and sensing devices."

"Mike, your training has come to an end for now. You have mastered many of the skills there is to learn. You will continue to develop your abilities and other trainings the club has for you. I am made proud. You will be an excellent heir to me and my father legacy. Tonight, is not a time to give mercy to our enemy. This enemy is intent to kill us and our families. They are evil and exist solely for power, pleasure, and wealth. The means to their goals does not matter to them."

"There is good and there is bad in this world. Given enough time, people may be led from the bad, to become good. Time is not what we have plenty of. They chose their paths, as we have chosen ours. When a cancer is in the body, we cut it out. Tonight, we cut the cancer out."

Cheryl stood by the door to close and accidently listened in on the conversation. She was aware it was not proper and had every intention step away, until she overheard their plan. A tiny sound made inside was amplified outside, when the door was left opened. Many people were not aware of this fact. Cheryl happened on that discovery by accident the night two men attacked the cabin. Standing outside, she overheard the conversation her mom was having with Cho, concerning Mike's condition.

Both Cho and Mike felt a strange awareness to a presence nearby. Mike walked over to the cabin's door opening it wide, quickly. Cheryl was standing by the bike until the meeting ended. Mike thought, maybe her presence was why Cho and he felt an awareness of someone.

Cho told Mike, "be ready when I returned. Also, Mike, cancel your supper with Bobby's family." Cho walked by Cheryl nodding his head, straddled his bike speeding away.

After Cho rode off, Cheryl saw her opportunity. She decided to pry some intel she overheard between Master Cho and Mike. Mike met her at the front door. Something was up. He knew Cheryl well enough to know, when she had something on her mind.

"So, Mike, what up with Cho being so secretly?

Cheryl, you know full well, I cannot discuss the club's business."

"I ain't asking for you to tell me their business, all I am asking is if there another event coming."

"Well, I guess there is no harm in telling you, there is a new event coming soon. That all. So, don't make a big deal out of what you think is going down. It's just another small task Cho wants me to accompany him on. You know, to learn from watching him. Just training for me."

Cheryl thinking to herself, "hmm, just training my butt. This night I'm going to follow along. I could use some training myself."

Mike saw Cheryl's smirk creeping across her face and had second thoughts on what he said to her. Maybe she overheard Cho and my conversation. Even if she did, she knows better than to go and blab the news around." Mike pondered with his concerns, before asking Cheryl to show him how to ride the bike.

"Well silly, hop on and watch me drive over to Bobby's family. You best tell them the news in person."

"Huh," Mike was startled hearing Cheryl take him to Bobby's family. Cho told him to cancel the meal. "Hmm, how did Cheryl know I was going to do that?"

Cheryl quickly realized her slip and immediately responded with a follow up about the meal. "Mike, Bobby's mom wants me to bring you over for a discussion, after you and Cho finished. She is concerned with his training. Bobby had been coming home with bruises and bloody hands."

Mike felt a bit uneasy. "Cheryl quick explanation fit her not knowing the truth for tonight and her ease dropping on our conversation."

At Bobby's house, several mothers were attending. Bobby's mom was going to inquire in the morning her concerns. Cho's sudden request for them to leave, had her change her mind. When the women left the cabin, she took time to tell Cheryl to bring Mike over. Arriving at Booby's home, both Cheryl and Mike are met at the front door. Cheryl asked Bobby's mom, if she could remain with Mike. "It is private," she replied. Cheryl made a good point; I have to drive Mike to Madd's house for training. She was invited inside. Most of the questions the mothers centered around, Why their children have sores and bruises coming from practice. They never had those injuries while training with Marcus.

Mike had a good explanation for each mother's concern they addressed to him. "Let me explain, I teach them to survive, not just to fight. We have some serious problems in the area. Several of your children may not be alive right now. What I teach them is to prepare them for real life occurrences. If you feel this is too dangerous and my training methods are wrong, then remove your child from my training class. I will not train anyone who does not have your approval." Mike waited for a response. None was given.

"I guarantee right now, your children can deal with the next time, they are attacked. If you feel they do not need this training and you can protect them without my assistance is your choice. Once they stop training, I will not accept them back."

The women spoke for several minutes among themselves. After an hour passed, they decided to have their children continue training. How could any not want their child to be safe. They are in a club wrought with danger was advocated by all. Unknowing to all the mothers their softly spoken comments were easily heard by Mike.

Cho reported to Chopper after leaving Mike and Cheryl at the cabin. At the clubhouse, Mike's training the children was discussed. Cho responded, "he is doing a great job."

Chopper said, "I am aware of his teaching progress. From all aspects, he is doing a great job. Our wives seemed concerned. Bell had a discussion with them and told them to speak with Mike. Bell reminded them all of their unique lifestyle in this club. Marcus was asked to train the children for any situations. He did a great job;

Mike is adding to that training. Remember how his training saved many of your children recently. Just think if your child had a tiny part of that skill, it was Bell's reply to those mother's concerns."

Jack knife went over the manor's terrain on this new threat asking Cho, "how can we best assist you and Mike?"

"Jack, your task is; secure all entries and exits for escape. Be prepared for a copter landing. From our intel, a helicopter was seen landing within the manor's compound. Keep hidden. We will set off their mines and few of ours. Mike is at Madd's lab collecting timers. When you hear them go off, Mike and I should have the compound secured. Most of the guards should be dead."

Chopper stands, "the front gate will blow at the same time of the explosions. We move in quick."

Razor stands, "make sure you have vests on and plenty of ammo. We are going to make one hell of a statement. If anyone surrenders, gather all into the main room. No one, this night will leave the house, unless we tell you otherwise. Remember, our family lives are at risk. They have the intentions to rid the area of us. They want to establish their power base. We are preventing that from happening. If one man gets away and contacts their backers, it can go bad.

Waiting for any questions, Razor begins explaining the second half of the plan. "We have discovered who, the police contacts are, and the only politician involved. This information discovered will be exposed to the public. Cho will do a follow up, when the time is right. Tonight, we will have our eyes and ears glued on manor compound."

Once the meeting ended, Chopper pulls Cho, Mike, Razor, and Jack aside. That politician is going to screw everything we do this night. Razor, contact the Director. We got to nix what we can, now, before this gets big. No body is going to like that.

THE MANORHOUSE

Darkness was a key for Cho and Mike's entry into the compound. The night provided the proper conditions. No stars and moon could pierce the clouds that blanketed the sky.

Mike was first to assail up over the wall. Quickly running across the street jumping unto the trunk of a tree by the wall. From the trunk, he ricocheted over the concrete wall. Not once did any part of his body came close to touching it. Softly, Mike landed on the grass in a crouched position. He waited until Cho had done the same. Both squatted peering across the wooded area. Cho watched Mike carefully attempting to assess if his injuries gave him trouble. Nothing was seen to persuade him Mike was unfit to complete the mission.

The woods were dense with underbrush. It offered a difficult terrain for any to cross, but not for Cho and Mike. Both of them made only a few yards before coming to a sudden stop. Each felt the sensors nearby. Some were lasers and others were cameras. Mike realigned the lasers and Cho took on the cameras. Each knew where to walk to avoid being seen. Cho set a timer with explosive to each camera.

After each device was set, Cho and Mike crept slowly toward the lawn. Mines had been planted from their information. It was easy to avoid setting them off. It was like a cold spot existed under their feet coming close to a mine. A little white paint was sprayed over each mine giving notice to others. A clear path was visible to the bikers where to step. One timer was left behind. "Each mine is planted close together. One goes off, all will go off," Mike signaled Cho

Cho whispered to Mike, "amateurs."

Cho pointed for Mike to follow along the lawn to the house. Three guards were walking along the edge. Bushes were nearby. Mike

245

quickly crawled to the house, then leaped up onto a tree. He swung to another tree making his way through the branches getting within range to make a leap. From the tree, he flipped onto a lower limb near one of the guards. His foot redirected the guard's head 360 degrees around. Before the second guard turned to return to his position, Mike was waiting. With the guard's gun and hat worn, standing in the position, Mike waited for the second guard.

Before realizing the guard was not the same man; Mike shoved the rifle under his chin. His chin went up, then back, then down, it dangled long enough to keep the third guard becoming suspicious. Then fell to the ground with a thump. The thump came after Mike met the third guard.

The third guard saw Mike advance, he knew it wasn't one of the two guards this night. He saw Mike running at him. It was a kid running toward him. Why was a kid on this compound running at me, he thought? The question never got an answer. It did get a response. Mike flew like a bird, a big bird, none the less, a kid was flying is what the third guard saw. The snap of Mike's leg was quick. It separated the third from the fourth vertebrate in the guard's neck. No push back came that usually followed with an impact from his kick to the guard's body. The kick was like snapping two fingers together to make a pop. Neck popped just like the two fingers snapping.

Cho watched Mike make the flying kick perfectly to the guard's neck. Quick, precise, beautifully well executed. "He has come far." Cho had made a report to the leaders before the night mission concerning Mike's training the children. Cho quietly kept watch Mike training his students. He had to be careful how close he came to the training, fearing Mike would sense his presence. He didn't watched Mike fearing he would teach his new students the secrets of his art, but because Chopper requested him to do so.

Cho made his way to the kennels with a hop, skip, and short jump. The dogs began barking. It ended quickly, once the raw steak was thrown over the fence. In the steak was a fast-acting drug. Cho stopped by the Vets early that day. Anytime dogs were present on an adventure, Cho made it a prime part of his preparations to stop by the Vet.

One guard was present, when the two dogs barked. By the second yip, the guard fell asleep from a more powerful drug than given to the dogs. Cho used his knockout punch on the handlers. The dogs woke several hours later, the handler preferred to sleep longer; much, much longer.

Mike swiftly set two timers near the front door. Another by a window Mike was peering in. Several guards were sitting at a table playing a card game. Mike recognized the game Magic introduced to him. Mike left, he didn't want to interrupt the man closest to the window winning streak. He made his way to the Gate. Cho was already hiding in a bush by the gate. He was about to strike, until seeing his son walk up the drive.

A third timer was left at the gate. Two guards saw a kid walking up the road inside the compound. It was weird, the way Mike sash-shayed up to the gate. He acted, if he living in the manor. Both guards knew, that was not the case. What really sold them, was the kid whistling a tune. One guard acted first. He held his hand out to halt the kid. Mike stopped. One question was permitted from the lips of that guard. Cho waited, watching Mike's approach the gate. He was about to do them in, instead waited for Mike to get close.

Cho left his concealment spot to witness a guard advancing on Mike. The guard dropped like a rock with a kick. Cho stood beside the second guard staring down the road at Mike. Cho abated any attempt to neutralize both guards. He was curious how long for both guards to realize they were not alone at the gate. Soon, that number increased to a fourth person when Mike arrived at the gate. Both Cho and Mike seeding each other waited for the other to strike. Time was short, both struck at the same time.

Cho decided on a simple grab around his guard's neck. Quickly driving the head back and downward. The guards back snapped coming to a sudden stop on Cho's knee.

Mike preferred a more difficult method for his attack. The man facing him had a gun pointed in his face. Quickly, Mike seized the barrel, then sidestep around the guard Mike lifting the rifle barrel upward. The rest of the rifle was still in the guard's hand. Only the barrel made a wickedly curved bend aiming back to the guard's face.

A gasping sound exited the guard's mouth watching the barrel make a weird bend. Another gasp followed when the barrel was pointing directly at his face. The third gasp came once he realized the gun wasn't fired into his face. The fourth and final gasp was his dying breath feeling the barrel enter through his mouth and continued it bending down his throat.

"Mike, you do have a flare for the artistic method, you bring to your foes, Cho softly said.

Mike, smiled. Both Cho and Mike ran with the speed of a cheetah to the rear of the house. On the road leading to the manor, a lone bike approached. A girl stopped half a mile from the place Cho and Mike leaped over the wall inside the manor. Cheryl wore an all-black outfit. She was about to climb up the wall. An explosion occurred. Then, several more. Quickly, she decided to get over the wall. She followed the wall until coming near the front gate. From her position, saw Cho snap the spine of a man. Then watched Mike execute his gun barrel feat.

Cheryl saw Cho turn, looking in her direction. She was well hidden behind bushes. "He never would see me in a million years," she thought. Watching Mike, she wondered, "was he going to show the class that technique."

Cho sensed a body near him. His senses had become so acute, he was capable of recognizing many of the people he known for some time. "Cheryl somehow followed us here. She is hidden well, Cho thought. Can't deal with this at the moment. Mike might react and right now, is not the time to reprimand her."

Mike, also sensed a person in the bushes. He felt, he knew the presence. He feared he was right. He hoped it wasn't who he thought it might be. He knew Cho was aware of the presence. If Cho did nothing, then, he would do nothing. Mike hoped they would not need to. It could jeopardize our mission."

After viewing the scene unfold at the gate, Cheryl wisely came to the same conclusion as Mike and Cho. She was way out of her league. She decided to remain behind the bushes waiting until an opportune time to quietly leave unnoticed had arrived. She hoped. Explosions everywhere, all at the same time occurred.

Chopper's bikers were coming through the gate and closing in on all sides advancing to the walls. Mike and Cho were in the manor. The bomb Mike set near the window, took out the three playing cards and two two men stopped to watch a play one man was about to win a large pot. Mike saw the big winner, also several cards under the table he palmed.

One man guarding the front door was buried after the explosion. The ceiling came down on him. Two men were upstairs guarding the leader's room. This night, he was entertaining two women guests. The explosion coincided with his. A climax he never experience again.

Another guest in the kitchen was going through the refrigerator for a snack. He was having trouble finding what he needed for his sandwich. Ever since he lost his eye, he had trouble adjusting. He was always careful eating after the broken jaw, the kid gave him at his home. It caused losing most of his of teeth. Leader man constantly was heard cussing every time he wanted his favorite food. Dam crumbs kept getting under his false teeth, was one remarks heard by his crew before the warehouse explosion.

One-eyed came to the manor a day after contacting his old friend. They been doing business for years. Leader man needed a place to hang for a while. The warehouse scene and searching for that dam kid depleted most of his resources. Not to mention, his money was gone. His friend provided a passport and a bag of cash. In the morning, a plane would be waiting. In Mexico, One Eye figured to hide-out, until the search for him ended.

As soon as One Eye heard the explosion, one thought entered his mind. "They found me." Quick, he dropped his sandwich running to his room. Next, he grabbed the bag of cash on his bed, then ran to the basement. Racing down the steps, he heard the main room explosion. A hidden release switch laid near the ceiling, pressing it, opened the door. The entrance led beyond the wall. A car was parked there. It was an emergency escape route for such an occasion.

One Eye pondered whether to wait for his friend before exiting the tunnel. One minute seemed like a fair amount of time for his friend to get to the tunnel and to the car. One Eye drove off exactly one-minute wait time elapsed.

Upstairs, Cho advanced. Mike followed taking out the second man left by Cho. Cho took the one closer to the bedroom door. With a palm thrust, the door slammed opened from the impact. The leader man had enough time to achieve a climax atop of his lady. He turned spotting a small man flying across the distance from the door onto his back.

Cho delivered a most potent finger jab into the back of the Leader. A loud nauseating gasped exited him. Blood flowed through the chest cavity exiting on the other end, on the lady, he was a top. Cho's finger couldn't make the distance through the chest, the force of the blow was similar to a bullet entering a body exploding out an exit hole. Death was quick.

Mike yelled to Cho. "At the window." Mike stood watching a man standing near a car beyond the woods. Cho came to his side quick. Both looked at the man by the car. He had One eye.

Outside, several guards raced from the garage and another house believed a bunk house for the Leader's guards. Swiftly, Cho and Mike came flying through the second-floor window onto the ground. Each parted in two directions, Mike reached the bunk house and Cho arrived at the garage. Bikers were converging from the gate to both their positions.

Both Cho and Mike began taking out one guard then another pouring out both places. The bikers sat atop of their bikes watching how effortlessly Cho and Mike worked.

Mike struck one guard with a kick, then a sweep followed by a multitude of punches. One straight punch to the nose, then a back fist to the side temple, a double combination spin back fist followed with a hooking punch. One strike on each person. Each hit was all it took. Five hits, five dead men.

Cho gave a slightly different method attack for his viewers. Four men ran from the garage. Each man aligned with the man in front. A neat line of four men ran out and into Cho. One punch, that's all, like dominoes, four men tilted back falling to the ground.

Chopper gets off his bike, Cho was walking over to Mike. "Cho, why was it necessary for us to even show? If you two continue this, where is the fun for the rest of us?" Before Chopper could get a replied from Cho, his bikers still mounted began a loud round of applauds. Many made comments.

"What a show." "Dam, that happened to quick, Cho." "Do it again, just slower." "Hey Mike, way to go, boy, you and Cho make one hell of a team, came shouts to both Cho and Mike from the watching bikers.

Cho had been with the club from the beginning. Few of his friends ever had an opportunity to see him in action. Usually, Cho would go in and do his thing. Sometimes, it was necessary for the bikers to assist. To many or too far apart were Cho's targets for any bikers to get a view of his real potential.

"Okay, everyone, get this place cleaned up," Chopper commanded.

Cho pulls Chopper over to one side. "Chopper, One Eye was spotted leaving over the wall, in a car. It appears he is heading to the airport."

Thinking for a second, Chopper replied, "Cho, the airport is far from here. We should get to him before he gets there."

Mike interrupted Chopper, "sorry Chopper, there is another airport closer."

Both Chopper and Cho spoke the same time. "Our airport, we use."

Thinking quick, both Cho and Chopper make a quick calculation for the time allotted One Eye to get to the airport. "Five minutes tops," Chopper spoke first.

Mike speaks up for a second time. "It is too late, if he has a plane ready for take-off."

Chopper recalls a plane in a hanger Pilot once told him. "Cho, it was kept topped off and ready to fly, waiting for a call. My first thought was some millionaire's plane. Now, "I think it's some millionaires drug dealer's plane." Above a small plane was heard flying. Cho and Mike glanced up. The plane was coming from the direction of their small airport.

"I will get Pilot to find out its course," Chopper said watching the plane fly away.

Meanwhile, Cheryl watched the entire biker club ride through the main gate. Once all were through, she hastily darted out the open gates and down the road. She arrived at her bike stashed under some shrubs.

"I made good time running down the road," she thought. "Thank you, Mike, for all that running you made us do lifting her bike from under the shrubs." Soon, she was quickly riding back in the opposite direction from the manor.

Chopper, Cho, and Mike were swiftly heading to the airport. Mike rode on the back of Cho's bike. Cho laughingly called back to Mike, "when you think you going to learn to ride that bike of yours?"

Mike replied, "I haven't got the money to buy gas for it."

Cho reached into his pocket handing Mike two quarters. "With that tiny bike, this should be enough to fill her up."

"Ha, ha," chuckled Mike.

At the airport, Chopper rode to the hanger Pilot lived. It was large enough for four small planes to shelter in. Both bikes parked by the office door. Inside was a back room with a bed, small kitchen, table, several chairs, and a T.V. Pilot was a loner. It wasn't cause of the constant gasoline odor on him or the shoddy beard. Nor was it his pocked scarred face or the nasty tobacco wad he always was chewing on. It was simply, he did not want to be around bitchy women.

The door slammed opened; Chopper entered. Pilot was up and at the door with a 45-cal. pistol at the ready. Seeing Chopper, he quickly lowered the gun.

"What's the dam hurry, why you go and slams my door? I only got that door and no spare."

"One question, I need answering right now, Pilot. Did a plane just leave?"

"Yeah, just no more than five minutes ago."

"Quick, do you know it's destination."

Thinking Pilot says, "no, but wait a few minutes, I can git that's info soon enough from a flight manifest."

"Quickly Pilot," Chopper commanded.

OZ

Pilot gits to his phone and make a call to the tower. After several questions, pilot turns to Chopper. "Mexico."

Cho turns to Mike, "get ready for a trip to Mexico, soon, Mike. It will take some time checking with ours contacts down there, but until that, we have some cops to answer for their misdeeds and one politician to have a talk with. Cho, that shouldn't be a problem with you finding out what we need to know from him."

Cho agrees. Turning to Mike, "Mike my son, this time you will accompany me to talk with this politician. It is time to learn some more secrets about pressure points."

"Before we leave Cho, I need to tell you something," Mike meekly speaks.

"What is it, Mike?"

"Well, back at the compound, I sensed a familiar presence at the gate. The night before, when you were at the cabin discussing the plan for this night, I had the same sense. When I walked out the door, Cheryl was standing by my bike. I thought nothing about it. I did have some suspicions, but Cheryl answered my queries satisfactorily. I didn't feel it right to be weary enough to bring this to your attention."

"Yes Mike, I too sensed a presence at the gate. I sensed it was Cheryl. I have learned to recognize many people from my chi senses. I now believe your senses have grown considerable for you age. Do you want me to have a talk with her?'"

No Cho, she is my student and friend. Tomorrow is my class day for training."

Driving into a gas station, a girl rode to the side. The store was a Quickie with gas. It was on the road to the airport. One that was rarely traveled. This night, the rode had many riders.

Cheryl met with her classmates early that day and discussed what she over-heard at the cabin. They wanted in on her plans. Plans that would ultimately bring all of them into a new sphere of danger. At the station, there was five bikes parked. Cheryl had stopped at the station prior to the entrance into the manor by Cho and Mike. Her friends, Cheryl commanded them to remain behind. She went scouting ahead to the manor. Before leaving the store, her crew wanted to

253

follow. Cheryl had time to think about what she done, letting them in on the attack. She was having second thoughts on what she was going to do.

"Listen everyone, if we all show up at the compound alerting what our fathers are attempting, we could get them killed. Maybe, it would be better if I go ahead and check out the situation, before the rest of you come? Wait here for my return."

"Come on Cheryl, we all agreed to the plan," Bobby rebutted. "Yeah, Lou said, we agreed; besides, it is too late and we came this far already."

"Look, I know we all agreed, but like I said, if we show up and spoil the attack; well, do you want to go home and explain what we done to your parents," remarked Cheryl.

All the students pondered what Cheryl said. "Okay, okay Liddea replied, we will wait here." Lou interjected, "for thirty minutes." Macy just nodded his okay to Lou's idea.

"I should be back soon, now, don't come down that road until I returned, please," Cheryl begged them.

Cheryl left the station and her friends standing by their bikes. She was over the wall and at the gate within ten minutes. Everything was happening fast. Cho and Mike took out the guards, then scurried to the manor. After the last explosion, Cheryl was climbing back over the wall to her bike. Some gun fire was heard driving back to the station. Arriving, all her friends heard the explosions and shots. They quickly gathered around her bike coming to a halt.

"What is all that gun fire? Are they attacking the compound? We just got here. they shouldn't have begun this early. What is happening? Did something go wrong, early?" Cheryl had to stop the bombardment of the questions pouring out of her friends.

"Hold on a second, give me a moment to get off my bike. Yes, the attack is happening. No, nothing went wrong. Cho and Mike were over the wall and took out many guards."

"Did you see them do that, Cheryl," Macy asked? "Yes, I did." "How?" Well, it was fast, I had little time to see just how. Cho got one man standing at the gate. He never knew Cho was standing there. The guard was so busy watching Mike walk toward the gate.

One of the guards pointed a rifle at Mike, Cho put him down. The guard's head slammed into the concrete. It was awful to see brains splattering everywhere."

"Did the first guard shoot Mike, Cheryl?"

"No, Liddea, Mike grabbed the rifle barrel and bent it around into the guard's mouth."

"Wait, you telling us Mike bent a rifle barrel in a circle shoving it down the guard's mouth?"

"Yep Bobby, that is exactly what I am telling you. Before the guard could swallow, he pulled the trigger while his rifle barrel went down his mouth. An explosion came out between his legs. I thought the brains splattering the concrete was horrific but that was nasty." Before Cheryl finished her story, the attack was over. Many of the bikers finished applauding Cho and Mike.

Everyone went in the store to get a soda to wash down what they heard. Two bikes roared passing the store just as the students came out of the store. Cheryl saw Chopper and Cho with Mike on the back of his bike. She thanked the stars they entered the store when they had.

Mike felt his chi tingle and quickly took a fast glance over his shoulder. He saw Cheryl getting on her bike and five others at a store they just passed.

THE DAY OF RECKONING

Just before ten P.M. two bikers stopped in front of the cabin. Three riders dismounted walking to the front door. The door was open. A light was shining from the lantern seated on the table. Chopper was unprepared for the strange events coming from the cabin. He heard the stories, but as yet, not had the experience of seeing it actual happening. On the wall, over the bed was written a message," well done".

"Does this happen most of the time, Mike?"

"Yes Chopper, every time I enter the cabin."

"Is it true this ghost, spirit, has a name?"

"Yes, his name is Mister Casper. Please use his name properly when you address him. He can be temple mental when you are not respectful to him."

"Hmm, I see your point, Mike. Okay Cho it will take some time before all the answers needed, before you and Mike leave to visit our politician and his police friends."

The door shuts, Chopper turns to see it latched. Then turns back to face Cho and Mike. It was that time between him turning to the door and returning to face Cho listening on to his talking points when he saw a new message on the wall.

""Where you going"?"

"Hey, did you see that." Chopper stopped before continuing his talking points. His fear levels rose with every spooky happening in the cabin. Cho noticed the subtle word stuttering in his speaking.

Mike spotted the message after Mister Casper wrote on the wall. Mike learned, if you take your eyes off the wall, Mister Casper had something to ask, he waited until you weren't looking.

Chopper tried to think of an appropriately excuse to need to leave, but his words were slow coming. Cho spoke up. "Chopper, I figure it will take several weeks, maybe by early winter. School will be starting soon. No one will miss either of us. By the time kids are established in school, we will be long gone."

"Yes, yes, your right Cho. The way our women been giving Mike their attention, it would be the proper time to take off."

"May I make a suggestion, Chopper?"

"Sure, sure Mike, what, what do you want to say?" Chopper spoke with his eyes glued over the bed staring at the wall, without looking at either Cho or Mike

"Maybe sir, it would be best if this plan remains between the three of us."

Cho steps in, "that is a good point my son is making, Chopper. It does seem of late our plans have been seeping out. I'm not accusing anyone, but no one really needs to know what and when we decide to leave."

"Maybe you are right, Cho." A message appears written on the wall, "he is right."

"See Chopper, Mister Casper agrees with Mike's suggestion."

"Well, I ain't arguing with no ghost, on this point. Then, if all agree, looking toward the wall, Chopper says and that includes Mister Casper, it is done."

Early in the morning after Cho and Mike's run, practice, and breakfast, Bell, Miriam delivered, Cho left. The women waited until Mike's students arrived. They watched them start their run, then left.

Returning to the cabin after a rough obstacle run through the woods, Mike calls for a time out. This, Mike never did and to all, it meant something they feared. He must know about their plans to follow him to the manor. They were right. Mike stared at them for five minutes, not saying a word. Then it began.

"I know you all meant well and maybe thought, in some weird fashion your following Cho and myself to the manor, you could aid us. I am sure Cheryl expressed some of the things she witnessed to you. Chopper has not heard of any of this, as yet. Now, you all know the rules and know to follow them. There is a severe consequence doing otherwise. You put this whole mission in great harm. Many people lives were at stake that night. Not just your fathers and the evil men we went after. You do not know this and for good reason. That evil group of men planned on killing everyone one in this club. That included all the mothers and children." Mike paused to allow his students to digest what he said.

"They wanted to make a statement to all the gangs around this town. Taking us all out would have put them on top of the heap. If you showed up, the plan would have been canceled. This evil gang would be alerted to our intentions. That night may have been our night, after that."

Most of Mike's students begged for him to forgive them. Some plead for him not to tell their parents. One begged to not tell Chopper or Cho. Mike listened to their pleas.

"I am sorry, Cho knows what you did. We both were aware of Cheryl hiding in the bushes near the gate."

Cheryl was shocked learning Cho and Mike were aware of her being at the gate.

"We spotted your bikes at the store. Before you ask how we know this, it is part of our training. You are not even close to the level Cho and I possess. It is not my intentions to train you in this way. You will receive much in the way, to prepare you."

"What Cho and I had done that night is a way of life many of you would not want in your life. It is only for a few. We are going into danger every time we leave here. Every day, we may die. Our enemies grow in number. Their hatred grows. They seek revenge, if they ever capture us. Do any of you understand what will happen to each of us, when that happens. Do you," Mike hammered it home with a stern commanding voice? "We live to serve you, the club, our families, and country. Most of all God, to rid the world of evil."

"I will continue to train you, but let it be known from this day forward, never will you try anything to endanger us all. If you do, I will assure you, it will be the last thing you ever do. That are the rules. You got a second chance today. Never will there be a third chance."

The meaning was clear. Every eye stared toward Cheryl. Mike called her to one side. They entered the cabin. On the wall was a message to Cheryl. "Last chance, Cheryl."

Cheryl saw the words and begged Mike forgiveness. Mike gave her a hug. I cannot save you the next time, Cheryl. Your fate is in your own hands. I pray you have learned this lesson. Now, go outside and lead the class in their drills. I will be out soon."

After Cheryl walks out the door, Mike walks over to the wall. The door shuts. Speaking softly, Mike addresses Mister Casper. "Sorry to have written on your wall, I wanted to drive the point home to Cheryl." Mike erased the words he wrote. After he removed his words, new words appeared.

"Glad you did".

Diner invitations started to dwindle after the manor attack. Many bikers returning home were allowed to stay for some family time. Chopper saw the need for his men to be with their families. That night reinforced their fears of an enemy attack to everyone's families.

Mike was at the cabin by himself. Not even Bone nor Penny stopped by. Diner was on him, to provide.

"Well Mister Casper, I do believe we are enjoying fish for the night."

Down to the river, Mike went. After removing his clothes, he entered the cold waters waist deep walking along the riverbanks edges. Apparently, on this day, the fish wanted a day off. Mike crawled out of the river wet to the bone. "No fish for supper," silently saying to himself.

Donning his clothes, Mike walks back to the cabin. Inside, Mike told Mister Casper, "water for super." Cho stayed late at the clubhouse. He assumed Cheryl and some ladies might drop by. He was wrong. When Cho returned to the cabin that night, Mike was asleep. Cho went back to his place. He noticed the empty plate on the table. Neither was there any aroma of food cooked.

Cho lived in a small house at the end of a street leading to nowhere. Most of the time, living alone. He never thought to tell Mike about his girlfriend. She was a stewardess on an Atlanta airline. Many times, she dropped in unexpectantly, then leaving the next day. That was the wonderful thing about their relationship. No ties, Cho was too busy to further their relationship.

That night, Cho planned on telling Mike. That was the reason he remained at the clubhouse late into the night. He couldn't gather the courage to tell Mike. Besides, Mike had been here for a while. It was enough time to tell him. Now, much time had passed. How is he going to tell his son about his home. He could have stayed there. Now, if I tell him, he might consider he was not wanted in my house. I know he would understand and not make me feel horrible. Still, this should be easy. Why can't I bring myself to tell him? This thought kept running over and over in Cho mind this night.

THE GIRL FRIEND TROUBLE

The next day Mike arose with a belly growled, something he had grown accustomed too, until the wives changed that. Them bringing him meals everyday was easy to get used too. It has been a long time since he felt the pangs of hunger. He sat at the table, before his morning run waiting for Cho. It was Cho's habit to be on time. When he wasn't, Mike knew some other reasons had detained him. Mike would take off alone.

Returning back to the cabin, no one was waiting with a basket of hot food. Mike thinking, if I want food, I need to wangle for my breakfast. After an hour wading through the cold river again, he returned to shore without so much of a stubbed toe. After getting dressed and no teaching planned for his students, Mike had a date at Rita's house for Spanish lessons. Arriving at the house, he was greeted with an aroma of bacon and eggs.

Maybe, Mike thought, if he made it there in time, they asked him to join them. Knocking on the door, Madd answered leaving to his lab. Chopper asked him to get some special explosives ready for a mission.

"Hey Mike, you up early. If you came sooner, Rita would make breakfast for you."

"I am always up before six to begin my training. Cho is very adamant about me rising early."

"Oh well, have a good day. I hear my wife said you got to be fluent in Spanish quickly."

Before Madd got to his bike Rita called for Mike to enter. Rita was finishing washing the dishes in the kitchen and heard his voice.

Going inside, Mike realized he was not going to be invited for break-fast. Rita was beginning to scour her frying pan. Mike walks up to her, "Mrs. Rita, would you like me to wash the pan for you?"

Why thank you Mike. That would be helpful. Madd rarely assists me in this kind of chores. In fact, I nearly have to pull his teeth to get him to put out the thrash. Remember to always speak Spanish in my home.

Mike saw the trash can full by the back door. I will be glad to take the thrash out, once I finish with this pan. Before the morning had ended Mrs. Rita managed to have Mike clean the bathroom tub and toilet bowl. Then made a comment, "my yard is the worse in the neighbor." Mike ended the day cutting the grass.

After the yard was mowed and the edging done, Mrs. Rita mentioned her hedging had to match the manicured yard. Mrs. Rita remarked, "how can you cut the grass and not have the bushes cut. After the clipping and cleaning done in the yard, Mrs. Rita came outside to review Mike's work.

"See Mike, this made the yard so much nicer." All this she, said in Spanish. Mike knew half of what she said, smiled to give her the impression he understood everything Mrs. Rita said. She smiled back.

Noon came, Mike just finishing the yard work when Mrs. Rita said, "Mike, can you come back later, I have a meeting with some of the other ladies for lunch." Mike nodded without saying a word, then left. His belly still growling.

Having no money to buy food, Mike began scouring the area for soda bottles. Several of the kids were playing near the street in a puddle of water. Both boys made small ships to sail in the makeshift pond.

Mike set his bottles aside near the street. Thinking to himself, the bottles should be safe in the ditch, until I find several more. "I sure don't want those kids telling their brothers, and sisters, or moms, they saw me looking for soda bottles. Mike recalled the story got around that night of the hot mustard event, I forayed soda bottles to buy food on my travel home. I don't want no pity or to have people think they need to feed me. I ain't going to be a burden to anyone," Mike thought.

Down the street Mike found several bottles to add to his total. Returning back to the spot he hid his bottles, they were gone. The two boys sailing homemade ships were coming up the road Mike was on. Both of the boys were drinking sodas and eating from a bag of potato chips.

Seeing Mike with bottles in his hands, one boy quickly remarked, "I see you got the same idea as we did. We found some bottles stacked in the ditch, and decided to cash them in for some goodies at the store."

Mike spent an hour looking for those few bottles he found. Not enough to buy much. He walked down the street collecting additional bottles. This time he hid the bottles under a tree, safe from prying eyes and little boys.

The path to the cabin was ahead. Mike decided to do some gathering before returning to Rita's home for Spanish lessons. Shortly, he spotted some blackberries. Quickly, Mike had a handful of berries. Just as shortly, ate them all. "Better than an empty belly," Mike said softly.

Back at Rita's home, Mike sat on the porch. Within the hour Mrs. Rita returned home. The rest of the day, until five, was spent on lessons.

"Mike from now on every day, you will speak only Spanish." Mike did even to anyone coming to visit Rita, he spoke Spanish. To his amazement, Cho stopped by to get him, Mike tried out his Spanish. Cho answered with fluent Spanish.

Back at the cabin Cho had Mike sit down. They were not going on their run, instead, Cho wanted to get something off his chest.

"Mike, I should have told you this before I brought you to the clubhouse, from your home. I kept putting this off."

Mike was a bit puzzled to where Cho was leading the conversation. Cho sensed Mike apprehensions building. Thinking it is best to just say what he was intending to say, without all the wandering about.

"Mike, I have a girlfriend. She lives at my house several miles from here."

Mike felt a sense of relief hearing that. "Cho, I always thought we were both alone. I gave up my family to protect them. I figured you had no family ties to protect them from harm's way. I never thought you had a girlfriend. It really, never occurred to me."

"Mike, is that a problem between the two of us. I know you have no family around and live alone for the most part. I thought about asking you to move in with me. You seemed very determined to be by yourself coming here?"

Mike pondered the words Cho was speaking. He wanted to tell Cho; it was because he didn't want anyone to feel sorry for him. After what Cheryl said the first night, fears he would be a burden would cause more trouble for himself. Instead, Mike replied, "yes Cho, I prefer to live alone. I worry about people coming around. I fear they may come into harm's way."

Cho could sense there was something Mike was holding back from him. He decided not to press the issue. Somethings are best not discuss, until the time is right. This is not the right time. Mike, my son has been hurt and needs time to heal from the news I dropped on him."

Cho noticed no aroma in the cabin of a hot meal permeating in the air. He heard some children speak about Mike looking for soda bottles. They came inside the store he was in to buy food for his girls arrival this night. The kids were buying more snacks with bottles they found in bushes. One comment alerted Cho they made.

"Mike was looking for soda bottles, like us. He must be hungry." Another boy replied, "yeah, we got lucky. Twice in the same day, we found soda bottles. Mike should hang out with us.'"

Mike, I have an idea, would you like to meet my girl tonight. You know, for diner. She has been gone for three days and I spoke much about you to her."

"Thanks Cho, I would love to but tonight is your first day with her. I cannot impose on you two. I will be fine. Go be with her. Maybe tomorrow will be a better time for us to meet?"

Cho could sense Mike did not want to go. "Okay, then will you allow me to drop off some groceries. Most of the bikers were given time to be with their families, by Chopper. You might not be getting those good meals for a time."

Mike nodded okay. "See you in thirty minutes. Cho wanted Mike to ride with him. Again, this would be pushing him, when what he wanted most was some time alone. Quickly, Cho went to town and bought Mike a bucket of fried chicken.

Back at the cabin, Mike smelled the chicken before Cho walked in. A look of amazement crossed Mike's face. Cho said, "eat; It's okay to have this once in a while. Besides, you must be hungry, not having supper last night or any meal today." Mike looked at Cho with even more amazement.

"Mike last night I came by. Your clothes were wet hanging outside. That meant you went fishing. No aroma of supper lingered in the cabin. You were mighty tired and asleep when I entered. Today, I came by after you left too Rita's for your lessons. I was going to take you to breakfast. I noticed no cars, nor aroma of a breakfast in the cabin, again. I was coming here to tell you what was worrying me, then I smelled nothing. This evening, I returned to talk to you, no smell of supper. I assumed you been going hungry for several days. When you come to my home, Laura, my girl friend is an chef. She can cook better than any woman or restaurant you ever been too. You are going to get stuffed. She likes it when I fill my belly. I will tell her about how you live. better be prepared to eat. She will not be pleased seeing you not eating her food."

That night, Mike had no visitors. Cheryl didn't come by. In the morning, all seven students arrived. He was finishing his run; they were waiting on the path. After three hours of a tough workout, they left. Cheryl remained. Taking Cheryl by her hand, asked her," Cheryl, today I want you to teach me about the bike. I will be making a trip using it. I surely don't want to break down on the road."

Cheryl looked stunned hearing Mike say, "he was going on a trip" As far as she knew, no assignment was set for either Cho or Mike. By the end of the day, Mike was well acquainted with the bike's operations.

Mike told Cheryl, " for next few days I am going to keep the bike and practice. Cheryl, I know you really enjoy using my bike and after my trip, you can have it back. To care of for, like you have been." Mike could sense her feeling for losing her bike.

Cheryl quickly tried to hide those feelings from Mike wanting his bike. "No, no, it's your bike, Mike. But this trip, I thought you and Cho wasn't going on any assignments for a while? Chopper told everyone to take a few weeks off."

"Well Cheryl, Mike hesitated on what he didn't want to tell anyone about, what he had planned. Especially after the news Cho dumped on him. Cheryl, I kind of wanted to go home and see my mom and sisters. I might bring my dog back with me."

"You mean that dog you found tied to a tree, the one you thought was killed by a car on your journey home. What was his name, Beau, Bingo?"

"No Cheryl, his name is Boo. It gets lonely out here sometimes and besides, we had been through a lot and I miss him."

"Mike, how far is your home from here?"

Maybe two hours or less. I rode with Cho here, after I was informed of your dad and Teddy bears deaths. I wasn't paying much attention to the time coming here. To be honest, I am not sure where here is, compared to where my town is at. I guess, I will eventually get there. I did walk from Virginia to Georgia without a map."

"Mike, a thought came to me."

"Yes Cheryl.

"Well, would you be alright with a companion to your home?"

Mike pondered for a minute before replying, "sure, that would be a good idea."

"You thinking maybe Cho?"

"No, he has a girlfriend. She came back from her trip. Cho said, "she would be here for a week. I figure he would want to spend some alone time with her," Mike replied.

Cheryl stared at Mike. "You are a little dense, aren't you?"

"What you mean by that, Cheryl?"

"I meant, me going with you to see your mom and sisters, dummy."

"Well, I didn't think about that. I would like the company, but your mom might have a say in that?"

"No worry, mom knows you can take care of me."

"Yes, but she might not want you to be riding with a boy to some other city without."

"Without what?" Cheryl looks at Mike with both hands on her hips and two eyes daring him to say the next words, she figured he was going to imply. "You do want me to come, don't you, Mike?"

Mike did want her to go but really didn't want her to meet his mom, if she was not sober. Cheryl heard Mike talk about his mother and them barely making a living with her drinking, smoking, and nasty mean talk. Some of the kids heard their families tell stories. It wasn't long before Cheryl pieced together her fabrication of Mike's home.

"Before I agree Cheryl to you coming along, I need to discuss this with Cho, Chopper, and you with your mom."

"If my mom's say it is okay, why do you need to tell Cho and Chopper? Can't you go wherever you want without asking permission?"

"Cheryl, they need to know where I go, because they been caring for me and it is the proper thing to do. If they have a reason for me not to leave right now, I must respect their decision. I am part of this club and Chopper and Cho are my superiors."

"Okay, then I will ask my mom tonight. No need to get in a huff, Mike."

"Good, I will talk to Chopper and Cho at the clubhouse today."

After Spanish lessons, Mike went straight to the clubhouse after making a detour to Bone's home. Penny answered the door. Seeing Mike was a surprise.

"Hello Penny, Mike greeted her opening the door. Is Bone in?"

"Sure, I will go get him. Come in and sit." Inside was a fancy décor. Penny had a flare for decorating.

"May I get you a drink?"

"Yes, please." Mike sat gazing about the room. Their home looked like one would see in a magazine. Shortly, Penny returned with a glass of cola and cookies. Mike hadn't had breakfast and as of late, rarely had any meals. Those cookies smelled good, he swiftly devoured four from the plate. Penny saw how fast they flew off the plate and went back to replenish the fast-emptying plate. When she got back, the plate was cleared.

Bone came from the garage with oily hands. Bone towered over everyone in the club. Penny made him shave his beard. She looked like a child standing next to him with her red flowing hair. Before he could greet Mike, Penny had him wash up. Returning, Penny resupplied the plate with more cookies.

"Hey kid, this is the first time you came to visit. What's the occasion? Bone slaps Mike on his back. Every time he did that Mike's back was left with a huge red paw print for the rest of the day. Not to say the slap rattled every bone in his body."

"Bone, can this be kept between the two of us," Mike asked in a querying way to him.

"Sure kid."

"Bone, Cho just told me about his girlfriend. I was a little upset. I figured, he and I were alone. I gave up my family, to, keep them safe and figured it was the same with him. I'm not mad or upset. God, I am glad he has a girlfriend. It is lonely, the way we have to live."

"Hey Kid, I never knew or thought much about how Cho lived or how that might affect you. I thought you wanted to live like that, alone."

"Bone, no one wants to be alone, all the time. I don't, and I know Cho doesn't. I just thought, we had each other to provide friendship, you know?"

"Yeah kid, I get the drift. I thought you knew Cho had a girlfriend. We all thought you wanted to live out in the woods, alone."

Mike's eyes began to tear up as he started to tell Bone the true reasons, he been keeping inside. Penny stood by the kitchen listening what they were discussing. As it was later known, Penny was somewhat of a snoop.

"Bone, please don't tell anyone, what I am telling you. I lost my dad and Cho, you, and Chopper, I kind of, you know look to as, a, a."

"Mike, I get it. I too lost my old man when I was young. Bone puts his arm around Mike. Kid, I feel the same way to you. I know Cho does and thinks of you as his son, Chopper, Jack knife, and Razor, also think of you as part of their family. You ain't alone, Mike. You got family; we are here whenever you need us. We want you to feel, you can come and talk to any of us about anything. You just know this; Cho and you are tight. That's why he had a hard time trying to tell you about his girl."

"How you know that Bone?"

"Dang kid. Cho and I, along with the others have talked to Cho about this for weeks. He been scared silly to tell you. He been worrying, you take it wrong."

"Really Bone?"

"Is that what's this is about?"

"Some of it, I want to take a trip to see my mom and sisters. Would you think anyone will have any objections, if I leave in a day or two. Cho got his girl and the rest of you have your families and me, I sure don't want to be in the way. I know you going to tell me, I am not in any way. Family and club family, well, they are different, Bone. I been feeling alone and miss my family. Yeah, I know you are thinking how we live, but it's the way we grew up, Bone. I was thinking about bringing my dog back with me. Someone to keep me company at nights."

"Well Kid, I'm pretty sure Chopper won't like it much and Cho, well Cho. Chopper knows you can take care of yourself. Training time doesn't mean training all the time. Sometimes, it is a good thing to take a break. God knows you could use one. Chopper should agree."

"Well Bone, there is one little problem," Bone looked at Mike wondering what it could be. Leaving to ride home was a big deal. Most of the clubs threats has recently is no longer a concern. At least, not at the present."

Bone looked at Mike's face and hair. Mike, is this about the way you look? Most of your hair has grown back. That burn on your face is nearly healed. The other things won't be seen, unless you do a strip tease in front of your friends and family."

"Bone, Cheryl wants to come along. She plans on asking her mom. If she agrees, can she go? I felt bad telling her, I wanted my bike back to make the trip."

"Mike, I should not be telling you this, right now. But maybe, it might solve a problem. That manor you and Cho went to. Well, it had a whole bunch of cash stashed in a back room. Chopper planned on giving the club members some extra cash for the holidays and whatever. Mike, you should be getting some. Why don't you allow me to buy Cheryl a bike for her own? When the money comes in, you pay me back. What you say about that?"

"Would you? When?"

"The bike will be at the cabin in the morning. Is that soon enough?" Mike reaches to grab hold of Bone.

"Now, you go to the house and talk to Chopper. Cho should be there, before you get there, Mike."

Mike leaves the house and Penny steps out of the kitchen. Mike knew she was in the kitchen and thought about leaving, saying nothing to Bone. He wanted it to be a private conversation. Penny was listening. Mike began blabbering and found he couldn't stop talking. Besides, what Bone just told him, Mike did not care if she overheard. Cheryl will get a bike.

Mike left Bone's home riding directly to Susan's home. A bike drove in her driveway. Cheryl ran to the front door. Cheryl grabbed Mike's hand leading him inside. She was feeling ecstasy thinking about the trip Mike said she could go on. This was her sign, he cared for her. She would meet his family. How could they not like her. In Cheryl's mind, Mike was hers. If he liked her, so does all his family. Not once did Cheryl consider others may have different feeling. This could interfere with her plans in unexpectantly ways.

Quickly, Cheryl went to her room. Her mom was sitting at the table sipping on a third cup of coffee. Mike must have been to Bone's home by now. Cheryl figures finish packing her clothes for the trip. Cheryl dashed up the stairs so fast not noticing the worry lines across her mom's face. Cheryl return from her room panting and anxious for mom to announce she can go. Thinking, "It had to be good news, she knew Mike could keep her safe and be respectful toward her. Besides, it will be a two-day trip at most. Mom would never say no?"

Ten minutes past from the time Cheryl jetted off her bike, ran up to her room, and down to Susan sitting at the kitchen table sipping on her first cup of coffee. Mike had not gone to Bone's home Bone his concerns. His concerns centered on Susan's answer. If she said it was fine for Cheryl to leave with him to visit his family, then he would stop at Bone's home.

Cheryl spoke to her mom, once she stopped her panting. Susan feared what words Cheryl was going to say. She been watching Cheryl's growing liking Mike. She never wanted her child to live the kind of life, she had with Stephen. She saw Cheryl grow up in this lifestyle and secretly thought one day, Stephen and her would settle away from this life. With his death, her dreams diminish. The club provided a good income for her and Cheryl. This was Susan's thoughts when Cheryl stood facing her. Do I dare leave taking Cheryl away from her friends and this way of life, she has grown up in?"

"Mom, mom Mike wants to take a trip back home. He asked me to come along. He wants me to meet his family. Isn't that great? It will be two days at the most. You know Mike is a good person and capable of taking care of me."

Susan looked at two glowing brown eyes filled with her stepdaughter's heart's desire. "I once felt that way. It was a beautiful life, the first ten years with Stephen," reflected Susan looking at Cheryl.

"You said, "Mike asked you to go with him?" Several weeks ago, me and Mike had a sit down at the cabin. Cheryl just left; Bell was at my side. I spoke frankly to Mike about my concerns for Cheryl. I told Mike how Cheryl felt about him. I told him, I saw them kissing in the park that first night he came to supper. I told him, what I told Cheryl. "Mike, I believe you are dangerous and any life with you would bring her a lot of pain and hurt." To my surprise, Mike agreed with me. He gave me his word, if anything changed in their relationship, he would come sit down and discuss it with me. My feelings about a relationship was a concern for him and he would honor my wishes."

"Mike had not come to talk to me. Could he have broken his promise to me? I heard Cheryl say, "Mike asked her to go with him." This, he should have come to me and discussed, before it was ever mentioned to Cheryl?"

Mike rode to Susan's home with one worry plaguing his thoughts. I told Susan, "I would discuss any new changes in their relationship with her. This sudden trip was not considered with Cheryl in mind. Somehow, I was in a situation that got out of control from me. Cheryl made her decision and somehow convince me into letting her come. Now, I have to face Susan. I knew Cheryl would blab it out, before I had an opportunity to discuss the trip with Susan. After riding to Bone's home, I decided it was more important to go to Susan's home.

Both Susan and Cheryl heard the bike in the driveway. Cheryl ran to the door. Mike came in and went directly to Susan. Susan spoke to Cheryl waiting to hear mom agree to the trip.

"Cheryl, please go to the park and wait until Mike and I have our talk."

"Mom, I am a grown woman and do not need to be treated like a girl. "Cheryl stomped out the door knowing what the look in her mom's eyes meant, then the same look coming from Mike's eyes. It was no use saying anything. That one thing, she knew about her mom."

Mike asked to sit down. Susan offered him a cup of coffee. "No thank you. Miss Susan, I remember telling you about anything concerning Cheryl and myself would be discussed, before any decisions were made. This trip, I intend to go on was not with Cheryl in mind. I was going to make it alone. I needed time to do some reflections. This morning, Cho told me he has a girlfriend. I thought we both gave up our families, to keep them safe."

Susan sat quietly listening to Mike. She knew how pushy Cheryl can be at times. What Mike was saying fit Cheryl's ways of getting her way. That eased Susan's mind."

"Bone and I discussed this, and I feel much better. I hope this conversation, remains private. I realized I should get over here, before I request my trip with Chopper and Cho. To be honest with you, I would be pleased to have her along. But, also pleased if she didn't. I hope that makes sense to you? It doesn't much make sense to me."

Susan saw the pickle Mike was in. He cared for Cheryl, but lacked the conviction to commit to any long-term relationship. He knew Cheryl's feelings. Cheryl said, Mike did not want to put anyone he cares about, in harm's way. Susan knew what was best. Allowing Cheryl to accompany Mike to visit his family would solve two problems. Either way, she would win. One; she still had Cheryl loves and not anger that could drive a wedge between them. Two; they would have time to be alone. Their true feeling could be revealed on that trip.

Mike was nearly floored with Susan's approval. Secretly, he hoped she would not. This gave him some mixed feelings. Susan saw Mike expression, knowing she made the right decision. It was Cheryl and not Mike with a puppy love crush. Mike's feelings would begin to make Cheryl understand this, in time.

"Mike, go to the clubhouse now. I will tell Cheryl."

Mike left and soon was at the clubhouse. At Susan home, a phone rang. Susan answered the call, before calling Cheryl.

"Hello," Penny answered back. "Susan, Mike was just here."

"I know Penny, he stopped here and just left. We had a discussion concerning his trip. Cheryl wanted to go."

"Good, then you told him she wasn't going on the trip."

"No, Penny. In fact, I gave them my approval."

"What?"

Listen, Cheryl is my daughter and I know what is best for her. I appreciate your concerns and informing me about Mike coming over. This is what Cheryl needs. Me, I don't want my daughter hating me and do things behind my back. This way we can always communicate. Cheryl is in love and this short trip will help both decide the best course to take. Mike and I have had talks concerning just this. He is aware of the danger Cho and he faces every time they are on a mission.

"Susan, I like Mike a lot and I want him to be happy. God knows he has done a lot for this club since being here. But that is your daughter. Being with Mike could put her in danger."

"Penny, you chose to be with Bone. He has the same dangers Mike has. We all do."

"I guess you are right. Love causes us all to do things we know better. Besides, she has one tough man. If he couldn't take care of her, who could? He's even training her. Those kids are better than most of their parents in fighting skills."

"Thanks for understanding Penny."

Chopper, Razor, Cho, and Jack Knife was at the clubhouse when Mike drove up. Bone called ahead. Chopper was prepared for their meeting. Bone informed Chopper about getting Cheryl a bike. He told Mike, he would loan him the money. Then made mention his slip telling Mike about the cash found at the manor.

Cho arrived just before Mike. The trip was new to him. He felt Mike's decision could be good for him. He wished Mike first came to him.

Entering the clubhouse, Mike saw all the leaders waiting for him. Bone came a few minutes later. On the bar was sandwiches. Cho mentioned Mike had few moms, lately bringing meals to him. Mike was back searching for food in the woods and streets. To look at him, he hadn't eaten food for days. He wasn't having much success foraging," replied Cho to the leaders.

Hello Mike, come in. Mike knew the word got back to the leadership. He half expected it, when he left Susan's home. Word had a way of getting to Chopper, pretty quick.

Mike spoke first. Turning to Cho was Mike's first choice. " Father Cho, after you left the cabin, I suddenly felt a need to see my mom. This has been coming ever since I returned from the city. I held back my feelings until we had that discussion. It made me realize everyone needs to have someone in their lives. You are my father, Sifu, and best friend. I love you and respect you most of all. I do not need to tell you that. You know my heart. I want everyone here to know this."

"Chopper, Bell, Razor, Bone, and Jack Knife were with me in my worst times. You fought alongside of me. Your friendship and strong feeling for me is returned many times over by me. I have grown to consider you my family more so, than I do with my own family. Still, I need to see them. I have to know they are well."

Mike pauses waiting for any rebut. No one said a word. Mike continued. "I need to take this trip for my own benefit. The next assignment could be a long time between chances to see my mom. I asked you to allow me to leave."

Chopper had already discussed Mike seeing his family and was going to tell him to take some time to visit them. He talked to Cho days ago after giving everyone time off to be with their families.

"Mike, you have every one's blessing to go."

"Chopper, there is one more request I would like you to approve. I had a talk with Cheryl's mom, Susan. She has given her permission for Cheryl to go with me. I talked to Bone about asking you to allow me to buy Cheryl a bike. I wasn't sure how to pay for one. Bone told me, he would loan me the money. I planned on asking, Cho first. Mike turned to look at Cho mentioning the bike. I would work any job to earn money to pay Bone back."

Mike was careful not to mention the cash found at the manor. It was not his right to ask. Besides, he did not want to get Bone in trouble for leaking the news to him.

Cho spoke first to Mike. "Mike, my son, Bone is a good friend to both of us, but, that decision belongs to me. You are my son and my responsibility. If you want a bike for Cheryl, I will provide for that. Bone, thank you for your wiliness to help Mike."

Bone nods his approval. He knew what Cho meant. His feeling was not in the least hurt from Cho rebut. Mike sensed Cho had no hurt feeling. Cho patted Mike on his back.

"Mike, my son, I know you will be careful on this trip. Know I will be thinking of you. Also know this, if you get into trouble while you are away, there will be hell to pay when you return."

Chopper motioned Cho back, so he could speak. "Mike, Cheryl may go. You will be responsible for your actions. You will protect her and make sure she is still innocent. Do you understand my meaning on this matter?"

"Yes sir."

"Bone can you get Mike a Bike to give to Cheryl?"

Bone replied, "it is on its way from the dealer. Should be here within the hour. Cho, I had the bike charged to your account, before I came here," Bone replied.

Mike was amazed hearing Bone say that to Cho. "Why would he charge the bike to Cho, then telling me, he was going to loan me the money. Suddenly Mike understood much more than before. Many things were becoming clear, now. This is a family in more ways than he realized."

"When you plan on leaving Mike," Chopper asked?

"I was hoping to leave first thing in the morning. Susan planned on dropping Cheryl off at the cabin. I told Susan, I had a bike for her and wanted to surprise Cheryl. I figured if you said no to her going on the trip, the bike would soften the bad news."

Chopper smiled, everyone laughed. Mike had all this planned." Good, eat some sandwiches. You should have a good appetite with all this planning you been up to."

Mike grabbed two sandwiches, and turned to walk out to his bike. Cho stopped him, to walk together. Outside Cho said, "Mike, never go and talk with others before you talk to me, first. That hurt me that you went to Bone."

Mike replied, "I was coming to see you when Cheryl brought up the trip. After that, I dropped her off at her mom's. Bone was down the street and I wanted to feel out what Chopper thought. I figured, if Bone told me, it was no way Chopper was going to allow me to take a trip, I figured, I would tell you, and you could prepared the way with Chopper."

"So, let me get this straight. Going to Bone to get the feel for Chopper, you had assumed I was going to allow you to take this trip?"

"Yes Sir."

"Well, I give you credit, I would have agreed. Just tell me one thing, Mike. What made you so sure I was?"

"Cho, your girlfriend was here."

"Okay."

"Well, her being here and you not seeing her for some time, it figured. You want some alone time without some snot-nose kid hanging around."

"Okay, how did you know it been a while since I saw her last?"

"Oh, that was easy, after you told me you had a girlfriend. All the pieces fitted. You started to stay at the cabin when she wasn't here, you would stay gone, unless the moms showed up and brought me breakfast."

"What makes you think my girlfriend doesn't make me my breakfast?"

"Well, since you get to the cabin so early, I just figured she was still in bed, when you left."

"Chopper was right, you done a whole lot of planning, ha, ha, ha. Just do me a favor, keep in contact with me. I want to hear from you every day, please."

"I will Cho."

Mike straddles his bike and quickly rode to Cheryl house. Susan had just informed Cheryl, she could go. Cheryl when Mike returns, and only if Chopper gave the go, you can go. You need to promise me, you will call me every day."

"I promise ma."

A bike roared into the driveway. Mike walked to the house. Cheryl heard the bike and recognized it's familiar roar. She watched Mike slowly make his way to the front door. Her heart sank. From the way he was coming to the front door, Cheryl knew Chopper had said no.

Just as Mike got to the door, Cheryl opened the door. "He said no, didn't he?" Susan heard the disappointment in Cheryl voice. She called for him to come to the kitchen.

Mike said nothing walking to the kitchen. Sit Mike, Susan said. In a way she was happy Chopper told Mike no.

"Susan, Cheryl, Mike said, turning to face Cheryl. Chopper gave his approval."

Cheryl punched Mike hard on his shoulder. "Dang you, the way you were walking and acting, we thought he said no."

Susan's heart sank a little, but she had decided it was for the best.

"Miss Susan, would you bring Cheryl to the cabin early in the morning. I would drop by and get her, but I was told to wait until some word was sent to me. When the word comes, I want to get on the road quickly."

Cheryl, quick go fetch your things, I will take them to the cabin and tie them to the bike. I need to make ready myself. Cheryl ran up the stairs. Mike quickly told Susan the real reason for her to be brought to the cabin.

"Miss Susan, I have a surprise for her coming by in the morning. It's a new bike." Susan sat back and gasped.

"Mike, she will be overjoyed. How you wangle the money to get her a bike?"

"I'll explain that to you when you show up. I want you in on her surprise."

Quick as a wink, Cheryl had her bag in hand. Before Mike could leave, Susan wanted to say something to him.

"I know you are excited to see your mom, and rightly so, but Mike, you have been in a terrible fight and hurt badly from a bomb blast. I don't think you realize that you still bear the marks from that blast."

Mike grabs his face. It has been itching of late. Every day he would wash his face and never once thought of the damage caused by the blast. There was no mirror in the cabin. Mike looked around for a mirror. Susan fretted, she said to much.

"Mike, the damage will heal, then there will be no sign of the blast marks on your face." Susan tried her best to prepare Mike for what he apparently had not been aware of.

Most of the kids knew about Mike's damage resulting at the warehouse and seen him many times. They were accustomed like everyone to Mike's disfigurement.

Slowly, Mike walked to the bathroom holding his hands to his face. Cheryl wanted to be with him, when he saw his face. Susan held her back. In the restroom Mike stood looking down. Slowly, he raised his head. A reflection of that day was still evident. One side of his face was darken with many small cuts crisscrossing his face. One large cut loomed over his brow. On that side, most of his hair was shorten. It showed some signs of growing back. The two sides looked different. In a way, he feared the worst and what he saw was a lot so bad as he feared.

Returning back to the kitchen, Mike read the expressions on both Cheryl and Susan faces. He smiled to them. "From the way you were telling me about my face, it really had me worry."

"You mean it didn't get you upset," Cheryl said.

"A little Cheryl, but it will heal, why worry on it. I am still me. I am just glad it wasn't worse."

"Mike before you go see your mom, we need to tend to the differences. Your mom wasn't prepared for this. It could cause some emotional outburst."

"What would you have me do, Susan?"

"Just sit here." Susan motions to Cheryl to go get the clippers. Shortly, Mike had a towel wrapped around his neck. Susan cut the long side enough to make the different appear like a new style of haircut. Opening her purse, she covers the rough area on his face with some color makeup.

"See Cheryl how I apply this to his face. You will need to do this before Mike walks into his house before he sees his mother."

Cheryl nodded to her request. Mike wondered what his friends would say. When Susan finished, she took her compact mirror out of her purse. Handing it to Mike, flipping it open. Mike was suddenly struck dumbfoundedly. To his astonishment, it hardly appeared he was ever in a bomb blast.

"This is remarkable Miss Susan," Mike said in awe.

"Good," Susan handed the make-up over to Cheryl. You are in charge of his face."

Mike stands to leave. He reaches over to give Susan a hug, then to Cheryl. Susan had a strange tingle from Mike's hug. She looked at Mike, he was several years younger than her. Still, their ages were less apart than the age was between Stephen and her getting marriage.

At the cabin, a bike was sitting in front of the door. "That was fast," Mike thought perusing the new bike. "This is a real good bike.

In fact, it was far better than mine." Mike was given a rebuilt bike requested by Cho. Cho had little plans for him to use it. He wanted him to know how to ride a bike, when the time called for it.

That night, a short message read on the wall. "How long?"

"Mister Casper, I will be gone for two days, maybe three, no more, Mike replied to the message on the wall. Thinking to himself, Mike thought Mister Casper was being worse than Cho, Bell, and Susan all wrapped up together. He was more like a mother, than a companion.

THE TRIP

Five o'clock in the morning, Mike was up. He went to the river jumping in. He had a bar of soap. He found out it was faster to just jump in with a bar of soap than to fill his shower bag hauling water from the river. Mike just got dressed, when he heard a car approaching up the path.

The car stopped near the front door. Mike had put the new bike on the side of the cabin away from the path. When Susan drove up, the bike was not present. Susan thought Mike may have not gotten the bike, before the trip. Cheryl jumped out of the car. Mike had to stop her.

Mike shouted to Cheryl, stand there, don't move. In fact, you will need to turn around. Cheryl looked confused. She turned around. Mike went to the side of the cabin. He brought the bike into view, then told Cheryl to turn. She did and said nothing.

She saw the bike. She thought it was Mike's bike. His bike wasn't seen. Mike left the bike by Cheryl, then went back to the side of the cabin fetching his bike. Cheryl looked confused.

Susan spoke up. "Mike got you, your own bike Cheryl. Still, she looked confused. Cheryl, that is your bike to keep. Aren't you going to thank Mike for the gift," Susan gave her a hug. The hug woke Cheryl from her trance.

"Oh my, it's mine, really mine." Cheryl looked from Susan back to Mike then to Susan and back to Mike.

"Well, get on the bike, Mike cried out. I plan on leaving soon as I close up the cabin."

"Just get going you two, Susan told Mike. I might change my mind." Cheryl runs back to her mom giving her a big hug. Quickly, she hopped on her bike. With one stomp on the pedal, it revved up.

Down the path she took off. Mike stopped near Susan thanking her. "I will take care of her. Then, mounted his used repaired bike and drove off giving Susan one last wave goodbye. Before the main road, Cheryl halted waiting for Mike. Together riding down the road.

South of Atlanta, Mike motions to Cheryl to pull over. "Cheryl, I have only been down this road once. I think this is the correct road to drive."

You silly person, last night, mom and I sat up checking a map out for the trip. She showed me the best way to your hometown. Just follow me."

Less than two hours, Macon loomed ahead. Cheryl signaled Mike to turn on the bypass. Within minutes both turned off the interstate heading to Mike's town. Entering the city limits, Mike knew they would pass the Rama theater. It was too early for anyone to see a movie, but the crew should be inside preparing for the first showing. None the less, he signaled Cheryl to turn into the parking lot. Then signaled Cheryl to follow him onto a back road.

Soon, they turned into a subdivision. It had many duplexes. Most looked worn down. At a corner was a duplex, it looked empty. Mike stopped and pointed to Cheryl. That is my, our home.

Cheryl said nothing. Her thoughts were easy to read to Mike. Waiting to drive up to the house, Mike heard a familiar sound. It was yipping coming from a small dog. Quickly, Mike pulled up to the house. He was off his bike and at the front door in a flash. Cheryl remained on her bike. Susan told her, "when they arrived, let Mike go in first. He will come and get you, when he sees his mom."

Mike knocked on the door again after the first knock failed to get a response. The yipping got louder. It was Boo yipping. Mike knew his sound anywhere. Mike tried the doorknob. It turned. Mike called to his mom, entering.

"Hey, anyone home." Mom was on the cough. She was sleeping. Beer cans littered the table. Mike knew immediately why the door was not answered.

Dodie walked out of the kitchen, after finished cleaning. She saw her brother standing in the doorway. At first, she wasn't sure if it was him. He looked different. Boo was jumping up and down at

Mike's feet. Mike picked him up, he licked on Mike for minutes. Mike looked at Boo, he was on the porky side.

"Boo, didn't I tell you, I would return. I missed you so much." Dodie hearing Mike's response to Boo runs over giving Mike a hug.

"Mike, I am so sorry telling you to leave. I was scared."

"I know Dodie. I know you were scared but that didn't mean you were wrong. I knew I had to leave. I wanted to tell you this before I left. You were not home, when I left."

"I put that money away, as you told me to. Sharon did as well. Mike, mom found Sharon's money. She took most of it. Sharon told me, she hid some in several places. Mom was always finding her money. Mom knew I didn't work, figuring I did not have any money. I would wake mom, but as you can see, it will be a while before we can. If we do so early, it could start her yelling."

"Dodie, did mom worry much, when she found out I left?"

"She got mad, Mike. She thought she was going to lose her government money. So far, nothing has happened to the check."

"Nothing else, Dodie?"

"She gets drunk and asked several times, when you were getting home? She thinks you are still working at the Rama."

Cheryl comes up the steps to the front door. Dodie noticed her presence. Mike felt the room tense up. Mike turns knowing Cheryl is at the door. "Come in Cheryl. Dodie, this is my girlfriend. Her mom, Susan was the wife of Stephen. You met him the day Mitch and I tangled with the three bikers at the door. By the way, how is Mitch?"

"Oh, we are still dating. I think he wants to marry me?"

"Really, that is good news," Mike replied with a glee.

"Where is Sharon, Dodie?"

"She is working at the Krystal, in town. It is new. She got hired on the first day. She should be home later."

"Where is this Krystal," Mike asked Dodie?

"On Watson. You must have passed it coming home?"

"No, we came the back way."

"Mike, are you here to stay?"

"No Dodie, just for a day, maybe two. I will need to get back. I have a job. Cheryl breaks in.

"Yes Dodie, Mike is doing really well. He is highly respected by all the people he works for. Mike is a hero to many of them. He."

Mike stopped Cheryl from praising him further. Thanks Cheryl, for all the praise, but my family really doesn't want to hear all of that. Dodie, do you want to ride with me, to go see Sharon?"

"No, I'll stay here."

Cheryl saw the disappointment in Mike when his sister did not want to ride with him. Mike rode on the main road toward the Rama. Before getting to the Rama, the Krystal was on the opposite side of the road. Cheryl and Mike walked inside the burger joint. Mike immediately spotted his sister. She was at the counter taking orders.

After a short wait with two people ahead of him, Mike stood looking at his twin. She took his order and gave him a ticket. Mike walked over to a table Cheryl picked out.

"Mike, Cheryl said, didn't she say something to you?"

"No. I don't think she recognized me. You know, with this new hair style and make up on my face. At the Rama theater parking lot they halted on their bikes. Cheryl told Mike before leaving the lot to let her do his face.

The order was called out. Mike got up walking over to the counter. Sharon had the bag in her hand. When Mike took the bag, it suddenly hit her. She knew that person. Looking hard at his face, she saw her brother. She cried out. Everyone turned to see her grabbing him.

"Mike, wait here, I'll go and asked by boss for some time off. Soon, both Mike and Sharon shared a table with Cheryl. Many questions poured out of her. Sharon wasn't present when some of the attacks took place at their home.

Cheryl knew Sharon was Mike's twin sister. Looking at Sharon Cheryl could not see any similarities. She had blonde hair; Mike's hair was brown. Her face looked more like her moms, while Mike looks like his older sister, Dodie. Both had brown hair, brown eyes and the same turned up cute nose. Sharon had hazel eyes. The one thing both have in common, both were the same height. His older sister was a few inches taller than either of them.

Mike quickly brought her up to date. "Sharon that last attack by the three bikers was when Mitch aided me. Did Dodie tell you any of what happened?"

"Yes, she said some, not much. She told me she told you, you had to leave. I got really mad at her. What right did she have to make you leave. After she got the money, you left us, her fears left, and she quickly regretted telling you to leave. How long you going to stay? You are not going off, are you?"

"Why you asked me that, Sharon?"

"Well, I got eyes, is this your girlfriend?"

"Oh, I'm sorry, this is Cheryl." Cheryl told her about Mike and held back what she tried to tell Dodie, when Mike stopped her." Sharon sat amazed listening to Cheryl admiration describing her brothers deeds. Mike allowed her to speak on some of his activities but made sure she left out the missions he been on and the warehouse incident.

"She is pretty," Sharon telling Mike.

"Thank you, Sharon, so are you. Mike and I will stay for a day. He is needed back at the business."

"Yes Sharon, I am an important member of the company," Mike responded.

"He is that Sharon," Cheryl was fast to point out.

"Are you going to be home, when I get off, Mike?"

"Yes, we will come by later, when mom is awake."

"Oh," Sharon's reply hearing mom was sleeping. She knew what that meant.

"Cheryl and I will need to find a place to stay for tonight."

"Why not stay at home?" Sharon realized her mistake as soon as she said it. First, no extra room, and Mike made it clear, Cheryl and him were friends and no more by his tone." Sharon knew her brother better than his mother or sister. They were fraternal twins but had a link between them, that his other sister did not possess.

After many minutes passed, Mike and Cheryl left. Once they got two room at the motel down the road it was time for the theater to open. Mike parked in his old parking place, when he worked at the Rama. That spot he parked with his old car.

Both Cheryl and he walked to the front door. Tad was out front. He just opened the door. Turning around hearing people approach, he stood staring at Mike.

"Oh my, is that really you, Mike?"

"Yep Tad."

Looking at Mike since his leaving came a shock seeing Mike with a different look. When Mike left, Tad felt sure, that was for the last time. Now standing in front of him, there he was.

Mike saw the Tad was giving him. "Tad, we had that fight with the gang from Atlanta. We almost ended the threat. The Leader man, called One Eye now, he got away again."

Cheryl spoke up, "Mike different tell you that his gang is destroyed, and that man has left the country."

"Is that how your face got that way, Mike?"

"Yes Tad. There was a bomb blast. I got caught in the door near the blast. I am told this will heal in time with little scarring. My hair will grow back in time."

Lindsey walks over at the group talking to Tad. She recognized Mike right off. Quickly cries out his name. Mike turns to see her. Lindsey almost screamed, seeing one side of his face turning to her.

Lindsey gives Mike a huge hug. She couldn't look at him in his eyes. Cheryl notice her apprehension. "It is okay Lindsey; Mike was in an accident and he will fully recover."

"What kind of accident causes those marks?"

Mike signaled to Cheryl it was okay to speak freely about what happened. Cheryl explains the cuts. Then, before she could finish telling Lindsey, Rusty and Melvin come over. Connie and Pretty Debbie show up. Soon, many of Mike's friends arrived. Lindsey went in the booth making some calls. Before the hour passed, almost everyone that night at the haunted house was present in front of the theater.

Tad had to break up the welcoming to get the Rama ready for business. It was one of those slow days. When the evening shift came to replace the early shift Mike and Cheryl met almost the entire crew working with Mike.

There were some new faces replacing the old, they went to their workstations. Many of the crew stayed with both of them until the nine o'clock show. The main questions after continuously retelling of the bomb blast markings covering his face, was if it is okay to tell others about the haunted house?

"Look, you can tell people the story but leave out people being killed. You can say there was a huge fight and you all ran the group off. That is all. Anything other than that will cause a whole bunch of people concerns. They are the type you want to remain clear of. Anything of what happened that night, will open doors you wish you never opened. Remember, people still are looking for me and my friends."

The second question most asked Mike, "do you plan on staying." Then the third, "who is the girl?" Pretty Debbie asked that question. Cheryl caught the intent. Mike played dumb. Either way, nothing was said about them again. Cheryl made it clear what Mike was to her, when she kept hold of his arm.

Mike and Cheryl left going back to his home. Mom was up and had her first drink. Dodie told her, Mike was home. Mike rode up to the front. Cheryl was told to remain outside, until asked to come in. Mike and Sharon explained a ton to Cheryl at the Krystal. Mike felt unsure of his mom's condition and him showing up after being gone for some time.

Mike entered the door, Mitch was there. Dodie asked him to stay, when Mike came home. Mitch wanted to be there, when Mike came home. Much was needed asking by him.

Mike walks through the door. Mom saw Mike enter. Mike kept his face turned from her gaze. Dodie and Mitch saw the full extent for the first time. Dodie grabbed hold of Mitch's arm. Mike walks over to mom giving her a hug. "Where have you been?"

"I been working mom. I got a good job in the big city."

"You do; can you send us some money? The bills are getting large."

"Mom, I am an apprentice and my pay his barely enough for me, right now. I have been told, it will become much better, before the year is out."

"Mike remember, all we have to live on is your check and if you are gone, we can lose that money."

"Mom, I am going to school and will have my boss send you the info for the government, it they require any."

Cheryl wanted to be in the house with Mike. She waited for a minute, then got off her bike, then went to the porch, next standing at the door when Mike told mom about his job. Cheryl quickly stepped back outside. She remained there, until Mike called to her. Mike was aware she was at the door. He also knew, she stepped back out.

"Mom, this is Cheryl; he been wanting to meet you." Mom looks at Cheryl, as a thief taking her boy away, or rather a check away. She did what was expected greeting Cheryl kindly. Both Cheryl, Mike, Dodie, and Mitch knew better. Sharon walks in.

Sharon had a sack of burgers. Hearing about Sharon's brother returning home gave a sack for a family reunion. Everyone dug in. Boo sat on Mike's lap. Mike gave him the first burger.

Mom made a comment. "I see Boo is still your dog."

"Yes mom, he is. I plan on taking him with me." Mike thought about letting Boo stay. Then had a vision of his mom drunk and asleep on the couch. She wasn't going to miss him, and Boo didn't need getting fed candy for his meals. Boo seemed happy with that.

After everyone finish eating and mom eating two burgers followed with a beer, Mitch asked to talk to Mike outside.

On the porch, he asked about the gang. "Mike fill me in on the gang."

Mitch, the gang is destroyed. All their members are dead except one leader. He is known as One Eye. He is the same thug that attacked this house. The other leader is dead. Master Cho did him in. I was caught in a blast at their warehouse hangout.

After returning to the clubhouse and getting me patched up, the Rider learned about his where-abouts. We went to the manor in force taking the compound down. One Eye unfortunately made his escape. We know where he went. The Riders are preparing to leave for Mexico, in pursuit. I wanted to see my family before leaving.

Mike, you involved in fighting? Weren't you afraid? What experience do you have?"

Mitch, recall when I was here. Those three thugs attacked the house, Dodie was held captive. You smashed a car window ending one of the thugs and me, I took out the others. You told me that was the most incredible thing you ever witness. Well, my skills are even greater now. I am in par equal to Master Cho. I have been on several missions with him. It was Master Cho and myself that entered the manor ending that new threat.

Cheryl listened tentatively to Mike's brief explanation on the events taking place at the manor she seen with her own eyes. Her patients listening to Mike describe the event with little fanfare, irked her. Again, she butted into Mike's conversation.

"He did more than that. He killed many men with his bare hands. I saw him at the gate. He rammed a rifle barrel down a guard's throat; after bending the barrel. Both him and Master Cho charged the manor fighting many guards with guns. Not one guard came near pulling the trigger to end either Master Cho or Mikes days. They moved like lightning from one man, then another. Within seconds, twelve men laid at their feet. Neither Master Cho or Mike broke a sweat. Our riders sat on their bikes watching the scene. If they wanted to help, they couldn't. The fighting ending so quick. Their bikes were running. Once the rides were stopped the fighting ending. Every Rider applauded both of them. It was amazing to see."

"Cheryl enough. You said to much. Go to your bike and wait for me." I am sorry you heard all that. Cheryl is a big fan. She doesn't like it when I down play any of the stuff, I done. Now, what is so important to tell me outside our house, Mitch?"

Mike, you being the only male in the family and your mom not always coherent, I thought it proper to ask you. I been seeing Dodie for a year. I love her. I want, well, I was thinking of marrying her. I didn't want to elope, not telling someone in the family. Your mom worries about the income loss. I told Dodie we would help any way we could. I got a good job on base. The pay is not great right now. I expect to get a pay raise soon. When I get the raise, I want Dodie and me to get married.

Mike eagerly gave Mitch his approval. "Great by me, Mitch. About the money, I learned after the manor home event, I was to come into money. Our group raided the manor finding a ton of cash. I will be getting some. I don't know how much? I really have little need for money, the club takes care of all my needs. I will send some money or ask Master Cho to send monies on a monthly schedule. Dodie handled the money mom got from the government. I want her to receive the money and continue paying the bills. The money I send will include her salary. I think, once she is married with her own family it is only right, she get paid for working." Mitch agreed and thanked Mike, then asked Mike, about his training. That came as a surprise to Mike. He gave Mitch a vague response to his questions. Mitched asked about Stephen. Mike remembered; Mitch never knew about Stephen's death nor did his own family. The only person to know, was Tad at the Rama Theater. Quickly, Mike explains to him about Stephen.

"Stephen was killed along with Teddy Bear. They were ambushed by the gang, we destroyed. Cheryl is his daughter. She blamed me for their deaths. Later, she learned what happened and why I was not to blame. Seems she has been tagging after me ever since. We are tight, but not romantically. Well, not by me." Mitch nods understanding his relationship with the girl Mike was with.

"You want to know about my training. This I cannot talk about. It is secret. I will tell you this, I am the heir to this martial arts system. It is hundreds of years old. It is considered the deadliest of all the arts. My body is trained day and night. I can do things unbelievable to those that witness either Master Cho or myself in action. So, fear not for my safety and calm any fears my sisters have. Master Cho is my step father and will die before any harms comes to me." Mitch nods not knowing how to except hearing what Mike said to him.

"Look Mitch, I really don't know when I can come back. I will be on a mission soon. How long and where, I am, I'm not at liberty to tell you. Besides, knowing that will not do anyone any good."

"Mike, I guess you are with the bikers."

"Yes."

"Are they treating you good?"

"Mitch, I am learning many things. I have a pilot's license, I am a weapons expert, learning to speak Spanish, taught magic tricks and how to escape almost any way you can tie a person up. Also, I live in a haunted cabin. Yeah Mitch, you can say I was doing good. There is one thing missing. My family and Boo. I could use some companionship, living alone. The bikers are my family, now."

"I thought you and Cheryl were, you know, more than a girlfriend?"

"No Mitch, her mom would kill me. We are very good friends. I eat at their home once in a while. I take turns eating at all the biker's home. Every morning one lady will bring me breakfast. They worry about me more than anyone. It has become a contention with the men in the club, their pampering me. Master Cho put his foot down, demanding they stop pampering me. Chopper our club leader decided, they could bring me meals but not to interfere with Master Cho training. Cheryl is a member of my class. I teach them martial arts. Master Cho deemed it necessary after several incidents around the neighborhood, the Rider's families live. I teach them the basis and not the secret art I am learning."

"Oh, I see." Mike understood the underlying meaning Mitch meant to say but had the good manners not to say.

That night after both Mike and Cheryl said goodbye, they returned to the Rama. Tad asked him to stop in. Mike said to Tad, "they planned on leaving the next day."

Mike returned before the last show ended. All three stood outside under the marquee discussing Mike plans. Tad patted Boo on his head. Boo remembered Tad. Suddenly, a sound alerted Mike's sharp senses. It came from the roof top over the jewelry store Mike last worked.

Mike signals Tad and Cheryl to remain quiet. Lindsey walks out of her booth. Rusty and Bob came outside waiting by the doors. The movie was about to end. They opened the door for the patrons to leave. Mike spotted movement on the roof top.

Then came a crashing sound barely heard by all of the workers standing outside the theater. Quickly, Mike tells them what is occurring. Quick, someone call the police. The jewelry store is being robbed. Boo was handed to Cheryl. Mike dashed off.

People started pouring out of the double doors. Everyone stopped. One patron spotted a person scoot up a wall. Then, the person ran across the six-foot wall toward the stores. Everyone turned hearing the man shout, "hey, look at that person. He leaped up on that six-foot wall. Everyone turned and saw an incredible feat. The person jumped up onto the theater wall and bounced off landing atop of a six-foot high wall, the same wall, Bob saw Mike jab his fingertip into.

With that leap onto the top of the six-foot wall the person ran doing a handstand somersault with an astonishing forward flip to the roof top of the shopping center. Mike followed the edge closest to the frontage of the stores. The sound came from the rear of the jewelry store.

Every patron exiting the theater were on the streets watching some crazy kid run across the rooftop. Mike saw one man reach down a hole. He was pulling his partner up through the opening. The roof top had a portal to enter the jewelry store onto the roof; the axe was used to pry it open. When that failed, they pounded on it. That was the noise Mike heard.

"Thinking, Mike said, "that was their first mistake. The second mistake was him being present when they decided to break into the store. The third mistake was the store he was working in, before leaving with Master Cho. The fourth mistake, he was highly trained. The final and costly mistake was they tried to fight me off with that pickaxe."

Soon, a scream came off the roof. It was followed by a man flying through the air. The scream got louder, when the flying man realized, he was going to miss the roof top. He was going to the street without a ladder. that was okay, Mike thought, the second man with the axe got the point. He also got a flight to the road with his partner. Both lived. The crowd went wild. Shouts of delight filled the air.

Cheryl turned to Tad and the Rama crew. "You asked what his job was. That should answer your questions."

Mike walked to the edge of the rooftop looking down at a large crowd watching. He was amazed to see all the people standing around the two men. "Neither were seriously hurt. Well, maybe a broken leg, or elbow. Might be a hip. No not a hip, definitely two concussions, Mike ponder to himself deciding not to tell anyone.

Mike flung both the robbers in a way, that should have them hit the pavement with the least damage. Well, what he thought should be the least damage before deciding how to fling them down. The only problem was the second man tried to change Mike's plan for his impact. His panic caused the flight down to the ground to be modified. Both arms were to be spread out in front of the man, like superman. Instead, the crook decided he wanted to land using his arms to catch the pavement. His arms felt the full impact of the drop. Both elbows dislocated from the shoulders, also at the elbows. Later, it was noted the wrist shattered on both hands.

Mike decided to do a double forward flip to the ground from the roof. "Might as give them a good show, since they all saw what happened."

Mike did the flip not just to amuse the crowd, but to take their eyes off of his appearance. The crowd focused on the flip and not the face. When the police arrived, no one could give a good description of the man, who stopped a robbery. No one from the Rama said a word. They had plenty to tell the police about the double forward flip the man made from the high roof top. Some mentioned the incredible climb Mike made up to the roof.

Both Cheryl and Mike quietly got on their bikes and rode off to Atlanta. They slept somewhere off the road. Mike brought his backpack. Cheryl slept peaceful and Mike stay awake with his thoughts. Boo laid on Mike's chest.

NOT THE END

EPILOG

BOOK 4

Rumble in the Jungle

Two people just arrived in a small Mexican town. After weeks of investigation to search for the where about of One-Eye their search ended. Problems arose as soon as they arrived. Cheryl and two of her friends followed Mike for the second time. Mike found out, Cho and he had to separate. Cho faced a town of Cartel Drug soldiers bent on killing him. Mike located his friends to only have them take a river trip they believed would take them to the next town. That river raft trip put them and the tourist in the hands of vicious pirates. Both Cho and Mike faced odds that quickly tested their skills. What Mike did next, made him into a legend.

Mike ventured down a river knowingly was loaded with menacing pirates at every turn. He wasn't alone, Jack with his seal team tagged along. It wouldn't belong until him and the seal teams were forced to separate. Mike went alone after those that held Cheryl hostage. That was not the only danger that laid ahead. It was a fight every inch of the treacherous path he and Cheryl were on.

Both Cheryl and Mike were going to wish Jack and his seals came with them. That would not happen until they reached the valley of the pyramid. An army awaited.

PREVIOUS BOOKS WRITTEN

Published

1. Oz Book 1: One Fine Adventure
2. Oz Book 2: Rama Rowdies
3. Oz Book 3: Battle in Atlanta
4. Oz Book 4: Rumble in the Jungle
5. Oz Book 5: Desert Storm
6. Oz Book 6: Wicked City

PENDING PUBLISHING

7. Oz Book 7: Tranquil Forest
8. Oz Book 8: Ghost of Past
9. Oz Book 9: The Gift
10. Oz Book 10: Voodoo Queen
11. Oz Book 11: Alien Agenda
12. Oz Book 12: Sensei's Dilemma
13. Oz Book 13: Wisp of the Willow
14. Oz Book 14: Time Loop
15. Oz Book 15: Invisible Assassins
16. Oz Book 16: The Arcturian Orb
17. Oz Book 17: Horizon to Oblivion
18. Quest for the Children of the Amazons

ABOUT THE AUTHOR

Michael Osborne a son of a Robert F Osborne Navy Chief Torpedoman and a southern belle Evelyn Spivey both deceased. One of three siblings and a twin to one. The only sibling to graduate High School and College. He graduated with a BS in Geology from Ga. Southwestern College and later received a MS in Educational Science from Ft. Valley State College. Created his own business doing clock repair which he learned from a local jeweler. He entered the U.S. Navy and deplored on a WES PAC, then completed twenty-one years total active and reserves attaining the same rank of his father Chief Instrument man. Michael went on to earn several black belts in several Martial Arts disciplines as well as certification in sport diving. He set many goals for himself and strived to achieve each one.

He refers himself to people as an over educated fool. He trained on various office machines, postal machines, copiers, engraving, jeweler repair, projectionist. When he is not busy he builds scaled hand crafted wooden ships, winning many firsts at State Fair. One of my greatest achievements was being a grade school teacher. The other was marrying my wife Dorothy, my partner and friend for life, so far thirty-eight years. He has written two unpublished books. This book was his first attempt in having published a book. In this book I hope the many adventures and some of my life lessons can inspires others to take the bull by the horns and do it.

Printed in the USA
CPSIA information can be obtained
at www.ICGtesting.com
LVHW020739210923
758747LV00010B/184

9 781961 017979